To Mari;
I love you
husband. Enjoy the
book!
[signature]

GREEN GRASS

RED STREETS

A NOVEL BY

Toni M. Judd

WESTON PUBLISHING
URBANA, ILLINOIS

ISBN 1-889463-42-6

Cover design by Patrick Doiel

Library of Congress Cataloging-in-Publication Data

Judd, Toni M.,
      Green Grass, Red Streets: a young lawyer's journey of
  love, intrigue and hope/Toni M. Judd
        p. cm.
        ISBN 1-889463-42-6
  1. Title. 2. Judd, Toni M. 3. Adult Fiction

                                  98-094180
                                  CIP

---

03 02 01 00 99

10 9 8 7 6 5 4 3 2 1

ACKNOWLEDGMENTS

I dedicate this book to my mother, the woman who believed in me from the day I was born; my best friend, who knew I could write before I did.

I also give special thanks to the two doctors who went beyond their training in medicine by providing a distraught daughter hope and their valuable time. Thank you for saving my mother's life, Dr. James McGill and Dr. Michael Kraus.

To my husband and boys: there were many days I could have played, but I didn't. You're my inspiration.

To Dee Henderson from Golden Apple Press for providing valuable editorial experience on the early drafts of this book; and Kim Albert, who generously helped type and retype without complaint. (It was only two and a half years of edits!)

I am also extremely grateful to Jennifer Littlepage Spencer for the art on the book cover and her never-ending talents.

Many of the later changes go directly to Ann Kempner Fisher, professional editor and screen writer. She gave me a fair and honest evaluation, yet left me with the confidence I could make it a better book. Thanks!

Patrick Doiel of Doiel Graphics, I will always be thankful for your first-rate publishing skills, sound advice and experience. May we do books two and three together as well.

Lastly, to my dear friends and family, who listened to me, read the book, listened to me, read the book, I thank you from the bottom of my heart.

C H A P T E R
I

I am alone. There are no lights or windows. This is room I know all too well, the downstairs closet. Today, I'm lucky. I could've been in the basement, a place that's dirty and cold and smells like mildew. When he locks me down there, I'm really scared.

Here, I'm safe. More importantly, I won't go hungry. Last week I hid a candy bar in one of Jack's old shoes and a can of pop in my mother's coat.

When I grow up, I'm going to help kids like me. Maybe I'll become a secret agent and spy on dads who are mean to their daughters. Maybe I'll even become a cop. My dad's a cop, a man who upholds the law. His law is a bad law. My punishment is living with him in this house, this house of horrors.

Whatever my mom and dad may think, I'm not a bad girl. I try my best to be good. I can't help it if I'm smarter than they are. My mother always says, "You should conduct yourself like a proper lady." Sometimes I try so hard to sit up straight, my back hurts. Why should proper ladies sit still anyway?

I daydream a lot, to hide from them, to hide my secret, creating a fairy-tale world where I'm loved, anywhere but here, here where they hate me so.

Standing up in the narrow space under the stairs, I hunt for my pop. Right away I smell my mom's perfume. This should comfort me, but it doesn't.

My favorite red jacket is lying discarded on the floor. I've outgrown this thing, but I keep it hidden so they can't give it away. From its pocket, I retrieve the book I took out of the library and my handy flashlight. Settling down in the corner, the candy bar immediately takes care of my empty stomach. Now warm and safe in my coat, I leave this world and enter the glorious world of books.

Hatred silently creeps its way into my cozy spot. Quickly I hide my book behind my back so he can't see it. I know what he wants, what he always wants. He's searching for my soul.

This black shadowy creature waits. Its terrifying presence begins a slow, insidious move, reaching out to corner me. Like a frightened rabbit caught in a cage, I'm trapped and powerless.

The spirit manifests the face of my father upon its demonic form. Without warning, evil penetrates my body. He beckons me forward by giving me a look you would give someone you cared for, someone you loved. His is a false love. In his hand, he carries the bottle I have learned to hate.

A blinding flash cuts sharply across the ceiling. My world shifts from the closet to a place of water. I'm older now, and I've only been here once. This is a place where God might live, or perhaps it's a place of magic. There's a lake that reflects the clouds and white, snow-capped mountains. When the sun begins to set, the sky turns to orange-colored streaks, and the birds, now black, wing their way to a safe haven.

The moon slowly emerges from the water, shimmering a path that can only lead to heaven. Caught under its spell, it implores me to follow. Overcome with nature's peaceful beauty, I walk to the edge of the sandy shoreline. The tranquil moment is suddenly shattered by a fierce wave.

Without warning, a calculated hand reaches out and shoves me below the dark, murky surface. As my lungs begin to burn for air, I'm fighting for my life. The hand that imprisoned me slowly releases its grasp. His laughter taunts me as my body races toward the surface.

His voice repeats the same words, "You're a slut. Do you hear me, girl?" Out of breath, I crawl back to shore, ignoring him. "Look at me when I'm talking to you," he demands. He grabs my chin, forcing me to look into his bloodshot eyes. "You're a slut just like your mother. A good for nothing slut. You knew I'd come for you. You've been expecting me. Come. Take my hand. Join me in this spiritual darkness where there is no forgiveness, no escape from the fires of hell!"

* * *

The water is gone. Instead, I am lying on a hard, slippery surface. My hair is too heavy and tangled. Still laden with fear, I struggle to get up. Momentarily blinded and confused, I shade my eyes to focus, once again, upon my father's face. He gives me a disarming smile not unlike the ones we shared when I was a child and he taught me to ride a bike. The smile, too, is false.

As he slowly removes his coat, a .38 caliber handgun is pointed directly at me from across the room. His toying with me has ended. I try to scream. My cries of fear are soundless. I try to beg, but words fail to come out of my mouth.

Once again, he shouts the word, "Slut," and without hesitating, pulls the trigger.

Raising my arms to protect myself, I see a flash and billowing smoke. Out of the corner of my eye, a radiant light emerges, blocking my view. Why can't I feel the pain I know should be mine?

I smile. I'm no longer afraid. I recognize the light. It's my guardian angel, someone whose life is more precious than my own. My brother, Jack. He smiles back.

His head turns toward my father in confusion. Brain tissue from the back of his head splatters across the room. As his hands reach out to hold me, he stumbles. I lunge forward, placing my arms around his chest, and, together, we fall to the floor.

Again, I can't breathe. I am drowning in my brother's blood.

* * *

Oh, God, it's happening again. The wet bed sheets have twisted so tightly around my body, I can't move. In despair, I automatically turn toward the side of the bed that once provided security and comfort. The man I married was no longer there. Like everyone else who had been close to me, he is gone, rid of me similar to the way you'd discard an old piece of furniture.

Seeking an invisible solace, I place my head upon his forgotten pillow. Inhaling deeply, I sniff out a reminder of his presence. Stupid, woman, get a grip, I say to myself, kicking the covers off the bed.

Determined to ignore my heartache, I try to picture my brother the way he was before my father accidentally shot him, but

I can't. The nightmare is still too vivid. It's been ten years, ten years of merely surviving.

Jack, who was six years older than me, had always been my hero. I adored him. I wanted to be his shadow. He wanted his younger sister to stop following him. He loved me and was often sweet to me, but, like most older siblings, much of the time I was the thorn in his side.

No wonder my husband left me. Who could blame him? I didn't deserve his love, or was it love? They say love is blind. Blind? It's fantasy. That's what it is...pure fantasy.

I move to the side of the bed to switch on the light. My eyes instinctively search for the blue crystal bird, Jack's gift, my source of strength. Holding its cold, smooth surface protectively in my hand, I close my eyes and wipe a tear from my cheek. Knowing I am under the watchful eyes of my dead brother, I smile, drifting back to another time, now only a memory.

* * *

There were three or four strategic hiding places I had as a child. One of them was where you could almost touch the sky. Back then, trees were better than friends. My special tree was situated in a park a couple of blocks from my home.

It wasn't easy being alone in a neighborhood like mine. People were jammed in what I jokingly called, "Matchbox Metropolis." I know it's a tongue twister, and that's why I liked it.

I grew up in a typical middle class neighborhood, an ugly row of uniform houses all boxed together, completely void of charm -- unless, of course, you try to disguise this fact by planting flowers and shrubs, and painting your house a bright yellow the way my mother had done.

`On a sunny, warm afternoon, climbing down from my special tree, I hear a squawking noise. Following the source, I find a baby bird. Terribly upset by Tiffany, the Siamese cat, who wants it for dinner, I gently pick it up, cradling it in my hands. Tiffany slowly walks away, giving me a haughty look of disdain.

Reaching my house with the bird cupped gently in my hands, my father jumps out from around the corner and startles me. "Slow down," he said, grabbing my arm. "What have you got there, young lady?" Reluctantly, I show it to him.

"It's a baby bird," I answered. He took it out of my hand, examining it.

"That's not a bird. It's a damn starling!" He threw it against the wall, killing it instantly

"They're dirty birds. At least that one won't be around to build a nest in my gutters," he said, wiping his hands with the clean handkerchief in his pocket. As if I'd once again disappointed him, he muttered under his breath, walked to his squad car and drove away.

My brother, who had witnessed the incident, came up from behind me. He tried to get my attention by waving his hands in front of my face. I was unresponsive and still in shock. What made my father react that way? Why was he so cruel? It was my fault. I killed the baby bird.

With the unanswered questions still lingering in my mind, Jack held me as close as older brothers are willing to do while I cried in his arms.

A couple of days later, he came to my tree. "Is it Lady Anne or Princess Anne this afternoon? Or maybe you're hoping you were switched at birth. Come down. I have something to show you." He was right. I was too busy pretending to be a fairy princess who had been kidnapped by her now phony parents, and, quite naturally, he was part of the conspiracy.

Then I noticed he had something he was hiding behind his back. Before I had a chance to ask, he raised it above his head taunting me. It was a wrapped present, a rare occasion indeed.

With a sense of excitement, none-too-princess-like I scrambled down my tree. I could sense his pride as he handed me the gift. Tearing the paper as fast as I could, I opened it. Inside was a blue crystal bird. It was about the size of my palm. Raising it to the sky, it glistened in the sunlight. "I'll call it my bluebird of happiness," I said, dancing. "Oh, Jack, it's so beautiful."

"I saw it in a garage sale," he said, uncomfortably shy. "You know how we get those bargains right before they pack it up. It's not a real bird, but at least Dad can't hurt this one." He put his arm around me, and we headed for home.

"Wait, I forgot my shoes." Once again, I scrambled up the tree. They were too small. My mother insisted I wear them anyway. She hated my dirty feet. I dropped them toward Jack. In one swift movement, they were in his hands.

Sliding back down, he placed them next to my feet. "Come on, Cinderella, put them on or you'll be put in the dungeon." I ignored his advice, picking them up and throwing them nonchalantly over my shoulder. He started to scold me, but changed his mind. We walked along the sidewalk, I with my special gift and he in quiet reflection.

A couple of blocks later, he suddenly stopped. I

knew he had something on his mind, something really important to say. He was so tall and straight, my Jack. I tried to be solemn, but I couldn't help it. He was like some general about to lecture his troops, consisting of one. I started to protest, but he put his finger to my lips.

"Annie, I want you to promise me something," he said, with authority in his voice. The truth was I would have done just about anything for him, the dishes, taken out the garbage, even cleaned his room.

"Anything, Jack," I said, holding my trophy as if it were a blue diamond.

Jack turned to face me and said, "Raise your right hand." I complied, even though I thought he was being silly. "Promise me that you'll learn to find love in this world."

Now that certainly was a strange promise. Love? What did I know about that particular subject?

"Are you all right?" I asked, giggling and checking his forehead for a fever.

My bossy brother gave me a dirty look and said, "It's not funny. I'm being serious. Do it!"

"Okay, Jack, whatever you say. For you, I'll vow to find love." He shook his head and pointed his finger.

"No, Annie, that's not good enough, not just love, love in this world."

Confused, I stood up nice and straight and did as he asked. "All right. I, Princess Anne Elizabeth Stevens, do solemnly promise to find love in this world."

Finally satisfied I had said the proper words, he smiled. "Okay, rebel princess, come on. I'll race you home." He beat me by what seemed a good half block, the no-good creep.

* * *

I opened my eyes and kissed the bird's smooth surface. God, do I miss you. Oh, Jack, why? Why? If only I hadn't called you that night, you'd be alive.

I found love all right. Damn men. They both had deserted me. But that's not what you meant, was it, dear Jack? Oh, how I need you, how I've always needed you.

A tear rolled down my cheek. With the back of my hand, I wiped it away, turned off the light, and knew a peaceful sleep would once again elude me.

* * *

As usual, I was ten minutes late. If it hadn't been for the awful bout of morning sickness and the suffocating heat in my apartment, I would've been on time. The blasted air conditioner was still on the blink. Even after thirty minutes of blow drying, my hair was still damp. I should threaten the rotten landlord with bodily harm or, better yet, sue his butt for breach of contract; of course, the lawyer in me had stubbornly refused to sign the lease.

With a sense of pride, I paused to look up at the white stone building which housed my new workplace, the United States District Court. Monolithic in structure, it was set back from the street by fifteen or so concrete steps. It had been built in a neoclassical design with a bold use of metal and limestone. The building's exterior had recently undergone some restoration. The windows were tinted charcoal and most likely bullet proofed, reflecting the traditional designs of the past yet consciously adjusting to the needs of present-day life.

Today was one of those major milestones occurring only once or twice in a person's life. Waitressing for the meager tip money, and the late-night shifts as a receptionist at the university's hotel were behind me. Those jobs were merely the stepping stones toward my goal, toward my final metamorphosis.

I had spent the summer studying for the bar exam. Other than volunteering at Legal Aid and clerking for a law firm part time, this was my first *real* job. My only concern now was making it up these steps without losing my breakfast. Slightly winded at the top, I stopped to examine my reflection in the massive steel and glass doors.

I saw a confident young woman, although I certainly didn't feel it. The person staring back at me was tall and slender, 26 years old, with a thick mass of dark curls that no comb could control. Today, I had it pulled back in a clasp, a few tendrils had escaped and were curling around my face.

My mode of dress was what I jokingly referred to as the "granola look." However, this was not due to a lack of style, it was due, sadly, to a lack of funds. My entire wardrobe consisted of old, worn-out, dependable pieces of clothing from my high school days or simple garage sale rejects.

With trepidation, I lifted my chin, took another deep breath, and opened the door. Immediately, two court security officers in black uniforms wearing guns on their belts smiled politely. Nervously, I placed my purse and briefcase on the conveyer belt.

"Hi, I'm Anne Stevens, Judge Rosenthal's new law clerk."

The two men looked at each other and shrugged their shoulders. "Sorry. You should check with Mrs. Michaels. She's the judge's secretary. No one's told us anything."

I was put through the grueling task of passing through the metal detector several times. After a short striptease, including my shoes and hair barrette, I walked through one more time. The machine continued to beep that loathsome sound.

Puzzled, I shrugged my shoulders and looked at the man with the wand. "I'm sorry, ma'am, but are you wearing an underwire bra?" I blushed and nodded affirmatively. He placed the wand around this corresponding region of my anatomy and without saying another word waved me through.

Feeling thoroughly askew and quite irritated, I was directed to the elevator, which would take me to the third floor courtrooms.

Upon exiting, I wandered anxiously through a quiet, narrow corridor of dark, cherry wood not unlike the way I saw Dorothy doing it in the Wizard of Oz. I nervously chuckled to myself. At least I didn't have my hair in pigtails and a blue-and-white checkered dress with red-sparkling, magical shoes.

Glancing at my shoes, I was relieved to discover they were the black pumps I had hastily retrieved from my closet this morning. Perhaps I should have wished for those red magical shoes after all.

At last, I stopped at a door. The bronze doorplate read, "Joseph Rosenthal, U.S. District Judge." The Wizard I was about to encounter was a federal judge.

Before entering Oz's office, I made a last attempt at straightening my skirt and fussing with my hair. The speaker phone startled me.

"May I help you?" an irritated voice on the other end asked.

Mortified the camera had caught me primping, I cleared my throat and responded, "Yes. I'm Anne Stevens, the new law clerk." What I really felt like saying was: "This is Dorothy. I want to go home to Kansas." The voice on the intercom interrupted my musing.

"Who?" It asked.

Feeling totally put out, I continued in a louder tone of voice, "My name is Anne Stevens. I'm the judge's new law clerk. Apparently, there's been some misunderstanding."

The voice sounded a little more reassuring. "Oh, Miss Stevens.

You're right. We weren't expecting you. When you hear the buzzer, please turn the knob on the door. It sometimes sticks; so give it a good push."

Giving it a hefty shove, I stumbled forward into the office. Embarrassed, but regaining my balance, I looked up and smiled at a very attractive, young woman, 30 years or so, with dark hair and a petite figure. She was dressed in a very expensive-looking navy blue suit. She approached me and placed her manicured hand in mine, giving me a hearty handshake.

"Miss Stevens, I'm sorry. My name is Jan Michaels, Judge Rosenthal's secretary. I've talked to you a couple times on the phone."

She turned and walked back to her desk. "Fred told us not to expect you until the 1st of September. I'm sorry, but Judge Rosenthal isn't here to greet you personally. The lucky man is on a well-deserved vacation."

"When do you expect him back?" I asked, hiding my disappointment.

"Oh, he left Friday. He'll be back on the 1st, the day we all thought you were going to start."

The Fred to whom Mrs. Michaels referred was my co-clerk. Along with several hundred applicants, I had applied for this job at the beginning of my second year of law school. District courts hire their clerks a couple years in advance. Depending on the judge's preference, clerkships generally last one to two years. I was told Fred had agreed on two years. I had been given my choice and decided to stay one.

Still standing next to her, I tried to clear up the confusion. "Well, Fred must have misunderstood. I told him on the phone two weeks ago I would start on the 15th of August."

Mrs. Michaels waved her hand reassuringly. "It's all right. It's really not a problem. Fred's a practical joker. I wouldn't be at all surprised if he played this dirty trick on you so your first day here would be, shall we say, a memorable one."

She opened a filing cabinet next to her desk.   "We've all been the victims of his harmless pranks, including the judge himself."   Having found the file, she turned and walked toward a rear door. "Come, I'll show you where to go."

We approached a door in the back of the room.   Before we entered, she stopped and turned to face me.

"I don't recall whether you were given a tour when you came for your interview. You probably met Aaron and Mark. Unfortunately, the law clerks are still sharing an office. Thank goodness, it's a large room. If you don't want to look at Fred, I'll see what we can do about finding some dividers. I think I spotted a couple of them in the basement the other day."

Placing her hand upon my arm, she hesitated for a couple of seconds before she spoke. "There's no way I can fully prepare you for what you're about to encounter. Really, we ought to put a sign on the door that says, 'Beware of Fred the Incorrigible.' He's not the neatest and cleanest guy in the world, nor the most organized. However, after your first impression wears off, he's not so bad."

She walked over to another filing cabinet and pulled out a slip of paper.   "I have two sons at home just like him. I'd say maturity-wise he's on their level. I don't think you'll change his ugly ways, but you might develop some kind of truce -- or perhaps seek your own revenge."

Mrs. Michaels extended her arm, handing me a file. "Well, anyway, I wish you luck. For the past several years we've had nothing but male law clerks. It's nice to see another woman's face. Here. Fill this out and then place it in that folder," she said, pulling another piece of paper out of another folder and handing it to me.

"It's self-explanatory. When you're done, I'll put it in your personnel file."

Mrs. Michaels pointed her finger along the aisle. "Oh, one more thing. We're a little more laid back when the judge is gone. Relax. You'll find we're all like one big, happy, dysfunctional family. Now, go and give that *boy* a run for his money."

She held open the door allowing me to enter. I spotted rows upon rows of law books divided in sections. "Turn right at the last book shelf. You'll see the door to your office." She was about to say something else, but changed her mind. "Oh, I'll need you to sign a few more records to indicate your start-up date. It'll probably take a couple of weeks to get paid." She gave me a conspiratorial smile and a thumbs-up sign, then shut the door.

The library was so quiet. I felt comfortable and at home here. Many nights after class, I would often sit and read. I liked the older books with the smooth-bound mahogany covers. I enjoyed the smell of them, something computers failed to provide. They often reminded me of mystery novels. I was seeking refuge in a place that always provided me escape. It's true I'm an odd duck, but libraries are a lot of people's sanctuaries.

It's Fred who was about to have a problem with me. I hated people who played dirty tricks on others. Thanks to Nick, my ex-husband, I was still a very angry woman. My brother used to tell me anger was a wasted emotion. Naturally, he was wrong. Anger was one of my best attributes and oftentimes resulted in my greatest accomplishments.

Hadn't my husband once told me I would make a lousy lawyer? I was about to prove him wrong. I was sure I had passed the bar exam. Of course, I hadn't received the results yet, but I knew it to be true.

As I came to the last row of books, I spotted his door, or I suppose *our* door. Entering as cautiously as possible, I glanced around the room. Sitting at a desk was a young man, mid-20s, dark hair, brown eyes, and a nice beard. The earphones on his head were connected to a disc player. He attempted to sing something I thought I recognized from the Grateful Dead, or if it wasn't the Grateful Dead, anyone listening to him would have wanted it that way. At the same time, he picked up a Nerf ball and shot it into a plastic hoop attached to the wall.

He certainly wasn't dressed like any of the lawyers I had seen. He wore a pair of jeans with holes at the knees and a T-shirt I can only assume was for my benefit. It said, 'All men are created equal. Women should stay in the kitchen.'

The dirtiest looking tennis shoes I'd ever seen were nonchalantly propped on top of his desk. Except for the grungy clothes, he reminded me of one of those cute Talmudic-scholar types. His muscular physique was extremely noticeable.

Not surprised to see me standing there, he took the headphones off. He had a small gold-hooped earring in his left ear. Ignoring him, I looked around the room. Jan's earlier description was an understatement.

The mess immediately struck a raw nerve. There were comic strips randomly tacked to several pegboards; and nailed to the wall was a picture of Elvis surrounded in hideous black velvet.

Four very large and spectacularly stuffed birds were perched on the tops of bookshelves. Later, I found out these poor birds were long-forgotten trial exhibits from an old criminal case. A taxidermist had been charged with violating the national wildlife laws for stuffing species protected under the federal statutes. Who knows how many years those majestic birds had sat upon those bookcases, glassily gazing out upon an office where there were no trees, no predators to disturb their ineffectual stare.

Inspecting the room, I noticed case files strewn on a couple of chairs. Some were stacked in the corner, and still others were sitting in piles haphazardly on the desktop, what there was of a desktop.

Fast-food wrappers rolled in balls, leftovers from meals possibly eaten sometime in this century, were scattered around the floor, discarded reminders of a long-forgotten game of garbage basketball.

As Fred stood up to approach me, there was an evil gleam in his large, brown eyes and a smile that bespoke his treachery. I ignored his outstretched hand. Seemingly unaffected by my rebuff, he smirked, sat back down, and propped his dirty feet back on his desk. "So you finally made it, Stevens," he said as he glanced at his watch. "A little late, aren't you? Oh, by the way, how did you like the welcoming committee?

"Thanks to my landlord and you, I've had the morning from hell. Why didn't someone warn me? Although, I must confess, Mrs. Michaels made a *minor* attempt at it."

Leaning over his desk, I pointed my finger close to his face. "Just remember, two can play your games. There's always revenge, perhaps murder."

Fred sat back in his chair and chuckled. "Murder? You don't even know me, and yet you're already plotting my demise. I'm making progress." He licked his fingers dotting an X in the air. "Chalk one up for ol' Fred here. I do believe I'm going to like you, Annie. Just remember, *'In taking revenge, a woman is but even with her enemy; but in passing it over, she is superior.'*"

At least he's not a complete moron. I knew that quote and I knew it wasn't meant for a woman's revenge. Should I impress him or was he worth the trouble? I folded my arms giving him a withering stare.

"Revenge is a kind of wild justice; which the more man's nature runs to, the more ought law to weed it out. Certainly in taking revenge a man is but even with his enemy; but in passing it over, he is superior; for it is a prince's part to pardon. This is certain, man that studieth revenge keeps his own wounds green, which otherwise

would heal and do well."

"Francis Bacon also said, and, of course, I will take it out of context: *'Young men are fitter for execution than for counsel.'* Furthermore, my name is Anne. Don't call me Annie."

Fred placed the earphones back on his ears. "Since you understand this revenge philosophy thing so well, I assume you'll take the I-wish-to-murder-Fred look off your face by heeding his first advice and excluding the latter. And, by the way, I'll call you whatever I want."

He then gave me one of those men-who-are-pleased-with-themselves smiles and shook his head. "Boy, it's nice to have a skirt around here. Aaron, the last law clerk, was a slob. As you can see, I'm a conformist. Hopefully, your woman's touch will straighten this place up."

I moved to stand in awe at the front of Fred's desk. "Who would believe it? Is it only this morning or will you be a major pain in the lower part of my anatomy for the rest of my clerkship? If you think I came here to be your housekeeper, forget it!"

I walked over and placed one of the chairs between our desks. "From now on, there will be a line drawn between your half of this room and mine so your filth stays on your side. In fact, Jan and I will soon be hunting for a much-needed wall divider."

"Annie, my dear, where have you come from? You're an adult. You can use the words 'pain in the ass' without getting punished. And the answer to your question is: yes, I suppose I will be a pain in *your* ass. And since we're on the subject, you're a woman; and, as such, I can assume the lower part of my anatomy will be stinging as well."

Fred couldn't have known how close he'd come to understanding me. He was right. The word "ass" would have been forbidden in my home, a trip to the basement. In so many ways, I was still a child suffering from my father's dominance.

Assuming the other desk belonged to me, I walked toward it and placed the papers Mrs. Michaels had given me to fill out on the printer. "Here. These must be yours," I said, picking up the cases stacked in my chair and placing them on his desk.

"Sorry. Those belong to you. Before the judge comes back, you need to read through them, check the cites, and write a bench memo. Don't forget to include both sides of the arguments and type it up so the judge can make a decision and rule. If you don't believe me, ask the clerks downstairs. Or better yet, check the docket. Oh, and by the way, enjoy yourself, Sweetheart," he said with a slow emphasis on that demeaning word.

Retrieving the files I had wanted to throw at him, I once again crossed the line. "Is this another one of your practical jokes?" I asked, balancing the pile in my arms. Fred shrugged his shoulders and ignored me.

Those files could not possibly be mine. Sure enough, I found out those were just a handful of the many cases I was required to keep track of. The law clerks divided them up on an even/odd basis. I was assigned the even-numbered cases, totaling several hundred.

Fred, not bothering to answer, wadded up a piece of paper and flung it toward an already overflowing basket. "As you just pointed out, you didn't come here expecting to be my housekeeper. Now, do you want to change your mind?"

Shaking my head, I took a deep breath in frustration. "No, but I think we need to hire one. I hope you're going to show me the ropes around here without any more of your *juvenile* pranks."

I wadded up a half-eaten thing on my desk and grimaced when I saw a gray molding piece of bread sticking out of its wrapper. Flinging it toward the wastebasket on his side of the room, my aim met its mark. Reaching for a handkerchief, I wiped my hands, smoothed my skirt and sat down in my chair.

"By the way, you don't know me yet. I'm a nonconformist."

Fred turned his back on me, pretending to be more interested in his computer. "Once you get settled in, we'll sit down and go through your cases. It's really not that tough. I'm sure you'll get the hang of it."

I found an empty drawer for my purse, then started digging through the piles. The rest of the day I spent asking plenty of questions. I discovered the other employees in the office were normal types, warm and friendly. Not completely trusting Fred, I got a general description of my job duties from Mrs. Michaels. That day marked the beginning of "practicing law, neophyte style," which means accepting the fact I'm still an idiot law student.

C H A P T E R
II

After a few weeks, the Wizard made his first appearance. The courthouse brimmed with activity. Prior to his arrival, everyone had been somewhat laid back. Today, the parking lot was full and the chaos apparent.

Lawyers were dressed in their business garb. The docket was filled with motions and trials to be heard throughout the month. Jurors were corralled in the jury assembly room awaiting their orders. The schedule indicated we had six *voir dire* examinations, which are really jury selections. *"Voir Dire"* is a French word that means "to speak the truth."

Jurors are asked questions regarding their backgrounds, competency, interests, et cetera. After this has been accomplished, the lawyers conduct what is called 'peremptory challenges.' There's no rhyme or reason to this methodology. A juror could be dismissed simply for having red hair. Once done, the jurors and the lawyers go home and await their trial date.

It took about a week, but Fred and I had settled our hostility through compromise, which meant he cleaned up his half of the room and I forgave him for the T-shirt, the bad jokes, and the chauvinistic remarks. He continued to call me Annie. I gave up. At least the rest of the staff called me Anne.

The two weeks of quiet activity preparing for this day were over. Even Fred dressed up for the occasion. He looked quite handsome in his dark navy suit. I felt dowdy and uncomfortable. My clothes didn't fit me like they used to. I was definitely going to have to do something about my wardrobe and soon.

When I sat down, I couldn't breathe. I was constantly unfastening buttons. The judge's court reporter taught me an ingenious maneuver. I could loosen the side of my skirt by threading a rubber band through the buttonhole. As long as I wore a jacket, it worked perfectly.

The Wizard took the very moment I was fiddling with my clothes to walk out of his chambers and greet his public. He was a very tall and distinguished-looking man, possibly in his mid-fifties. He had gray hair at the temples and a medium build. Propped halfway down his nose was a pair of conservative brown reading glasses. He wore an expensively tailored suit with a crisp, white shirt and red paisley tie.

He quickly discovered me and gave me the signal to follow him. Smiling uncomfortably at the others, I swallowed hard and walked past the milieu in Mrs. Michael's room and down the hall to his chambers.

Once there, the judge extended his hand, and I shook it. "It's a pleasure to meet you once again, Anne. I can see by your bench memos that Fred has shown you the ropes."

Without waiting for my response, he took a sip of his morning coffee and sat down. He motioned for me to do the same. As I sat uncomfortably in the chair, he jokingly referred to my first day. "I hear you had an interesting start. It's all my fault. I'm truly sorry. Someone in this office should have warned you. It's a shame you have to share an office with such a scalawag."

Grabbing hold of the armchair, I tried not to fidget -- another one of those bad habits when I'm nervous. The judge, ignoring my uneasiness, stretched out his hand to retrieve a file from the long conference table.

"When the GSA built this building, there was only one judge and one law clerk. Now, with this extraordinary caseload, my hope is to have another district judge on staff soon. Try not to let those nasty habits of Fred's bother you too much. Believe me, I'd go insane if I had to share the same quarters with him. I have to say, for all his faults, he is an incredibly talented and gifted staff attorney."

Judge Rosenthal seemed like an amiable guy. In law school, judges were revered. I wondered how it felt to have all that power, the power to change people's lives forever. In today's society, they were the only true autocrats in existence. This was my first official day working with one. I was exceptionally proud to be a part of his team.

* * *

Soon after the trials had begun, I was notified by mail that I had passed the bar exam. It was nice to have it confirmed in black and white.

As my clerkship continued and the days turned into months, the three of us became steadfast friends. The judge, who by the way was now only a mere mortal and no longer the divine Wizard, would go to lunch with Fred and me and listen patiently as we argued incessantly about the issues involving the afternoon's hearings.

Our opinions on the law became a battleground of political aspersions cast from one to the other...as if Fred's caustic, conceited, and argumentative tone could change my mind.

On those days, the judge attempted to provide a counterbalance to our enthusiasm by pointing out where we had erred, or patting us on the back when something we did met with his approval.

Also, while reading the briefs, I couldn't help but be struck by the attorneys' pursuit of the dollar over the interests of their client. Not to denigrate my own profession, but occasionally I noticed a frivolous and unnecessary motion or two filed to increase some lawyer's already burgeoning billable hours.

The man who sat upon his bench cared about every one of these cases. Oftentimes, I would see him leave the courthouse with a drawn and weary face, especially when he sentenced first-time drug offenders. Due to the mandatory Sentencing Guidelines passed in 1987, the judges' jobs were now quite perfunctory. Individual justice was a thing of the past. The days when a federal judge could give what they believed to be a just and appropriate sentence were long gone.

Most of these cases were black youths caught up in the web that crack created. We called them "the drugs and guns cases." This problem was on a national level. That's why Congress decided to usurp the judicial branch in the hopes of eliminating disparate sentences given out by some judges, thus, concentrating their efforts toward punishment and deterrence. It was another ploy in the political arena which got them votes for being tough on crime, and at the same time crammed correctional institutions so that our tax dollars couldn't keep up with the ever-increasing need for new jails. Rehabilitation was a penological goal of the past.

Fred and I, although sometimes ideological foes, got along. Occasionally an outburst of victory came from my mouth and could be heard through the halls beating Fred at his own game, Nerf basketball. I also discovered a serious side to Fred. He liked to make you think he was this down-to-earth practical joker, some normal type of guy, void of brains.   In fact, the judge was right.   He was quite talented, a gifted child, like myself, who had accelerated through grade school and high school.

Unlike me, he had traveled the world, taking his time deciding on his life's work. He had a master's degree in finance from Princeton and a law degree from Yale. He was an only child whose parents were divorced and spoiled him terribly. His father was a senior member of a large prestigious law firm in Chicago; and, quite naturally, he was bound to follow in his father's footsteps.

I tolerated his pigsty, and he was patient with my first-time pregnant woman's woes.   Cussing became a large part of our vocabulary. It helped take the edge off the stress.

Some of the most interesting parts of this pregnancy were the bathroom trips.   There was no convenience store, grocery store, hardware store, or McDonald's restaurant I had not hit. Every place I went and every trip I took, a bathroom was a prerequisite.

* * *

I was five months pregnant when I received a call at home from my low-life ex-husband. Such an awful word, "ex-husband." The title alone was a constant reminder of the guilt I felt at having failed. "Low-life," however, gives me a self-serving satisfaction without the implication of a past mistake.

An ever-enduring aspect of my character is refusing to admit defeat. Giving up simply because the man in my life wanted out didn't seem fair. What did he know? After all, he was just some idiotic fool who didn't know what he wanted out of life. I, on the other hand, knew exactly what he needed. He needed me.

Nick and I had literally grown up together. With my mother's permission, we got married. He was nineteen, and I had reached the ripe old age of seventeen and a half. I was alone and desperate, and he was -- well, how should I put it? Horny. The first couple of years were what I would term 'the robust-craving-for-lust years,' carnality at its best.

Unfortunately the reality of our immaturity soon took a hand in our marriage. We were both going to college at the same time. I would work a semester; then he would work a semester. Instead of studying, he started going out nights with his college buddies. His grades began to suffer.

Like your typical maladjusted male, his roving eye would catch a voluptuous nympho or two at one of those pick-up joints and her abounding generosity would keep him away from me for a couple of nights. Of course, he would always come crawling back begging forgiveness, proclaiming his love for me. Like the alcoholic who says I'll never take another drink, my masochistic belief in my need of him, plus the fact that I would be alone, forgave his dirty betrayal.

* * *

On the telephone, the former love of my life told me he had some very important matters to discuss concerning the baby. Secretly, I was thrilled to hear from him, but in a perverse way I hoped he was suffering as much as I was.

In my heart, what I truly wanted was for him to finally admit he still loved me and wanted to start over. The majority of my lifetime had been spent depending on his love and support. He was my rock. Unfortunately, we both grew up and he fell off his stone pedestal, and instead of a halo, he had grown some ugly-looking horns.

My apartment was in a red brick building that had an old security system with a buzzer you pressed on the mailbox to get the occupant's attention. Upon entering the foyer, you had to walk carefully over the once colorful ceramic tiles, no longer a geometrical design, more like the long-forgotten pieces of a jigsaw puzzle.

Taking a hurried glance around the living room, I jokingly thought to myself, "He certainly wasn't coming after our worldly possessions." At this moment, they consisted of a broken couch, one folding table with four chairs, which served as a makeshift kitchen table, and a bed which was really a mattress on the floor. I ran around the apartment straightening the pillows. Of course, that took only a couple of seconds. I quickly brushed my teeth, combed my hair, and put on a little makeup.

A few minutes later the buzzer rang. Nick must have been around the corner. As soon as I opened the door, my confidence was dashed. Nick wasn't coming home. He was saying good-bye.

A large knapsack was slung over his shoulder. In his hand, he held what looked to be an airline ticket and some papers. Not wanting to hear what he had to say, I was tempted to slam the door in his face. I looked into those beautiful, rotten, green eyes. Damn, he still took my breath away. He was the type of man you wanted to hate because he had it all: good looks, a sense of humor, a keen intellect. I was especially vulnerable when he wore a pair of tight blue jeans like the ones he had on now.

When he smiled, his swarthy complexion and perfectly straight teeth made women turn their heads at least once or twice. He also had on one of the few luxury items I had ever purchased, his brown leather bomber jacket and a pair of hiking boots. In these boots, he was at least 6'4".

There was guilt written on his face. Entering the apartment, he came straight to the point. "I'm sorry, Anne. I'm leaving. I've got a job in Texas. The oil company wants me there in two days. There's an exploration team leaving for the South Sea requiring a man with my background. I was actually hired over the Internet without a formal interview. Can you believe my luck?"

"Oh, here." As if they were an afterthought, he handed me the papers. "These are for you. "

Mystified, I took the papers from his hand. "What are they?" I asked.

Nick was visibly uncomfortable. "They're legal papers giving up my parental rights. It wasn't my idea to have this kid. It's your baby."

The way he said "your baby" made me want to bust that handsome face into a billion pieces. I carefully placed my hands along the sides of my skirt to control my temper. "Are you insane? Do you have any idea what you're doing?"

Fidgeting with his knapsack, he reluctantly gave it up and placed it on the floor. He looked like he'd rather be anywhere, anywhere but here with me.

"I know what I'm doing," he said impatiently. "I realized a long time ago I'm not the man to make you happy. Trust me. No man can do that."

Nick came forward and placed his hands on my shoulders. He turned me toward the direction of the mirror hanging on the wall. "Look at yourself. You don't need me. That woman in there has finally grown up. You're no longer a child."

Then he absentmindedly placed a kiss on my cheek. I desperately wanted him to hold me. Instead, he saw the yearning in my face and quickly let me go.

Not wanting to hear my comment on his lack of compassion,

he sat down in one of the folding chairs and ignored me. I walked into the kitchen and poured myself a glass of water. Several minutes passed in uncomfortable silence. Rubbing his hands along his face, Nick was ill at ease.

"We never should have gotten married," he said in a callous tone of voice.

"Yeah, you're right. We were both too young." He was surprised to hear me say that.

"I had nowhere to go, no place to call home. But you stood by me, didn't you, Nick? What would I have done without you?"

He held out his hand. There wasn't a thing I could do. I walked toward him and placed mine in his. I didn't have it in me to refuse him.

"It's true," he said. "You needed me then, or at least I thought you did. Nevertheless, you would've survived. Probably better than *we* did. Yet, you never complained. We had nothing." He glanced around the room and chuckled. "At least not in a tangible sense. Nothing's changed, has it?"

He laughed at his joke. I didn't think it was very funny. He was beginning to feel a little more comfortable with me. Reaching over, he placed me on his lap and moved my chin to meet his gaze.

"You see, my dear, you don't know what the word 'happiness' means. Oh, you'll occasionally smile, but it never seems to reach your eyes. I suppose I'm partly to blame. I didn't know how to help you find the answers. I let you hide from the world, from yourself. I was wrong. I see that now."

Nick's tone changed to one admonishing a small child. "Anne, since I won't be giving you any more advice, I would like you to listen to me for a couple of seconds." I knew I was in for one of his long lectures. I took a frustrated breath.

"You've turned your mind and your heart inward."

"Wait a minute, Nick. That's what I'm trying to tell you."

"Listen! That's one of your problems. I'm trying to give you some sound advice here. Stop living for the sake of living. Every time you feel happy, don't think you've robbed your brother of his happiness. You of all people deserve to be happy. Jack would have wanted it for you. Get him out of your system. If you don't, you'll never be free. You're what I call an HD."

"What's that?" I asked.

"A human downer," he answered. "You've been like this noose tied around my neck, and now I'm free. I like myself again."

It wasn't easy to hear him say this. He was right. Since his leaving, I too had changed. Perhaps I could make him understand. It's true. I didn't know how to have fun, his kind of fun. Making friends and partying all night seemed so unproductive.

"I'm sorry, Nick. But you're wrong. I'm working through this guilt and I am capable of happiness. It's just taken me a lot longer to figure it out."

Placing his hands around my large waist, he pulled me against him. Unbalanced, I fell into his chest. I was embarrassed. There was no concealing the fact I was big and pregnant and nearing the end of my second trimester. Damn, I was such a fool. I still wanted him. Reluctantly, I disentangled myself from his embrace.

Nick almost seemed disappointed. "You know, I've always had trouble keeping my hands off that gorgeous body of yours," he said, totally aware of my desire for him.

Even though, a couple of seconds ago, I was incapable of it, I chuckled. Damn, I still loved him. He wasn't all bad, being irresponsible was part of his charm. I gave up and let the tears roll down my face.

"Divorce obviously becomes you. You're laughing," he said tapping my arm. I guess he didn't recognize hysteria when he saw it.

"You're better off without me. After you graduated from law school, I thought we'd travel together, finally have some fun, live life out of a car or something. Not this pregnancy fiasco. Believe me, I'm not equipped to be anyone's father."

Realizing I had married a different type of man, I made one last attempt. "Giving me up is one thing, Nick, but giving up your own flesh and blood -- what kind of a man does that?"

"What do you want me to say? I'm a man who puts his happiness before anyone else's, someone selfish. At least I'm honest enough to know the baby deserves a better father than me."

Nick stood up as if to leave. "Look, there's no excuse for my behavior. It's a waste of time to argue about this. My mind is made up. I want out."

Giving him a look of disgust, I turned my back. I wanted him to leave. This seemed to anger him all the more. His voice raised a couple of octaves. "Damn you. Don't look at me like that. In this day and age only a fool has an unwanted pregnancy."

"You bastard," I screamed. "What's that supposed to mean? If I abort this baby, you'll stay with me?"

Nick shook his head. "No, that's not what I meant. You're the fool responsible for this fiasco, not me. Why in the hell don't they give men the birth control pill?"

That cinched it. He deserved a couple of blows to the head. Nick grabbed my hand just as I was about to punch his nose into the nether regions of his brain. He held my fist in check; so I kicked him in the shin. It didn't hurt him. It hurt me. I had kicked the hard, leather sole of his boot.

"Damn you to hell, Nicholas John Stevens. That hurt," I said, rubbing my swollen foot. At that moment, I hated him. He had a child's rudimentary understanding of life. Anything too complex, exit stage left. For once in my life, that's exactly where I wanted him. The qualities I thought I loved had never existed. That wasn't quite true. They existed in my fantasy world, my projections of who he was. It was my miscalculation of his character flaws that put me here. It was all my fault.

"You know, Nick, if I were a vindictive woman, I could track you down and make you pay child support for the rest of your life. These ridiculous papers in my hand won't erase that fact."

Defeated, he released his hold. Regaining my balance, I again sat down at the table. Still angry but in a much quieter tone, I added, "If you wanted to travel, why didn't you say so? Communication, Nick. Do you know what the word means? No, you don't. It means open your damn mouth and say what you want. I sure as hell can't read your mind. If it's fun you want, by all means, let's go. Try to understand. The stupid woman in me still loves you. The smarter woman in me hates you. Damn you, I hate you!" I said, hitting him in the arm. "Damn you, I love you. A part of me always will."

I wiped the tears flowing freely down my face. "Don't you see? Marriage is never simple. It's not supposed to be. You have to be willing to give and take and fight when you want to give up. Besides, what's wrong with you? You're acting like some spoiled brat and there's nothing I can do about it. Where's the man I thought I married?"

Nick remained silent, not answering me.

"You're right about one thing," I said. "Our marriage was a disaster. God knows it was hard enough without adding all the other crap we had to deal with. Look at what we did. There was no one to help us through college and hand those diplomas to us on a silver platter. We worked hard. If we got through that, we can get through anything."

I couldn't keep the regret out of my voice. "Oh, Nick, you've kept me sane and stood by me all these years. Don't you see? That's what marriage is all about."

Trying not to plead too hard, I placed my hand in his. "Look, for the first time in our life, I have a real job and our bills are somewhat caught up. Money will no longer be a problem."

Nick, frustrated, shook his head and sat back down. We were both playing musical chairs. In frustration, he gripped my shoulders a little too roughly.

"Can't you see? It's always about you. It's never about me. It's over. Try getting it through that thick skull of yours."

"Damn you, Nick, look at me! This thing between us will never be over. Never. You take your last long look and remember this day for the rest of your life."

He refused to look me in the eye. Giving up, I released my hold and turned away. I was too angry to care.

"Don't come back," I said with finality in my voice. It was over, and I had to accept it.

"When you walk out that door, there will be no changing your mind. This baby and I are out of your life for good. Tracking you down will be the last thing I'll do."

I turned to face him for the last time. I had always forgiven him, always took what he was able to give. There was no love not worth having, or at least that's what I had come to expect. I deserved more.

"You know, Nick, the funny thing is you're the one who's pathetic. It's true. I actually feel sorry for you."

He was growing tired of the fight and weary of the conversation. As if dismissing me, he stood up to leave.

"I guess that's the way you see it," he whispered with no hint of regret. "I'm sorry for hurting you. You're probably right. It will never be truly over. In my own way, I'll always love you, Anne."

He once again came toward me and raised my chin to meet his face. I saw tears in his eyes. Perhaps there was some human compassion in the man and he wasn't a total loss.

"You're the sister I never had. I'm going to miss you," he said apologetically.

I suppressed the urge to spit in his face and began to chuckle.

"Don't laugh," he scolded. I wasn't laughing. I was shaking with anger. He pulled me to him. I buried my head in his coat not wanting to listen. "You've always been my best friend, the sister I never had. You're a hell of a woman, Anne, a good woman. Just no longer mine. You'll make a fine lawyer someday." He caught my surprised look.

"I should have known the minute I told you not to go to law school that's where you'd head."

He raised my hand to his lips and placed a kiss in my palm. "You're always trying to fight for the misbegotten garbage who have no life. When you walk down a sidewalk, you pick up the broken pieces of glass. I'd say don't waste your time, but you'd never listen."

He gave me one last hug similar to the type you would give an old relative. "You think you can change the world. Good luck to you. Put those blinders on and never see the true filth that sits outside your window at night. I'm glad I won't be around when you realize there's not a damn thing you can do about it."

With the back of his hand, he wiped away one of my tears.

"For once in your life, do something for me. Let me go. Please."

Placing a lingering kiss upon my lips, he turned and picked up his knapsack. "Perhaps you're right and I am throwing away the best thing that ever happened to me. Try to understand. I would suffocate with the life you have planned for us."

I felt physically and emotionally drained. Still not able to give up, I made one last attempt. "Can't we at least be friends? You can write to me, call me, check up on us from time to time."

Nick, impervious to my pleas, had that look of finality and stubborn pride. His need for freedom was what had brought him here and that was all he wanted.

"No," he said, frustrated by my lack of understanding. "I

want out. Permanently. No strings attached. No child. Nothing. You're pregnant and I'm sorry for that. To make it easier to raise this kid, I stopped by to drop off those."

Nick pointed to the papers lying on the table and looked into my eyes. For a couple of seconds, we just stood there without saying anything. "Good-bye," he said. "Have a nice life."

I mimicked his voice. "Good-bye. Have a nice life. You're leaving for good, and that's the best you can do?"

He turned his back on me and headed for the door. "That's it," he said, looking me squarely in the face. A couple of seconds later, he shut the door.

Without thinking, I walked toward the window. I foolishly watched as he took the final steps out of my life, that spineless creature who meant everything to me, my best friend, my champion, my rock. I saw a rugged, good-looking man who loved the outdoors. I loved that face, that body, those hands. I needed those arms. Or did I? He might as well have ripped my heart out and taken it with him. Damn him. I was completely alone, once again abandoned. Perhaps it was my fault after all.

There was a life, our life, growing inside of me. Nick was right about one thing. I stopped taking the pill on purpose. I knew this day would come. There, I had finally said it. I wanted this child. I wanted it because I needed to belong somewhere. I needed a sense of family so long denied me. Folly or not, it was our flesh and blood, now my flesh and blood.

As though the baby sensed its mother's pain, I felt a soft nudge against the side of my abdomen. Soon there would be someone else in my life, someone to love, someone to hold, someone who wouldn't run out on me...die on me. Damn you all for leaving!

I had a habit of speaking to this baby. "This isn't exactly what I would have wanted for you, no father. Oh, hell. Who needs a man? Not me, sweet baby. Most of the ones I've known have been useless sacks of shit anyway. Unlike me, you'll never experience a day of your life without knowing you're loved.

"We're going to show him. Don't you worry. And you bet we're going to have fun. I solemnly swear I'll never take you for granted, to take living so seriously. I will listen to you when no one else will, give you advice and joy like no one else can."

As I continued to foolishly stare out the window, I caught my last sight of Nick as he rounded the street corner. To hell with him. I was free. I no longer needed the safety nets of his protection.

"I feel sorry for you, you son of a bitch. I hope to God someday you'll realize what you missed out on. Too bad. When you finally figure it out, it will be too late. Good-bye, Nick. 'Have a nice life,' my ass. You have a lousy life, you mother-fucking jerk. You traitor. You scumbag."

CHAPTER
III

This morning was one of those December, chill-you-to-the-bone days. I recognized the symptom. It was competing with my heart.

After Nick had left, I spent the night awake feeling sorry for myself. In fact, I didn't have the strength for work. I called in sick. It wasn't a lie.

Grabbing for what was left in the tissue box, I blew my nose. The phone rang. After all these years without one of these obnoxious contraptions, whatever had compelled me to finally get one? I tried to ignore it, but it kept on ringing. I knew who it was.

"Hello." I sounded hoarse, like I had a cold.

"Annie, is that you?" I ignored the question.

"I called you at work, and you weren't there. Nick didn't come home last night, did he? Oh, you poor dear. Well, ol' Mattie here happens to have the cure for broken hearts. I'll be right over."

I started to protest, but the phone went dead. It was typical Mattie. Staying out of my business was not her style.

* * *

The first time I met this paragon of femininity was about a year ago. Before ever setting eyes upon her, this woman had been nicknamed "the psychic experience" by several of my colleagues at the Legal Aid Department. Mattie was what we lawyers call *pro bono* work, one of those charity causes you do for free.

When she called the department, I was a third-year law student who had just volunteered a couple of hours a day. She was set to pick on the next female staff member. Oh, yes, it had to be a woman. She admired women and distrusted men. Right now, we certainly had that in common. Her feministic belief for a woman to succeed in life was simple: "Do better work than any other man in your field. "

Just the mention of Mattie Turner's name brought forth fits of despair, coupled with laughter. All of them seemed to have a "Turner" story of their own to tell.

The department personnel conspired and, fortunately or unfortunately, gave Mattie my name. I hadn't known it then. This was to be a morning that would forever change my life, the morning Mattie Turner came looking for me.

I heard her before I saw her. A demanding voice was yelling my name. "Anne Stevens. Anne Stevens. I wish to speak to Anne Stevens!"

The experienced receptionist smiled and ducked under her desk. I didn't know whether she was teasing her or whether she was truly intimidated by her. Mattie, used to the routine, began to talk first.

"No, I didn't make an appointment, you numbskull. You know who I am, and you know what I want. Please don't waste my time."

Straightening her jacket, the entire office could hear her complaint. "I have rights, young lady. I'm a very busy woman, and I don't have time for this nonsense. Just direct me to Anne Stevens. Never mind. I'll find her myself."

The receptionist quickly pointed a finger in my direction. I watched the woman as she searched the room.

"Oh, there she is." She left the waiting area and headed toward my desk. She waved to several members of the department as she passed them. They all turned their heads and looked over at me with sympathetic smiles on their faces.

Mattie Turner didn't seem so tough. I really expected someone the size of the Jolly Green Giant. She was, in fact, quite petite. She was a striking black woman with flawless skin. She had on a nice-looking hunter green jacket with gold buttons down the front. Her hair was streaked with gray and piled in a bun. A tortoise shell comb was having some trouble keeping all of her hair piled on top of her head.

She kept mumbling as she approached. "This place is always a madhouse. Don't you people have better things to do with your life? Go find a job, volunteer, do something worthwhile."

Unconcerned by the attention she was receiving, she limped her way through the crowd. I found out later she had fallen off a ladder painting the outside windows of her house. She was using a cane to aid her in her quest to find me.

A little voice in the back of my brain said, "Quick, duck under the desk, too." Unfortunately, I failed to listen to it. Finally, she stopped at my desk. "You're Anne Stevens, aren't you?"

"Yes, Miss Turner, I am. As soon as I'm finished with this young woman." I pointed to the person that had previously been sitting in the chair. There was no one there. Perhaps that cane of hers was a magic wand, and she used it on my vanishing client.

Strangely enough, all the other people in the room had also moved aside.

Slightly winded, Mattie sat down and took the newly-vacated seat. She reached in her handbag for her glasses. Placing them on her nose, and with the aid of her cane, she leaned into my desk, taking a closer look at me.

"First things first, Miss Stevens," she said, gazing directly into my face. "Before I will accept your help, I need to take a good look at you. Come here a little closer." For some unknown reason, I did what she asked.

"I want you to know I'm an excellent judge of character. When I look into a person's eyes, I can see what's inside."

Rolling my eyes at her, I looked around at the others still watching and gave them one of those you-have-got-to-be-joking looks.

"It's true. Pay no attention to them. They're your typical unbelievers. Trust me. I'll know immediately whether you're a genuine person or a phony."

I looked at my colleagues, shrugging my shoulders.

"Do your ears work? Stop looking at those other people. They've been through it, too. They've failed miserably." Instead of shaking my hand and saying, "Hello. My name is Mattie Turner," we were engaged in a small battle of wills.

Not wanting her to get the upper hand or think she had some authority over me, at first I didn't do what she asked. Eventually I couldn't help it. I began scrutinizing her in the same manner she was scrutinizing me. Don't ask me why. I learned later that weird and wonderful things happen to you when you're around this crazy woman.

A couple of seconds elapsed in silence. Mattie, not I, inevitably broke the dueling match.

"Young lady, with that auburn hair and dark green eyes you're beautiful. You don't know it yet, do you? You're a strange combination, stubborn yet sensitive, insecure yet strong. It suits you. You're one of a kind, Annie Stevens."

She saw the nameplate on my desk. "That's right. You're Annie to me." I started to protest. She raised her hand, taking her fingers to her lips. "Ah, that uptight expression is bad for your constitution. Wipe it off your face right now before you get permanent wrinkles like mine. I've dealt with your kind before. When I taught school, I could always spot the special ones. I hope you like a good challenge."

I tried not to smile. It wasn't every day someone thought I was special. "There's just a touch of humor below the surface. You definitely need to work on that. It's rarely used, but it's locked away. I'll bring it out of you. Don't you worry about that."

She lifted the glasses off her nose, running her eyes down the front of my blouse. "Judging by your clothes, you're paying for your own education. No Jewish father? I've met a few of them here. Too spoiled for their own good. Take my word for it. You don't need one. Lack of money builds strength of character."

I thought she was through mocking me. I was wrong. "Most people find you unfriendly.   It's not because you're a snob; it's because you're unsure of yourself, isn't it? You're extremely intelligent -- another fine attribute that will often get a woman in trouble."

Mattie was not ready to shut up. She put her glasses back on her nose and turned her head toward the picture frame of a baby girl sitting on my desk. "Not yours, the coloring is all wrong." I nodded. I usually sat around the corner at a different desk.

She scraped her chair, leaning in closer. "Oh, yes, there's more than meets the eye here, something secretive," she said whispering. "You're hiding -- oh, yes, you're hiding guilt. I recognize the symptom. Perhaps old family skeletons? Remember, no one can say of his house, there is no trouble here. It's quite true, you know. It's an old Oriental proverb."

The shocked expression on my face registered her accuracy. "Oh, I see, touched a sore nerve, did I? So, you know pain and have experienced some kind of tragedy. Even now you're resenting the fact I'm right. Don't worry. It's none of my business. I, too, have my scars. I'll never invade your privacy -- at least not until I've gotten to know you better. I'm sorry to say it, Miss Stevens, but it's in the cards. We're destined for a deep and lasting friendship."

Had she just psychoanalyzed me or given me a psychic reading? I wasn't sure. It was my turn to get even.

"Miss Turner, I, too, have done my homework." I was about to give the lady a dose of her own medicine. I picked up my pencil and legal pad, writing her name on the top of the page.

"Miss Madeline Sterling Turner, most of my colleagues here find you exasperating. At the same time, they admire your tenacity and spirit. No one pushes you around and gets away with it, do they? I've been told you're a retired schoolteacher. Now that I've met you, I can't help but think you don't exactly fit the mold. CEO of a large corporation would be more in line with your character. Or, better yet, a dictator in a small foreign country."

Imitating the way she raised her nose when she compared my clothing, I did the same. "You dress in expensive clothes and have a keen eye for beautiful things. You bought them yourself, didn't you? Too bad. No rich husband."

The humor in Mattie's eyes lit her face. She was about to say something. I touched her arm and shook my head.

"I'm not done. It's still my turn. My sources tell me you fought against the system in the '60s. You rode buses like Rosa Parks. Only no one gave it a thought to take your seat." I moved closer to her and whispered in her ear. "Actually, that's a piece of nonsense made up by colleagues here after they got to know you better. After meeting you, there must be some truth to it."

Mattie winked at the others and shook her fingers at them. I continued with my assessment. "You don't trust anyone. You have delusions of persecution that are built up primarily by your own paranoia. Everyone is out to get you, aren't they, Miss Turner?"

Placing her file on my desk, I leaned back in my chair. "They tell me you're brave enough to fight off the street gangs. In fact, that's why you're here. You're also a philanthropist. You've made it your main objective in life, badgering the city council for zoning so you can convert your home into a youth home for young blacks who need your education, love, and support."

I put my pen down and waited for her response. She said nothing. It took me a couple of seconds to realize she was waiting for me to continue.

"I'm sorry. Are you through?" She asked, sarcastically. "I didn't want to interrupt your diatribe of my character flaws. Surely you have more to say."

"I'm through. Say what you came here to say and let me get back to work." I said, with more rudeness than I intended.

Mattie Turner stood without using her cane. With her chin raised, she turned slowly so everyone in the room could hear. The mayhem usually associated with this office was not there. It was quiet. There were several people waiting for her reaction.

"Good afternoon, my former colleagues. My reputation certainly precedes me." She gave them all a coy smile. Everyone chuckled. They started to go back to their work. She held up her hand expecting their full attention.

"No matter what you people may think, I still want to do my work. You all want to be lawyers. You're young and idealistic. Remember, enthusiasm decreases as our experience increases. Do your work well, use your heart along with what you do best. Indifference never wrote great works. Indifference will never change your lives."

Their silence was similar to that of young pupils in a classroom whose teacher had just given them a good balling out. Mattie sat down and turned her attention back to me. I smiled and nodded my head. I knew I was going to like this woman. I was well on my way to admiring her spirit.

"You're right. Your reputation *does* precede you. Many people here say they've tried to help, but you're such a pain in the neck no one can work with you."

I took a sheet of paper from my desk drawer and placed it on the table. "Personally, Miss Turner, I don't care whether you're a paranoid schizophrenic or you have delusions of little creatures from outer space at your door, those children need people like you. At least that seems to be the consensus of everyone here. We're not your enemy. We want what you want. But I've also been told you're rude, totally out of control, and you're your own worst enemy. The city council has tried to help you."

"Help me? Baloney! Let me show you a thing or two, Miss Know-it-all." She laid her glasses on the desk.

Opening her purse, she handed me a couple of documents. "Here, Miss Stevens, take a good look at these. One more thing, I'm not here to win a Miss Congeniality award. I'm here to pick your brain and use you like I have everybody else. However, I must admit you've impressed me. In my life, that rarely happens."

She leaned into her chair and whispered in my ear. "I'll let you in on a little secret. I tend to like bitchy women." I was surprised she had pegged me in that way, but I didn't say anything. I had rehearsed this speech and she knew it.

She poured the contents of her purse out on my desk and found an electronic organizer about the size of a small book. I had no opportunity to read the papers in my hand. She continud to intrigue me as she went on with her complaints.

"How do you like my computer terminal? I can download the information from my home computer. Pretty cool, huh?" She took her pen and pressed a couple of buttons on the small screen. "Last October they asked me to put in a wheelchair ramp. I did. Now, they want me to install a sprinkler system in my house. Well, they can stick that sprinkler system where the sun won't shine. I simply can't afford it. They're also griping about my stair rails of all things. Those damn stair rails have been in that house over eighty years now. Surely they'll be around for another eighty."

She turned the organizer off and put it back in her purse. "Miss Stevens, to tell you the truth, they're wearing me out. I'm tired. I can't take much more of this. They've abused me, demanded things of me, and I can't physically do it anymore."

Mattie raised her head toward the ceiling. "Oh, but, Lord, how I've tried. You've obviously done your homework. It's not the first time something like this has happened. Why can't they see the good in what's going to come out of this? What's wrong with changing a few of these kids's lives? All I'm trying to do is put a little human dignity back in my neighborhood. Sprinkler systems, my ass. They're all a bunch of prickly white folks who could care less what's happening in our community."

She leaned on her cane and pointed her finger at me. "Well, young lady, are you willing to help me conquer those city demons? I think it's people like you who can make this project work. As for trusting people, you're right. I don't. Believe me, I have my own reasons which are none of your concern. If you lived in my neighborhood, you'd understand. In fact, I'd like you to see it. Will you come to dinner?"

The queen had invited me into her domain, even though it was common knowledge people who had known her for years never saw the inside of her house.

Without commenting, I attempted to read the papers she

handed me. After all, I didn't have time for this. I had an assignment due in Con. Law. Mattie pulled out a twenty-dollar bill and placed it in my hand.

"What's this for?" I asked.

Mattie ignored my question, collecting the contents of her pocketbook. She groaned using her cane to pull herself up from the chair. "Damn, it's hell to grow old. I need a new body. Know any doctors doing body transplants? The money is for dinner, silly. Meet me at six o'clock. Here's my address."

She handed me her business card. It read: Madeline Turner, 1601 Holloway Street, Occupation: teacher. In the corner in small print it said, "Children may close their eyes to advice, but you can open their eyes with example."

I looked up and smiled. She winked back. "Just pick up one of those roasted chickens at the grocery store and a couple of salads, but only if they appear fresh. I hate brown lettuce."

As an afterthought, she added, "Oh, and a decent bottle of wine. I love dry reds or whites. It makes no difference as long as they are *very* dry. None of this sweet crap for me. Here, I better give you another twenty.   An occasion like this calls for *grand cru classe*."

There was a gleam of mischief in her eyes. She backed away from my desk and frowned. "And take that surprised look off your face, Miss Stevens. Believe me, deary, you don't want me to cook. Some of the cans in my cupboard date back to the 1960s. We'd probably die of botulism. I keep saying I'm going to throw them away, but that depression child in me can't. But you're right about that paranoia. Who knows, we might be under nuclear attack someday and botulism would probably beat starvation."

Still holding the money in my outstretched hand, I asked, "Why me?"

"Let's just say you remind me of myself at your age. Besides,

I could use some intellectual stimulation. I'll expect to see you promptly at six o'clock." She glanced at her watch. "Oh, damn, I've got to run. That's a joke. I can barely walk."

As an afterthought, she whispered, "I have one more place to go without an appointment. Well, it's been an interesting afternoon. By the way, you can call me Mattie. Have a nice day, Annie."

Without waiting for my response, she picked up her cane and left, never giving me a chance to turn down her invitation. Still holding the money in my hand, I knew Queen Madeline Sterling Turner had been the victor of round one.

* * *

That evening I obeyed her instructions to the letter. Turning the corner onto Holloway Street promptly at six o'clock, I pulled alongside the drive. I was astonished at the size of her home.

There were window boxes with an array of colorful flowers all along the upper floor balconies. A profusion of perennials and annuals reflected a superb attention to detail and color. It had a wide veranda that wound its way across the front porch to the east side.

At one time, it must have been magestic in its ancient setting. It needed a quiet park with women in fine dresses carrying parasols. It was astonishing to find such a historical-looking home existing in such a neglected neighborhood. As if to protect itself from the crime in the streets, a black wrought iron fence surrounded the grounds.

She must have been watching for me. The front gate opened electronically. I drove my decrepit car onto a newly, blacktopped driveway. I got out and walked to the front of the house carrying our dinner. Mattie wobbled toward me. She greeted me before I had a chance to take a closer look at the beauty of her home.

"Miss Turner, this house is gorgeous. However do you manage it in this neighborhood?" I asked, hoping I didn't sound too pretentious.

"Stop this 'Miss Turner' nonsense. I told you my name is Mattie. It's a pretty incredible old place, isn't it? I call it Mattie's albatross."

As we walked toward the front porch, she turned toward the drive. "How do you like my new advanced security system? I can't have my kids wandering around in the streets, now can I? Besides, I'm like a kid in a candy store. I just love these electronic gizmos." She pressed a button and the gate closed. "Unfortunately, they confound me at least half the time. I suppose it gives me something to do."

We walked up the sidewalk to the front porch. She quickly grabbed my arm. "Oh, be careful. Don't step on my sidewalk. The cleaning solution will mess up your shoes." On the ground was a large metal section of fence.

"You should have seen it. It was all bent up and rusted. Incredible, isn't it? It looks brand new."

Mattie pushed the front door open allowing dinner and me to enter first. "I guess you forgot to buy a remote for your door," I said sarcastically.

"Oh, no, didn't you see James?" She pointed to a man in a ball cap sitting on the sofa. "Oh, that man. He's so lazy." She walked over to him and picked him up. He was a plastic dummy filled with air. It was kind of eerie. He looked just like a real man dressed like a construction worker, shoes and all. "Best kind of man to have around. He keeps his opinions to himself."

She positioned him back on her couch, bending his leg to cross the other. "People who might be too curious think I have company. It's a nice security measure for a lonely female."

I turned back toward the hallway. A circular staircase

immediately caught my eye. The grand foyer opened directly into a spacious room with a vaulted ceiling. Oddly, there was no furniture, but the hardwood floors gleamed as if they were made of glass.

Mattie took the food. "I've been working on that floor for a couple of weeks now. It's amazing what a determined woman and some power tools can do, isn't it?" I noticed her chin raise a few notches or two as I continued to follow her. I suppose she was waiting for a compliment, but I was too overwhelmed to say anything.

Avoiding the great room, we walked down a dark narrow hallway. "This house belonged to my great grandmother who, I am told, was an extraordinary woman. She married a very old but wealthy man. Not long after they married, the good Lord took him away. My mother always suspected my great grandmother had something to do with his precipitous death. He died so unexpectedly. Only Great Grandma knows the truth and her secret died with her."

I was having trouble following her story. Mattie fumbled for the light switch. "My mother said the old lady despised men. I think it's a family trait. Even though she was a young woman when the old man died, she never remarried. Anyway, that bright and intelligent woman left the house to the women in the Sterling family. You called me that this morning. My mother's maiden name was Sterling. Even if my mother had blessed her with a great grandson, the house could only be inherited by a woman heir. Quite the feminist, huh?"

Mattie was dressed in a lovely, dark purple dress. A set of old-fashioned flapper beads from the 1920's hung around her neck. She wore a pair of black suede boots. Looking at her, you would never guess her age. Her hair was neatly plaited at the back of her head. Her skin was absolutely flawless. She was still a very lovely woman.

With dinner in her arms, the queen flipped the light switch.

She might not know how to cook, but she sure set a lovely table.

Several candles sat in antique etched sterling silver candelabras on the dinner table. She had a centerpiece of blue flowers that matched a set of blue and silver china, obviously quite valuable. The room was lit by a spectacular crystal chandelier, its prisms refracting rainbow of colors on the walls and ceiling, achieving a sense of intimacy despite the room's size.

There was a huge stone fireplace with a magnificent brass mirror above the mantel reflecting the refined appointments of the room. Vivid blue fabric hung at the windows and on the chairs were matching seat covers. A Louis XV clock ticked away the hour.

I was spellbound. This room was like a fairy godmother's private dining room. I looked at my simple navy blue skirt and shabby black cardigan. It was out of my league. Someone had forgotten to send me Cinderella's gown.

Like the woman herself, Mattie's home reflected her warmth and charm. She gave no explanation for her elaborate setting. She lit a match and went about the room lighting some of the magnificent candles.

"I'll be right back. Make yourself comfortable," she said, almost burning her fingers on the match. She blew it out, leaving the room in a small trail of smoke.

It was obvious she wanted to impress me. Why? As if on cue, she returned with a large platter and quickly assembled our meal. We ate roasted chicken from the grocery store on plates fit for queens.

For the first time in my life, I talked openly to someone other than Nick. Prior to Mattie, I had always been reserved around strangers. After two bottles of wine, I didn't care. Yes, I did, but I knew she liked me.

During this time, I was also having marital problems and desperately needed someone to confide in. I even told her about my father and my dreams and hopes for the future, why I went to law school. This was the same night I stopped taking birth control. It wasn't Mattie's suggestion. I knew Nick would leave me. The thought of *alone* scared me more than I was capable of admitting. It didn't take a psychic reading to know that we needed each other and we were going to be good friends.

Ironically, she told me she'd spent the last few years of her life behind the walls of her own home, too afraid to open her door or cross the street. She jokingly referred to it as her "agoraphobia phase." Oddly enough, it wasn't present in the woman I saw today. Mattie was blessed with a fierce inner strength and a courageous spirit.

The streets outside this enchanting fortress were not safe. She told me of her fears and what it was like to live here. Through her description, it was as if I could hear the shots of gunfire, ever present, ever pervasive. She explained to me how the kids were used to those frightening sounds; and, much more horrifying, they were used to the deaths that so often struck their playmates.

After thanking her for a lovely dinner, I got in my car and waved good-bye. I caught myself listening to her sounds of night. Pulling out of the driveway, a shiver ran down my spine. Turning the corner, I glanced in my rear-view mirror. Two young boys were exchanging small talk on the street corner. I saw one of them give the other a greeting. The smaller boy, possibly ten, placed something in the other's pocket.

There was no power against the evil that permeated Mattie's streets -- the streets of gangs. Men who held the drug had the power to snuff out human lives. The sheer evil of this activity was compounding itself, casting a dark menacing shadow over Holloway Street and, indeed, throughout the nation.

This epidemic demoralized the human spirit; and because of crack cocaine, human compassion was nonexistent. It was like driving through another world, a world where a white person like me could get shot for simply being white.   I must be insane.

Mattie and I hadn't even touched on the issue of bigotry. For so many centuries, humans have found companionship in their own kind, and breaking that barrier would always be more than difficult. Was I stupid enough to help Mattie in a world in which I would never belong?

Mattie's cause was about to be *our* cause. Together, we were to fight the perilous injustices that put children at risk on her streets and to protect the lost souls that even now were succumbing to the power of the drug.

Hopefully, someday when she gazed out her window, she could feel a sense of peace, no longer worried that the glass would be shattered by a straying bullet. Mattie needed a lot of people on her side. She could not take her streets back alone. Unfortunately, no one was standing in line. This was bigger than feeling sorry for myself. This was what Jack would have wanted. I had agreed to become her champion, someone to do her grunt work.

* * *

Months slipped by, and the battle with the city council persisted. Her neighbors were too afraid and unwilling to fight. In fact, meeting after meeting they showed up before the council challenging our petition for zoning. Perhaps they were being paid by the same stench that rotted the streets.   Time after time, we walked away disappointed.

However, a few weeks ago, we had achieved our first victory. Thankfully a couple of concerned police officers urged them to pass the referendum. Thanks to a white Irish cop named Murphy, the council finally gave us the permit to open Mattie's house.

No one seeking refuge at her doorstep was going to be turned away. It was to be a place that provided sanctuary and, yes, of course, a lot of love.

Mattie's battles had just begun. She was rich, but not rich enough. At the present time, she was selling off all the beautiful furniture and antiques she'd inherited. She told me, "They're just useless old objects that are no longer important. What am I going to do with them? Take them to my grave?"

It depressed me to watch the appraisers go through her items piece by piece. I felt she was selling a piece of herself, her history. I suppose having never experienced a sense of family made those things important in my eyes. Not in Mattie's. She saw a greater treasure in helping others.

As we took a final walk through the empty house one night, she put her arm around me and said, "Annie, my dear, don't you see? In this life, we must not only give what we have; we must also give what we are. And right now it's what we are that'll make a difference to those children."

Mattie was doing just that. Instead of sterling and crystal, there were functional, tough pieces of furniture and bunk beds, books, food; everything necessary to get this home functioning.

Other mounting problems were the families in the neighborhood. They were angry and afraid. Who could blame them? The gangs on the street had the power to destroy their homes or kill their children. She needed help. Still none was forthcoming. Everyday she lived in constant fear of retaliation.

C H A P T E R
IV

"Annie, are you in there? Open this door this instant," Mattie demanded, pounding the door. The nosy pain in the neck had come to cheer me up. Well, that was going to be impossible.

Frustrated by her intrusion, I thought I'd let her stand out there awhile. "Are you going to open this door?" She yelled. "If not, I'm going to break it down."

Afraid of complaining neighbors, I reluctantly did what she asked. With several packages in her hand, she ignored my unwelcoming face and entered my apartment.

"Don't give me that look, young lady." Placing the grocery sack on the folding table, she took out her purchases one at a time. Junk food more aptly described what she had brought.

"You need a friend." She handed me a chocolate bar. "I have just the cure for a broken heart – only you can't drink it, so I will. One more thing. I couldn't carry everything up here at once. I'll be right back."

A few minutes later Mattie came back carrying James, the dummy. "That's right. James won't break your heart. See. I knew I'd get you to smile. He's the type of guy we women can handle.

He'll cheer us both up." She positioned James on the couch and headed for the kitchen. Uncorking the bottle, she took a swig of the cure she had promised and patted the spot next to James on my broken couch where I was to sit. It was a little crowded.

"Now, tell me what that jerk of a husband had to say." She whispered in James's ear. "What'd you say, dear? You agree men are jerks. Yes, that's right, dear."

As I told her all the gory details, I continued to cry. She got drunk and spent the night.

* * *

It took several days for me to feel human again. I suppose it should have been more having wasted ten years on the deadbeat.

Without Mattie's guidance, I don't think I'd have made it. The holidays were particularly rough. She kept coming over with what I began to call her "care packages." She ordered a fruitcake from a catalog. I didn't have the heart to tell her I couldn't stand fruitcakes. I'd slice off small pieces at a time, sending it down the garbage disposal. The old thing grumbled, but it would eat it.

A couple of nights a week she'd stop by with tickets to a movie, telling me to lose myself in Harrison Ford's arms or Denzel Washington's gorgeous brown eyes. "Nothing like a good fantasy to take your mind off your broken heart," she'd say.

The Christmas tree she gave me came equipped with lights and ornaments. It was one of those old silver-tinseled things she'd bought at a church flea market many years before. It was ugly, but how it could cheer me up.

Before Mattie left on her mysterious vacation--I suspected it was with some secret boyfriend, but she wasn't telling--she gave me a beautifully embroidered handkerchief with my initials on it. The card read: "Annie, when you're through using this, call me. A newspaper clipping fell out of the card. In her handwriting in black ink it said, "If you keep this quote in mind, you should feel better in no time:

The institution of marriage makes a parasite of woman, an absolute dependent. It incapacitates her for life's struggle, annihilates her social consciousness, paralyzes her imagination, and then imposes its gracious protection, which is in reality a snare, a travesty on human character.

Love, the strongest and deepest element in all lives, the harbinger of hope, of joy, of ecstasy; love, the definer of all laws, of all conventions; love, the freest, the most powerful molder of human destiny; how can such an all-compelling force be synonymous with that poor little state -- and church-begotten word, marriage?"

She was right. Marriage sucked.

* * *

Fred, too, bought me interesting guaranteed-to-mend-a-broken-heart purchases. Actually, they were more along the lines of improving "Annie's culinary skills." Of course, Anne had no desire to learn. However, this did not deter Fred.

A full set of new stainless steel pots and pans sat unused in my cupboard along with the classic two-quart batter bowl with a lid accompanied by recipes and instruction booklets. I used the bowl under my kitchen sink to catch the water from my leaky faucet.

Before he left to celebrate Hanukkah in North Carolina, he dropped by with a bread and pizza baking stone. I almost hit him with it.

"A whole new world of delicious pizza and bread baking is at your fingertips, and the product has a warranty of one full year from the date of purchase!" he proclaimed, placing it on top of my counter.

It was then I finally figured it out. Fred had a new girlfriend working in a kitchen appliance store.

With the two of them gone, I was really alone. The best I could do was keep Mattie's handkerchief readily available and stay out of everyone else's way. That's exactly what I did. I had sent a card to my mother. There was no response. I was used to it.

When I was a child and everyone else was happily planning family dinners and gifts for their loved ones, my parents were usually playing some hate game of their own. It was called "Family Jeopardy." We were the ones in jeopardy of spending our Christmas holidays in solitary confinement.

On these occasions Jack and I would ignore them and celebrate by ourselves. We would pool our savings together and sneak off to our favorite restaurant, McDonald's. We'd play games, make something creative out of cardboard or paper plates. We even had a theme. If the gift did not make you laugh, you had to eat it. Jack had given me a *papier mache'* onion. Eventually, I laughed, but not before I'd taken a bite. At least it was a stab at something festive. I couldn't even do that. You can't be festive alone. I heard only the echoes of my lonely heart.

* * *

December was finally over. January had arrived. As if to tantalize me, a couple of days ago, the sun had been shining, the birds had been chirping, and the temperature was delightful. But now the bitter cold was back bringing with it snow and freezing rain.

With lawyer-like cunning, I planned on dropping a bomb on poor Fred. Since Nick's departure, at least one night a week we would get together for a pizza or a movie. He even bought me a ticket to my first college basketball game. I actually enjoyed myself.

My best approach was to use his sympathetic feelings toward me to my best advantage. Cautiously approaching Fred's desk, I removed a file from a chair and sat down in front of him. He was preparing an order on a motion for summary judgment which had been heard last week by Judge Rosenthal.

"Fred, I need to ask you a big favor. Can I talk to you seriously for a second?" He ignored me.

Patiently waiting, I watched as he typed the final paragraph to the order. "Just one more sentence and I'll be right with you," he said, paying close attention to the computer screen.

This gave me the opportunity to think about my game plan. How was I going to hit the unsuspecting Fred with this one? Okay. Just come out and ask it.

"Okay. What's on your mind?" Fred asked, as he turned toward me, taking a sip of his coffee.

I tensed in my chair, then blurted out the question. "Fred, will you take Lamaze classes with me? I desperately need a partner." Some innovative lawyer I would make some day.

For a few seconds, Fred didn't speak. The wrinkles on his forehead and the look of incredulity on his face caused me to get up and move to my half of the room. Damn, I never did get one of those room dividers. Perplexed, he wondered if he had heard me correctly. "You want me to do *what?*"

I calmly asked him again. "Will you take Lamaze classes with me?" Using my hands to ward off another outburst, I continued. "Just wait. Before you get all bent out of shape and say no, I only need you for a temporary replacement. I got up the courage to call my mother. She has agreed to be with me on the big day, but she can't make it to the classes. Please, they're only two times a week for four weeks. Please. I need you. Don't worry," I said, attempting to convince him, "I promise I'm not asking you to hold my hand through labor or anything. Just hold my hand through a couple of Lamaze classes."

For the first time in several months, Fred was speechless. He tried to squirm his way out of it by passing the buck. "Can't you find a girlfriend to take these classes with you? Why me?"

"Do you know of one girlfriend I have?" I asked. "You're the one with all the girlfriends. Maybe I should ask Miss Gadget Queen. Oh, I forgot. You broke up with her last week."

Of course, there was Mattie, but Fred didn't know about her. She was my secret. Mattie had seemed uncomfortable at the prospect. Besides, she was so busy. Two nights a week would be a hardship for her.

I moved closer toward his desk and began to plead. "I'm sorry, but there isn't anyone else to ask. You and Judge Rosenthal are it. He already thinks the best place for me is at home in bed. Truly, I don't think he could handle it. Please, Fred. I'm desperate and if you refuse me, I'm going to pop the same question to him."

I could see Fred's mind churning up ways in which to extricate himself. I was prepared to beg. "Please, Fred. I can't do this by myself. I'd feel too humiliated. I'll be stuck with all these loving couples and then me, alone, totally isolated, no one who cares for me."

I tried another approach. "If you were in this situation, I'd do it for you."

Fred gave me a withering look and laughed loudly. "If you did that for me, I wouldn't have to work another day in my life. Since I would be the first pregnant man in history, I could spend every afternoon on the golf course."

Putting on my best hoity-toity performance, I stood up and headed for the door. "Fine. This isn't a joking matter. I'll do it myself. In fact, I'm not that desperate. I was prepared to beg, but I won't. I'll come up with someone else. Forget I asked you!"

Fred rolled his eyes. "Oh, don't start whining. I can't stand females who whine. I'll do it, but on one condition. I take that back, two conditions," he said, holding two fingers in the air.

"What's that?" I asked, with a sigh of relief.

He relaxed in his chair, propping his feet on his desk. "I get one home-cooked meal with all these pots and pans I've been buying you, and I will not be in the labor room. No way. No way. Never. If you make a solemn promise I'll never have to witness this birthing thing, I'll do it. It's bad enough I may have to participate in this wholesome event with the woman I marry someday."

A mischievous light entered his eyes, as he chuckled to himself. "After all, what are you really asking me to do? I might enjoy sitting on the floor with you, surrounded by a couple of pillows, and, God forbid, more pregnant women."

An evil grin crossed his face. He threw a Nerf ball at me. I ducked. It hit one of the birds sitting on the shelf. "I suppose I could find some satisfaction in watching you lie there, breathing heavily, big as life, embarrassed, completely humbled. Oh, what a sexual fantasy. It sends shivers of revulsion up my spine."

Then another horrifying thought occurred to him. "Oh, by the way, how much of this is going to cut into my social life?"

"It's every Tuesday and Thursday night for four weeks," I answered.

Fred, somewhat resigned to his task, went back to his computer. "Darn, if it's this Tuesday I'm going to miss my mother's fine cooking and the Wake Forest/North Carolina basketball game."

Fred's mother took him out to dinner every Tuesday night. She was a single woman, a college professor. When she divorced Fred's father, she swore off the apparatus they call a stove. Tuesday night was her way of keeping tabs on her only son. As for the road to the Final Four, who cared? Obviously, he did. His betting sheets were strung out all over his desk.

Well, lucky me, I had my Lamaze partner. Now all I had to do was put up with Fred two nights a week for four weeks. Could I do it?

* * *

The first two classes went well. Fred was oddly cooperative. He didn't tell everyone he was not the father, or announce that my husband had ditched me. Occasionally a satisfied grin lit up his face as he imitated my panting. Of course, I knew a complacent Fred was not in the cards when I suggested this.

"Take long deep breaths. That's it. Deeply, slowly, in and out, in and out," the instructor said.

With Fred there, I was too self-conscious. Honestly, I did try. It's just that at inopportune moments, Fred whispered to me. "Annie, slowly in and out, in and out." I couldn't help but crack up laughing. "Oh, Annie, please save me from this nightmare. Where is Cindy Crawford when you need her?"

Let me say, Fred and I did not win the most popular couple in the class award. The man found Lamaze classes way too much fun.

We were three weeks into this ridiculous ordeal when they announced the next session would include a trip to the hospital, and, of course, a sensational movie on childbirth.

Fred's punctual arrival was enough to arouse my suspicions. He drove me to the hospital and pulled up at the front door. He turned in his seat, giving me a guilty look. "Annie, I'm sorry, but I have to go somewhere else tonight. I'll be back to pick you up in a couple of hours."

Actually, I didn't care. In fact, I was so huge I had become a part of the "great beyond." With luck I'd make it out of his car without a crane. A bargain was a bargain.

"It's okay, Fred," I said, in a tired voice. "I'll catch a ride with the instructor or call a taxi." Finally relieved to be standing on the curb, I took a deep breath and turned my back to him.

"Hey, aren't you angry with me, pissed off, anything?" He asked, yelling out the window. "You're not even going to accuse me of letting you down? Wow, you're actually letting me off the hook. I don't believe it."

Ignoring his guilty outbursts, I straightened my shoulders and slowly began walking toward the double doors. "You're right. I'm letting you off the hook," I yelled back at him. "I know you're a wimp. The thought of watching that disgusting movie horrifies me, too." Actually I was looking forward to it. Those breathing exercises were boring me to tears.

"Is Andrea giving you a hard time again?" She was the latest femme fatale in his never-ending love life. When he introduced me, the ball-like portion of her eyes shot withering daggers in my direction. Most of his girlfriends disliked me. She was different. She despised me. Who could blame her? I was taking Fred from her sweet loving arms two nights a week.

I could see it on his face. Andrea had turned the heat up and he was entangled in two conflicting emotions. Fred jumped out of his car and came toward me grumbling. "Stop. Damn it. You always win, you bitch. You look at me with those rotten green eyes of yours and all of a sudden I'm the one who's the asshole. In your weakened state, I can't seem to refuse you anything. Why is it women seem to have that effect on men? It must be in our nature, spawned from the Neolithic Age. 'I'm squaw. You man. Sit down and bark like dog.' Women, why the hell do we intelligent men put up with them?"

I started to tell him it had something to do with that thing between his legs, but he halted my explanation.

"No, don't say it, Miss Never Sex. This bulge here promises my women infinite bliss and everlasting thrills. Just ask them."

"Oh, right," I said sarcastically, "that's why most of the smart ones dump you. Miss Never Sex, huh, how do you think I got in this predicament?"

"If you're asking me, the sperm bank or the immaculate conception seems plausible," Fred replied.

Still mumbling, he went and parked the car. I chuckled to myself as I waited for him on the bench by the front door. Walking toward me, he was still muttering under his breath. "Lead the way," he demanded, helping me to my feet. Feeling triumphant, I turned and walked through the double doors. We were just stepping into the foyer when my water broke. I stopped unexpectedly and Fred bumped into my back.

Puzzled by the holdup, he started to complain. I looked at the floor, confirming my worst fear. He grabbed hold of my hand and ushered me over to one of the couches in the waiting room.

"Oh, dear, what are we going to do? Sit down," he ordered in a loud voice. "I'll find somebody who can clean up this mess and get you some help." The last thing I wanted to do was sit down, but I did what I was told.

Fred sprinted anxiously down the hall. I started giggling. The look on Fred's startled face when my water broke was too funny. Perhaps I was going mad. It's true I was embarrassed. My clothes were soaking wet. The baby wasn't due for three more weeks. I was supposed to see some damn movie on delivering the thing.

Other than old movies where the women all look like Princess Grace on this happy occasion, I had no knowledge of what the delivery room even looked like. Didn't I need a suitcase? I wasn't even packed.

Oh no, my mother. Oh, dear, she had at least a three-hour

drive. Fred, I promised him *no* childbirth. Oh well, I was a great one for promises. Hadn't I promised the father of this child "no children"? Oh, boy, that was too funny. I started giggling again.

I had to get control. The best way to accomplish this was to talk some sense into me. Calm down, Anne. Don't get hysterical. My mother will make it. Everything will be all right. Didn't doctors and nurses tell you it takes hours before your first baby is born? Maybe there's still time to catch that flick. Or if they would let me go home, I could pack my bag.

Damn, doctors. They're all a bunch of liars. Even the Lamaze instructor said first-time babies were generally born after your due date. That's it. I'm getting out of here while there's still time to get these things done.

As I started to get up, I felt my first contraction. It wasn't a flutter. They were supposed to start slowly. All the books said so. This one started at the bottom and moved up my stomach like some huge rolling pin.

Fred came running back with an entourage of blue coats. The look of concern on his face was so sweet. The laid-back, no-cares image he constantly portrayed had vanished. He was showing signs of panic, too. He patted me on the hand, doing his best to reassure me.

The staff helped me into a wheelchair and rolled me to labor and delivery on the third floor. Fred, for once, was silent. I handed him a piece of paper with my mother's telephone number. Hopefully, she was home. It was a Thursday night. Nothing happened on Thursday nights, right?

After a few questions from admissions, they found me a room. Fred left to find a telephone. The nurse handed me a hospital gown, told me to take off all my clothes. "Relax," she said, "first-time babies usually take some time." I figured this baby was not the ordinary type. It was mine, wasn't it?

"Have you had any contractions?" she asked, as she did a pelvic exam.

"I've had a huge one!" I replied. She looked at me skeptically and without much sympathy.

"You're going to be fine, Miss Stevens. Let's hook you up to the external fetal monitor."

She attached some wire electrodes to my stomach. I could hear the baby's heartbeat, reassuring me everything was all right. What an incredible sound!

"Sounds great to me," she said, tucking the covers around my legs. "I've got to leave now to call the doctor." She put away my clothes, leaving me alone. I closed my eyes and took a deep breath.

While Fred was gone, I had a few more contractions. Major or minor, I certainly couldn't tell. I should not have made fun of my Lamaze instructor. Why didn't I listen? The hell with concentrate, count, focus, and breathe. I thought the best thing to do was hire someone to blast it out. I was only a tad nervous and a little out of control.

Fred came back wearing a hospital gown. At least he wasn't wandering the halls proclaiming, "Get me out of here. I'm not the father." Despite my own anxieties, I couldn't help but laugh. He looked ridiculous in that garb.

Fred had a stethoscope around his neck. Changing his voice into one of those deep-throated doctor types, he playfully came forward and placed the cold thing on my chest pretending to listen. "Ah, so methinks the lady has a heart. Could have fooled me."

Placing the instrument in my ears, he said, "Hear it? 'Thump. Thump. Thump.' It's saying, 'Let Fred go home. Let Fred go home.'"

As if he'd been around one of these monitors all his life, he checked the tape and shrugged his shoulders. "Looks fine to Dr. Fred. Not a monster in there after all."

Actually, I didn't care whether he went home or not. "It's all right," I whispered. "Fred can go home. Fred can go home," I replied as tears welled up in my eyes.

Temporarily resigned to his fate, he pulled up a chair, grabbed the remote, hunting for his basketball game. I hollered at him, but he turned a deaf ear. The next contraction arrived; and Fred, although not very sympathetic, took my hand while keeping one eye on the game. "Can't you see you're distracting me? Pipe down. I can't hear the announcer."

I gave him one of my "behave yourself" looks. He burst out laughing. "Okay. Look at me. Here. Focus. Take hold of my hand. Breathe. Come on. You can do it." He demonstrated the breathing technique practiced at Lamaze. "Breathe." He slowly blew out the air with me. "See. You can do it. Come on. Count with me."

After the contraction abated, he walked up and down the room yelping. "Did you have to squeeze so damn hard?" He held up his hand and pointed to it. "Look at this. Every bone in this hand is now broken. Try to ease up on this poor thing, will you?"

A light bulb went on in his brain. "Never mind. If you squeeze a little harder, I can sue your ass and collect disability for the rest of my life. Maybe that's not such a bad idea. I might even become your nanny, and Junior and I can go to the golf course every day."

"Lawyers don't need their hands," I said, rolling my eyes. "They just need a mouth like yours. Pain. Did you say *you're* in pain? I beg you to change places with me, Sweetie. Furthermore, by the time I pay off my student loans and raise Junior, nanny money will be a dream. Besides, what makes you think he's a Junior?"

Still holding his sore hand, he pondered for a moment. "I hope it's a boy. God forbid it's a girl. She would probably end up with your traits. Would you like me to list them? Let's see: Opinionated, like most women, extremely loud, major major stubborn, sometimes bitchy, and totally closed and narrow- minded to other more intelligent and enlightened opinions, such as mine."

I repositioned myself on the bed and grabbed a pillow placing it across my chest. "If you had anything to say that was even slightly insightful, I might listen. But basketball, golf, and the sweater some big-chested woman is wearing are not my idea of intellectually enlightening nor remotely stimulating."

At that moment, the doctor walked into the room. Dr. Rebecca Langworth was a very young and attractive woman. I knew Fred would be pleasantly surprised. She wore the usual doctor's garb. Too bad, too. Her chest size was obscured by the white coat and stethoscope hanging around her neck.

I had chosen Dr. Langworth because she was the newest OB-GYN physician on staff. Her patient load was smaller, so it was easier to make an appointment, get in, and get out fast.

In general, I hated all doctors and hospitals. They were good places to avoid. Sick people died in them every day. Just walking in the door raised my blood pressure to an alarming level, and the smell alone brought forth an instantaneous gag.

Be that as it may, I was unhappily confined here. Labor prevented my escape. I was definitely unable to extricate myself from this dilemma, and for the time being, I was going to try to like her. After all, she was the only one who could get me out of this mess. Counting on Fred was a fanatical person's nightmare.

Dr. Langworth frowned at Fred. He gave her the most annoying philanderer's smile. Seemingly unimpressed, she gave him a quick wave of dismissal to leave the room so she could examine me. He gave her one of those you're-a-fine-looking-female eyeballs; the kind that immediately turns a woman off, and left the room.

The doctor examined the paper emitting from the machine. "Your baby has a good strong heartbeat. Not to worry," she said, as she patted my arm. "Move down to the end of the bed and let's take a look. Come on, scoot down a little more." I reluctantly did as she suggested.

"This might hurt a little," she said, as she put on her sterile latex gloves. Before poking and prodding, doctors always tell you, 'It's going to hurt a little.' As usual, that hurt bit was an understatement. Why don't they just tell you they are about to cause you extreme pain and discomfort?

The result of the examination confirmed my worst fears. Big deal. I was in labor. Of course, I already knew that.

"You're five centimeters dilated," she said, tossing the gloves in the metal trash can.

"Could I have a couple of pain killers or perhaps some dynamite?" I joked.

She laughed and said, "Maybe a little something to ease your nerves." She wrote something down and handed my chart to my nurse.

"I'll be back in about an hour to check on your progress. You'll be fine. Try to relax." She put the pen in her coat pocket. Her beeper went off. "Sorry, I've got to run." She didn't look back as she opened the door, waving good-bye.

Alone again, I waited impatiently for those drugs. In the let-mother-nature-take-its-course category, I was an utter failure. The reason for Lamaze and the instructions in heavy breathing was so you could get through a contraction without using pain killers. It was something some sadistic misogynist doctor thought up, and I'd bet every red cent I had he was a man. Personally, I wasn't about to buy that hogwash.

Like mothers in the '50s, I rather liked the idea of getting knocked out and waking up to discover I had a baby. Furthermore, if I was the baby and I had to come out of that birth canal, a few drugs along the way might feel pretty darn good.

Only one task remained. I had to have this baby as quickly as possible and get out of here. I debated jumping up and down. In fact, I unhooked the monitor and got out of bed. While I walked, I thought to myself, "Darn. Nothing. It didn't fall out."

The room was hot. I gripped the bedframe. Oh, God, the next contraction lasted about four centuries. I panicked and quickly got back into bed. Where was Fred? Probably flirting with the nurse who had my drugs.

After what seemed an eternity, Fred and the obnoxious woman -- I mean nurse, entered the room. She had this nerve-wracking giggle. I was right. They were whispering, triumphing in their never-to-be-found intellectual capacities.

My rhetorical comment was one of absolute disdain, "How can you two stand there gawking at each other while I'm dying? You two can go out with each other after I'm dead." I grabbed hold of the nurse's jacket. "Right now, I want that drug."

The nurse took the stance of a mother speaking with a small child and patted me on the shoulder. "Miss Stevens, get control of yourself. Relax. Why don't you try directing some of that anger and sarcasm toward the pain?"

Sick of her, I was ready to show her a few facts about pain. "Relax," I replied sarcastically. "Tell me. How is that possible when I am being ripped apart?"

Fred shook his head. "Annie, you're only having a baby." He said, embarrassed by my lack of self-control. "It's nothing new. Women have been doing this for centuries."

I raised my voice and threw the pillow at him. "If you don't want to change places with me, get the hell out of here! Beat it!"

The nurse took the needle off the tray and stuck it none too gently into my arm. For the first time, I felt I was calming down, floating. It was as if a warm shower had spread over my face and down the length of my body. Closing my eyes, I fell asleep.

I was hearing some poor woman moaning in the room next to

me. As I was coming to, I realized I was that poor soul, and my relief had been short-lived.

The next contraction came much more rapidly. I grabbed the bed rail and began panting. Each new wave brought forth a new intensity. Thanks to Fred, my foul mouth had moved upward from the "A" word to the "F" word. I began using it with increased frequency.

My body wasn't going to tolerate much more of this. Wimp or no wimp, I wasn't going to make it. After the contraction subsided, I started to cry. Fred sympathetically put his arms around me. He held me while I slobbered on his shirt. He was actually offering support.

"Annie, you are a very headstrong woman. Women do survive, and the Annie I know is no quitter."

He placed a kiss on my forehead and held my hand. "Look at me. Concentrate. Strength in adversity has always been one of your more annoying traits. If you take it like a man, you can beat this."

I recalled the T-shirt he wore the first time I met him. 'All men are created equal. Women should stay in the kitchen.' Giving him the evil eye, I began to squeeze the hell out of his hand. Men should have babies. I'd stay in the kitchen forever if only men would have babies.

For several seconds, Fred's face contorted with pain as my ferocious contractions continued. "We'll get through it together," he mumbled. "Go ahead and break every finger I have. I promise you I won't sue, at least not today."

After a couple of hours, the contractions stopped, and I was fully dilated. The desire to push began. Looking up at the clock, it was ten o'clock. I thought, well, I'm going to have this baby in a couple of minutes. I was still pushing at one o'clock in the morning.

Somewhere in this span of time, my mother arrived. For the first time in many years, she was a welcome sight. More often than not we were at battle stations, but today was different. We were a united front, and the three of us worked well as a team. From time to time, she placed a cool refreshing cloth over my very hot forehead.

Finally exhaustion set in. I could not push. I was totally out of strength and too tired to care. I started ignoring the contractions. The doctor said, "All right, Anne. Fine. If you can't do this, you're off to have a C-section. Come on, woman, give me everything you've got. All I need is one more strong push."

The contraction came, but I let it pass.

"I can't," I yelled.

"Yes, you can. You don't want a C-section. Now, damn it, push!"

Later on, I found out that maneuver was often used by OB-GYN doctors. It's their way of getting the patient motivated again so they can go home to their own beds.

Fred grabbed hold of one leg and a nurse held the other. I pushed as hard as I was able. The doctor grabbed something that looked like a vacuum cleaner and placed it on the baby's head. Fred grimaced and jokingly said, "Maybe we should call the baby Hoover."

With the pressure from Hoover, the bond of mother-to-child unity was broken. I gave birth to a huge, nine-pound, screaming baby boy.

Mere words cannot express the elation I felt. Surprisingly, I was no longer tired. I felt a new surge of energy, an overwhelming faith in myself. It was as if I, too, had been reborn. I gazed upon the most incredible sight I had ever beheld. My son. Oddly enough, I had not perished.

CHAPTER
V

Unable to sleep and too sore to move, I spent the rest of the night hypnotized by the miracle I had created. He was like a hunger I could not get enough of. The nurse came in and wheeled him off to check his vital signs and his diaper. I lay back on my pillow, still fully awake. My vocal chords wanted to sing; my spirit wanted to soar. Without thinking, Helen Reddy's song came out of my mouth. "I am Woman, hear me roar..."

Fred opened the door. He had been standing there long enough to hear me boisterously move into the third verse when I spotted his shadow. Caught in the act, there wasn't much I could say.

He laughed so hard he was about to drop my overnight bag and flowers on the floor. "Lady, you will never again make fun of my attempts to sing like Jerry Garcia. Believe me, Reddy has no competition. I can't believe my ears," he said, as tears rolled down his face. "Annie, if I forget everything else about you, I will always remember this moment."

Still chuckling to himself, he moved into the middle of the room, placing my bag on a chair. He couldn't stop laughing. It was contagious. My face turned red as a beet. I began laughing with him.

He was right. I couldn't carry a tune if my life depended on it.

"Don't you laugh at me, Mr. Levine." I said, pulling the covers up over my head. "You should have seen your face when my water broke last night. I didn't know those scrawny legs of yours could move so fast."

Attempting to regain my composure, I patted the bed for him to sit. "What are you doing here? Aren't you worn out? What time is it? It's seven a.m. Way to early for you."

Still smiling, he bent down and kissed my cheek. "Enough with all the questions already. It's not every day I witness the birth of a child. It was quite an experience. You know, there's something about holding a new baby. It kind of puts life into perspective."

He sat down on the bed, taking my hand. "Annie, you may think this is strange coming from me, but I'm glad I stayed. I tried to take a nap, but I couldn't sleep. Thank you for welching on your promise. It was somehow refreshing--yeah that's the word, 'refreshing.'"

Fred, seemingly proud of himself, kissed my hand. "It was good to see the two of you together. Your mother is a knockout. To hear you describe her, I thought she was some Ice Queen. By the way, I dropped her off at your place. When I stopped by to grab a few of your things, she was still sound asleep."

As an afterthought, Fred began to chuckle again. No longer finding him funny, I impatiently covered my ears. "Will you stop it already? You're going to wake up the entire hospital. Never mind. No one sleeps here anyway."

"Oh, Annie, I can't help it. You're a head case. How many mothers do you suppose ask their doctors after labor and delivery to see their placenta? God, that was a nasty-looking thing."

Fred was referring to the request I had made of the doctor immediately after delivery. He was right. She had looked at me rather oddly, but was quite obliging.

Taking the maroon-colored thing out of the silver bowl, I noticed it was about the size of a large water balloon. As she stuck her hands inside this amazing contraption, she pointed out to me what she called the 'vascular chorionic villi.' This permitted the exchange of materials by diffusion without direct contact between fetal and maternal blood. What that really meant was it provided my baby with the oxygen and necessary nutrients it needed in order to sustain life. Fred and my mother both thought I was nuts.

He handed me a slip of paper. "Oh, I almost forgot. This was taped on your front door. It looked important so I stuck it in with the rest of your things. Why don't you join the almost 21st Century and get an answering machine like everyone else?"

"Why would I want an answering machine? I can't stand the phone. It's a waste of good money. If they want me badly enough, they'll call me back."

Puzzled, I examined the piece of paper he had handed me. Ironically, it was a note requesting me to come to this very hospital. Apparently, last night an ambulance had taken Mattie to the emergency room.

Fred could see the concern on my face. "She's all right," he said reassuring me.

"How do you know?" I asked.

"I checked at the nurse's station on the second floor. Miss Mattie Turner, whoever she is, is resting comfortably. So you are holding out on me. You *do* have a girlfriend in this town. Why didn't you ask her to be your Lamaze partner?"

I placed the slip of paper on the table. "To tell you the truth, I did give it some thought. Believe me, I'd have never asked Judge Rosenthal. That was just my way of gaining your sympathy. Anyway, it doesn't matter now. I had you, didn't I?"

Fred took the flowers into the bathroom and came back with them piled in a pink plastic pitcher.

"Here, these are for you," he said handing them to me. I was touched. I smelled their sweet scent. A couple of them fell out of the pitcher, landing on my lap. Briefly, his hand found mine. I held it for a couple of seconds too long. As I hastened to clean up the mess, our eyes met. I saw tenderness and desire before the shield of his discomfort took hold. I cleared my throat. He picked up the mess then opened the blinds on the window. Whatever this was about, he wasn't going there and neither was I.

"Honestly, you'll like Mattie Turner," I said, breaking the uncomfortable silence. "She's the most obstinate woman I've ever met. She also has more stamina than women three times her age. Every time I visit her I get a desperate urge to take a nap. You'll see what I mean. The woman is a walking steamroller."

Fred gave me one of his I-think-I-have-met-a-woman-like-this-before looks.

"You're right. She's a major pain in the *ass*."

Without saying another word, he headed toward the door. "Well, I'm off to see Jack. That is his name, isn't it? Also, if you're up to finding this Mattie Turner, I suppose I'll have to find a wheelchair."

More than happy to send him off to get my precious son, I settled into bed. "Baby Jack is in the nursery. He had a dirty diaper. They had to check his stool. I have to admit, his bowel movements are rather peculiar looking. I'm not sure I can handle this. Do you suppose there's something wrong?"

"How would I know?" Fred said, wrinkling his nose. "I'm no expert on baby stool samples. Ask your pediatrician, my dear."

Ignoring Fred's suggestion, I covered my jello stomach with a pillow. "In a couple of hours he won't be a very happy camper. He's going to get the, you know, snip, snip. Oh, why did I decide to have him circumcised? I am a cruel, cruel mother. Do you suppose it will hurt a lot?"

Fred reached down between his legs and imitated the pain. "Pure agony."

"Gee, thanks for the moral support."

"Moral support, you better believe it. You'll owe me for the rest of your life. Someday it will be payback time. For now, get your rest."

Several minutes had passed since Fred went to see the baby. I hoped and prayed nothing too serious had happened to Mattie. My imagination kept getting the better of me. Oh God, perhaps she had been shot and was lying downstairs wounded.

A week or so earlier someone had thrown a Molotov cocktail through her window. Fortunately, it didn't explode. The chilly reception she was receiving from her neighbors had not died.

Too impatient to wait any longer, I called the nurse myself and asked for a wheelchair. Slowly, I struggled out of bed. Let's just say I wasn't exactly sprinting, but I could walk like some poor wounded animal.

Mattie was going to be thrilled with Jack Alexander Stevens. If ever there was a grandmother for him, she definitely fit the bill. Her loyalty was unquestionable. My mother's was another story.

There was a lot of commotion going on in the hallway. Fred and the nurse approached with a couple of wheelchairs and were now dueling outside my door. I placed my bathrobe around my hospital gown and gently crawled back on top of the bed to await the victor. Fred must have won because I could hear his voice reassuring the nurse he would take care of me.

He pushed my door open with the chair. "Can't you wait?" he said with a disgruntled look on his face. "I told you I'd take you downstairs. I wasn't even flirting with the cute nurse from last night. I checked. She's gone. Will you ever understand the word 'patience'?"

The exasperated Fred came over to my bedside and locked the

wheelchair in place. Then he, not too gently, picked me up and placed me in the seat.

"You're breaking my back. When are you supposed to lose this post-partum baggage anyway?"

Paranoid and insecure enough about my body, I did not respond to his annoying question. An older, more mature nurse obligingly brought in the baby, and Fred put us on the elevator in the hopes of finding Mattie's room.

* * *

The room was dark and quiet. At first I didn't think there was anyone there. As we moved around the curtain, I saw her. Electrodes were attached to the upper portion of her chest. A heart monitor was flashing a constant steady light. An IV tube was attached to her left hand.

Her pale, drawn face told me something was wrong. Was she dying? Oh, please, dear God, don't you dare do that to me.

There was a frailness to her in sleep that didn't exist when she was awake. Perhaps it was because she had so much energy and authority.

When she was at home, she wore an old flannel shirt and men's coveralls. That was another thing I learned about Mattie. In public, she wore St. John suits with very expensive jewelry. In the winter, she wore an old beaver coat that weighed more than she did. She told me it had been passed down from her sweet great grandmother, the murderess.

She once told me age meant freedom and respectability, age to me should mean challenges. I often thought about this comment. I disagreed with her. She was right that life was a challenge, but I would never experience freedom until the angels received me into their happy home of everlasting joy above. That's what I really believed. That's when I would truly be free. Why was I being so morbid? I had Jack. I was no longer alone.

Hopefully, that was not where Mattie was heading. Of course, I wasn't sure about God either. Besides, age meant decrepit bones and wrinkled skin, and Mattie was a far cry from either. Oh, God, please let me hear that ingratiating voice.

Fred grabbed my arm and helped me out of the chair. Slowly, I moved toward her bed and placed my sleeping baby on the pillow next to her. The movement must have disturbed her because she instantly opened her eyes. A lazy smile touched her face. This gave me some reassurance she was okay, but I was still worried.

I placed my hand in hers and gave it a squeeze. She turned to get a closer look at Jack. "Oh, Annie, the baby is so beautiful. Boy or girl?"

"A boy. Mattie Turner, meet Jack Alexander Stevens. He was born last night. He weighs nine pounds, three ounces. You're right. He's beautiful. He looks like the Gerber baby. All the other babies in this hospital look so puny. Wouldn't you know I'd have the monster. I thought they were supposed to have cone heads."

Fred gave me one of those calm down hand signals. I knew my mouth was motoring along, but I couldn't help it. Mattie struggled to a sitting position. Fred helped her raise her bed and adjust her pillows, then, holding Jack, placed him in her waiting arms.

Aware of Fred for the first time, Mattie grabbed him by the arm. "Who is this? Oh, I hope you're my new doctor. You're much better looking than that old fart that's been treating me. You don't have the look of the hospital staff around here. Let me guess. You're the Lamaze partner. Fred, isn't it? Annie's told me so much about you."

Before Fred could properly introduce himself, Mattie continued talking.

"By the way, how did she do? Funny, I didn't hear her screams on this floor. I've been putting up with those moans and groans of hers for months now. The walls of this hospital are still intact," she said, feigning surprise.

"Oh, yeah, you haven't seen the fourth floor," he said, winking at Mattie. "The maintenance men arrived early this morning to fix the mortar."

Mattie chuckled, and Fred extended his hand. "Miss Turner, my name is Fred Levine. It's a privilege to meet you. I'm the poor soul who's been Annie's slave would more aptly describe my role."

I waved them both off and went back to studying Mattie's face. Even though she seemed pesky enough, you could still see the telltale signs of fatigue. I finally asked the question uppermost in my mind.

"Mattie, why are you here? What the hell happened to you?"

Ignoring me, she continued to gaze into Jack's sleeping face. I knew she'd probably lie anyway. "Never mind. I'm going to find your doctor."

I started toward the door. "Stop, young lady! I guess you could say I've had a slight heart attack."

I gave her an exasperated sigh. She scowled.

"There's nothing to worry about. You know how these doctors are. They saw my insurance policy; so now they're running every test known to mankind. As if being sixty-six years old isn't bad enough. That's it. Go out there and tell those idiots I'm suffering from old age. I have too much work to do and I want to go home."

"That's the problem," I said impatiently. "Damn you, Mattie, slow down. I'd bet a million dollars you haven't told the doctor what you've really been up to. Where is he? I've got a few things to say to him."

"I'm not that daft," she said waving her hand. "If I told him the truth, he'd put me in the nut ward. Don't worry, Annie. I'm not on my deathbed yet. I'll know when the Good Lord wants me. Besides, he'd be insane to take me before my kids get help."

Mattie gently caressed the baby's cheek. "He's so precious, so tiny. Oh, Jack Alexander, what kind of miracle child will you be? Knowing your mother, as I do, I'm sure you're going to be a marvelous pain in the neck."

Fred nodded his head in agreement. "I second that motion. Only it's much lower than the neck. What do you say, Mattie, shall we lease him out to some poor unsuspecting couple who'd want a little baby with a sweet disposition instead of the hellion we know he will become if the mother has anything to do with it?"

I pointed a finger at both of them. "It's an honest-to-God privilege to have Baby Jack and me in your company. I can't imagine why we are associating with the likes of you."

Unfortunately, my hormones were out of whack, and I started to cry. "Besides, it's so incredibly sweet to see you hold the greatest miracle that ever existed in my life -- or, for that matter, on the face of this earth. I can't seem to take my eyes off him. God, he's so beautiful."

Mattie looked at Fred. "Well, at least she didn't add the entire universe. Oh, Annie, you thank your lucky stars every day for this little bundle here. This child is a gift from God."

Mattie was right. For the first time in my life, I felt a sense of belonging, a purity words could not explain. It was like a warm creeping tenderness which had me on edge. I'm not talking about the peace I would soon lack on the nights with no sleep. I'm talking about a peace recognized only by my subconscious after experiencing this miraculous event.

Mattie barged in, interrupting my thoughts. "If I have to unexpectedly leave this earth, I was going to saddle you with my house."

"Oh, no." I said. "I'm too busy."

"I'd have loved to croak and leave you with this mess," she replied. "Of course, you were supposed to honor me by naming the house after me. It was to be called 'Mattie's House.' You'd be doing all this work instead of me. Damn it, anyway. I guess I have to get off my deathbed. Oh, and, by the way, I'm still going to call it Mattie's House."

She was too excited to stop talking. "Annie, do you realize that the easy work is almost done? Fred, go tell the doctor that's what's wrong with me. I took stupid pills on my 66th birthday. Look at me. I could be leading the good life, retirement and social security. I wouldn't even have to spend my own money."

Mattie looked down at the baby again. "Annie, I can't have you lollygagging around my house. It's too dangerous. If something happened, I'd never forgive myself. You're fired. I guess I'll have to live a few more years and fight my own battles. Poop. I thought I had a scapegoat. How about you, Fred, darling? You sure look like scapegoat material to me."

"Oh, I am," Fred replied. "Just ask Annie. She knows how to twist me around her little finger and hide good friends like you behind her back."

Mattie did not pursue Fred's last comment. Instead, she took my hand. "All kidding aside, I can't ask you to take any more chances with me. It just won't work."

I was getting tired of this nonsensical conversation. "Mattie, first of all, if you died on me, I'd figure out a way to haunt you back for the rest of your ghost-walking life. You're never going to leave that albatross to me. You're right about one thing. The easy part is over. The tough part is about to begin. Come to think of it. You're right. Fred here is somewhat manageable. It just takes a little manipulation to mold him into a decent human being."

Fred was about to protest. I grabbed his hand before he had a chance and continued holding Mattie's. With a look of sincere gratitude, I hung on to both of them and once again began to cry.

"I thank you both from the bottom of my heart for being my friends and putting up with me these last few months. Mattie, thank you for not dying. And thank you for demonstrating to me what good friends can do to enrich my life. You're right. I am blessed, and I love you both."

With tears falling down my face, I carefully got back in my wheelchair. "Come on, Fred, let's get out of this room so Mattie can get her much deserved rest. Put Baby Jack on my lap, please." Fred complied with my wishes.

"Oh, and, Mattie, we still have a lot of work to do, you know. And as for firing me, you can't fire someone who's not on the payroll. Like I said, get some rest. I'll see you tomorrow."

Waving good-bye, the three of us left the room. Mattie was right. At this moment, she could be sitting on a beach in Florida living the good life. If someone in the world had to take idiot pills, I was glad it was her.

The mortality table was not on Mattie's side. What was I talking about? She was likely to outlive me. I shivered at the thought of losing her. With Baby Jack in my arms, I realized how imperative it was my stay on this planet would last at least another twenty or thirty years. Hers, too.

CHAPTER
VI

F red wheeled us back to my room just as my mother appeared in the doorway. She was a handsome woman. Most people would say she was beautiful. It was artificial, something like an ornament with all the glow on the outside and nothing on the inside.

She was a successful buyer for several department stores in the Midwest. She was quite young looking considering all the abuse my father had put her through. She carried herself with style and class and displayed no vulnerability. I could barely remember a time when my mother had a wrinkle in her dress or a hair out of place. Her makeup was always impeccable.

Despite that outer gloss, there existed an extreme detachment to reality. She never looked to the future. It was like she was stuck in a fog, blinding her to anything that might lay ahead. You could say for most of my life she had withdrawn from me. It had been eight years since I had last set eyes on her. Eight years of what I called "her duty letters," her way of feigning some concern for my welfare.

After finally installing a telephone in my apartment, I mustered up the courage to call. I was too ashamed to write about Nick and me. It was something you shouldn't tell mothers in a letter. We had a long and disjointed conversation. It was at that time she reluctantly agreed to be here for her grandchild's birth.

Fred walked over and handed the baby to my mother. Without again complaining about my weight, he picked me up and carried me to the bed.

"If you don't mind, milady, this poor starving servant wishes to depart this place for a well-deserved nap and some chow. Is there anything else your royal highness would like from this lowly and humble servant? I'll be around later tonight. If you need me, call; provided I wake up, of course."

His absence left a gap, an instantaneous silence. I watched my mother closely as she held Jack's tiny hand.. She was captivated by him, too. For as long as I can remember, I waited and hoped my mother would do that to me. Hold me. Hug me. Feel something. I learned to accept the fact it would never happen.

Jealous by her interest in my son, I shattered the precious moment between them. "For your information, I'm naming the baby Jack." I replied with more indignation in my tone than was necessary.

Disappointed I had interrupted her thoughts, she shrugged. "What do you want me to say?" She asked. "I figured you would. Keep in mind, Anne, I'm tired of the animosity between us, and quite honestly, I don't have the stamina for it anymore." If only she meant what she said. She'd said things like this too many times in the past to be true. I learned at a very early age parents say what you want to hear and what they should be saying as good parents, but saying is not doing.

"Oh, I forgot to tell you. I'm sorry I can't stay. Most of my vacation was spent traveling in Europe with George. The shows for the summer season are just around the corner, and work is piling up." George was not her boyfriend. He was her boss. They were not really vacationing; they were on buying trips.

"You sure picked a lousy time to have this baby," she

remarked.

"Thanks for the help, Mother." I pretended indifference. "I stupidly hoped you'd stick around, teach me to change diapers or something. Don't worry. I'm not going to beg." She gave me a blank stare, devoid of guilt.

My voice was tight with anger. "Oh, never mind. When you want to see us, call. We aren't going anywhere, especially not Europe."

She ignored the sarcasm. "I wish you would have waited. Being a single mother is such a huge responsibility."

I continued giving her one of those thousand disappointed and impatient faces I reserved specifically for her.

"What's done is done. 'If the path be beautiful, let us not ask where it leads.'" It was a quote I'd heard long ago.

As usual, she ignored me, choosing not to understand my message.

"You have your father's face," she said matter of factly. "It reminds me of too many nights with a bloody lip, and my hopes and prayers he'd never return. I wanted his head blown off long before he blew it off. I can't expect you to understand."

I did understand, but I was too tired to fight. Why had I put myself through this? She had filled her life with resentment and hate. There wasn't any room for me.

"I've never understood you," I said, disguising the hurt in my voice. "As far as you're concerned, I'm as dead as Jack. He was the only one in your life, your proud and devoted son. Can't you see I miss him as much as you do? Even Daddy, despite all his mood swings, knew I was alive. Occasionally, he made up for his bouts of ugliness, kissed me, bought me a small gift, or even held my hand. But not you. What did I do to deserve your contempt?"

My eyes filled with tears. My mother's remained dry. She had shed them long ago.

"Why do you hate me so?" After all these years, I had finally asked. Watching my mother carefully, I noted her discomfort.

"I don't hate you, Anne. What's love anyway? It's an emotion I find impossible to feel. Your father beat it out of me long ago."

Once again she looked down at her grandson, tracing her finger along his arm. "In my own way, I am proud of you. I'm jealous. I've always been a failure. Not you. You turned your hatred of me into your strength. It's funny, isn't it? You've become worthy without my approval. You're a fighter. In many ways, I'm as good as dead. We all deal with grief in different ways."

My mother stood silently erect. An uncontrolled tear rolled down my cheek. It was a waste of time. This baby wasn't going to change our relationship one iota.

She glanced at her watch. "Well, I have to get going. Take good care of yourself and the baby. Good-bye, Anne."

I wiped the tears from my face. "It's finally okay with me, Mother. It's true. I will never understand you, especially now after having my own child. Love for him just kind of flows. Funny, yours never did with me. There's nothing I can do about it. I took that reality check a long time ago. I'm letting you off the hook. I've come to terms with Nick's departure, and I came to terms with yours a long time ago. The truth is you've never said hello; so good-bye should be easy. Good-bye, mother."

"Don't be so cruel. It's been nine years. I'm getting better. Just don't push me." She took one last look at Jack and gave him a kiss on the cheek.

"Keep him safe." She placed him in my arms and wiped a tear off my cheek. With a cold stare from me, she left the room. I closed my eyes and took a deep breath. Why was I so upset? How could she still have the power to hurt me? The truth was I still loved her. I felt sorry for her. It was getting to be a habit, feeling sorry for the people who were supposed to love me.

Jack opened his eyes. I was aware I held nothing but a bundle of innocence, pure, clean, and fresh. Do you suppose evil was hiding somewhere in the depths of his soul? No, I didn't think so. My father was evil. I was a part of his DNA, and I wasn't evil. Perhaps he became evil because of her, drawn toward the bottle because of her.

I buried my face in his blanket. "Please God, if there really is a God, don't let him be plagued by the pain and guilt that will forever haunt my soul."

Closing my eyes, I conjured up an image of the brother I remembered. "Please, Jack, Mom's right. Keep him safe. You're not here, and it's all my fault. Oh, how I miss you."

I remembered Jack's smile, the way his legs would fly across the field as I threw him one of my fast balls, the many nights shooting hoops in the driveway. I remembered the days when we'd sneak some change out of the cookie jar and head for ice cream. I can hear his laughter and see the mischief in his eyes as he tickled me into submission. I could feel his arms around my shoulders. Once again, I felt Jack's warmth.

* * *

No sensation I ever felt was as good as the one I got from simply being Jack Alexander Steven's mother. After a month's leave, I sadly returned to work. Sometimes Baby Jack would come with me. When he did, the judge and my co-workers found one excuse after another to come and play with him. He had a sweet disposition and a charming smile, a baby with a real knack for bringing out the best in people.

Mattie was released from the hospital a couple of days after me. She hadn't bothered to slow down. The stubborn woman was hard at work. The builders had finally finished the section that would hold an enormous library. A seemingly endless array of books, study materials, tables and chairs were stacked in piles on the floor. Busts of such notable people as Shakespeare, Abraham Lincoln, Martin Luther King sat patiently on top of the fireplace mantel awaiting their place among the vast shelves of knowledge.

Several months ago, Mattie had built a small greenhouse in her backyard so the kids could plant their seeds and watch the flowers grow. Oftentimes, I found her in her vegetable garden wearing those dirty men's coveralls and a big ugly hat, which most of the time sat crookedly on her head.

Mattie's funds were dissipating rapidly. I found a couple of organizations willing to donate some of their time and effort as volunteers, but it wasn't going to be enough.

Several complaints had been lodged through the city council. It was too late. We had our zoning. We suspected the gang's handiwork, but what we mainly got from them were curses and statements like, "Get out of here, you ol' bitch. I can show you the way to the cemetery. Mind your own business."

This was not encouraging, but it's funny how much harder you work every time someone says something like that or spits on your front lawn.

In order to reach these children, she had to get parental support, or at least the modified version, be it grandmother or their doped-up parents.

Tonight was going to be the big neighborhood meeting. People from all walks of life were asked to attend. We wanted social workers, teachers, coaches, ministers, city council members, volunteers, and people from organizations and churches interested in improving the plight of minority children.

We had sent letters throughout the city asking for input as far as methods of entertainment, teaching skills, anything necessary in running a proper youth home.

We didn't receive a single response. Oh, I forgot. There was one. It read: "You's people have no idea what you's doing. All you's going to get is your fancy ass killed. Get out of here and take that white trash with you."

That evening, Jack and I had arrived a few minutes early. Mattie's house was ready! You could spot the evidence of her hard-earned accomplishments everywhere. The floors were immaculate. The electrical system was finally working. Thanks to her, I even learned how to connect a fixture to the ceiling. As I flipped the switch, I was relieved to find it still worked. I felt so honored to have been a part of it all.

Hopefully, this would be Mattie's night. As I watched the visitors arrive, I felt uncomfortable. Perhaps, I was experiencing reverse discrimination. It looked like I was to be the only white person present.

Speaking of that remarkable woman, I watched her descend the stairs. Dressed in a royal blue suit, she had the air of a congresswoman. If only this night was not filled with bitterness and disappointment.

People slowly entered the doors. It was impossible to tell what their motives were. Were they here to help or destroy? Most of the women were dressed in blue jeans and T-shirts. The older men wore dark-colored cotton pants and button-down shirts. The younger generation must've stayed at home. The majority of the guests were middle-aged or above.

Mattie, in her suit of armor, met them with her typical grace. Friend or foe, she was ready to do battle.

To my surprise, the house filled with people quickly. Uncomfortably holding my chin up, I took my seat next to Mattie as she called the meeting to order. She stood and was about to open her mouth when a woman in her middle thirties raised her fist and began shouting.

"Who do you uppity bitches think you are? I have my own youth home. Take care of my kids just fine, I do. I don't see anyone here helping *me* out. I could use the bucks, too."

On the streets she was known as "Mama Goose." Teenagers hung around her house ready to do her bidding. They fetched anything she asked for, including heroin, meth and crack cocaine.

The stories coming out of there were terrifying. So far, the authorities had been unable to arrest her. They couldn't find a teenager willing to testify against her.

She pointed her fat ugly fist at Mattie. "You've been a fancy-ass bitch ever since you was a kid. Up here nice and proper livin' in this fancy house, thinkin' you's better than all us. You ain't. Lady Turner, can't you see? No one here wants to help. Ya ain't welcome here."

Some of the men yelled words of encouragement. One woman angrily stood up against Mama Goose. She wasn't exactly trying to defend Mattie, but she had lost one of her sons to her drug house.

"Mama Goose, shut that big mouth of yours up. Zip it. Do you hear me, fat girl? Ain't nobody goin' to give you no money. We all knows what you do to those poor kids, what you did to my Malcolm. I ain't afraid of you. I got nothin' left to lose. You killed my Malcolm, or at least he's as good as dead, smoking crack around your house. Thanks to you, he'll be lucky if he sees his 18th birthday. Yeah, your kids need help all right. They need you in a grave six feet under."

Mama Goose shoved her way through the crowd. The crazy mother pulled out a revolver, and instinctively everyone clamored for the gun. All havoc broke loose. Mattie shouted, but couldn't be heard as they kicked and screamed and everyone hit the ground for cover.

Mattie and I ducked under the table. A man the size of a house entered the skirmish and grabbed the gun from Malcolm's mother. It took a gunshot in Mattie's newly-painted ceiling to calm them down. Afterwards, most of the crowd headed toward the door. Mattie crawled out from underneath the table pushing her way to the front door.

"Please, stay. If not for me, at least for your children's sake," Mattie said, pleading with them to stop. No one was listening.

Finally, this huge man who still had the gun in his right hand yelled, "Where do ya think you're all going? Stop! Listen! Maybe if this lady had been around here before now, Mrs. Williams, your Malcolm wouldn't be lost," he said, as he pulled Mama Goose off the floor where she lay sprawled on Malcolm's mother.

Mama Goose straightened her shabby clothes, wiped her bloody lip with a tissue she had pulled from her bra, and headed for the door. Before she left, she turned, giving a murderous look to the people in her way.

"You, despicable people deserve what you get," she said with a clenched fist. "Good luck, Lady Turner. Look at the scum you's been a wastin' your money on." You could hear her evil laugh as she walked across the porch.

The crowd formed a line to leave. The large man moved to block the door. "She's here to help our kids," he yelled. "Why do y'all want to turn away? Who doesn't have a kid out there in trouble? There ain't none of you goin' to raise your hand. Who hasn't watched your own kid pass dope right in front of your faces? How many of you have taken their blood money? We see it, but what do we do about it? Nothing! Nothing!" he said, pounding a big heavy foot on Mattie's polished floor.

"Wake up, stupid people! We're living in a fuckin hellhole. Maybe the only path out is being handed to us. Doesn't that beat all?

She's not a man spouting off how brave he is. She's a woman! If that's what y'all think she is, just some fancy bitch meddling, then go ahead and leave. She ain't no fancy bitch anymore. All her money's been spent on us, a bunch of no-good bums, wasters, just like Mama Goose said."

He raised his hands above his head, circling the room. "It was spent on this. Take a good look." He left the doorway and pushed his way through the crowd and stood at the top of the stairway. His booming voice could be heard throughout the room.

"Take a good look. It's the ticket to our children's freedom. This house, these books, these chairs, tickets to freedom."

The man walked back to Mattie who was still blocking the door. He turned once again to the crowd. "This here government and no rich white folks are goin' to help us. She's invited the whole city here tonight. I see one white woman. Ain't no white folks here who wants to see this community do good. We'll take their jobs and move into their neighborhoods. Ain't no white folk want that. Never have been, never will."

"That's not true," I said, surprising myself. The stares in the room turned instantly toward me. I wanted to hide as I saw their disdain and felt their hostility. I was a white, meddling do-gooder. Why would they listen to me?

"Let's be fair," I said. "This is not about black or white. This is about children. It's our problem. I think you give most of us white folks a bad rap. We're busy just like you raising our own families. The trouble is volunteering takes time. We need you! We need your time."

I couldn't help but wish I had stayed safely next to the wall. I tried not to look at their faces. My voice quivered to a whisper.

"Why are we still so ignorant? It's true. I'm not black. Mattie Turner is my friend and she needs your help. I'm not important. If I can't be of use to her, then I'll be the one to leave. You stay."

"This young lady here is right," the man said, as he once again took control of the crowd. I silently and gratefully went back to my corner.

"Good God, what's it going to take to finally wake you people up? We're the ones responsible for what's goin' on around here." Grabbing Mattie by the hand, he placed his large one in hers. "This lady might be some nutty old woman for sure. Spending her last dime on us, believing there's still some humanity left in us."

Mattie poked him in the arm as the crowd laughed. "She's nuts all right. But, people, it's them kind of nuts we need. Y'all came to see this woman fail. Well, I won't let her."

He pointed his finger at several of the women in the crowd. "I know for a fact Helen and Nettie over there came for the show. They came to see this house and what Mattie has done to it. You should be ashamed of yourselves. This isn't about interior decorating."

The women he referred to mumbled under their breaths.

"It's a damn shame, too. For once in your lives, get smart. I'm tired of mowing lawns, washing cars, collecting garbage, whatever I can to find work – work good enough for a black man. I'm sick to death of my own ignorance. Look around. Don't you ever want more? If not for yourself, think about your kids. Mrs. Williams, you say you've lost Malcolm, but he's not dead yet. Unless you want to stand next to his grave, you of all people should sign that piece of paper over there."

He picked Mattie up and carried her to the center of the room. "Here she is, folks. Here's the lady that can change this rotten, stinking dump we live in."

Gently, almost reverently, he put Mattie back on firmer ground. "If we don't find a way to keep our kids off drugs and away from these gangs, they're lost. We've lost. We brothers and sisters have to get off our dead asses. We have to find the courage to fight.

There are a lot of you women here who need a man's help because your man is either in prison or gone. You women folk is doing our jobs. Wake up! Sign on with Mattie here and give these kids some role models. She needs you. Your kids need her."

People began whispering and talking among themselves. A couple of the ladies moved toward Mattie. I watched her greet them warmly with an outstretched hand. Tears of happiness welled up in my eyes. For the first time in two years, I felt a glimmer of hope. Perhaps Mattie's dream could become a reality after all.

"I'll get LaTisha in this here school if I have to box her ears to do it," a middle-aged woman said, signing her name on the list of volunteers. Several women nodded in agreement. I sat down next to the folding table and took their names. One at a time the volunteer list was signed.

Most of the signatures belonged to women. However, there were a couple of men who approached the table interested enough to sign their names.

"Miss Turner, if I could use your garage, I could bring over a few tools. I'm a carpenter, ma'am, by trade. I could teach at night."

Secretaries, seamstresses, and cooks; all of them came forward to volunteer. These people were not coaches, social workers, psychologists, doctors, or trained police officers. They were common citizens with diverse backgrounds. Hopefully, they were brave enough to stick by their commitments.

After a tour of the house and some store-bought refreshments, everyone left. Mattie closed the door. The hulking man, whose name I still didn't know, lingered in the hall.

I left to get Jack who was playing in the nursery. Mattie had provided babysitting services for anyone wishing to attend the meeting. If I'd known about the danger, I would have left him at home. Jack was happily playing with a couple of teenagers. With

Jack and the diaper bag in my arm, I returned to the foyer. I was still overwhelmed by his speech.

"Thank you," I said, proud to shake his hand. "You have no idea how much Mattie and I appreciate your support. I don't know what we'd have done without you. Unfortunately, we're going to have to mend the ceiling, but we're forever indebted to you, sir."

He let out a rip-roaring laugh. "My dear Miss Stevens, you ain't indebted to me. My name is Moses. They call me Earnest Moses or Grizzly for short. I'm the bouncer at Freddie's Tap down the street."

Mattie came back into the room. She handed him cold hard cash. She was paying the man off. I was shocked. Had Mattie paid Grizzly Moses to be her bodyguard?

He smiled as he stuck the money in his wallet. Mattie put her arm around him and gave him a hug. "Thanks, Moses, Honey. You did a real fine job. I do believe you have the knack for show business, son."

Grizzly tipped his hat, and politely bowed his head. "It's been a pleasure. I must admit you're one smart lady. I truly enjoyed spouting every last word of that speech you wrote. Did you notice? I even added a few of my own words."

"I noticed you added that "ol' lady" bit, too," she said, slapping him on the arm. "Your speech was better than mine. On second thought, give me that money back. Consider it a donation. In fact, I'm feeling pretty damn young right now thanks to you."

He nodded in agreement. "Keep the money. I was only teasing. You're still a good-lookin' broad. That you are, sweet Mattie. Well, glad to be of service, ladies. Anytime you need me, you know where to find me. Good luck. I hope you can do some good in this neighborhood. Used to be a mighty fine place. That it was. That it was," he said, playfully teasing Jack with a set of keys in his pocket. Jack giggled.

Grizzly Moses jumped down the front steps. I shut the door and dropped to the floor. Jack crawled away. Mattie, laughing uncontrollably leaned on the wall and sat down next to us. Placing my hands around her neck, I squeezed. "Damn, you're a cunning witch, Miss Turner. I'd use the "b" word but Jack's here. That was definitely diabolical."

I gently let go of her neck and then punched her in the arm. "I'll have to keep a close eye on you. You'll have the generals shaking in their Nike's."

Mattie smiled coyly and slowly got up from the floor. "God needed Moses to find the Promised Land for his people. Honey, we needed Moses for the very same reason. If Moses was good enough for Him, Moses is good enough for us."

We picked up the rest of the debris and threw it in a garbage bag. Walking Jack and me to the gate, she happily waved good-bye.

C H A P T E R
VII

In a few weeks, Fred and I would leave the U.S. District Court and enter the dog-eat-dog world of practicing law. I say, "practicing law" because when I started at the courthouse my intentions were quite different. Originally my plan was to stick with what I knew best, libraries. Lawyers were needed in libraries, too.

It wasn't the thought of clients that terrified me. It was standing in front of a judge and jury. My brain, due partly to my anxieties, had a habit of malfunctioning in the presence of others.

It was Mattie's pushing and her shopping abilities which changed my turtle-like ways and gave me wings. Of course, I was getting used to it. It was hard to be a chameleon when I was the only one with white skin.

Thanks to her, I had shed my bag-lady looks for something professional. My weight was back to where it was before the baby, 125 pounds give or take, and there was this fancy new hair cut that swept along my forehead to go with the clothes.

While in court, I would sit in my chair and study the members of my own profession. This was much better than a trial advocacy class. This was the real thing with the cast being real people in big trouble. T.V. court was sensationalism. This was mostly boredom in technicolor.

The good lawyers were most often the ones who displayed a down-to-earth cunning and were charismatic in their attitudes. They'd take the time to be polite, quickly honing in on their opponent's weaknesses. Like a good politician, they would twist the facts to their best advantage. Of course, always with a smile, those pearly-white smiles that belied large summed verdicts and early retirement.

Mattie told me I had an honest face and a keen sense of right and wrong. What she was really saying to me, "I need you to find me the kids who are in trouble. Where else but in a courtroom? *We* need to help them." What's with this "we" thing? It was my ass and not hers who'd undoubtedly fail. She pushed and I gave in.

Several months ago, I reluctantly gave up my library job and accepted a position with the Public Defender's Office. In her opinion -- I mean my opinion -- this was the quickest way to get the real hands-on trial experience I supposedly craved, and, at the same time, find her those unwanted children.

Fred was on his way to the Windy City, Chicago. He had a job in his father's large firm, what lawyers call "sweatshops." These places usually consisted of lavish marble reception areas with 25-foot-tall Ficus trees and large brass framed portraits of the "respected ones," those who had gone to their vast beloved courtroom in the sky.

Fred had a glass cubicle for an office along with hundreds of other overworked lawyers where he would practice the art of evasiveness, which is really known as the art of constantly annoying other lawyers, dragging things out, and billing lots of hours.

And, if you were good enough, your first trial would be perhaps five years down the road. The upside of this unbearable existence was the mighty dollar. Fred was going to make a lot of dough. The downside, of course, to this job: fun, women, and a life outside the office would be nonexistent.

Anything to ward off doomsday, Fred talked about becoming my nanny, taking Jack to the golf course. He even tried to convince Mattie to hire him as a basketball coach. There was only one problem. Most of the older kids could play a lot better than he could.

* * *

The final day of life as a law clerk arrived. Poor, unfortunate Fred was not heading for Chicago yet. His dear grandmother had given him a gift after graduation, a trip. The poor man was heading to Australia, New Zealand, Thailand, and Japan. He claimed that in Thailand, beautiful women would sleep on a rug at the foot of your bed and do whatever you asked of them. He had even shown me a picture of one of them. She was, indeed, beautiful. Of course, it was a travel brochure beckoning him to her waiting arms.

Besides, at the last minute, he decided to take his girlfriend. She and that Thai woman would hopefully give him some trouble.

To say a final good-bye, the judge called us into his office. He wanted it to be a secret, but it wasn't.

Everyone yelled, "Surprise!" Without really being surprised, I was still overcome with emotion, another trait I still could not shake off. Did this happen to all new mothers? I was a highly-strung, out-of-control, hormonal woman, and Baby Jack was almost five months old. When would it end?

When I saw their smiling, familiar faces, it warmed my heart. I, of course, burst into tears. All the other women followed my lead. I was going to miss this place. In many ways these people had become my family. In a weird sense, the courthouse was a second home.

We ate cake and opened gifts. I gave Fred a rug I had woven myself for the Thai woman in his dreams. One of Mattie's volunteers owned a loom and had taught several of us women how to use it. What she was really conducting was a free therapy session with a lot of mixed-up females, myself included.

He gave me a gavel engraved with my name on it. It read, "To a very dear friend: Twenty years from now you will be more disappointed by the things you didn't do. So throw off the bowlines. Sail away from the safe harbor. Catch the trade winds in your sails. Explore. Dream. Discover." He had vacation on the brain. I wanted to go, too. I was touched and would treasure it always.

Fred and I walked out the doors of the courthouse for the last time. It was a sad occasion. The unknown always seems daunting, but I had learned a long time ago to expect the unexpected on the road through life. I tried not to cry. We walked toward the parking lot and stopped to look up at the old structure. With fondness, I gazed at the massive white stone. Fred was silent. I already missed its protection.

* * *

The next evening, I drove Fred and the latest love-of-his-life to the airport. Actually, he was loaning me his car, so dropping him off was the polite thing to do. I suspected he let me borrow it because he wanted to ensure Baby Jack was still alive when he returned.

My rattletrap car was on its ninth life. Fred was convinced Baby Jack and I would be stranded along the roadside some night depending on some serial killer for a ride.

As we got out of the car at the airport, he bent down to the carseat and kissed Jack. I have always been lousy at good-byes. There should be some rule about them. Personally, if they had to happen, they should be done via telephones or fax machines -- better yet, an old-fashioned letter.

The truth of the matter was I didn't want to say good-bye to Fred. I loved his irresistible, obnoxious face. Should I kiss him in front of his girlfriend? Should I shake his hand? I felt so uncomfortable. Fred made the first move. He put his arms gently around me and gave me a polite kiss on the cheek. I was obviously in the sister-of-the-month category.

"Have a nice life." I said, punching his arm. I figured if my ex-husband, Nick, could say it to me, it was good enough for Fred.

He was puzzled. "Have a nice life? What kind of corny thing is that to say? I'll be back in a couple months, if not to see Baby Jack, at least to pick up my car."

Reminding him of his precious treasure, he pointed his finger in my face. "Annie, dear, try not to run into anything, and once in a while see that it gets a bath."

"I'll treat it the same way I treated Old Betsy," I joked. "Come on, Fred. What do you expect from me? Are you telling me you want me to actually *wash* this thing?"

Fred balled up his fist as if to punch me in the face. I pulled his fist away. "All right. Say no more. I'll just treat *your* car like you do *our* office space. I'll take it through one of those car washes, you know, the kind that works automatically. Not to worry. How hard can it be? I'm sure I'll figure it out."

"Please don't," he begged. "At least use one of the sprayer

stalls." He took one last look at his gleaming car and patted it on the hood. "Don't you dare ruin this fine finish. I must be nuts. Why do I let you use me like this?"

Whenever I was around, the girlfriends gave one of those "let's get out of here" stares, and that's just what she was doing. Fred quickly got the message and picked up her bags.

"You two have a nice time," I yelled through the busy hubbub of airport traffic. I placed my hand on my heart and said, "Thanks for letting me borrow your precious car. Thanks for everything. I know I've been a pain in the *ass*, but isn't Jack worth it?"

Fred smiled as he, too, remembered the first day we had met. "You'll always be a pain in my ass. Take care and, please, try to stay out of trouble."

Pretending not to understand his advice, I shrugged my shoulders and waved good-bye. Heading toward the revolving door, he waved back. I took one last look at Fred's back as he entered the airport terminal.

I sadly opened the door and sat down. Baby Jack was wide-awake. Looking at me, a smile lit his tiny face. "We're certainly not off to Australia or Thailand. Sorry, you're stuck with me, babe. Where shall we go? Istanbul? Paris? How about Mattie's house? I'm getting depressed."

* * *

During the months that followed, Madagascar would have been preferable. Every day a constant stream of spiritless souls would enter the Public Defender's Office. I thought the legal aid office had them. I was wrong.

On Monday mornings the place was jammed with foul-smelling alcoholics or drug addicts who had been arrested during the weekend. On Tuesday, you could still smell the stench from the stale alcohol and sweaty bodies. Startling to me was how case-hardened I had become in such a short time. Warehousing them seemed to be the only solution. Most of the time I was grateful they were behind bars.

Every once in a while someone came along who had some redemption material. As planned, Mattie pulled up at the curb preaching community service work. So far she had two young girls picked up for shoplifting and three young boys who refused to go to school. When faced with jail or Mattie, the choice was easy. It was working beautifully.

* * *

"I need to see a lawyer. Please, young lady!" I looked out my office door and down the hall. A large black woman was quite upset and yelling at the receptionist.

"It's urgent. I needs help. Can't you see I'm about to have a nervous breakdown? Listen to me. I'm in deep shit!"

Most of my associates were in court, so, resigned to my fate, I walked down the hall and motioned the receptionist to buzz the lady through. As she approached me, I observed her to be in her mid 60s, a large, ample woman with a huge bosom. She entered my office and collapsed into the seat in front of my desk.

Out of breath and sweating profusely, she wiped her brow with a very used and shriveled up Kleenex. Obligingly, I handed her a clean one. Without saying a word, she blew her nose reverberating the sound off the walls and shaking the photographs of Jack nailed there.

Her white cotton shirt looked like it had been put in the dark clothes wash too many times. Her top button was hanging together by a thread revealing a dirty, gray-looking bra.

She had a bruised and swollen lip. A tiny drop of blood had not yet coagulated and was still dripping down the left side of her mouth. Ready to direct her to the women's shelter, I reached for the phone. She said something unintelligible and grabbed the phone out of my hand.

"No. Lady, don't you dare touch that phone. I'm in trouble. They're after me." She looked around expecting someone to barge into the office any second.

"All right. Calm down. I won't touch the phone. Relax. Tell me what's happened."

She burst into a new round of tears and took a couple of deep breaths before answering my question. Words flew out of her mouth so fast I had trouble understanding her.

"Damn it. I told that bastard if he called me a bitch one more time I was gonna let him have it. I've been waitin on that bastard hand and foot for eleven years. Look at me!"

She pointed to her face. "This ain't no beauty face. He's hit me one too many times. He doesn't even call me by my name. 'Bitch, get this. Bitch, get that.' I just couldn't stand it no more. A person has a right to lose her mind after being treated so badly. Let me tell ya, I'd heard it for the last time."

Fearing a confession, I raised my hands and tried to interrupt her. "Wait a minute." She ignored me and tried to speak again. "Shut up!" I yelled. She finally stopped her babbling. "If you've done something wrong, don't tell me!"

She seemed puzzled and searched my face for answers. More tears trickled down her face. "Why the hell not? You're my lawyer, ain't ya?"

"Quite frankly, no. I haven't been appointed to represent you and –"

She interrupted me. "I'm appointin' you! I needs help. I ain't some rich lady. I don't have no money to hire me some fancy dude."

Tomorrow I would find some humor in this conversation, but today I had a job to do. "All right. I'll do what I can. I suppose you can go ahead and tell me what happened."

She reached for another tissue, taking a deep breath. "That's the last time ol' Willie ever calls me bitch. For eleven years, I've put up with his bullshit. Call the police. They'll tell you who I am. They've saved my life more times than I can count." She took another deep breath and started to hiccup. "Got any water? " I left the room and came back with a paper cup. She downed the water in one gulp, wiping her mouth with the back of her hand.

"Thanks. Willie was sitting pretty as you please in his lounge chair ordering me around. He said, 'Bitch, get me another beer. Bitch, make me some food.' I left him and sat in my kitchen getting angrier and angrier. Don't really know why I did it. It was like some evil force entered my body and done took it over. Kind of like time was a runnin out on me. If I didn't end his life, he'd end mine."

She cleared her throat, her voice increasing a couple of octaves. "I went to the sink, poured me a large pan of water, and put it on the stove to boil. Hating that son-of-a-bitch, I opened the cabinet and looked for a box of macaroni and cheese. That's all I was a gonna do. That's when I looked at the top shelf and noticed a bottle of Karo syrup. Like I said, this evil thought just started happenin' to my brain, like I had no control. It was like that bottle was callin' me. I grabbed a kitchen chair, pulled it down, and poured the bottle into the pot." She took the paper cup and smashed it between her hands.

"While the pot boiled, I was a listenin' to the son-of-a-bitch call me names. There comes a point when you can't take it no more. He didn't do nothin' to redeem hisself. He kept yelling, 'Bitch, where is that beer? Bring me that Goddamn beer, ol' lady. How many times do I have to tell you to get off that fat ass of yours? Good for nothin' bitch!

"He came into the kitchen and went to the refrigerator hisself. 'Damn lazy bitch.' He slapped me across the face and went back to watching T.V. I thought about that pot. Then I says to myself, if he calls me bitch one more time he'll be sorry. 'Bitch, where's that food?' I picked up that pot of boiling syrup, marched into the livin' room and dumped it on his lap. You should've seen the look on his face. I shocked the hell out of him." She slapped her hand on her knee and chuckled.

"I called 911 before I left the bastard. He was still breathing when I walked out that door for good!"

Her voice lowered to a whisper as she leaned closer to me. "Oh, God, have you ever smelled burning flesh? It stinks, not a pretty smell. I hope that rotten skin of his melts right off his bones. I should've threw it at his mouth. Shut him up for good, wouldn't it? I don't know whether I killed him or not. Probably shut him up for good anyway. The police are out there looking for me. I called my neighbor, told her what I'd done, and she told me to come here."

"She gave you excellent advice." I said, reassuring her. "Running away is not the answer." Who was I to give advice? I'd been running all my life. I was too overcome to ask questions. All I could think about were my own parents, the belt hanging on the wall next to the back door, my mother's bloody lip, the makeup she wore to disguise the bruises. I needed to concentrate on this woman's problems, not my own.

I hadn't asked the lady her name. "Let's start with some background information, shall we?" I was back to playing the part of a lawyer. "Have you ever been arrested?"

"Haven't you been listenin to me?" She wiped the sweat off her neck. "Willie and me ...we go way back. We've been drinkin and fightin, my goodness, for eleven years. Every week the police pays us a visit to our house. I've been in pain. Oh, forget it," she said, waving her hand. "You'll never understand. I've got me a couple of battery charges and I've written some bad checks. Other than that, I'm pretty clean. Oh, yeah, they got me for shoplifting when I was just a kid."

I took out my legal pad and pen. "Let's start over. I'm sorry. This is a very serious matter. I didn't get your name."

"Oh, I'm sorry. I completely forgot my manners. My name is Georgia Harriet Wilson," she said, extending her hand. "Lived with that man and never married him. Shoulda left when I still had a good-lookin body. Too late now. I'll probably go to jail...die in jail. I took about all a human being had a right to take. The bastard's name is Willard Dixon. Everyone calls him Willie." She picked up my phone. "Go ahead. Call the police. What are ya waitin' for? I'm ready."

I took the phone out of her hand and dialed the Sheriff's Department. After the interview, I took Georgia over to the police station myself so she could turn herself in.

Prior to Georgia, I had been assigned mainly drunk driving cases and misdemeanors. She opened the door to my first felony. Occasionally, the associates in my office asked me how the Karo syrup case was coming along. Their snickers could be heard as they walked down the hall. I didn't think it was funny. I had a job to do. I swore on my brother's grave to take care of people like her, women who could not take care of themselves, women like my mother, beaten by the same man who vowed to love her. How much abuse did it take to finally burn your man with a pot of Karo syrup? I spent many weeks filing the proper motions and planning my strategy.

* * *

In Mattie's life, things were becoming a little more hectic.

Her problems were still the same: seemingly hopeless, no funds, and not enough kids. A couple weeks ago, she had assembled some baby cribs and, with the help of her new carpenter, they finished the day care center. In that determined way of hers, she was walking through the neighborhood knocking on doors, passing out flyers, and letting the young women know she was available to watch any child whose mother was willing to go to school or get a job.

At first, many of these single mothers used her so they could run around a bit. Mattie put a halt to that in a hurry. She insisted on proof of their enrollment. A class schedule or a quick phone call to the employer cured the problem.

Right now, she was taking care of at least a half a dozen three and four year old girls and boys. She was still baffled as to what she'd do with the women who had a night job. They obviously needed her in the evening, but so far she hadn't given up her sleep. I suspected I would hear about *that* any day now.

The number of teenagers who entered her home varied. They were slowly warming to her generosity. If a parent had been drunk or had thrown them out, they would come to her for food. So far she hadn't convinced them of their need for her love, affection and sound motherly advice.

Fortunately for Mattie, a teenager's life was always in a hormonal turmoil so she counted on that to befriend them. She was convinced the "geniuses of the new millennium" would eventually listen. It was only a matter of time.

I, on the other hand, was finally discovering what it meant to have a real sense of home. I had purchased a house from a client of Fred's father. It was a two-story stucco, situated in a mostly white, middle class neighborhood. It had a big screened-in porch which faced the street.

It desperately needed a new coat of paint and a new roof. On today's market it was what you would call "a fixer-upper." My greatest enthusiasm for the house was in its hardwood floors. They were in perfect condition. The kitchen needed to be renovated, but I took off the old doors and painted the interior a dark green. Without cabinet fronts, the few dishes and plates I possessed were exposed, adding a pleasing and contrasting color to the walls.

There was now a burgundy-colored couch, a couple of mahogany coffee tables added to my list of material possessions. I'd found them in a garage sale. A large cream-colored area rug in the living room was placed in front of the fireplace.

Mattie insisted on a housewarming party. It was the first party I had ever thrown. She and a couple of the volunteers, Eunice and Martha, who by the way were excellent cooks, made the hors d'oeuvres. My co-workers surprised me with two matching table lamps to go with the couch. Fred came back from his long vacation and surprised me by bringing my mother.

"How are you, my dear? This is for you." My mother handed me a large bouquet of cut flowers. Before I had time to grasp any implications this visit meant, Mattie came swooping into the room.

"So you're Annie's mother,"she said, shaking her hand. "It's a pleasure to finally meet you. Fred told me you were coming." Mattie noted my discomfort and took over. "Your daughter seems to be speechless. Here. Let me get you a drink."

I was the one who needed the drink. The evening had just turned into a disaster. I gave Fred an angry stare and, grabbing him by the arm, escorted him into the bathroom.

"If you wanted to get me alone, this is a pretty strange place. Come here. Give me a hug," he said, resting his hand on my shoulder.

"What do you think you're doing?" I asked removing the hand.

"Would you be referring to your mother?" he asked innocently. "I told her I was coming down and asked her if she'd be interested in riding along. I thought the daughter might like to see her mother, not to mention the grandson who needs his only grandmother. What can I say? She wanted to come. You know, Annie, for an intelligent woman you're missing the boat where your mother's concerned. Let bygones be bygones. She's a very nice woman."

"She's not a very nice woman. She only pretends to be for your sake." Frustrated, I turned my back on him.

"Really? That's not the impression I get. It's time to forgive her, Annie. She needs your forgiveness. You need to forgive. That's all I've got to say in the matter. Now, if you'll excuse me, I'm going to go and enjoy myself." He put his hand on the door knob, then changed his mind.

"Come here," he said, drawing me to him. "You need her in your life, Annie." He put his finger up against my lips. "I know you don't want to hear it. Think it over. I'm giving you good advice." He kissed me on the forehead, then closed the door in my face.

I should have popped Fred in the nose. The enthusiasm I felt at the beginning of this evening was over. Putting on my pretend face, I opened the door. I wasn't ready to accept his advice, nor deal with these issues. Why couldn't the jerk just leave us both alone.

When I entered the living room, Jack was giggling at his grandmother. She glanced toward me and smiled. " He's adorable."

She could say, "I'm sorry to barge in on you like this." She could say, "I shouldn't have come." She could say, "I've missed you, Anne. It's been so long." None of these things were said. None of these things mattered. If they didn't, why was I so upset? I suppose what mattered was she was here at all. What was she trying to prove?

The house was getting crowded. This wasn't the time to have it out with my mother. This was the time for small talk with friends. My mother could wait. The guests were enjoying themselves.

The party broke off at about one in the morning. Fred spent

most of the evening ignoring me.

Before they left, my mother hugged Jack, then me. It was the first time she'd done that in over a decade. "I'll see you two later," she said smiling. I wondered what that meant. Eight years from now or a couple of months, who knew?

The place was beginning to look like a home. It was still rather empty, but I liked it that way. One of the rooms on the first floor I nicknamed the Schwinn room. It was a nifty place to keep my old bicycle. I abhor clutter; but at the same time, I could receive a gold medal for being guilty of never throwing things away. I was not a pack rat, just a lazy bum.

Baby Jack was turning into a butterball. His face would light up at the sight of me, oh, how proud and privileged I felt. He could crawl to the couch, lift himself up, and walk along its edge. I hoped those thunder thighs would disappear once he became a little more active. The strength it took to raise those wobbly legs off the ground made me pant right along with him.

Fred was now working fourteen hour days in his sweatshop. At least once a week, he'd call. We steered clear from the topic of my mother. He mostly complained about the stratospheric egos he had to put up with in other less civilized law firms. Sometimes he came down on the weekends. Thank goodness, it was alone.

During these times, Mattie put him to work with one project or another at her house, and we'd bump into each other in passing. Our relationship was strained, but I cared too much to have a major fight. I forgave him. He forgave me. Why wasn't it as simple with my mother?

For the past couple of months, Georgia had been out on bond and living at Willie's house. There was no one there to pay the rent so naturally she was evicted. Homeless, I picked her up and found a bed at the women's shelter. Perhaps I should have taken her to Mattie's. I didn't want to burden her. Georgia had been an alcoholic her entire life. She would call me at nights, still drunk and crying. There were some cases too hopeless even for Mattie's special talents.

The women's shelter was clean and warm. It lacked the charm of Mattie's house, but it beat a jail cell. I watched Georgia unpack her belongings. On the twin-sized bed assigned to her, she laid out the meager contents of her life. Placing the well-worn clothes in the drawers next to the bed, she took a piece of old newspaper out of her jacket pocket.

"Here, Miss Stevens, this is for you," she said, handing the package to me.

I had told her many times before to call me Anne. She wouldn't do it. I tried to place it back in her hands. She shook her head.

"No, I want you to have this. It's the only thing worth anything, the only thing alcohol hasn't destroyed in my life. Please you've done so much for me. It'd probably get stolen here."

Reluctantly, I opened the gift. Inside was a gold and silver pocket watch. Georgia took it from me and showed me how to open the cover. When the lid flipped open, music filled the room. I recognized the tune. 'What a Wonderful World' -- the one thing that had always been denied her. The one thing that had always been denied me – until now.

* * *

Willie had been transferred to a burn unit in a health care facility and was not doing very well. His prognosis for a full recovery was bleak. The poor man had been so badly burned he was undergoing daily treatments of skin peels and skin grafts. This process removed good skin tissue in other parts of his body and transferred them to the areas where raw tissue was exposed. I was told by the hospital staff this was a slow and painful process.

The pictures of Willie's body were horrifying. His skin, no longer black, was now pink and white. The splash marks from the syrup went all the way up to his neck. To make matters worse, the main area taking the brunt of the hot liquid was his penis and thighs. Parts of his skin in those areas oozed large patches of dark yellow pus.

Georgia had been charged by the State's Attorney's Office with attempted murder. It is common for women who have been verbally and physically abused to visit the person who abused them. Georgia was no exception. She was visiting him on a regular basis.

Willie tried to persuade the prosecutor not to charge her. This attempt had been futile. I was filing a motion to suppress to get the pictures thrown out of court because of their prejudicial nature.

In the end, I lost the motion. Willie was refusing to testify against her, but the prosecutor confident of a conviction did not care. The pictures alone and Georgia's confession to her neighbor were probably enough to send her away.

All our attempts for a continuance failed. On the first day of opening statements, the couple had been seen holding hands in the elevator. Willie could barely walk, but he stood by Georgia throughout the trial ranting about this unfair process and proclaiming her innocence.

Neither Willie's testimony that Georgia did it in self-defense or my closing argument worked. The jury found her guilty anyway. Georgia's bond was revoked because the presumption of innocence no longer applied.

The court security officer loomed over our table. Georgia looked at me and patted my hand. Still too stunned to take in the full impact of her predicament, she thanked me. I should have told her about the appeal process, but I was too overwhelmed. It wasn't that

I had lost a case. I had lost a friend, a human being who'd now be just another number in an institution.

Only once did she turn toward the back of the courtroom. With tears in her eyes, she dutifully placed her arms behind her back. Willie smiled and waved a final good-bye.

I'll never get used to the sound handcuffs make as the metal clicks adjust themselves to a person's wrist size. It's one of those sounds that cause you to thank your lucky stars it's someone else. It's one of those sounds that sends goosebumps down your spine. No matter what crime the client committed, you can't help but feel saddened by their plight.

In sorrow, I turned to find Willie. He took his handkerchief from his jacket pocket and wiped the tears rolling down his cheeks. Georgia was quietly escorted out of the courtroom. I shook the prosecutor's hand without any enthusiasm. When I had gathered my file, I turned to speak to Willie. He had vanished.

Later that evening, I got a call from the police department. Willie had gone home and put a gun to his head. He was permanently at peace and Georgia was facing a minimum fifteen years in prison. A few months ago she had said it herself. She was sixty-four years old and would probably die in prison.

From time to time, I would take her only treasure out of my pocket. I flipped the delicate gold cover. "It's a Wonderful World" played its magical melody.

C H A P T E R
VIII

After Georgia's trial, I was assigned a greater number of felony cases. This afternoon, my client, Jason Reed, was charged with burglary. He had been caught stealing a T.V. from a middle class neighborhood and was up for sentencing. He was a black male, nineteen years old with large, brown, wide-set eyes, light-colored skin, and a clear complexion. He had a muscular build and was quite tall. He was extremely polite, and quite ordinary looking until you saw him smile. He had gorgeous straight white teeth. Unfortunately, those smiles would never reach his eyes and were very, very rare.

His mother was dead. His father was listed as unknown. No family appeared in the courtroom on the two occasions we had hearings. I liked him a lot. I suppose he struck a chord of familiarity in me. Unlike most of my young clients, he had graduated from high school and scored 150 on his IQ test. The prosecutor and I worked out what we called a "plea bargain," a deal.

We sat quietly in the courtroom while Judge Morris read Jason's presentence report. Puzzled, he glanced in my direction.

"Miss Stevens, it says here Mr. Reed is not employed. I don't have a disagreement with counsels' plea negotiations; however, I am concerned with this defendant's employment history. He seems to be a bright and capable young man. What gives? Why can't he find a job?"

I leaned over and whispered to Jason. "Your Honor, may I call Mr. Reed to the stand?"

"You may," he said opening a drawer to find a pen. "Please proceed."

The defendant approached the bench, raised his right hand, and was sworn. Standing next to the podium, I could sense Jason's nervousness. I began my direct examination.

"Please state your name for the record, Mr. Reed."

Jason tried not to fidget in his chair. "Jason Reed."

"Mr. Reed, have there been any significant changes in your life since the presentence report was written?"

"Yes, ma'am." He pulled out a sheet of paper and handed it to the bailiff.

"Can you explain to the court what those changes involve?"

"I'm working part-time at Mattie's House. I've applied for night school. That's my application. I want to get my associate's degree in landscape architecture. Your Honor, sir, I'm doing my best to get my life back on the right track."

I sat back down. "I have no further questions."

With no cross-examination from the prosecutor, the judge instructed Jason to step down and resume his seat at the table. Looking somewhat self-defeated, the judge shook his head in frustration.

"Miss Stevens, isn't Mattie Turner's house getting a little overcrowded? Last week you told me DeAngelo Wilken was mowing the lawn. Tina Goodwin was a daycare instructor and Maurice Sampson desperately needed to refinish the upstairs floors in the house. What, pray tell, are you telling me now?"

I started to speak, but the judge interrupted me. "Let me guess. Mr. Reed cleans the basement and the front porch. I haven't heard that one yet," he said sarcastically.

Maintaining my composure, I responded, "No, Your Honor, when he's not needed at Miss Turner's house, I employ him, sir. He's great with kids. I recently purchased a house. It needs a lot of work. I'm paying him to mow the lawn, paint the fence, those types of things. Oh, and he takes the recyclables from both houses to the distribution center."

The judge shut the file, shook his head, and calmly began to sentence my client.

"Mr. Reed, please approach the bench."

Jason and I approached.

"You have the right to make a statement regarding your sentence. If you wish to make such a statement, you may."

Jason stood and looked straight at the judge. "Your Honor, sir, I'm sorry. You won't see me in this courtroom again."

"That is my fondest wish, Mr. Reed." The judge placed his reading glasses on his head and picked up his file. "It is the judgment of this court that the defendant, James Reed, be sentenced to three years probation and 24 hours community service work to commence forthwith at the youth home known as 'Mattie's House.'" Also, this defendant is further sentenced to three hours of jail time, which is to begin this morning."

Pointing his finger at Jason, the judge's tone became sterner. "Young man, consider yourself lucky. If it weren't for Miss Stevens, you would be doing time in the penitentiary. It's only because this is your first adult offense that you get this break. However, Mr. Reed, you do have a lousy juvenile record. If I see your face in my courtroom again, I'll not be so lenient."

Then Judge Morris stood and headed toward his chamber door. "Miss Stevens, I could use someone at my house. Do you suppose when Mr. Reed finishes his chores, he could wash my car and mow my lawn?"

Jason overheard his comment. "Your Honor, I would be happy to help you. And, of course, there will be no charge."

The judge smiled. "They'd put me in the slammer for accepting a bribe if I took advantage of your offer. All kidding aside, Miss Stevens, from what I've heard, Miss Turner is making some progress. We need people like her in this community. Keep up the good work. Please see that you keep your charges out of my courtroom."

As he began to walk toward the chamber door, he turned. "Oh, may I make one more suggestion?"

I bowed my head and smiled. "I could always use the advice of an esteemed and reputable jurist."

"You're running out of places to put these defendants. Next time try finding them legitimate jobs."

"Your Honor, you are quite mistaken. These are legitimate jobs."

That afternoon, walking down the courthouse steps, I felt a sense of satisfaction. I was gaining the self-esteem to practice competent law. Most of the time it didn't matter what I had to say. But, sometimes a judge actually listened to me...like today...and Jason could walk the streets a free man. Those days felt good.

Most people think only the rich get set free. What's called "justice" today is hiring a good competent defense lawyer, beat the system, and get acquitted. In a media sense, that seemed true. Since the O.J. Simpson trial, the citizens of this country had taken an interest in courtroom drama. We were turning into very cynical individuals. How many times would a no-good politician get reprimanded or acquitted?

In a legal sense, justice is supposed to apply to all, rich or poor, white, black or whatever color you happen to be. The word implies a sense of moral rightness and fairness. More often than not, I believed in the system. I observed the machinations of its inner core work and, honestly, I was proud to be a part of it.

Like most things in life, it periodically failed.

* * *

As I sat watching Jack's modest attempts at crawling, the phone rang. It was a tired-sounding Mattie.

"I need to get out of here before I go crazy," she protested.

"Is there anything wrong?" I asked.

"No. Annie, dear. I need a break. None of this roasted chicken crap. Pick me up and take me out to dinner. Since you're the working woman and the only one presently earning any decent money, it should be your treat."

Famished myself, I felt I could use a break, too. I agreed to pick her up at 6:30. After I made the arrangements with one of my neighbors to baby-sit, I drove to her home. I felt guilty about leaving Jack. I worked so hard during the day, the nights became our special time. I shook off the feeling and pulled up at Mattie's house in good spirits.

It was the middle of October, a brisk, pleasant evening. A light, cool breeze and signs of autumn were in the air. Glancing at the sky, I could not find a moon. The stars were shining brilliantly.

I was overjoyed at the prospect of spending an evening with Mattie in pursuit of frolic and fun for a change. My life resembled an eggbeater. I was being whisked by a crying baby, work, volunteering at Mattie's, crying baby, work, volunteering. Alone was a forgotten experience.

Poor Mattie was even worse off. A good night's sleep was a thing of the past. The cardiologist should strangle her. Better yet, I needed to strangle her. I watched her as she tiptoed down the stairs two at a time. She kept looking behind her, expecting one of the kids to need her at the last second. Mattie plopped herself beside me, winded and out of breath.

"What do you think of my new look?" She asked, closing the car door. Touching the rows of colorful beads, she patted the mop on her head. Her hairstyle was not the only thing different. The gray streaks were now the color of dark burgundy. She was also dressed in a long plaid skirt with a black turtleneck. As if the beads on her head weren't enough, around her neck she wore a couple of strands of gold and steel animals on a pink satin chord. Her feet were laced up in a pair of black velvet granny boots.

"Well, am I ever going to get your answer? What do you think?"

"I'm too stunned to reply," I said, not sure whether to give her an honest answer.

"Oh, come now. We could be sisters, don't you think?" The beads in her hair made a clicking sound as they flew in my face.

"Don't push your luck," I said, teasing her. "You might be able to pass as my mother, mid 40s -- I take that back. She's going to be fifty this year. Sister's pushing it a bit."

"The kids talked me into it." She pulled down the visor and glanced at her reflection. "The color is supposed to come out when I wash it. I sat for hours while they braided this mop. Oh, and check this out," Mattie was full of enthusiasm. She opened the bright red coat she carried under her arm. Black houses and faces were painted all over the wool material. The children had signed their names under each piece of artwork.

"What do you think? Pretty adorable, isn't it? Just wait and see. I'll bet a lot of grandmothers will want to buy one. Trust me. They're going to be a big hit at the next fund drive."

"Not a bad idea. Put Jack's name on one, and I'll buy it."

Mattie chatted while I drove to a lovely Italian restaurant on the west side of town. For once, we didn't talk about child rearing and happenings at home. In no time at all, one bottle of wine was gone. I wasn't used to alcohol. I had tried it when I was married to Nick and hated the taste. Fear of turning into my father had kept me good and away from it. With Mattie, it was different. I was comfortable. The warmth spread slowly through my body. It had been years since I felt so relaxed.

Mattie held up the empty bottle and the waiter brought over another. Thank goodness, the food arrived. We ate our delicious pasta in silence.

Toward the middle of the second bottle, we moved the discussion to politics and current events. Too depressing and boring, the subject changed abruptly to sex.

"Annie, I think it's high time you found yourself a man. Perhaps someone your own age or maybe a little older. Have you looked in a mirror lately? You're a knockout. You should be having sex at least twice a week, maybe three times."

I was embarrassed and shocked by her boldness. "Since you look twenty years younger, does that mean someone your age should have it at least once a week?" I asked, mocking her.

"You're right," Mattie said. "What's age got to do with it? Maybe no boyfriend counts for something."

"Tell me, Mattie, do I ever pry into your personal life?" I asked.

"Why would you? I'm boring. I don't have a personal life," she said with a sigh, putting her elbow on the table and her hand to her chin.

"I don't either," I said, wiping the spaghetti sauce off my mouth. "Let's see. Should I pick some man out of a crowd and take him home?" I turned and assessed the competition in the room. "Maybe that guy over there. What do you think? Maybe his wallet is as big as his stomach."

"Shame on you," Mattie scolded.

"How about that cutie pie over there?" Mattie pointed to a short, skinny guy wearing black glasses.

"No way, much too short. He probably suffers from Napoleonic syndrome or short male complex, whatever they call it." Mattie turned around to check out the other side of the room.

"Stop it! We're misbehaving. We've made fun of short people, fat people, oh look, there's one that's too skinny. Do you see anybody else we can abase with our criticisms? Besides, I like my freedom. I don't want to take care of another child. That's what they are, you know. What I need is a 6'5" male with his tongue cut out. Someone like James, the dummy only flesh and blood.."

Picking up the wineglass, Mattie almost choked on what was left in the glass. "You'd miss what that tongue could do," she said, with a gleam in her eye.

I laughed so hard I almost fell out of my chair. "My you are a wicked woman tonight."

"I can't help it. I've been locked up in that house too long. When I was your age, I used to walk down the streets checking men out. Who am I kidding. I could do it today if I had the time. I'd look them over and say to myself, 'You look good. Oh, and so do you. I'll have an affair with you, but not with you. Wow, now he's a handsome guy. But you're too handsome. I won't have an affair with you because you'd be having affairs with the entire female population. I don't know, though, maybe I should reconsider. Damn you're good looking, maybe tomorrow.'"

I halted her next retort. "Hold it. I don't want to hear this. If you recall, I'm used to infidelity. I recently got dumped by the award-winning philanderer of this century. Please, no good-looking ones. I'm still smarting from the jet lag."

I leaned toward her ear and came up with one of her beads. I removed it from my cheek putting it back in place. "This new hairdo must've done something to your brain. I'm disappointed in you. Why would I want to do something so utterly asinine? You're a fine one to talk. Some example you make. Where's your husband, girlfriend?"

Mattie was unaffected by my insult. Taking one last bite of her French bread, she washed it down with another large gulp of wine. "You're the foolish woman here. I'm too old and set in my ways. Get off that high horse of yours, or is it a dead horse?"

She moved into my face and looked deep into my eyes. "You're definitely acting like a dead horse."

Then she switched gears on me. "The kids today are no different. It totally astonishes me why every generation thinks they created the word "sex." In my heyday, believe you me, I had plenty of fun times. Come to think of it, maybe we did create it."

She placed her hand upon a wayward braid pushing it back where it belonged. "Maybe I should tie these things up. In those days, I was a damn good-looking woman. I could have it whenever I wanted it. Of course, we all can at that age. The greatest invention known to womankind is that pill. Darn it! I just needed it a decade sooner. I hated those rubbers. They always spoiled the fun. Of course, more for the man than for me. Come to think of it, why did I care?"

Mattie was enjoying herself and having too much fun with me. "Don't look at me like that."

"Look at you like what?"

"With that frown on your forehead. I'm telling you. They'll make nasty wrinkles some day. Where was I? Oh, we had to find a drugstore away from my neighborhood. Rubbers, what a stupid name for those contraptions. Rubbers. I hate the way it vibrates off your top lip in order to say it. Don't you think men get a certain amount of macho pride walking into a drugstore like they're off to retrieve some prize right out of a Cracker Jack box or something?" she said, leaning in her chair.

Personally, I disagreed with her but didn't say so. It's an uneasy experience no matter what sex you are. Even today I had trouble buying articles of feminine hygiene. Oh, God, now she had me doing it.

Mattie wasn't making sense and neither was I. Drinking lots of water seemed a better idea. "Another thing: our generation kept our mouths shut. We didn't go around bragging about some new position we should try. It was a private matter. A lady was treated like a lady. I still want my man to open my doors and pay for my suppers."

As if examining a complex problem, Mattie took another sip. "Actually, that's not quite true. Perhaps I am wrong and you're right." I was confused. I relished the fact that I could be right about something without having said a word.

"Look how nosy I've become in your life. Maybe my 'little mouth' back then should have been the 'big mouth' I have today. I was so darn shy. The older I get, the smarter I become. That's why it's necessary to spread this mouth around the world."

Mattie continued to reflect upon a past I did not know. Then a wicked smile crossed her lips. "Let me tell you something about myself that will truly shock you, my friend. I remember a time when I had sex with two different men on the same evening. Can you believe it?"

"Of course I can believe it. I can't even spot a wrinkle on that flawless face of yours. Second of all, please don't give me a blow-by-blow picture. Trust me, I believe you. Please spare me!"

She took my hand off her mouth and ignored my suggestion. "It happened like this. On Mondays, Wednesdays, and Fridays, I went out with Harry. On Tuesdays, Thursdays, and Saturdays, I went out with Bernie. For some stupid reason known only to Harry, he came on Bernie's day. I was in a panic. I couldn't let Harry know I was two-timing him. Annie, I was very deceitful in those days."

"You, Mattie Turner, deceitful?" I asked, pretending shock. "Deceitful, I'd believe. Shy, no. Truly you're joking. I can't imagine anything so preposterous."

"Shut up and listen to me," Mattie scolded. "It's not often a woman can pull that kind of a stunt and get away with it. Besides, I liked them both. They were both incredibly handsome. I couldn't keep my hands off either one of them. You know how it is when you're young. Your hormones are totally out of control. Oh, I'm sorry. You wouldn't know about that."

I shook my head and refused to give her the satisfaction of answering her smart aleck remark. Mattie grinned and turned her head to ignore me. I knew I was in for a long-winded tale. There was no shutting her up. Unfortunately, they oftentimes ended with unsolicited advice.

"Thinking back, it was one of the most exciting evenings I ever had," she said leaning too close to my ear. I supported her weight, positioning her back in the chair. "I had long, delicious sex with Harry, then quickly shuffled him out the door and got dressed again. It was just in the nick of time, too. Bernie arrived at my doorstep just as I was putting my stockings back on. That's another thing about your generation. I love panty hose. The pill and panty hose, what magnificent inventions. I hated those garter belts and those nasty marks they left on your thighs."

"Shhh, shut up! You're beginning to embarrass me."

I noticed a young couple staring in our direction and making comments about our table. "Forget panty hose, Mattie," I said growing impatient. "What happened? Did Bernie ever find out about Harry?"

"Not right away, but eventually I got caught. It was a good thing, too. My stomach was getting enormous. That month alone I gained ten pounds."

"Mattie, I don't care about garter belts and your weight gain. Get on with it."

"All right. All right. Back to my story. Then I went out with Bernie. We, too, had rapturous sex. 'Rapturous,' I love that word. It means it's better than just extraordinary. When you use it to describe some man in your life, you better watch out. It can only lead to misery."

Once again, she changed the subject. "So you see, my point being, Miss Goody Two Shoes, you have to move on. Get off the treadmill that goes nowhere." I was still having trouble following her. She frowned and leaned closer, almost touching my face.

"Your generation is lucky. It's because of all these contraptions you people have nowadays that we didn't have: washing machines, dryers, panty hose, birth control, cordless telephones, paper shredders, 30-inch screen TV's, stereos in surround sound. You don't know what you're missing. You need to move into the 21st Century, dearie."

"TV depresses me. As for paper shredders, I'm not a politician so I don't need one. I'm not even going to ask you why you need one. See how smart I've become, Miss Deceitful."

"Oh, now she's funny. You don't seem to understand their significance. We women received our true emancipation! It had nothing to do with wars and leaving us behind to fend for ourselves. It took gadgets doing important mundane things, easing our lives and bringing about our true freedom."

Mattie sat taller in her chair. She waved her hand, dismissing my ignorance. "Oh, well. Everyone needs to be a little wicked. It puts spice in your life. Trust me. You'll be more disappointed by the things you didn't do than by the things you did. Somebody said that. I don't know who. I adopted that philosophy years ago."

"You read it on the giant gavel Fred gave me. Remember? You need to start drinking some water, too." I tried to get back to the topic of discussion. "Who did you see on Sunday?"

"The Good Lord, of course. Every once in a while I would be overcome with guilt. On Sunday, I confessed all my sins so I could start anew on Monday. No, I'm kidding. On Sunday, after the Good Lord's sermon, I slept. I was too exhausted."

It was my turn to monopolize the conversation. "Since you're being so impertinent, I'm going to ask you another stupid question. I know it's vulgar, but I can't help myself."

Mattie, anticipating my question, interrupted me. "You white people always ask the same old question: Is it true, 'Once you have black you never go back'? Again, some macho black man must have made that idiom up."

Astonished by her accuracy, I replied, "How did you know?"

"Really, child. I thought I taught you better manners. In answer to your stupid question, honestly, how would I know? I've never desired anything else. Black men are the cutest men in the world! But I suppose men are the same everywhere. It wouldn't make a difference to me. It's my philosophy men are good for only one thing: Sex. In my entire life, I've never had the desire to chain myself to one. Once they put that ring around your finger, it's like tying a noose around your neck. They have you hook, line, and sinker."

That wasn't the first time I'd heard marriage described that way. I thought about Nick and wondered if he had finally found what he was looking for. Would he recognize the changes in me? If only he'd cared enough to stay.

"Pay attention. You know, Annie, it's a shame. I was a woman before my time. Back in my day, once you reached the ripe old age of 25, you were burdened with an 'old maid seal' stamped across your chest."

Mattie grinned and, once again, sat taller in her seat. "Personally, I wore it like a badge of honor. Other than children, I couldn't see any reason in the world to saddle myself with a man. The more I watched my girlfriends marry them, the more I knew I wasn't missing out on much. They don't want your happiness. They want their happiness. We women, who are supposedly free, must ask for permission, some kind of bondage thing. Our forefathers said it well. All men are created equal. To this day, men could care less about creating *equal* women."

Mattie was right. We needed more women in Congress, more women executives in corporations. We needed more people of different cultures running our country. That's what made it so beautiful. That's what made it so unique. I was Irish, German, Polish, and English. Mattie was African American, but who knew what white slave owners' blood was in her veins. We Americans were a mixed bag of many races, many colors. Why couldn't many of us see it for ourselves?

She waved her hands in front of my face, giving me the evil eye. "Will you pay attention? This is important." I gave her my best angelic smile and tried a little harder to follow her conversation.

"So, what did we women do? We go to work to be on an *equal* plane with men. What did we prove? We proved we can bring home a paycheck and in our spare time do all the chores and child bearing and child rearing we did before we had jobs. Stupid but equal. Stupid but equal, hogwash. That's what we are. We've created a generation of Super Moms. Anyway, my freedom is the best gift I can bestow upon myself. It's priceless."

Lowering her chin slightly, she wiped her mouth with a napkin. "My only regret in life was never being able to raise a child. Remember, Annie, men are worthless. Children are a gift from God. I don't have to tell you, do I?"

In total agreement, I nodded my head. "Mattie, you're right. It's a shame, too. You would have made one hell of a mother. But, let's face it, you're sure making up for lost time. How many crack babies are you taking care of right now? Two? Three?"

I slapped myself on the cheek. "Oops, I was not to discuss that house or anyone in it. Okay. Back to this boring subject. Let's talk about personal fantasies."

"Oh, I've got one," Mattie interrupted.

"Excuse me. It's not your turn. I've heard enough from you. Now don't laugh." Leaning back in my chair, I debated with myself whether I should tell her.

"Are you going to sit there all night, girl?" She asked impatiently.

"Oh, all right. It's really pretty silly. I've always had this endless curiosity about other cultures. I'm attracted to foreign men. I enjoy picturing myself with my own harem surrounded by Arabs, Hispanics, Middle Easterners, French men, and a couple of African Americans would be good, too. Of course, their mouths are taped shut and I'm the boss."

Pulling my seat out from behind me, I stood up and hit Mattie's shoulder, "Hey, I have an idea. Maybe we could set up a new platform for women's rights. Our bipartisan slogan and our prerequisite for membership would be: Women who have had sex with more than one race must commingle, and be willing to express all experiences in a *laissez-fair* fashion, of course."

Mattie pulled me back down on my seat. "Shhh, sit down and behave!"

"Me? You've misbehaved all night. Now those women would be a lot of fun, wouldn't they?" Mattie frowned, shook her head, then rolled her eyes.

"You're a constant surprise to me, Girl."

We laughed much too loudly. "Of course, you'll have to make up for lost time. Find yourself a white man," I said shoving her arm. "It's never too late. After all, we don't want any of these LaLeche women in our group. They think their kids need to breast-feed until they reach six. Forget them. They would be too boring for our kind."

"You don't like them because, you, Miss Natural Annie, failed the breast-feeding-mother-of-the-year award. Deep down you should admire those women. They're taking a stand and caring for their children; even breast-feeding causes, my narrow-minded friend, have their place in life."

Mattie stood to attention. "I can see it now. We'll march to Washington chanting. 'I pledge allegiance to my body and the United States of America, for which it stands, one woman, individual, on top of every race, regardless of nationality or creed." Mattie was laughing so hard she fell back in her chair and lost her balance.

I grabbed her by the arm to keep her from falling. As she fell into me, I whispered. "Mattie, I think we'd better leave. People are beginning to stare. There must be some decorum attached to my profession, you know. For instance, who's going to drive us home?"

Mattie waved her arm. "No problem. We'll call Jason, and he can pick us up. As for another bottle of wine, let's order."

With the few remaining brains I had left, I ordered her a cup of coffee. Mattie and I left the table and stumbled our way out of the restaurant. Recovering from the revolving door crash, we rubbed our swollen noses and walked outside.

Down the block we spotted a pay phone. We walked along the sidewalk using each other as a balance to keep ourselves vertical.

Twenty minutes later, our chauffeur-driven limousine turned the corner. Well, actually it was Mattie's rusty old blue Chevy, but who cares? Jason pulled up, got out, and opened the car door. He seemed more angry than disappointed by our behavior. Perhaps he had a date, and we interrupted something important. There was definitely a mysterious side to our Jason. He wasn't acting like himself at all. My brain was too befuddled to figure it out.

"Did you two have a good time? Get in this car and quit making spectacles of yourselves." He demanded.

Mattie turned, wrinkled her nose and looked at me.

"Spectacles. Speaking of spectacles, where are my spectacles? Annie, did I leave them at our table? Oh, no, here they are wrapped around my neck. It's okay. I have my spectacles. See."

Once we were settled, he slammed the car door and took off. He was acting like a brute. "All of this preaching you do and here you are, a couple of no-good drunks," he said, berating us. "I can get that at home. Where are my mentors now, ladies? I have half a mind to pull up to the police station and have you both arrested for drunk and disorderly."

Mattie yelled from the back seat. "Jason, don't be such a nincompoop. Shut up and drive us home, Mr. Sanctimonious. We don't need this self-righteous attitude of yours. We had some well-deserved fun tonight." Jason shook his head. "Don't shake that head at me. It makes me dizzy. Besides, you're stuck with us whether you like it or not."

Not another word was said, or at least I can't remember. I fell asleep in the front seat.

When the car stopped, I opened my eyes and saw a young woman frantically running down the steps. She cautiously looked around as she opened the car door.

"I'm so glad you're back! We're all so scared. Two young boys were shot to death. Oh, God, you should've been here! The kids are so upset. One was a little boy of about six and his older brother. Blood was all over the sidewalk. What are we going to do? It's getting closer. Damn it, say something! What are we going to do?"

Mattie hit the front steps at the same time I did. The house was in a turmoil. In the living room, the children and adults were all huddled around each other. None of them were successfully calming the other down. Some of these kids I hadn't seen before, others I knew very well.

What could Mattie possibly say? 'Don't worry. This won't happen again.' The reality was street gangs were everywhere. The respectable neighbors were moving out. The "best homes" and the "best parents" was fantasy here. These children were looking out for each other, abandoned by what I would call "no family."

Some of the younger kids ran to Mattie. She knelt down and hugged the two closest to her. That was another thing about Mattie. She always got down to their eye level.

"It's all right. Mattie's here. I'm so sorry. Take a couple of deep breaths. Now, close your eyes." The children did what they were told. "We can fight this thing by pretending we're not afraid. The key word here is 'pretend'. We have to stick together."

She kissed them all on the cheek and took them by the hand, moving them into the living room. The smaller ones she put on her lap. "I have an idea. Let's light a fire in the fireplace and say a prayer for those who died. Better yet, let's pray for the souls of these evil gang leaders, too. Maybe if we pray for them, we can somehow change them and in our own special way turn them into our friends."

Several of the older kids thought she was crazy. "Pray for them. You've got to be kidding! Somebody needs to shoot them the way the cowboys cleaned up Dodge."

Mattie shook her head. "No, children. It's wishful thinking, but we need to pray for our enemies."

One young girl was not convinced. She cried out in protest. Her name was Katisia. She was one of the older ones, fourteen years old, petite, with big brown eyes. She'd seen more than her fair share of dying.

"But, Mattie, those poor boys. You don't know what you're talkin' about. I was there. They were just standing there talkin' with some guy, doing their business. We need to get us some weapons so we can shoot them!"

Another young lady suggested, "Forget that, Katisia. We don't have no weapons. Let's hide! Quick, barricade the door!" She got up to run to the front entrance.

Jason grabbed the girl gently by the arm and said, "It's okay. The door is locked." Then he placed her next to Mattie who began to stroke the child's head.

"I don't want to die! My brother was killed by those creeps. Oh, God, I miss him. When will it stop? When will it be my turn?" The little girl put her head to her knees and cried.

At a loss for words, Mattie held the child, waiting for the tears to subside. She had more kids than her arms could handle.

"I'm so sorry," she said in a soothing voice. "I don't have the answers. I don't know what drives these madmen. Is it the power, the money, the drugs? It's worthless compared to human life."

Mattie struggled out of her pile of kids and knelt down beside them. "We must believe in God. We have to be willing to try our very best or they'll win. Don't you see? The more of us there are, the more hope we have of beating off their stench."

Jason came back with some firewood. He bent down and soon had a fire burning in the fireplace. Mattie and the children seemed pleased by its welcoming warmth. "Let's all stand up and hold hands."

The children and the adults formed a circle and grabbed hold of each other. Mattie closed her eyes and prayed.

"Dear God, tonight we come to You in fear, the fear that we, too, will become the victims of this war. Please give us the strength to overcome our fears. Martin Luther King once said, 'I have a dream.' Well, everyone in this room has a dream, too. The dream is freedom, the freedom to walk outside this door safe in the knowledge we won't be shot by one of our own; the dream that every child on this block gets a chance to make something of himself, the dream to build respectable lives with family and friends who won't shoot us in the back. Please give us the power to continue in our crusade."

Tears were streaming down the children's faces as Matttie gathered them in a tight circle. Did they understand? Jason and I were standing in the corner of the room observing. Without thinking, he placed his arms around me and cried.

"Are you all right, Jason?" I asked. He moved away from me, wiping the tears away.

"I can't handle it anymore, Annie," he said, unable to look me in the face. There was nothing I could say. I didn't know how any of us were going to handle it. For a long time, I put my arms around him, holding him, puzzled by his breakdown.

Mattie, too, was unable to console the children. They were all talking in unison. Attempting to regain some order, she changed her tone of voice.

"Kids, I have a secret to tell you. There was a time in my life when I was afraid, too. So afraid I couldn't walk out the door. I stayed in my house, shutting out the world. But I'm not afraid anymore. Do you know why?" The kids shook their heads.

"I have all of you. Since you've come into my life, I'm brave. I'm strong." She flexed her biceps which had more loose fat than muscle.

Some of the younger children laughed. The older kids gave Mattie one of those "you-have-got-to-be-kidding" looks. "Now don't you laugh, Phoebe," she said grabbing her by the arms and squeezing tight. "I'm a tough woman, a lucky woman. Yes, believe it or not, I can sleep at night, even with those jerks living down the street."

She danced her way over to the couch, grabbed a pillow, and laid down pretending to be asleep. She began to snore. Some of the kids smiled and some giggled, while others were not convinced. She propped her head up, and looked them each in the face with one eye open.

"You see, I'm not afraid of death. I'm afraid of not living. Since I've come to that understanding, they can no longer hurt me. I thank every one of you for putting your fears aside and giving me, giving us the chance to help you. Tanya, LaToya, Marguerite, and Phoebe, that's why we're here: To help you, to love you and to give you a chance to live."

The firelight was captured in Mattie's eyes. She looked like a witch, albeit a good witch. "I'll make each of you a solemn promise." She raised her right hand. Her voice could barely be heard.

"The promise is escape. Together we'll find the answers. But, again, it has to come from each of you," she said pointing to them one by one.

"You have to be a willing partner in my plan. Come here and sit down while I tell you a story. Please. Let's all make a small circle around this couch. It hurts these old bones sitting on the floor."

The children did her bidding and sat down. Mattie, in a low animated voice, began.

"This story is about a young man who grew up not far from here. He was born in a log cabin. His parents were very, very poor. During his first seven years in the wilds of Kentucky, the only thing he knew was how to spell his name and maybe a little math. In fact, he wasn't even close to being as smart as you all."

The children all looked suspiciously at each other not thoroughly convinced they were smart.

"But that wasn't good enough for him. Unlike most of his friends, he felt a sense of purpose. His friends were always calling him names and making fun of him. They told him he was a wastin' his time, readin' and learnin'. He ignored them and said to himself, 'I'll study and someday my chance will come.'

"Let's all say it together." The children began to chant, "I'll study and someday my chance will come." They continued to repeat it several times.

"This young man was so poor he couldn't even buy books. He borrowed everything he could get his hands on. It's been said that he once walked forty miles just to get one wee, small book. You see, this young man would do his chores by day and read in front of the fireplace 'til midnight. Those books brought him joy; joy that only your imagination can grasp.

"This young man loved those books more than anything else. Those very books gave him the power to hold conversations with the greatest minds of all the ages. He once said, 'The things I want to know are in these books. My best friend is the man who'll give me a book I ain't read.' Can any of you tell me the man's name?"

One young boy raised his hand.

"Yes, Parker." Mattie pointed to him.

"Martin Luther King," the young boy responded.

"Well, that's a good guess, but it's not the correct answer. The man to whom I refer wrote one of the most famous political speeches in American history. He became the 16th President of the United States."

She paused before divulging his name and then whispered, "His name was Abraham Lincoln. Do you all know the speech I'm talking about? It was called the Gettysburg Address. That speech changed this nation forever. He's the same man that put an end to slavery and, in so doing, changed *this* world."

You could have heard a pin drop. Jason and I smiled at each other. The children had listened to her story as if spellbound. One of the older boys raised his hand. His name was LeConte but everyone called him Buddy. His mother, Michelle, was one of the first women to volunteer on the night of the open house. She was in her early 30's, a petite woman with huge brown eyes. She was not beautiful, more like handsome. Like me, she had no self-assurance and no understanding of women's apparel. Frumpy is what I would call her mode of dress.

For the past eight years, she had a job sewing in a jacket factory. She had injured her hand and was presently receiving disability. On evenings, Mattie was secretly teaching her to read. In payment, Michelle was cooking. I stayed away on those nights. I think she shared our talent in the kitchen.

Buddy was what I'd call a child prodigy. He was an only child and his mother doted on him. Mattie had nicknamed him the million-question kid. He was exhausting us all. No one was surprised to see his hand waving in the air.

"Yes, Buddy," she said, with a hint of weariness in her voice.

"Mattie, have you ever noticed your heroes are all dead? Abraham Lincoln, Martin Luther King. They weren't all that smart. They got shot. Wouldn't they've been better off if they'd a went about their business and just ignored the country's problems? The same way we should mind our own business."

Mattie took another deep breath. "Buddy, I'm glad you asked me that. You're right. Who needs heroes anyway?" The kids gave her a confused look. "We do. That's who. This country needed their special gift, their strength in adversity, their belief that change was possible."

Mattie stood up and stretched her legs. "Take what's happening to us right now. It's not fair. And, as you've probably heard so many of us adults say, 'Life's not fair.' You should be outside playing, but you can't. You should have loving moms and dads, but most of them are too sick themselves to care for you. You should be able to walk to school without being ridiculed by others, but you can't. You should be able to leave your homes to play in the park, but you can't. Look around. This is where you're safe. Not with me, but with these; these are *your* books."

Mattie walked over to the shelf and picked one out and held it up for them to see. "See how wonderful it is? You don't have to walk miles to get them. They're here waiting, waiting to expand your life, waiting to take you to a new world. Without them, you might as well have been born brain dead."

Mattie laid the book down on the table. I recognized the face on the cover. It was Christopher Columbus. Was it a coincidence? Knowing Mattie, I doubted it. He was a man whose adventurous spirit had changed the world.

"We have to be strong. You put that pride where it belongs, in your heart. If they bust your nose, don't turn and fire a gun in their face. Instead, hold your head up and walk away."

The kids mumbled to themselves. Mattie moved closer. "You listen to me. I'll never teach you anything with attitudes like that. The answers are not in blowing some other kid's head off. Your escape is buried within yourselves. It's right here." She pointed to her head. "It's here in your brain."

"Put your hand where I'm pointing." They all did as she asked. "We each have one, you know," she said with a wink. "Only you, and you, and you, can achieve this escape route." She tickled the kids as she walked around them. They giggled.

"You might say to me, 'How will I make it? I'm too stupid. That's not true. None of you are stupid. You all have the answer. This thing I'm talking about is called individual power. The true test in measuring your strength is your own determination and hard work to succeed. There's no greater treasure in this world, no better gift that I could ever hand to you. Can you guess what it is?"

The girls and boys in the room shook their head.

Buddy raised his hand. "It's knowledge," he said proudly.

"You're right, my boy. Knowledge is the key to unlock the door that holds you to this place. You see, you're already smarter than I am." She walked over and knocked on one of the older girl's braided heads. The children began to laugh.

Their fears and their doubts were still painted across each of their sweet, worried faces. Perhaps Mattie had given them a sense of hope. More importantly, she certainly gave them a place to belong, a place to be loved.

Mattie quickly changed the subject. "Let's ditch this discussion and have some fun." Standing up, she looked for Jason and gave him a signal. Jason walked over to the bookcase and hit the on switch to the CD player. Music immediately filled the room. She got up, clapped her hands, and started dancing.

Mattie knew of another gift. Her ever-present grin and ongoing smile made her a natural with children. There was nothing like music to replace fear with laughter. She saw me standing alone in the corner and motioned me forward. "Come on, Girlfriend. Show me your stuff. I think it's a fact you white folks have no sense of rhythm. Here. Let me show you how."

In my case, she was right. Slowly and reluctantly, I danced my way forward. As I attempted to find a beat to the music, the children in the room burst into giggles. Mattie gyrated around the room, pulling up the kids one at a time. "Come on, guys. Your young bones could use a little exercise. Show me that thing you guys do nowadays."

Mattie looked at Jason who was quietly standing against the wall. He shook off whatever was bothering him and laughed. "Speaking of men who make fun of old women, get your little butt over here, young man."

Jason folded his arms shaking his head. "I need a partner. Come on over here and let's show them a thing or two." Jason was relucant. He moved to the center of the room, grabbing one of Mattie's hands. Putting his arm around her, they floated around the room. A few of the young girls turned a deep maroon color when he danced by them. Poor girls. Overactive hormones were dancing, too.

They were great kids, every one of them.

The beat changed to rap music. The kids loved it. After a couple more dances, Mattie turned down the stereo. "How about some hot chocolate?" We were all sweating.

"You're right. Let's make ice cream sundaes. Annie, go to the basement and find the chocolate sauce. Jason, I'm pooped. Keep entertaining the younger generation, will you? I need to sit down."

Turning the volume back up, Jason continued dancing. Mattie and the other women quietly danced their way toward the kitchen to grab a few snacks.

With the boisterous activity above, the basement seemed so quiet. I stumbled my way downstairs. Searching for the light switch, I was grabbed from behind. I froze as my arms were pulled behind my back.

A voice whispered clearly and firmly, "Lady, don't scream. I'm not going to hurt you."

I was too off-balanced to do much of anything. It was a man's voice, and judging by the way he held me, he was quite tall. He was strong and had no trouble keeping me in place.

"No funny business. If you scream, I'll have to hurt you. Do you understand?"

With difficulty, I nodded my head. As soon as he removed his hand from my mouth, I slammed my elbow into his rib cage. He cried out and staggered backwards, giving me enough time to bolt for the door at the top of the stairs. On my way up, he grabbed for my feet and tackled me, banging my ribs against the stairs.

My body landed hard on top of his. I tried to fight back, but he held my arms in a vice grip. "Damn it!" he said, "I won't hurt you. Stop it! Mattie knows me. Call her and I'll prove it to you. I swear."

"What do you take me for?" I asked, trying to control my fear.

Someone flipped on the basement light. He loosened his hold on me and I was able to wriggle free. "Call the police!" I yelled, as I rolled over and bounced back to my feet.

Mattie's appearance gave me the opportunity I needed to get the upper hand. I kicked him solidly in the groin. He groaned in pain. "Damn it, Mattie, get the hell out of here and call the police."

My attacker slowly struggled to his feet. I found a brick lying next to the stairwell and was ready to finish him off with a pulverizing blow to the head. Shielding the top of his head, he yelled, "Mattie, tell her I'm on your side before she kills me!"

Without saying a word, she took a seat on the stairs and tapped her knee with her hand. "Annie, dear, drop the brick," she instructed in a calm voice. "Please, there are children upstairs. I specifically remember sending you down for chocolate sauce, young lady, not a roll with Peter on my basement floor. Really now."

Confused, I moved as far away as I could from the stranger. The man gave her an evil grin and stood up.

"Surely you don't know this...this barbarian?" I asked.

"It's about time the two of you met. Annie, meet Peter Monroe Harrison," she said with pride.

Surprised, I covered my mouth. "You're Peter Harrison?" I was clearly disappointed. This monster was Mattie's hero, the man she worshiped? I dropped the brick.

"Mattie, has told me very little about you." I was no longer afraid but still panting.

He seemed equally put out, but extended his right hand to shake mine. "Under these circumstances, it certainly has not been a pleasure to meet you, Miss Stevens. She left out a few things while describing you, too."

Mattie walked to the lower landing and turned on another light taking a closer look at him. His clothes were covered with blood and dirt. He had a large laceration on his right arm that turned the left side of his shirt a crimson red. I was not responsible for that.

"God Almighty, what on earth have you been doing?" she asked, angrier than I had ever seen her. She started to beat his chest with her fists. "You're trying to get that bloody fool head of yours blown off, again? Damn you to hell! You're lucky it's just your arm and not your feeble skull."

Peter grabbed her attempting to prevent any further damage to his person. He looked imploringly at me. I shrugged my shoulders.

"You're hurting me. Can't you tell the woman loves me? I know now why the two of you are friends. You have a lot in common."

"Get your bloody ass over on that bed so I can get a better look at you!" She shoved him over to the cot in the corner of the room.

One of the kids started down the basement steps. I quickly grabbed the can of chocolate and switched off the light.

"Annie, are you down there? The kids are driving me crazy. Have you seen Mattie? We lost her, too."

I scooted the child up the stairs and told a lie. "No, I haven't. Let's get this chocolate cooking."

"You don't cook the chocolate. You pour it out of the can. The ice creams waiting for you."

"We'll try to find Mattie later," I said, taking the boy's hand. "I'm sure she's around here somewhere. Maybe she's in the bathroom. You know how those old ladies are. They take forever." The boy giggled. I wiped the sweat off my brow.

C H A P T E R
IX

The danger that lurked outside seemed faraway. When Mattie transformed the living room into a library, I worried it would lose some of its old-fashioned charm. I was wrong. She succeeded in combining the graciousness of the past with the necessities required in a youth home. The children sat in functional, but decorative chairs eating their ice cream. The Louis XV-style mantel had been painted a neutral tone with dark wood accents adding a muted rusticity that was warm and inviting.

We spent another hour filling their stomachs with ice cream and playing charades. If not ridding them of their fear, at least replacing it with understanding and love. Children had that uncanny ability to bounce back. I wasn't so quick to recover. Once they were calm, we put them to bed.

When everyone had gone home and the kids were finally asleep, we crept back into the kitchen. Mattie retrieved the first aid kit from the cupboard. I watched her thread a large needle.

"Don't tell me you're going to stitch his arm with that?" I

asked, totally appalled at her daring. "Haven't you ever heard of a butterfly bandage? This is not the Dark Ages, Dr. Turner."

"You're right. What he needs is a hospital," Mattie said, cutting the thread with her scissors. "Unfortunately, he'll be arrested. While you were upstairs, I got a good look at his arm. A bullet grazed him. It's only superficial."

"Did I hear you right? Did you say 'arrested'?"

After seeing for myself the bloody clothes the man wore, it did not take a rocket scientist to figure out what kind of trouble he was in. Mattie handed me the needle and walked to the refrigerator.

"Are you crazy? You can't harbor a fugitive. If they found him here, you could be charged, too." She found a bottle of water and some rags and placed them on the table.

"Oh, no, don't look at me!"

"You're right. We definitely can't keep him here. I have this dear, sweet friend who will do anything for ol' Mattie, including hiding a possible murder suspect in her own home until we can come up with a better plan."

"Murder suspect! Have you lost your marbles? I have a baby, not to mention a law license, which at the present time is my only source of income. Who's going to feed and take care of Jack while I'm in jail? Besides, I don't even have a car, and I'm a lot more sober than a few hours ago."

Ignoring me, she closed the first aid kit and wet one of the rags at the sink. "Peter is not a murderer."

"Oh, Mattie, you've convinced me. Of course, I'll hide him," I said with sarcasm. "Big deal. The police must have another opinion."

"There's more to this than you know. I purposely kept you in the dark. It's impossible now. I need your help. Peter needs your help. I don't have time for this. Oh, hell, stop hovering around me and sit down!"

Mattie ushered me over to the table and pressed me into the chair. She remained standing. "I'm going to talk fast so listen carefully. His name on the street is Reggie Parks. A few years back, I helped him out of the gutter and into one of those halfway houses. It not only changed his life, it changed mine. Peter graduated from college, moved to Detroit and got his master's degree in child psychology from Mercy. He's working on his thesis. Unfortunately, there's not enough spare time. For quite a while now, he's been working undercover infiltrating gangs."

I knew Mattie was getting help from someone named Peter and she would often sing his praises. What I never stopped to consider was his age.

"In order to earn their trust, you have to commit illegal acts." Mattie put her hands on her forehead, wiping away the sweat. "That's the bottom line. These things take time. He's been secretly convincing kids to leave. That's where I come in. Since it's too dangerous for them to stay here, I, and some other trusted volunteers around the country find what we call "safe houses." I guess you could say we've established an underground network."

"You're joking?" I could tell by the way she said it she wasn't. Mattie shrugged her shoulders. "And I thought you had enough to do," I said, shaking my head. "One of these days, Mattie, I'm going to leave you in these messes, and let you clean them up yourself. I ought to wring your neck."

"One of these days, I'll help you do it. But right now we need to take care of Peter. Come on. Let's see what we can do about fixing the poor boy's wounds."

"If I had any sense, I'd turn around and go home!"

Mattie carried her first aid kit and the rags. I took the needle and the bottle of water. She flipped the light switch with her elbow. Quietly, we descended the stairs. Peter, who had been lying on the cot, was momentarily blinded by the light. His face was pallid, almost ashen. He rose slowly and in obvious discomfort. He had taken off the gray sweatshirt he had worn earlier. The sleveless T-shirt he had on was clean but you could see a dark red stain on his upper hip where the blood had soaked through.

Mattie went directly to his bedside. She placed her hand on his lacerated arm to examine it. "Good. Dr. Turner's done a good job. It's stopped the bleeding,"she said with relief. She wiped his arm with the wet clean rag and I handed her the needle.

Peter took one look at what was in Mattie's hand and rose to leave. "You've got to be kidding! I'm not going to let you stitch me with that thing! Forget it. Just let me lie here for a while and I'll be fine. Otherwise, I'm out of here. Cops or no cops."

Mattie looked like a lady out of a Dickens' novel as she shoved him back on the cot.   "Don't be such a baby. Do you honestly think I'll enjoy this? I've never done this in my life -- except on an old doll. Her name was Candy. My father threw her against the wall and the stuffing fell out of her. It almost broke my heart, but I patched Candy up real fine."

Mattie affectionately patted his leg. "Don't worry, honey. Give me that damn arm and shut up! Unless you have a better idea."

Peter looked imploringly at me.

"I'm as astounded as you are," I said, totally surprised. "If you want to take your chances, the emergency room is still an option."

Since that wasn't a feasible alternative, he stuck his arm out in resignation. Mattie looked at me, took a deep breath, and began to stick the needle through his flesh.

"Ouch! I must be crazy!" Peter said, closing his eyes. Mattie concentrated on the arm, ignoring his discomfort. Peter closed his eyes and tried not to yell. I turned my back. It was too painful to watch.

"Damn it! At least in the movies, they put a stick in your

mouth or something," he said, clenching his fists, his face revealing his obvious discomfort. "Better yet, load me up with some booze. You guys sure reek of it. Ouch! Ouch!"

Mattie stuck it through his skin several more times. "Shhh, sit still. This is not exactly a pleasant task. Be grateful my queasy stomach hasn't brought up my dinner. Yet."

Several minutes later, the onerous task was complete. Given the extraordinary circumstances, I was impressed. Mattie and I studied his arm. Admiring her workmanship, she gently laid his arm back on his leg and unwrapped the gauze lying in the first aid kit.

"I don't suppose you sterilized that needle?" I asked.

She shook her head. "I completely forgot about it."

Peter closed his eyes and moaned. "Oh, God, please get me out of this nightmare. One mad woman is bad enough, but did you have to send two? Where's a real nice angel with a soothing touch when you need one?"

"It's late and I need to go home," I said, ignoring his joke. "Tell us what happened and how you're going to get yourself out of this mess."

"A little bossy, isn't she, Mattie? Must be taking lessons from you." Mattie finished wrapping Peter's arm and handed him the water bottle and a couple of aspirins.

"Annie's right. Talk! I've had all I can take for one night, too."

"It smells to me like you were out having a good time."

"We were out having some fun," Mattie replied. "Now stop stalling. Tell us what happened!"

"We'll talk tomorrow,." Peter said, lowering his head and picking up the wet rag to wipe the dried blood off his hands.

"We're not leaving here until you tell us what happened." she angrily demanded. "I'm tired and I want to go to bed."

"Forget it! I can't! Just leave me alone." Peter took a deep breath, burying his face in the pillow.

"What fool-brained, idiotic game have you been playing now?" She asked, with an evil gleam in her eyes. It was obvious these two knew each other well. Peter sat in silence.

"Oh, it's a fucking game all right. One that killed two innocent kids!" He looked at me, his voice almost a whisper. "I don't know how much Mattie has told you about me."

"Almost nothing," I answered.

"I thought it was a good idea to keep her out of this." Mattie wanted to give Peter some time to compose himself. She got off the box she was sitting on and walked toward a wall in the corner of the basement, pushing aside a metal shelf with empty boxes. A gray-paneled door opened toward the inside.

"You might as well know it all," she said as she turned on the light. I cautiously approached the door and looked inside. I saw a couple of cots, and a sink with an old-fashioned commode. The room was sparse but quite clean.

"We hide the children in here for a couple of days until we can find another home for them. Sadly enough, their parents are either addicted to drugs, or they think the kids ran away. I thought there would at least be a police inquiry or two, but nothing. So far, we've only had four kids in this bunker. Peter's only been around here for about six months. He travels a lot. Too much if you ask me. You're going to send me to my Heavenly Father yet!"

We walked back toward his cot and sat down again on our makeshift stools.

"I wish I'd been the one killed tonight. It's all my fault." Peter wiped his eyes with the corner of the bedsheet.

"We don't expect you to understand everything." Mattie said, shaking her head. I didn't understand anything. I was shocked, but there was no time to think about the consequences of this dangerous scheme, nor was I sure I wanted to hear what Peter was obviously not wanting to tell us.

"Sometimes they suspect some other gang of kidnapping them, killing them, or worse, selling the young girls off. It's too sick to imagine what those poor kids go through."

After a few minutes of silence, Peter began to speak. "A couple days ago, Rodney Thomas approached me, accusing me of kidnapping Deidre Morris."

Mattie turned to me, noting my confusion. "She's one of our kids. She left a couple of weeks ago. She's doing fine. I got a call from Atlas."

Peter seemed pleased. Evidently, they weren't going to tell me who this Atlas character was. I wasn't pushing. Quite frankly, I didn't want to know.

"Rodney said he had information concerning Deidre Morris's whereabouts, and I was responsible for her kidnapping. I'm sorry, Mattie. It seems we may have a spy. Someone is passing out some pretty reliable information. For the time being, we'll have to shut down. There's not much I can do on the streets. The police are looking for me, and they suspect I murdered Rodney Thomas."

Mattie and I looked at each other. "Rodney Thomas is dead?" we asked in unison.

Rodney Thomas was a well-known criminal, a man whose followers understood the meaning of violence. His random acts killed and maimed. He achieved his power through fear and his money through drug deals, bank robberies, thefts, and home invasions. You name it the man would do it. No one could catch him. No one would testify against him.

I began to understand the enormity of the situation. "Tell me why they think you're their number one suspect."

Peter, uncomfortable, squeezed the pillow on his lap. "I set up a meeting with Mitchell Reese and his older brother, Jeremy. Mitchell wanted to leave the streets, but he wouldn't go without

Jeremy. It was my job to talk his older brother into it. I failed them both."

Peter bent his head and placed his hands on his face. "Oh, God. I met them on the street corner as planned. Jeremy seemed on edge, almost hostile. A few seconds later, a white van pulled alongside the curb. The door panel opened; two guys with semi-automatic weapons aimed them at us."

His voice cracked as he began to explain. "It all happened so fast. Jeremy dropped to the ground, pulled out a revolver and shot at the guys in the van. I grabbed Mitchell and took cover behind a park bench. Jeremy was shot in the head. There wasn't much I could do for him. I'm sure he died instantly."

Peter was no longer able to control his emotions. Mattie moved toward the cot. Placing her head on his chest, she tried to comfort him.

I stayed in my seat knowing there was nothing to say, realizing the truth. These were two very brave people and I was an outsider. Several minutes passed. Peter looked at me with tears in his eyes.

"I'm sorry," he said wiping his face. "After the van left, Mitchell was still breathing. There was nothing I could do to save him. His brains were lying on the street beside me. Blood was everywhere. He kept saying, "Please, I don't want to die. Did they get my brother, Reggie? I don't want to die. Hold me. I don't want to die."

Peter's pain was too great. He could no longer speak. Tears streamed down his face. "Oh, Mattie, do you have any idea how tiny a six-year-old's body feels? I wanted to bring him here, here where we had plans for him. We could have saved them. He kept repeating those same words over and over until he couldn't say them anymore. He died in my arms. He was so wise, so smart...so scared. He loved his brother. He loved him enough to trust me. I was supposed to protect them."

Peter buried his face in the pillow. "It's all my fault. Damn it! I panicked. Some of the neighbors came out of their houses. They just stood there watching us. I started screaming. 'Take a good look at hate, people. Damn you all. Can't you see? We're killing off a part of ourselves. Why? Why? Why? All of this senseless dying.'"

Mattie looked at me then took a hold of Peter's hand, caressing it. "Shh, it's okay. It wasn't your fault. You tried to save them."

"I then heard the sirens. I placed Mitchell's body next to his brother's. Like a coward, I ran off. I left them. I failed them. Damn it. I failed them. I can't do this anymore! Please, tell me to stop, Mattie. Tell me to stop!"

Mattie, lost in her own thoughts, closed her tired eyes.

"There's nothing I can say to ease your pain, son. It's been a dreadful night. She raised her head toward the ceiling, clenching her fist. "Damn it, God, why are they always children?"

For several minutes, we sat in silence. There was no answer to her question. We moved the boxes back against the wall, not speaking. Mattie picked up the dirty pile of clothes lying on the floor.

"Why are the police looking for you?"I asked, still confused. "Who murdered Rodney Thomas?"

"That's the perplexing part of this whole disgusting night. So many people gathering around me, I panicked. When I heard the sirens, I ran to the bushes. I was about to head here when I tripped over another body. I turned it over. Rodney Thomas's throat had been cut from ear to ear. Come to think of it, he had a perfect view of the whole incident. He must have ordered the hit. Two of his men saw me coming out of the bushes. It's only a matter of time before they find me. Maybe a plastic surgeon will help. Right now, I'm too upset to care."

Pulling a handkerchief out of her side pocket, Mattie blew her nose. "I can't take much more, Peter. I won't! Do you hear me? I won't attend your funeral before my own."

Exhausted, she walked over to me and placed her hand on my shoulder. "It's not a good idea to hide Peter at your house. It's too dangerous. He's too dangerous."

Mattie turned to Peter and let out a heavy sigh. "We have to find our leak; and depending on what that person knows, we may all end up dead meat."

Peter defeated, lowered his head and placed his face in his hands.

"We're not giving up!" Mattie said, angrily. "You may have to leave for a while. Don't worry. I'll replace them with two other little boys. There are plenty of them out there. Do you understand what I'm trying to say? As much as we would like to, we can't save them all. We've got to keep the faith. Rest assured, they're in a safer place now."

Mattie left my side and walked toward Peter. "Annie, it's time for you to go home. I'll think of a plan in the morning. Besides, I'm so exhausted I can't think straight."

It suddenly dawned on me. She was up to her old tricks again. "I know what you're doing," I said, shaking my finger. "This fight isn't over by a long shot, is it? You don't need to use reverse psychology on me. I'm in this mess thanks to you, and I won't run out on you now."

I spotted humor in those mendacious eyes of hers. She had manipulated me right where she had wanted me all along.

Mattie put away the first aid kit and collected the bloody rags. "We've got work to do. Peter here looks like he's going to pass out. So am I. You can hide in that room over there and get some rest. I'll get you some clean clothes tomorrow night. "

She turned her attention back to me. "We'll have to move him, and quickly. Honestly, I'm sorry. I never wanted you to get mixed up in this."

As if something else suddenly occurred to her, Mattie stomped her foot. "Darn it. Your car is still at the restaurant. We'll have to get my old pickup truck started. Forget it. Jason is upstairs sleeping. We'll borrow his. I'll sneak in and get his keys and you can take it home. It's too late to get that old relic of mine out. Besides, I'm too tired to find the battery charger."

She pulled Peter to his feet. "Help me get him to that holding cell. Sorry, the Ritz is out of the question."

Peter shook off our assistance and walked into the room. He slowly, and quietly, lowered himself onto the cot. We waved good-bye. He ignored us.

Mattie shut the door and moved a heavy piece of concrete, matching the rest of the basement slabs, into place. Together, we moved the metal shelving unit across the secret door. You could not tell the room existed.

"How on earth did you get this built?" I asked, scolding her with my eyes. "No more surprises. Please, this is it, right?"

Mattie walked over to the cot and pulled off the sheets. Without saying anything, she handed me the first aid kit, the dirty clothes and bandages. With the evidence in our hands, we hit the basement steps and turned out the light.

"You're right. Keep it to yourself," I said, passing her in the hallway. "I don't want to know. Damn you. You're scaring me to death."

It occurred to me the fireplace was a good place to destroy the bloody shirt and rags. A small fire was still burning. As I placed the items onto the flames, it occurred to me I was destroying state's evidence. In the eyes of the law, I was now committing a wrongful act. I was an aider and abettor. I was obstructing the justice I had been sworn to uphold.

What justice had the children who died tonight received? If it weren't for people like Mattie and Peter, who would save them from the injustices of their birth?

C H A P T E R
X

Wrapped in Mattie's arms, I'm a little girl again. Only this time I find warmth and comfort. A strong sense of peace washes over me. I'm no longer hated. I am loved.

There's a knock on her door. A stranger with the face and body of a bird shrieks, "Come! We must save the children! We must save the children!"

He flies me to a nearby corner and drops me on a rooftop. The trees are eerily silent. No breeze rustles their branches. I look up the hill and see Mattie's children. They are running. I can see fear in their eyes. I know that fear.

Behind them walks the monsters of these streets. White powder floats like a fog, trapped in the air. In their eyes, I see the fires of hate. In the distance, gunshots are heard. Mattie's children scatter across the neighborhood seeking shelter.

Rust-colored water flows out of the sewers onto the street. Discarded pieces of paper, aluminum cans, and beer bottles join forces with the gushing current. The children are trapped. Their blood-soaked clothing poses a new kind of terror. They scream. I try to move. I'm powerless. I scream. No one hears me.

* * *

I take a deep breath to slow my heart rate. It's not dark. The morning sun penetrates through the cracks in the blinds. I'm safe in my bed. It was another nightmare. That's all I needed, a new one.

The wine had left me with an immediate desire to quench my thirst. Crawling to the bathroom, I realize who had awakened me. He was jabbering baby talk in his room. At least he wasn't crying. I slap a little water on my face, grimacing at my mutilated self in the mirror. I had slept a whole two hours. Thank goodness it was Saturday.

Entering Jack's bedroom, the purest of innocence greets me. I pick him up, giving him a big hug. Placing him on the floor, I talk to him as I change his diaper.

"Okay, Jack. You're going to have to give me some slack. Mama is not feeling well. Today you and I are off to the attic to do some heavy duty damage. Sounds like fun, doesn't it? I'll bet you're hungry. Let's see what we can find."

My head was pounding. I tried not to groan as I carried him to the living room. Thank God he still liked his swing. Cranking the handle, I took one last glance at his happy face and headed straight for the coffee pot. I found a bottle and some baby cereal. Opening the curtain into the living room, ugh, I immediately close my eyes.

The light pouring into the room was painful. Wouldn't you know it. This morning would be one of those beautiful fall days, chilly but sunny, spectacularly colorful.

One of the things I most hated about fall was its true beauty only lasted a couple of weeks. Why did I have to go and get myself hung over on such a gorgeous day? Half asleep, I fed Baby Jack his breakfast.

A pot of coffee gave me the extra boost I needed. Our daily ritual usually began with workout time. The only way I could stay in shape these days was to use Baby Jack as a playmate.

I lifted him above my head twenty or so times, and he slobbered and drooled down the front of my face. Placing him in front of me on the floor, I did my pushups. When I came close to the floor, I gave him a kiss. Again, he would giggle and slobber. It was a special part of our day. Honestly, we loved it. On this particular morning, I loved it a little less.

After about fifteen minutes of workout time, we usually went for a walk. Unfortunately, today's walk would have to wait. If Peter was to be my houseguest, I had work to do. Hideouts were my forte. Hadn't I spent my lifetime hiding from my parents? The logical place was the attic.

Jack and I climbed to the second floor and pulled down the stairs. Since the day I purchased this house, I had merely poked my head through the stair hole. If I remember correctly, a makeshift bed was already there. The previous owner had been too old to tear the bed apart to remove it. He had also left behind whatever he considered not worth the effort to pack.

Carrying Jack, a dust rag, and some sheets up the stairs, I fumbled around for the light switch. The room was not repulsive. There were two small windows at the north side of the house. Removing the dark paper stuck to the glass, I tried to open it. It was stuck.   I left Jack, ran to the downstairs closet, and retrieved the cleaning supplies and a small crowbar. A couple of seconds later, fresh air filled the room.

The ceiling was greatly slanted, but it was dry-walled. No nails were sticking out. Peter was going to find the quarters cramped but still more preferable than where he was.

I changed the sheets, swept the floor, and dusted off the lamp and table. The room smelled a bit like mildew, but at least it wasn't too hot. Having spruced up the room to the best of my ability, I carried Baby Jack down the ladder.

I was putting the attic stairs back in place when the doorbell rang. Sneezing, I grabbed the baby and we descended one more floor. Mattie bolted right past me heading toward the kitchen. I was feeling worn out from my housekeeping duties.

"Gee, I thought I wouldn't see you crawling out of bed until noon," I said, watching her help herself to my coffee.

"I'm used to no sleep." Matttie had on a pair of bluejeans with a blue and white checkered pullover shirt. Her braids were tied behind her head and fell loosely down her back.

"You rat," I said, not detecting any telltale signs of last night's fiasco on her face. "You don't even look hung over. Why is it you're the older woman here, and you look better than I do?"

She stuck her tongue out and raised her nose toward the ceiling. "It's because I'm a black woman who possesses terrific skin pigmentation," she replied, patting her cheekbones with her head held high.

"When you white folks have a rough evening, you all get those ugly red and blue hues." She studied my face. "And look at that purple puffiness around your eyes. I can handle my liquor better than you. Obviously, you have had little experience."

I stuck my tongue out and sat down on one of the stools at the kitchen counter. "Since I've met this nut woman, I'm making up for lost time. Oh, Mattie, leave me alone. I'm sick and I'm tired. And you're not funny. You should be hiding in your covers. How do you do it?"

She grabbed another cup from the cabinet and poured me a cup of coffee. "Well, child, it's like this. I figure if you can't find any humor in life, it's not worth living. It's what keeps you young. It's Mattie's magical potion. Suffering is just a part of life. I have been in tighter spots before. Don't worry."

Crossing to the living room, I picked the baby up and handed him to her. Jack gave her one of his brilliant smiles. "That's precisely what scares me," I said. "I don't like tight spots. I don't like taking chances. All my life, I've been hiding my feelings, hiding from people. Just once I would like to be ordinary, find some middle ground. How do you suppose I get there?"

Mattie held the baby in her arms and sat down next to me on one of the kitchen stools. "Trust me, Annie. The middle ground is boring. The reason you haven't found it is because you don't really want to. It's not your nature. Like me, you have a knack for getting yourself into scrapes."

She kissed Jack on the cheek and settled him down on her lap. "For instance, most people wouldn't dream of befriending someone like me, a nut, you say, who takes a house, turns it completely upside down, and all this, just to love on a few unwanted children. There's some DNA material present in your genes that gets masochistic satisfaction in challenges. When I first met you, you only thought you were afraid. Now you've proven yourself to yourself. It's simple. You're stuck. We're enmeshed in this -- what would you call it?"

"Hades sounds right to me! Lucky you and lucky me." Did this woman ever make sense? The funny thing is, she was beginning to make perfect sense. At first, I said nothing walking toward the cupboard to grab some water for Jack.

"Stuck is not exactly the word I would use. Entangled, trapped, might be better. And, as for simple, there's nothing simple about you. You're more like a nightmare -- yeah, a nightmare, Mattie. Please wake me up."

She waved her hand, dismissing my silly complaint. "Well,

we both know Peter didn't murder anyone."

"I know nothing of the sort. Peter looks like a murderer to me." Rubbing the bruises on my rump from the basement fiasco, I pulled my sweat pants down to show them to her. "Here. I'll show you the proof. Look at what that jerk did to me."

"As I recall, you weren't exactly Miss Demure," she said with an evil gleam in her eyes. "I rather enjoyed watching the two of you go at each other. I didn't know you had it in you. I'm rather proud of you. He's a pretty scary guy, you know."

"He scared the living daylights out of me!"

"Stay calm and we'll get Peter out of here in nothing flat."

Jack stretched his arms toward me wanting to be picked up. I placed him gently in my lap. He wasn't happy. He wanted Mattie's keys on the table. She handed them to him.

"You know, Mattie, even the mere thought of a secret underground society taking children away from their parents truly bothers me. Part of me condones it, but the other part still calls it conspiracy and kidnapping. You're right. I don't want to know about that side of your life. It's dangerous, idiotic, yet, incredibly heroic. You both scare the hell out of me. You're toying with fire and the way I see it you're going to get burned. This is for real."

I was hitting too close to home. Her own guilty conscience was revealing itself by the way she turned her eyes toward the counter top. "Yeah, yeah, yeah. Spare me the condemnation. Let's get down to the business at hand. What are we going to do with Peter?"

"I've dusted and cleaned the attic. It's still not the Ritz, but it's a lot nicer than where he is now. Did you check on him this morning? He is still alive, isn't he?"

Mattie shook her head. "It's too risky. By nightfall it shouldn't be too difficult. Before I shut the door last night, I forgot to restock. He's going to be starving. In his already weakened state, it can't be easy. Oh, well, no use worrying about that now."

I poured Mattie another cup of coffee. She took a large sip, choking it down. "By the way, here's my plan. At ten o'clock tonight, you park your car at my back door. I'll sneak him out and into your car. After that, you'll have to play it by ear. Be careful. Don't let any of your neighbors see you."

Then it suddenly occurred to me. "My car is still at the restaurant. Great spies we make."

"Speak for yourself. A couple of minutes ago, I dropped Jason off. You left your keys on my kitchen table. I figured in your delicate condition a nap would be more appropriate. Jason should be pulling up any time now."

Just then the door slammed shut. Jason walked in, said nothing to me, taking the baby from my arms. A rare smile transformed his face as he teased him. Jason was so gorgeous when he smiled -- if only he'd smile more often.

"Jason, next time don't make yourself so at home. Even Mattie rings the bell and waits until I greet her."

"Not true," Mattie replied indignantly. "I tried the knob and the door was locked."

He reached into his pocket and handed me my keys. I gave him the adult-who-knows-more stare. He returned my look with the the-kid-who's-smarter stare and rolled his eyes.

"Who borrowed my car last night without permission?" He asked. "You two are not exactly models of decorum. If I had a video camera, Miss Emily Post would be turning in her grave."

"Jason, you really scare me sometimes," Mattie muttered. "What have we done to you? What happened to the guy who was busted for theft six months ago? My mama used to always say, 'There's nothing worse than a reformed alcoholic.' I'm adding reformed burglar to the list. You're driving me crazy!"

Mattie grabbed him, pinching his cheek. "Don't get me

wrong. I like the staying out of trouble part, but I'd like to see a little of the old Jason Reed every once in a while. Stop being so holier-than-thou. It's good for the soul to kick up your heels, have some fun. It's another one of Mattie's magic philosophies. Flying like a bird's good, too."

"I think I understand your meaning," he said punching her lightly on the shoulder. "But, Mattie, every time I flew like a bird, some mean old nasty white policeman came along, snatched off those wings, and put me in a cage."

I laughed so hard I spit out my coffee. Should I tell them about the bird that came to the door in my dreams? Mattie was still unwilling to let him off the hook. "The next time you want to fly like a bird, be sure to call Annie or me. We'll be your guide. After all, we owe you for agreeing to pick us up. Oh, and thank you for being so gracious, kind, and completely understanding. Our drunken butts greatly appreciated it."

"That's okay." Jason replied. "When you were young, I bet you did have a lovely butt. In fact, if you looked real hard, I'm sure some old geezer out there's just dying to have it."

She placed her hands in a halting position. "Okay. Enough. Let's forget about last night. I want to go home and take a nap. We'll see you later, Annie. Please get some rest. Perhaps you'll stop by tonight. Only after a full recovery, of course."

Mattie turned and walked over to where the baby had fallen asleep on the floor surrounded by his toys. She scrambled around the pile and found her keys. "Oh, how utterly beautiful they are when they sleep. Pure innocence at work. If only we could bottle it. Now that would be a bona fide magic potion. I'll have to work on that in my laboratory."

"Where is your laboratory, Dr. Turner -- wait, let me guess. You have a secret passageway that leads to an underground cave."

"Good-bye, my dear," she said, kissing me on the cheek. "My

secret laboratory is none of your business." She grabbed her hand-painted jacket and walked out the door. Jason picked up his keys and followed her.

After they left, I tiptoed over to sneak a peek at the baby. He looked too comfortable to disturb. Instead of picking him up and carrying him to bed, I pulled another blanket and pillow off the couch and snuggled in next to him.

It was three o'clock in the afternoon when the baby and I were awakened by the telephone's shrill ring.

A familiar voice was on the other end. "Hello, stranger," Fred said. "What's for dinner tonight?"

Disoriented and a little confused, I said, "Dinner? What do you mean, dinner? Where are you?"

Fred's voice sounded indignant. "What do you mean where am I? I'm here at my mom's. I took her out to dinner last night and I figured you for a nice gourmet dinner tonight. I've come to collect what you already owe me. I told you I'd be in town this weekend."

Still a little confused, I cleared my throat. "Oh, I forgot. That was a month ago. It completely slipped my mind. A gourmet dinner, huh. Let's see. There's Campbell's soup and crackers."

"Real fine." Fred said, angrily. "Your best friend comes to town after working his fool head off and you forget. I'm crushed."

"Fred, I'm sorry. Mattie and I went out last night, too. If you want to know the truth, I woke up this morning with the fiercest headache and driest mouth I've ever had in my life. In fact, the baby and I were sleeping."

At that moment Baby Jack decided to scream the house down. Who could blame him?

"Do you hear that?" I asked. "I'll tell you what. All I've had today is some coffee and Jack needs fed. I'm starving, too. Do you think you could stop by and pick us up a pizza? I'll pay."

"What time does your royal highness wish the pizza man to

show up?"

"Why, immediately, sir." I said, smiling to myself. "Get that ass of yours over here. I'm dying to see you. I've missed you; and, honestly, I really could use a friend right now."

After hanging up, I went directly to the refrigerator to find the baby's formula. Screaming babies are not pleasant experiences on hangovers. I prepared the bottle and went back to hold him. I sat down in our favorite rocking chair and he grabbed the bottle.

"Slow down. I'm sorry, honey. Why did you let me sleep so long? You must have known how badly I needed it. By the way, what time did you go to bed last night? Did Hannah's mother play with you all night, too?"

After Baby Jack finished eating, he seemed content as I put him down to play with his toys on the floor. I walked over and opened the blinds.

The mid-afternoon's sun dipped westward, creating a shadowy ambiance in the room. I thought about the tragic events of the night before. Suppose Peter stays in Mattie's basement until his health improves? Maybe I should talk to Fred. I know what he'd say if I told him. He'd say I was out of my mind.

What I was about to do had to be the most asinine thing I had ever done. Mattie must have poured some psychotic nut juice in my wine again. I think I'd better find her laboratory before it's too late. Oh, Mattie, this is all your fault!

C H A P T E R
XI

I was rummaging through my empty refrigerator when the doorbell rang. Anticipating food, I ran to the front door. Happily, I opened it for Fred, the pizza man.

"What took you so long?" I asked. "I was beginning to think I had dreamed up that order." Fred didn't say a word as he headed straight for the kitchen with my terrific smelling pizza. After setting it on the counter top, ignoring me, he picked up the baby.

"Hi, there, little guy? How ya doing?"

"What am I, chopped liver?" I asked.

Fred picked up Jack and gave me a frustrated peck on the cheek. "No, you're a pain in the ass. Evidently, pizza takes longer at three o'clock in the afternoon. Most people eat at proper dinner hours. I waited thirty minutes for those morons to make it."

Fred reached into his pocket pulling out a new toy and handing it to Jack.

"You should move to Chicago. You can order anything, absolutely anything and it comes to your door. It'd be great for a non-cooking lazy bones like you."

Fred sat down and began bouncing Jack on his knee. "This baby gets more adorable every time I see him. Look how much he's grown. Mom's been feeding you too much. We need to get you mobile, kid. Take the weight gain right off." Then he winked at me.

"Your mom's looking pretty good." I looked awful. I had on a pair of gray sweats with my hair tied in a loose knot on the back of my head.

"Sure could use a bath, though. She smells like cigarette smoke, Jack."

I went directly to the pizza, ignoring him. "What do you want to drink? How about a glass of baby formula?"

"Mmm, baby formula. Sounds terrific." Jack was reaching for Fred's knees. Picking out a piece of pizza, I waited for him to tell me what he really wanted to drink.

"It's a Saturday night. Don't you have a bottle of wine or better yet some beer in this joint? I'm not going out to get any, so forget it."

"Ugh," I groaned. "I had enough wine last night to last me a lifetime. How about some Kool-Aid?" Bending deep into the refrigerator, I spotted a blottle lying on its side. "Oh wait, I think I see one." I walked back to him and handed him the bottle. "Here, have a beer."

"How old is it?" Fred asked, examining the label.

"How would I know?" I grabbed my half-eaten piece of pizza and talked with the food in my mouth. "Who cares anyway?"

"Because it probably came with the house. I'm sure you didn't buy it."

Hurt by his accusation, I protested. "For your information, it was left over from my party. Stop being so ungrateful."

"Me? Ungrateful? The man who goes out of his way for you?" I carried the box into the living room and put it on the floor. I went back and grabbed some napkins and a couple of paper plates. Fred took the blanket off the couch and spread the contents out like we were having a picnic on the floor.

While I devoured the pizza, Fred grabbed a toy from Jack. He placed him on his stomach, raising him above his head. Jack giggled. A good hour went by joking and laughing.

"Why don't you come home more often? This has been fun."

"This is not my home anymore, remember?" Fred reached over and tenderly touched my cheek. All I could think about was how messy I looked. I was devoid of makeup. My body was still perfumed with the cigarette smell from the night before. My mind began rushing to assemble what I saw on his face. Why was he staring at me in such a strange way?

It finally hit home. Stupid me. It was passion. I should know. Hadn't I been the one to watch those eyes go to work on all the other women in his life? This was an entirely new experience. They were fixed on me.

I broke the spell by quickly picking up a plate. Fred leaned over and grabbed my arm, stopping me. "It's okay, Annie. Relax. You're not ready and I'm not ready. 'Time is the greatest innovator.'"

As his eyes filled with mischief, he smiled and lightly put his arms around my shoulders. "No, don't say it. I know. Your hero, Mr. Francis Bacon, the philosopher, I shortened it again."

He closed his eyes, placing his hands over his ears. "Please, don't tell me the quote in its entirety." Smiling maliciously, I started to speak. He put his fingers to my lips.

"Shhh, be a smart woman. For once in your life, shut up."

I nervously started to stand up. He gently pulled me toward him. The warm glow in his eyes caught me by surprise. He smiled and I shivered.

"I can read the panic on your face. My dear, if you're going to be a good lawyer, you'll have to stop showing the world and me what's written all over it. Calm down. We're not dealing with anything heavy here. At least not for now. Think how I feel. You're scaring me more than I'm scaring you!"

"And why is that?"

I lost my balance and fell into his chest. "Think of all the broken hearts I'd miss out on." He gave me a quick hug and let me escape his hold. I rolled over on my side and came up on my knees. Fred turned his attention to Jack who gave him a big smile.

"Before I came over, I was beeped by my office. Maybe you're right. Technology stinks. I know I promised to spend the evening with you, but I can't. Some despicable jerk filed a preliminary injunction on one of my better-paying clients. You're off the hook. I hope you're not too disappointed. Besides, I won't be bothering you for at least a couple of weeks. The firm is sending me to New York."

He stood up and helped me to my feet. "New York, huh? Sounds like fun," I said jealously.

"Trust me. It's nothing. The big boss in mergers and acquisitions needs someone to handle the contractual grunt work. Lucky me. I'll be stuck in some fancy hotel room doing research all day and night while the old man goes off to breakfast, lunch, and dinner with the CEO's of two very big conglomerates."

He placed his hand on my chin. "Do you suppose that's what I want out of life, Annie? When I look at you, I don't think so. Thanks for the beer and the company."

Placing his hands gently behind my neck, he pulled me to him. Slowly and deliberately he pressed his lips hard against mine. His lips followed his hands as they caressed my neck. Without giving me a chance to speak, he withdrew his hold.

Reaching in his pocket, he smiled, handing me a gift. "No, don't say anything. Let me leave while I still have the strength."

He picked up Jack. "See you soon, big guy. Put only smiles on your mother's face. She's beautiful when she smiles." He put the baby down. Before he left, he blew me a kiss and shut the door.

Utterly confused, I wiped the sweat off my brow and glanced at what he had placed in my hand. Untying the bow seemed to take forever. Inside was a hand-blown paper weight. The clear glass was a bright blue-colored ocean with tropical fish. It was a magnificent piece of the sea, a moment of tranquility without the bad storms. A note in his handwriting was taped to the bottom. It read: "One's desire should never be met with disapproval."

Afraid, yet intrigued. Pleased, yet apprehensive. I placed the gift on the coffee table. I shook off the rest of my jitters and immediately began picking up the mess we had created.

Not long afterwards, I loaded Jack in the car and drove to Mattie's. Every light in the house was lit. 'Oh, no, not again,' I said to myself.

When I entered the foyer, the reason became clear. People were mingling. In fact, there were too many strangers to count. I spotted a petite woman named Eunice, whom I knew as one of the first volunteers at Mattie's, and asked her what was going on.

"Oh, Annie, our prayers have been answered," she said excitedly. "These people are from the Calvary Baptist Church. They're here to volunteer."

Before I had time to grasp her meaning, Mattie came floating by and gave me a quick hug. "Annie baby, it's finally happening. You're not going to believe it!" She jumped up and down almost doing a twist. Jubilation was written all over her face.

"Honey, we have money and we have help." She gave me a high five. "Hallelujah, mama!"

She raised her hands to the ceiling saying a silent prayer as she continued to dance. "Oh, Annie, I feel so wonderful. Tonight, step two of our plan has worked."

I didn't know we had any plans or steps. Perhaps I should ask her about three and four before it was too late.

"Didn't I tell you those two sweet boys would not die in vain?

If it weren't for them, these people would not be here."

At that moment, a tall man walked up the foyer steps and began to speak. A hush automatically filled the room. This time it was not Grizzly Moses. The man was in his late 40's, baldheaded, crisp white-collared shirt with a black jacket. He was heavyset with dark-brown skin and eyes that spoke of his kindness. There was something about him, something which went far deeper than his preaching. He immediately had everyone's attention.

"Ladies and Gentlemen, most of you know who I am. I'm the Reverend George Miles from the Calvary Baptist Church. The members of my congregation have asked me to speak. We are here tonight to welcome Mattie into our community. In the past we have been -- how shall I put it? Ignorant in refusing to help. In fact, almost hostile of her meddlesome ways."

The crowd laughed at his joke. "However, today, I feel a new found sense of hope. Your benevolence puts to shame our own unwillingness and lack of cooperation. We all need to do what we can to see to it this neighborhood gets rid of the pestilence which corrupts are streets. Mattie has told me what she needs most right now are charitable contributions. We need to help in any way we can. Of course, we'll all pray to Jesus to help us overcome this enormous problem."

His congregation moved a little forward and gathered closer around the foyer steps. "Come, my friends. We must figure out a way to take back our kids, and we need more than one woman in this neighborhood with the stamina and strength to stand up and be heard. My friends, I can't say this enough. It is time. It is time to stop fighting each other. It is time to stop closing our eyes and exterminating ourselves. We only have to wish it and we can change the world. My brethren, awaken our souls to the scourge upon our streets. Give us the strength to overcome our fear. Salvation can only be imminent if we work together."

I walked along the wall to get a good look at the crowd. They seemed like decent folks. Reverend Miles had a deep, strong voice. I found myself intrigued by him, wanting to listen, too.

"We can't keep dumping the problems on our schools. Education is not only about the textbooks. It's about caring what happens to these boys and girls. It's about us. We must become responsible adults. We need role models like Mattie to show us the way out.

He looked across the room, as if speaking to each of us. "Brothers and sisters, we are not dumb. The problem lies in the forbidden fruit: crack cocaine. If we can clear these children's heads of it, maybe they can learn to think again. Maybe we can be successful at putting them on a track that takes them out of hell and onto a path back home, a path to our Heavenly Father."

Reverend Miles closed his eyes and extended his hands. "Let's bow our heads tonight and pray for God's blessing. Please, give us the courage to fight the resistance."

After his prayer, most of the men and women went to Mattie, hugged her, and welcomed her into their fold.

A medium-built man dressed in casual clothes came forward and pointed an ugly finger at me. "Who's she? You don't belong here. Ain't no white folks who give a damn about us black folks. Who do you think put the crack in the hands of our kids? Take that white ass of yours home before I shove you home.!"

Mattie placed her body between the man and me, getting into the man's face. "Get out! There isn't a person in this room that shouldn't thank her for this roof over our heads."

Mattie turned toward the others in the room and placed her hand in mine. "If there is anyone here who feels the way this man does, get out! I need help to fight this foolish bigotry, not see it passed on."

Moving toward the middle of the room, she pulled me along.

"Damn it, people. Do something that's right for a change. I don't care what the color of the ass is that's going to help me do it. I'll take cream-colored and I'll take shades of walnut or mahogany, whatever." Then she smiled. "Although dead asses I can do without." The crowd didn't know whether to laugh at her joke or not. They stood quite still.

She continued to stand near the man that had caused the ruckus. "You, sir, defy the very principles for which I have spent my entire life fighting. Placing blame won't remedy our situation one iota. It's a no-where street, you foolish man. It's for petty scapegoats, drug addicts and alcoholics. Line up and listen to their excuses."

The stunned congregation began whispering. At that point, Reverend Miles approached the man and turned back to the crowd, raising his arms. "Calm down. It's all right, Frank," he said to the man standing next to him.

"He lost his oldest son in a shooting with the cops. He's naturally suspicious of white people. His heart is bitter. 'To err is human, to forgive divine,' my friend. But, Mattie's right."

Then he came toward me and grabbed my other hand. "I'm so sorry, dear lady." He said, kissing my hand. Then he turned to his congregation. "Whether we like it or not, whites and blacks are a part of this continent. We may have started out as their slaves, but it's only the black man who enslaves himself today. Please, people. We must learn to be tolerant. We must accept help, be it white, black, red, or green. The color of a man's skin has never measured the man...nor woman," he said bowing his head and winking at Matttie.

"It's what's inside that counts." His voice turned into a whisper. "It always has and it always will."

Reverend Miles looked into my eyes and I shivered. "If there is anyone among you who cannot accept this woman's help, I, too, wish to see you leave. Bigotry will not be tolerated and will not exist in the walls of my church. Is that clear?"

For a couple of seconds, everyone stood in silence. As if a revelation had suddenly occurred to him, his next words profoundly moved us all. "Be it white man or black man, men have lost their lives on this country's battlefield for the glorious cause of freedom. Surprisingly, even today we accept and get used to the oppression caused by the color of our skin. Yet, from our own people, we hide in our houses fearing for our lives. What's our life worth? Our poor kids can't play in their backyards?"

He walked over to the window, pulling back the curtain. "Look! Really look. See it for what it is. We have green grass, but red streets, the stains of our children's blood upon our sidewalks."

Was it a coincidence or a spiritual message from my nightmare? I could hear the regret in his voice. It was as if he sensed what I was thinking. He gave me a knowing smile. I had trouble swallowing.

"Whose fault is it? It's yours and yours and yours," he said, pointing to all of us. "We're to blame." He pointed his finger at me from across the room. "Be proud of her. It takes guts to be the only white person present. And if you can't accept these principles, then leave. We're intelligent human beings. Suffer the ill effects of bigotry no longer."

Was this possible? The women in the room gave me reassuring smiles. The men ignored me and said nothing. The most important thing happened: no one left.

Even the man who had given me all the grief approached.

"I'm sorry, ma'am," he said, extending his hand. I placed my white hand in his black. "The Reverend's right. I didn't mean no offense. It's hard losing a son."

"I have a son of my own, sir. I hope I'll never have to know how you feel." The man nodded his head in agreement and walked away.

If we could all come together in this small way, maybe it was still possible to come together as a nation. I felt hope and an incredible sense of euphoria.

C H A P T E R
XII

After the guests had left and the children were put to bed, peace was finally ours. We laid our heads back on the couch and felt the welcoming warmth from the dying embers of the fire. Jason closed the glass doors and yawned.

"Sorry, Mattie, but I'm going to bed. It's a wonderful thing that happened here tonight, isn't it?"

"You've got that right, Jason. It's a glorious thing that happened here tonight," she said, folding her hands in prayer.

"Good night, Mattie. Good night, Anne. Jack's asleep in his crib. Do you want me to help you load him in your car?"

"No. Thanks anyway. I'd like to sit and talk with Mattie for a while." Jason yawned, heading for the stairs.

Unfortunately, we still had work to do. We waited for Jason to shut the bedroom door before saying anything.

"Oh, Mattie dear, I think it's time to say good-bye to Reggie and hello to Peter Harrison," I said, whispering. She rolled her eyes thinking it was a dumb suggestion.

"The police are looking for Reggie Parks. If he removes the earring and shaves that savage-looking beard, Peter Harrison might look like a normal human being. With some professor-type glasses, no one will recognize him."

Mattie seemed unimpressed by my plan. She started to open her mouth, but I put my finger on her lips.

"Listen, if we can convince Peter to apply at the university, I bet they'd consider his application. After all, he's a graduate student, right? He said he wanted to quit. Don't you see? He can work on his Ph.D. and be a social worker right here under the gangs' very noses. Of course, that spy problem still scares me. Well, what do you think?"

At first, Mattie did not reply. She was busy thinking over my suggestion. "My mentoring must be rubbing off on you," she said frowning. "That's a stupendous idea."

She was silent for what seemed like several minutes. I could almost visualize the wheels turning in her own brain.

"You're absolutely right. Peter is a pro. There's nothing new about the man changing his identity. He does it as often as a chameleon changes colors. Reggie Parks is history. But as Peter Harrison, he'd never be questioned."

She relished the prospect of Peter's help. "Oh, God, I feel as light as air. I've been so upset. Here I was putting you in danger, the house in danger, and who knows what horrible plight could have been in store for Peter had he been discovered."

Mattie jumped off the couch and danced her way into the kitchen. She hummed as she began preparing a pile of sandwiches for the stowaway downstairs.

I checked on my sleeping baby in the crib and headed toward the basement. Approaching the room with caution, we rolled the shelves to the right of the secret door, then quietly moved the fake wall. We peered into the room and then tiptoed inside.

Peter Harrison had been asleep. He was trying to focus, getting his bearings straight. Glancing at us, he made his first verbal complaint of the night. "It's about time you rescued me from this hellhole. Are you sure you two aren't a couple of terrorists?"

Peter slowly raised his head and put his feet firmly on the floor. "Do you realize there wasn't one speck of food to be found in this room? Honestly, Mattie. Those poor kids. Do you starve them to death before you get them out of here?"

"I'm sorry, Peter. You weren't exactly a planned guest," Mattie replied. "The last two children ate everything I stashed away. I forgot to restock. Besides, your hunger was not worth taking any unnecessary risk."

Peter's nose picked up the aroma in Mattie's hands. He beckoned her forward. "It's all right. I'll forgive you. Please, while I'm still alive, come here."

Mattie put the plate on Peter's lap, and we watched him swallow a whole sandwich in one gulp. We both giggled.

"Oh, fine," he protested, "not only am I being starved to death by two depraved women, I'm also subjected to their ridicule. Gee, thanks."

Mattie groaned and sat down on the cot next to Peter. "I'll have you know we are not depraved women. We are true intellects possessed with a keen sense of strategical prowess. Plus, we're the only depraved guardian angels you're likely to get. So listen and keep that big mouth of yours shut. We've figured out a way to get you out of this mess."

Peter was more interested in his food. He started to talk with his mouth full. "Honestly, I've been thinking along those lines myself." He looked at me with concern on his face. "I will not jeopardize Anne's life nor her son's. The best thing to do is get my car out of storage and leave town as soon as possible. I can lay low in a hotel somewhere. You know as well as I do I'm used to living on the run."

Mattie looked at me and shook her head. "Do men ever

listen? I told you we had an ingenious plan. Now, shut up and eat while we talk. You're not going anywhere. I need your help. Something has happened here tonight."

Mattie clapped her hands and tapped him on the uninjured arm. "Oh, Peter, we've done it!"

Peter momentarily stopped eating and gave Mattie a confused look. "Done what?"

"The house was packed tonight. The entire congregation from the Calvary Baptist Church showed up. I wish you could've been there. Right now they are more angry than they are scared. Oh, the senselessness of it all. Don't you see? It's our job to keep them upset. You're the only one who can put this whole thing together."

Mattie rolled her eyes and whispered in my ear. "Annie, stop me. I think I just admitted to myself that I need a man's help. Ugh."

She turned her head back toward Peter and gave him an imploring stare. "You won't believe it, but Annie has come up with a fine solution. We are women possessed --

"Ah, that's the first thing you've said that makes sense. You are definitely possessed," he said, interrupting Mattie. She slapped his pointed finger aside.

"Unlike you men, we use our brains, not that thing between your legs."

"Leave the poor man alone," I admonished. "He's been through enough. You've also inherited the gift of gab," I said, impatiently. "Get on with it already."

Mattie walked over to a metal table by the sink and picked up a small hand mirror. She handed it to Peter. Puzzled, he shrugged his shoulders.

"It's simple. Tonight we say good-bye to Reggie Parks and hello to Peter Harrison. After we sneak you upstairs, young man, you're going to take a well-needed bath." Mattie held her nose. "And then you're going to cut off that disgusting ponytail and shave that beard. Annie here thinks you look like a murderer. The earring is definitely out. I'm going to place some scholarly-looking glasses on your head. And, lo and behold, we'll have Peter Harrison back. Reggie Parks will remain a fugitive for the rest of his life -- or for at least the time being."

Mattie laid her head on his chest. "Stop running, Peter! I'm begging you. Do something for yourself. Go back to school."

Placing the mirror on the table, we waited for his reaction to the plan. He sat in silence, eating his third sandwich, pondering his alternatives. Washing the food down with the bottle of water, he began to speak.

"It's not a bad idea. To be honest with you, I can't take much more of this. A part of me died last night. Maybe I should retire Reggie Parks for good."

He was right. Children weren't supposed to die. Mattie and Peter lived in a world to which I would never be a part, or at least I hoped I wouldn't.

"I know, Honey. I know," she said with sadness in her voice.

"Let's get out of here. You need to get some rest so your wounds can heal." Mattie looked worn out. She slowly raised her body off the cot. I stood up and pulled her up by the arm.

"Oh, Peter, I can't wait to have you here. With all these new strangers, you'll blend right in. Hopefully, there's still time to apply for the spring semester. Just think, you can finally get your Ph.D. It will be so wonderful."

Peter didn't say anything for awhile. "All right. Let's give it a try."

A little stiff, he slowly stood up and headed toward the door. "Sweet Mattie, please point me to that much-promised bath. I stink to high heaven."

We closed the secret door and tiptoed upstairs. Thank goodness no one was wandering the halls. After a long shower, Peter appeared at the door. Mattie had a razor in one hand and a pair of scissors in the other.

"Do I really have to shave this off? I have no idea what I'm going to find under all this hair. The last time I saw my face clean shaven I was engaged in wet dreams and unnatural hair growth."

Turning back toward the bathroom door, he looked in the mirror. "Oh well, good-bye, Reggie ol' pal."

Moans could be heard through the bathroom door. Afraid he might wake the children, Mattie knocked and told him to tone it down. Suddenly, we heard only running water. A short while later, Peter opened the door and waited for our response. He had on a pair of dark flannel boxers with no shirt.

Mattie was the first one to jump to her feet. She walked over to where he was standing and began to circle him. "Wow," she said, "you're not a bad lookin' guy, Mr. Peter Harrison. Now, get over there so I can do something with that ponytail."

Peter Harrison was a very handsome man, indeed. The pony tail intrigued me. It was terribly sexy. Underneath that beard was a finely-chiseled face. There was a kindness in the brown depths of those deep set eyes.

His skin was a flawless golden color. He had a solid muscular build and was a good four heads taller than me. Why hadn't I noticed any of this before? I was taking this *man* to my house to live with me. Boy, was I a foolish woman. He oozed sexuality. I got goose bumps just looking at him.

Mattie read my mind and smiled. I quickly raised my hand to stop her from cutting off his hair. "Perhaps you should leave it alone. What do you know about haircuts?"

Mattie held the scissors in the same way she held the needle last night. "Absolutely nothing. But I didn't know how to stitch somebody up yesterday either. I could shave it all off and put a big letter "P" on the back of your head. Of course, instead of Peter, it would stand for poop."

Peter immediately got off the bed, placed his hands on Mattie's hips, and shoved her back ever so lightly onto the bed.

"My male pride is damaged enough." He looked at himself in the bathroom mirror. "Annie's right. Tomorrow I'll take myself off to a proper barber," he said grimacing. "Do you have any idea who this man in the mirror is? Ugh, thank goodness I won't have to look at myself."

Mattie walked over to the other side of the room and placed her arm around his shoulder. "You're not so bad. In fact, you look rather nice. Almost like a normal human being, instead of some evil gang leader."

Mattie punched him. Peter grimaced. "Ouch, that hurts." The arm was obviously causing him pain.

"Of course, it does." Mattie replied. "And it will continue to hurt until it heals. Oh, that reminds me." She scrambled around in her jean pockets. Pulling out a plastic bottle of pills, she removed one out of the container. "Here, take this."

Peter gave her a puzzled look. "Don't worry. It's not poison. I reserve that for the people I really despise."

She placed her hand on his forehead. "No, really. It's just an antibiotic, silly. You're not saying anything, but I can tell you have a low-grade fever. You look flushed. We have to ward off infection, you know. Down the hatch, young man."

Peter dutifully took the pills. She walked over to her dresser and handed him a clean pair of blue jeans and a T-shirt. "Here. On my way home from Annie's this afternoon, Jason and I stopped at the shopping center and I bought this."

Peter stared at it suspiciously. "I told Jason the clothes were for me. Thank goodness, he wasn't paying any attention to the size. He knows I like to wear men's clothes, so I just explained to him I needed something to mosey around the house in. It's all right. He's always looking at me as if I am some alien from Mars. Anyway, we've got to destroy those rags you're wearing."

Mattie found a large pair of socks in her drawer and handed them to him. "You're going to have to go out and buy some normal person's clothes, Peter. No more gang paraphernalia."

At the same time, we both glanced at the tennis shoes he had carried up earlier. Dried blood was still caked on the top. Thank goodness they were leather. She pulled out a clean rag and did the best she could to wipe it off. The night's horrible reminder brought a silent chill to the room. The teasing was over. Peter turned his back and finished dressing.

We left the bedroom and tiptoed down the back stairs to the kitchen. Baby Jack was still sound asleep. After bundling him up, Mattie kissed Peter good-bye.

"It will be all right," she said, assuringly. "Try to get some rest. I'll burn the clothes after you leave. Now, get out of here."

Peter remained silent. There was nothing that would bring those boys back, and, above all else, that was Peter's wish.

Leaving the house, we headed for the car. I placed the baby in the restraints in the back seat. Peter glanced suspiciously around as if expecting someone to grab him.

It was after midnight. A clear, brisk breeze was coming from the west. The full moon and the stars had cast a gray glow on the ground. I glanced around the yard. No one was lurking in the dark shadows, nothing but the trees. Those menacing giants were standing with their branches outstretched beckoning. Feeling a cold shiver creep up my spine, I was quite happy to start the engine and leave.

Reaching our destination, I got the baby out of the car and carried him inside. As I carefully took his jacket off, I noticed he was awake, not crying, just staring at us as if to say, "Who's the guy behind you, Mom?" I went to the refrigerator, warmed up a bottle, and sat down in the rocker to feed him. Peter walked around, checking out his new accommodations.

He uncomfortably took a seat on the couch and began his assessment. "It's a little sparse, but it's cozy. I like this room. May I call you Annie?"

Someone who asked permission. That was unusual. "I'm getting used to it. Everyone else does."

"Annie's a good solid name. It makes you more human, perhaps sweeter, speaks of your kindness," he said, placing his hands behind his neck. "It suits you better than Anne. It's much too formal."

I ignored his assessment of my character and talked about the house. "I'm glad you like it. This is the only room downstairs with furniture. Unfortunately, your bed is in the attic. I changed the sheets and cleaned it up a bit. It's a little too small for someone over six foot. You'll have to get used to hunching."

After burping the baby, I carried him to his room. Peter, with nothing to do, followed closely behind. I checked his diaper and placed the almost sleeping baby into his crib. I pulled the cover around his small form and stopped to take one last look.

Peter came up from behind me and peeked in the crib. "Do they all look like that?"

"Like what?" I proudly responded. "Like there isn't anything more perfectly innocent? Yeah, I suspect they all look like that."

A silent peace crept into the room. Peter's mysterious dark eyes turned their attention to me. I stood transfixed. Indiscriminately a tingling sensation ran down my spine.

Again, that same foreboding entered my brain. Was I nuts? Mattie was right. I wasn't a nun after all. Although until tonight, I was certainly living like one. My hormones were short-circuiting. Okay, Annie, get control.

As my musing continued, Peter gently placed his hands on my shoulders. He smiled and his hypnotic eyes made me tremble. It was as if he were memorizing the contours of my face. He slowly moved forward and gave my cheek a feather-light caress. I closed my eyes and waited for his lips to touch mine. Nothing happened.

"I don't know what to say. Thank you seems so inadequate. I owe you a great deal. Was it only yesterday you thought I was some pernicious creep who was about to ravage and plunder your body?"

He raised his right hand to his chest. "I swear I'll never have to stoop to such a low, degrading act. Yes, I will admit I intend to seduce you, beautiful woman. Seduce you like no man has ever seduced you. Touch you like no man has ever touched you. Be wary of me, Annie."

Since I had to crane my neck to look up at those penetrating eyes, he bent down, placed his arms around my shoulders and held me close. He nuzzled my neck and quite deliberately and slowly placed light, tantalizing kisses just below my right earlobe. When I opened my eyes, he smiled seductively.

As if reading my thoughts, he took my hand and placed a small kiss on the inside of my palm. Smug as the cat that swallowed the canary, he walked away.

Slightly dazed and not fully recovered from the encounter, I turned to follow him. It wasn't as if I could throw his egomaniacal ass out. For that matter, why would I want to? I was trapped -- or was I? It was going to be an interesting couple of weeks. Somewhat stabilized, I entered the hallway. I showed Peter the attic stairs and, without saying a word, closed my bedroom door.

Suddenly restless, I ran to my bed to seek refuge under the covers. I smothered my giggle with one of my pillows. Yeah, I was excited. What a challenge Peter Harrison was going to make. Hmm, which of us would seduce whom? Perhaps he should be wary of me. What was I thinking? It was a bad idea. Men had always betrayed me.

C H A P T E R
XIII

Like most mornings, the alarm went off before I was ready to get up. There was no sun filtering into the room, just a gray dull light. Knowing it wasn't going to do me any good, I pull the covers over my head. It was quieter than normal. Jack must have slept through the night. With my eyes glued shut, I crawl out of bed looking for my bathrobe. I check my vicious-looking self in the bathroom mirror. Nothing was going to help this face.

Walking like the old lady I saw reflected there, I turned and headed for Jack's room. It was empty. Taking two steps at a time down the stairs, Jack was in his swing being tickled by Peter.

They both looked up and smiled, "It's okay, Mom. Relax. I fed the baby his bottle and changed his nasty diaper. I think I've lost my touch. When I used to change my sisters' diapers, I skipped the gagging part. I almost lost my breakfast."

My bathrobe was gaping open at the throat. I caught his eyes on my breasts. Self-consciously I tightened the belt around my waist, turning my back. For a moment, nothing was said.

"I really do know what I'm doing," he said, taking Jack out of his swing and passing him to me."

My baby came into my arms grinning. Giving Jack a ticklish kiss on the neck, he giggled.

"I was their mother, the housekeeper, the father, the teacher, the cook, the Band Aid kid -- you name it, I did it." He walked into the kitchen and poured me a cup of coffee.

"What are you talking about?" I asked confused.

"My brothers and sister, of course. I raised them. Oh, I hope you don't mind. I pretty much helped myself. By the way, unlike your happy son, you don't wake up all sunny-eyed and bushy-tailed, do you?"

He wore no shirt and the dark-colored boxers fit snugly around his waist. He stretched his lean body, his hands almost touching the ceiling His chest brushed against the sleeve of my bathrobe.

"The best part of the day is the morning." He parted the curtain overlooking the backyard. The sky was a light gray with a hint of sunlight coming through the clouds. A light breeze rustled the trees. The birds were busily eating the seed I put in the feeder a couple of nights ago.

"Look, it's not so bad. You can almost breathe the fresh air," he said witnessing my lack of enthusiasm and dropping the curtain.

Peter took Jack from my arms and placed him in the high chair, handing him an animal cracker. I headed toward the front door to retrieve the morning paper. I accidentally tripped on some area rug that was now lying along the dining room floor in front of the kitchen. It was a large open area and prior to today it had been hardwood floor.

"Oops. Sorry. I moved the rug from the hallway thinking it would spruce up the kitchen."

Ready to give him a piece of my mind, my eyes immediately caught the change in my kitchen. He had totally rearranged the cabinets, neatly stacking the plates, glasses, canned goods, foodstuffs, etc. I was annoyed. How was I going to find anything?

"I suppose you placed the canned goods in alphabetical order, too," I said sarcastically. "What time did you get up this morning?"

"I slept all day in that prison cell, remember. If you hate it, I'll put it back. Sorry. My compulsive nature is something I can't control."

"It's all right," I said not knowing why I was reassuring him. "Actually, it's quite an improvement," I lied.

I rummaged for the milk in the refrigerator and poured some in my coffee. "Don't worry. It won't take me long to trash it again. I hope you like to grocery shop as well. Oh, and cooking, did I tell you I make terrific pots of canned soups and tossed salads? Oh, and Kool-Aid. I like Kool-Aid."

"I can't wait to try it," Peter said, rinsing out his coffee cup and pouring himself a fresh cup.

"What time did Jack wake up?" I inquired.

"Oh, it was somewhere around 5:30. I heard him on the monitor while I was straightening up your kitchen.

I turned my back and glanced at Jack who had cookie all over his face. "Sorry you mama didn't hear you this morning, sweetie."

"Actually, we've been having a pretty good time. He's such a happy guy."

"Oh, I'd better get moving," I said suddenly aware of the time. I quickly left the kitchen and headed for the upstairs bathroom. "Don't worry about changing the baby's clothes. The baby-sitter will do that. Oh, by the way, you'll have the house to yourself. If you want something to do, paint the guest bedroom and leave my kitchen alone. The paint is in the garage. Maybe tonight, if your arm isn't too sore, we could move the bed from the attic into the spare room so you won't have to spend the next few weeks hunched over. Don't strain yourself. If it's too much, forget it."

"Excellent idea." Peter yelled back. "I practically crawled on my hands and knees to the bed last night. Mind you, I'm not complaining. It beats the hell out of Mattie's jail."

Showered and dressed, I went to the baby's room to retrieve the diaper bag. By the time I reached the kitchen, Peter had him bundled up. "I think I could get used to this," I said, impressed by his kindness. "First you clean my kitchen, then my kid's dirty pants, and now he's dressed and ready to go. You're scaring me. Are you truly a man or a woman in drag?"

"So she finds her sense of humor after a hot shower. I'll have to remember that," he said, handing me Jack.

Uncomfortable and running out of things to say, I took my baby and my briefcase. "Have a nice day. Try to stay out of trouble. Whatever it takes. You have my permission to clean anything you want."

Peter smiled, bent down, and kissed me on the cheek. "Thanks. It's a nice change for me as well. I do believe I could get used to this."

I frowned unsure whether I wanted to get used to this or not. He had me completely giddy and on edge.

"Don't worry. As long as you control the petrified look you're giving me, we'll get along fine. Don't freeze me out, Annie. There's nothing to be afraid of. Relax."

Ignoring his smug smile, I turned around and walked out the back door. Talking to myself, I put the baby into his car seat. "The man says relax. He's turning me and my house upside down and he wants me to relax. And what the hell was the kiss for? He's right. He gives me the jitters. Oh, baby, baby, what am I going to do?"

Startled, I turned to see Peter standing behind me. He had obviously overheard my muttering.

"You left this on the counter top," he said handing me Jack's blanket. I smiled and took it with a flushed face.

Ignoring his sheepish grin, I got in the car. He waved good-bye. Geez, what a complete ass I'm making of myself. I kept that thought to myself.

Arriving at work, I experienced the usual Monday morning ordeal. People were already packed in the reception area waiting their turn for a free lawyer. The Crimestoppers had a bulletin board hanging on the wall. There was already a drawn pictorial of Reggie Parks posted next to a wanted poster of a young white male who had robbed a liquor store.

Before entering the receptionist area, I took a closer look. Relieved that it didn't look like the man who was staying at my house, I shook my head and breathed a sigh of relief.

My hands were full of case files I had left in the car intending to work on them over the weekend, which, of course, I hadn't touched.

"Good morning, Miss Stevens," said Karen, our new receptionist. Kevin stood and gallantly opened the door, allowing me to pass.

"Thank you," I said, as Karen handed me my messages.

"I'm sorry I'm late," I said, walking down the hall. "You know how it is when you have kids." Kevin followed me down the hall sipping his coffee.

"Don't know how you do it. Single-parenting is rough." I could tell he wanted to talk because he bypassed his office and kept following me.

Kevin Doyle was my boss and one of those rare human beings who loved his job and enjoyed helping his clients. In the few months I had known him, I had never seen him angry. He had the uncanny ability to see a silver lining in everyone's character flaws. He believed criminals were people, too.

He was not yet bald, but his hair was quickly thinning at the top of his head. He was forty-two years old with a widening middle-aged girth. He smelled faintly of cologne. I'd say he was a happy individual with a doting wife and two children. Even the marriage seemed to be working.

He was also the same guy who taught me the important legal protocol, like what judge was sleeping around with what clerk and/or what prosecuting attorney would smile at you and then go for your carotid artery. He had a sense of humor and a sporting nature, a brilliant man of action.

Taking a seat in the chair across from my desk, Kevin opened the newspaper. On the front page were the pictures of Mitchell and Jeremy displayed across the top. I put my files on the desk trying to keep a stone face.

"Let's hope they catch these guys and they have enough money to afford their own attorney. I have a great deal of trouble representing the baby killers. Damn it. Those poor kids, fourteen and six. What kind of a sick world do we live in?"

Without waiting for my response, Kevin continued talking. "Can you believe it? Rodney Thomas is dead. I sure would like to represent the guy who allegedly killed him. Did you check out his picture? Cute, huh?" His picture, too, was on the front cover. Thank goodness it wasn't every day in this city three murders occurred in one weekend.

"What guts the man must have," Kevin said, shaking his head.

"What man?" I asked

"The guy who killed him, of course."

I placed the files and my briefcase on my desk. "How many white people do you suppose will read something like this weekend's tragedy and simply dismiss it because the killings occurred in a black ghetto?" I asked.

He hesitated before he answered. A file started to fall off the desk. Kevin grabbed it before it fell to the floor. He seemed to be listening to me and reading the file at the same time. Frustrated by his lack of enthusiasm for the conversation, I snapped at him.

"Excuse me, Kevin. Are you still here? If not, I have work to do."

Placing the file back on my desk, he shrugged his shoulders.

"We always have work to do. You're not going to change the world. That's the way it is."

He was forever telling me that. Once I knew I had his full attention, I changed the topic of discussion to something more positive. "Oh, Kevin, this weekend something wonderful happened. Mattie received some major help from the Calvary Baptist Church. You should have been there. Her community is finally getting the message."

"That's terrific." He took another sip of his coffee. "I'm glad for her and you."

"Where are all the black people fortunate enough to escape living in that hellhole? Why can't they help? Can't they see they need those role models?"

"Don't waste your breath talking to me. Look, I'm the guy who's been working in this stinking office for the last six years. I could be making real money, but I'm doing bigger and better things, like seeing to it the rejects no one cares about in this society receive a fair trial."

Before he could say anything else, I interrupted. "And speaking of 'fair trial' what the hell is that? Twelve white jurors convicting one black defendant. It isn't fair!" I said, putting my purse in my drawer and slamming it shut.

With a smug grin, he got up from the chair. "What happened? Did you get up on the wrong side of the bed this morning?"

Without waiting for my response, Kevin turned and left. A couple of seconds later, he stuck his head back into my office. "Let's work that liberal mind of yours into a real tizzy. While you were off last Friday, Benjamin Goldstein filed a warrant on the Lee Roberts and Joseph Gibbons case. He wants hair samples and sperm samples for the Paula Jennings rape case. He suspects that your two clients are responsible for that poor girl's narrow escape from death."

I stared at him speechlessly. Kevin shifted uneasily and smiled apologetically. "My sources tell me she's in the psychiatric ward almost comatose. I'm told there were no fingerprints found in her apartment."

I pulled out their file and looked at my watch. Kevin was not ready to leave. He kept talking. "Goldstein believes it's more than coincidence your clients were seen in the same area around the same time the rape occurred. In fact, they were arrested just a couple blocks away from the crime scene, weren't they?"

"Those boys aren't rapists. Armed robbers, maybe. Rapists, no. Furthermore, you can't obtain a warrant on mere supposition in this country, yet. If you want my opinion, this whole case stinks of race discrimination."

"What's new?" Kevin turned and headed down the hall. "Get this," I yelled, attempting to get his attention back.

"'At approximately 12:30 a.m. Officers Evans and Taylor, riding in an unmarked squad car, observed two black male subjects leaving a convenience store.' That's all they were doing, getting a couple of snacks around midnight. 'We followed the suspects' vehicle as it drove around campus.' It wouldn't have anything to do with the color of their skin, would it now?"

"Of course not. All black males at midnight are up to something criminal, didn't you know?"

"For ten minutes, they wait for the chance to pull them over and arrest them. Finally, and get this, the boys stop at a stop sign, but there's this invisible line."

I drew a picture for Kevin on my yellow legal pad to illustrate what the police officers observed.

"Supposedly, they rolled through this crosswalk here," pointing once again to my yellow pad. "Sin of all sins, isn't it? In fact, I drove that route myself. In order to get an unobstructed view, you have to move into the crosswalk before completing the turn.

That's exactly what they did."

"So they were pulled over for the nebulous traffic violation of the century. What's new?" Kevin asked.

"You can't leave yet," I told him as I stood up and walked around my desk. "Now, this part gets better. Unfortunately, but beneficial to my case, the police stopped the car with their guns drawn and their squad cars blocking both the front and back of my client's car. They were immediately told to raise their hands above their heads and exit the car. The officers found two handguns underneath the seat. At this very moment, I have a pending motion to suppress the evidence due to an unlawful search and seizure. What do you think? Do I have a chance?"

Kevin shrugged his shoulders. "If you get the right judge, he might dismiss it. It's a close call."

"Damn Goldstein." I said, hitting the file on my desk. "My clients are looking at a six-year mandatory sentence for possession of the guns. They did not rape her. And, of course, there are two confessions I want suppressed as well."

Kevin leaned his hand against the door and said, "Maybe we should quit our jobs and teach interrogation training in gang school," he suggested, jokingly.

I nodded. "You're right. The boys confessed to the police the guns belonged to them. Thugs, maybe. But rapists, no. At least, I hope not. Thanks for the tip, Kevin."

I sat back down in my chair to ponder my next move. I'd better make darn sure Goldstein doesn't get that warrant signed.

Tapping my fingers on the desk, I rose immediately from my chair. It suddenly occurred to me if Benjamin found Judge Palmer on a Monday morning he would likely be in his chambers suffering from his latest attack of hangover remorse. At this moment, I was entirely sympathetic.

I ran around Kevin almost colliding with him in the hallway.

"Judge Palmer just might forget about the Fourth Amendment and sign that warrant. See ya."

"I was wondering when you'd come to that conclusion," Kevin yelled, as I turned the corner.

The Public Defender's Office was in a different annex. I walked through the corridor and entered the marble foyer. The judge's chambers were on the third floor. Ignoring the elevator, I darted up the steps. Walking past the Treasurer's Office, I spotted Benjamin P. Goldstein, Esquire. It was my opinion, the "P" stood for peacock.

Goldstein was the First Assistant State's Attorney in charge of the criminal division. He was a peculiar man who always dressed like a prep school scholar. His horn-rimmed glasses were constantly slipping down his nose.

He was your typically conservative prosecutorial oaf whose abounding pleasure was getting off on his own accomplishments. It was true. The creep was talented and smart.

On the few occasions he was my opponent in court, people were automatically drawn to him. He could be charming and often manipulative. He played his role of saving the community from the scum bags of this earth brilliantly in court. I despised the man.

In my biased opinion, he used the power of his office irresponsibly, bordering on sleaze-bag tactics only fit for those we call criminals. I know it sounds harsh, but it always makes me feel good to say it. Puts my opponent in perspective.

Before they were charged, he was always a defendant's best friend. I had second chaired a murder trial with Kevin some time ago. The defendant had hired a hit man to brutally beat his wife for sleeping with his next door neighbor. Our defense was he hadn't wished her dead. Unfortunately, she suffered a heinous and brutal death.

Goldstein told the defendant during the initial interrogation

-193-

that he'd 'go easy' on him. The man believed him and confessed to hiring the guy. The defendant got it off his chest, and for a brief moment he probably felt better. Goldstein made the defendant feel good, all right; to the tune of asking the court for lethal injection. The jury found him guilty of second degree murder.

Goldstein saw me approach him. He straightened his jacket, automatically pushing his glasses back on his nose.

"Slow down," he ordered. "It's all right. I withdrew the warrant. I realized in my zeal to prosecute your clients, I couldn't risk the case being thrown out on a technicality. If they're truly the ones who raped Paula Jennings, I'll put their asses in jail without violating the Fourth Amendment."

I said nothing, turning my back to walk away. Goldstein grabbed my arm. Losing my balance, I fell against his chest. Regaining my equilibrium, I tried not to wipe his touch from my jacket. Eye level with his large nose always made me sick to my stomach.

"Anne, don't be angry. I apologize. In my haste to convict the bastards, I was wrong. Judge Palmer would have signed it, too," he murmured with a self-satisfied grin on his face.

Unaffected by his maladjusted conscience, I pulled my arm away from his grasp. "It's all right, Goldstein. The next time you try anything like that, I'll have your ass in court. There's always the ARDC." (The Attorney Registration and Disciplinary Commission.)

Smiling one of those rapscallion smiles of his, he ignored my threat. "We'll see. You're scaring me to death!" He said, holding his heart and pretending he was truly afraid. He took a handkerchief out of his pocket and began wiping his glasses.

"Oh, by the way, is there any chance I could get you to have dinner with me tomorrow night?"

"Why?" I asked.

"You're one of the few females that can intelligently provide me with a challenge, Anne dear.   You're also the only female in the courthouse who keeps refusing me. In fact, I'm not only infatuated with that brain of yours, I could enjoy what you hide under the suit as well."

"You know, I just happen to have a tape recorder in my jacket pocket." He cleared his throat, turning a beet red. I was thoroughly on the defensive and ready to nail his chauvinistic male pride to the wall.

"I'm only kidding. You're a cad, but you already know that. Trust me. I wouldn't devaluate myself by being seen with you. Besides, my social calendar is jam packed. My week nights are filled with male bonding of a different kind, trust me. You wouldn't appreciate it."

He glared at me in a perplexing way. Could it be I'd actually hurt his feelings? Who knows what ignominious thoughts were running through his pea-brain.

"Yes, it's totally scandalous. By the time I get home, I have approximately three hours to spend playing mommy. If you're interested, perhaps you can come by and change a few diapers or feed him this delicious-tasting baby food. He's always good for a romp or two on the floor. Of course, while you're doing that, there are several loads of laundry, a pile of dishes to wash, along with preparing for the next day's clean clothes, bottle, and diaper bag fill up. Truly, I'm a very exciting woman."

Benjamin Goldstein feigned injury by placing his hand once again upon his heart. I started to turn and walk away. "How much more rejection can one semi-attractive male take?"

"Please, " I said, backing away from him. "If you're going to take your life on my account, be sure to give me a call. I'll have some celebrating to do. Just think. If you're gone, who will I get to oppose me? Probably some other self-righteous *boy*. Although I must admit you surprised me. An adversary with a conscience. It's a change of pace I'm not used to. Maybe there's some redeeming quality in you yet. See you in court."

Walking back to my office, I shook my head in confusion. What was I doing? First, Mattie gets me drunk and tells me it's time to chase men again. Then Saturday afternoon Fred scares me half to death by kissing me on the lips. Not to mention that horseplay with Peter last night. And now Benjamin Goldstein asks me on a date. Maybe I should look in the mirror and see if I have "available" written all over my face.

Did I take some provocative pill in my sleep last weekend that suddenly changed me from an ugly duckling into a swan?

***

The rest of the day came and went without too many surprises. If there really is such a thing, it's what I'd call a regular day.

After picking up the baby, I approached home with a bit of apprehension. Having a guest living with me gave me the jitters. When I was married, I loved coming home to find someone there. Today, I wasn't sure how I felt.

Pulling the car into the garage, I was met with a pleasant surprise. The shrubs and bushes surrounding the house had been trimmed. The flowers that had died after the first freeze were gone. The garage never looked so immaculate. Perhaps it wasn't so bad to have someone around to do chores after all. Mattie was wrong. I needed a housekeeper not a man.

As I opened my door, the sensational aroma of food sent my senses soaring. Someone had actually used the stove and cooked. My poor house and I were in for a few shocks. I placed the diaper bag on the kitchen counter. Peter came over and happily took the baby from my arms. Astonished, I looked around the room.

"Where did you get all this stuff?" Old pictures I hadn't taken the time to go through when I moved here were now on the walls.

Having purchased the home in the summer, the tin thing blocking the hole in the fireplace had been detached. A cozy fire was pleasantly burning in the grate.

I was a new mom, so, of course, I had a few baby pictures cluttering up the mantel. Peter had gone through some of my old boxes and found a picture of my brother who was now sitting next to Baby Jack in a small brass frame.

"The resemblance is remarkable," he said, as he watched me walk over and trace my fingers along the metal frame.

"I should've put it there myself months ago. He's my brother," I said, studying his handsome face. Peter was right. I, too, could see a small resemblance.

"I found the candlesticks in an upstairs closet," he said, politely not questioning me about the man in the frame.

"They were a wedding present from my ex-husband's family. They were our only guests," I replied, not really wanting to be reminded of that day. Peter said nothing, sensing my discomfort.

In the center of the mantelpiece, a bright colorful vase had been beautifully arranged with a bouquet of autumn flowers. The effect he created was a soft, warm glow. Was this really my house? It wasn't 'House Beautiful', but, wow. He certainly had improved the place with the few possessions I owned.

Coming up behind me, he seemed a little nervous. "Do you like it, Annie?" he asked reluctantly. "I'm sorry, but I can't help myself. I have a knack for decorating."

I started to say something when I noticed there was an added piece of furniture in my dining room. I knew I didn't own it, nor had it been anywhere in this house when I left this morning.

"Oh, my! Where did this come from?" The table was

beautifully set for three people. He had taken my odd plates and had arranged them in a multi-colored order. With another bouquet of flowers and still more candles, it looked like an ad from a 'Modern Bride' table setting.

"That's your surprise. Mattie is coming over for dinner. Let her explain that one. Now, run upstairs and change into something more comfortable. I'll check on dinner and feed the baby so he's happy when our guest arrives."

Walking toward the hallway, I turned and hesitated. "What's upstairs? I'm almost afraid to find out."

"Don't worry." Peter shrugged. "I ran out of time. Jason helped me move the bed from the attic down to the guest bedroom. We had a lot of fun going through those boxes. It's amazing what people leave behind. Don't worry. I'll get to painting it tomorrow."

Relieved, to have found my bedroom just as I had left it, I quickly changed my clothes. I hit the bottom stair just as I heard Mattie's voice whispering to Peter.

"All right," I scolded, "I'm back. No whispering! What's up? What are you two plotting now?"

Mattie handed the wine bottle to Peter and gave me a welcoming smile. "Well, it's Cinderella. Don't bother to thank me, my dear. A couple of days ago one of the boys went rummaging around in the upstairs closet and found Aunt Rosie's table. There it was, deep in the back, as if it had been placed there yesterday. We went on a hunting expedition and found the legs. What do you think?"

"It's wonderful," I said running my hand along its smooth surface.

"Peter and Jason polished it up and placed it where it belongs. My mother hated it when I was a child. She thought it was gauche looking."

I walked toward Mattie and put my arms around her. "Thank

you." I said, kissing her on the cheek. "Ugly and gauche it is not. It's the most beautiful dining room table I've ever seen."

Reluctantly, I asked the obvious question. "Don't you think we should sell it and use the money for the kids?"

Mattie pulled out one of the matching chairs and sat down. "Don't be ridiculous. Aunt Rosie would roll over in her grave. It stays here. Lucky for you, I consider you part of my family. So be a gracious child and take it. It's a gift from my heart."

"Oh, stop it," I said on the verge of tears. "You've given me more than I've ever received from anyone in my entire life. I don't know what to say."

I picked Jack up and gave him a squeeze. "Oh, with one exception. Baby Jack is the greatest gift in the whole wide world."

Jack wiggled free from my hold. Obligingly, I placed him down at my feet. He attempted to crawl up the leg of a chair. He lost his balance and fell bumping his head. He started to cry. I picked him up, soothing his injured pride.

"Look at him. He's getting into everything. I'm going to have a heart attack before this is all over. How do you do it?"

"You take it one day at a time and thank the Lord for those days." She said, grabbing a carrot out of the salad bowl.

Peter went to the stereo and found a couple of old cassette tapes. Mattie took Jack and happily danced with him around the room. He was giggling in no time. Peter took me in his arms. A red flush crept up my face.

"I think the woman's finding her rhythm," Peter said, swinging me around in a circle. Peter laughed while Mattie curiously observed. I could read the woman's mind. She was right. He was too close for comfort.

I quickly changed partners. Jack was giggling as I headed for the playpen. He gave me a baleful glare as I surrounded him with toys. 'If I could talk, I would tell you to eat dirt. I want out,' he said with his eyes.

"I'm sorry, Jack. Your safe here. Besides, mom can eat in peace and keep an eye on you. Here. I'll get you a cracker."

I walked back to the kitchen and came back with a couple of saltine crackers. Jack took them with his greedy little hands and immediately placed one in his mouth. He seemed placated for the moment.

"Hurry. Let's eat," Peter said, impatiently. "The food is on the table."

Wandering into the now lovely dining room, he pulled the chairs out for us. "Peter, I didn't know you could be such a gentleman. Mattie, what more could I ask for? In our midst, we have a master chef, nanny, butler, housekeeper, interior decorator, and what do they call someone who takes care of the yard, a yardman?"

"No, Annie, a gardener. Yardman? What's a yardman?" Mattie asked.

"A yardman is the guy who hangs outside the prison doors in a penitentiary," Peter joked. "He watches the convicts. Thank goodness, I've never encountered one. Although if my luck doesn't hold out, it could be sooner than I think."

Mattie ignored his explanation, placing her napkin on her lap. "Enough of this silliness. Here. Take my hand. It's time to say a prayer of thanks and eat this chow."

We all joined hands and Mattie began praying. "Dear Lord, thank you for this heavenly-looking food. Annie and I have finally found us a man with the ability to cook. I know it's through your bounty that I did not die of botulism years ago. More importantly, thank you for sending me two incredibly talented and loving friends to aid me in fulfilling my dreams. Amen."

I noted Peter was missing a wine glass. Evidently he did not drink. He poured the wine into our glasses and picked up his glass of water for a toast.

"Although I'm not any good at prayers, I'd like to say something anyway. You women may be thanking me for the chores I did today, but it's the least I could do. I owe you my life. To Mattie and Annie, the best women connivers I have ever known. May I always get to share in their profound generosity. It is a privilege to sit at this new table and bask in such magnificent beauty."

"Oh, Peter, the table isn't all that glorious." Mattie protested. "But, if you mean us, let me tell you, use all those charming words on Annie. She's the one who needs to listen to them."

"Mattie, I do not. Behave," I scolded, "or you won't be invited to dinner again. Every time we get together and you see a bottle, your mouth won't shut up."

"She needs a man to provide her with some good, flamboyant sex. Show her what a real man can promise her," Mattie said with an evil grin.

I glared at her. "Mattie, please." She glared back.

"Oh, all right. It's none of my business. From here on out, I'll try to behave. I was just beginning to have some fun. Besides, I'm right. You need a few sparks flying to spice up that boring life of yours."

"Mattie, you have provided enough sparks in my life to light up the whole city. Spare me."

"I think you should both shut up and eat," Peter suggested, as he opened the casserole dish. When the steam subsided, I saw tiny corkscrew pastas with chicken and asparagus. Peter put the food on our plate. When I took a bite, there was a refreshing lemon taste to the chicken. Also, he had made a light salad with a sweet vinaigrette dressing. It was delicious.

After finishing the main course, Peter left the table. He returned proudly carrying a key lime pie. Billowing peaks of foamy meringue with slices of lime piled on top. "The dinner was low fat so indulge," Peter said, as he placed the dessert in front of our greedy faces. "Oh, I forgot the coffee."

"I think I could get used to this," I whispered to Mattie. Impressed by its presentation, I took a bite. "Wow. Who needs sex? This is what I call an orgasmic dessert."

"You're right," Mattie agreed, as a heaping mound went into her mouth. "This is wonderful."

Thankfully, the baby had not cried. It was the second hot meal I had eaten in several months.

After dinner, we all took our coffee into the living room where Jack slept peacefully in his playpen. We sat down on the floor next to my new cozy fireplace. Mattie and I were slightly intoxicated. The food, coupled with the warm glow from the flames, resulted in a drowsy feeling of contentment.

"What kind of mother am I?" I asked, glancing toward Jack. "I think he sleeps on the floor or in that playpen more than he sleeps in his bed."

Mattie ignored my silly remark and turned to Peter. "Oh, by the way, the head of the Psych Department called me back. He said he has an opening for a teaching assistant for the spring semester. Do you think you could do it? Don't dawdle. Get your butt over there. It seems you may get the chance to attend school and make a little money, provided you qualify, of course."

Peter grabbed one of the pillows off the couch and laid down. "Where do you find the time? This afternoon, there were at least ten people on your porch waiting for instructions. When I walked inside, there were a half a dozen more. The kids were going through old school books that arrived this morning from a man named Ferdinand, whom everyone suspects is some old boyfriend of yours. Who's Ferdinand, Mattie?"

"Don't you know your history, dear? Ferdinand Magellan. He was a Portuguese navigator who set out on a westward route to the Spice Islands. The poor man was killed in the Philippines. His ship, however, continued sailing and they completed the first circumnavigation of the world. The kids and I looked him up this afternoon. Tomorrow we should get another set of books from someone called Dante. I've been told there's an interesting and imaginary journey through Hell, Purgatory, and Paradise. I'm sure we'll find it fascinating."

"You're too clever for me, Mattie. Next I'll be reading the Divine Comedy myself." Peter said, taking a poker stick and adding another log to the fire.

"There are lots of things you don't know about me, boy. We women have a right to our secrets. Isn't that right, Annie dear?"

"Oh, all right." Peter said, throwing me a blanket to put around my legs. "I won't quarrel with you. I have an interesting book on Sputnik and the space race. Perhaps Neil Armstrong can send your next mysterious package. Forget it! Since you're from another planet, you'd be bored to tears."

Mattie changed her tone of voice to a soft whisper. "I come from a far distant galaxy. They plopped my miserable body on Earth because I did something wicked. It's so wicked I can't even tell my best friends. You see, I have this thing about the opposite sex. I let the men think I'm some helpless female. That's how I manipulate them into doing what I ask."

Mattie looked at her watch and stood up to leave. "I'm sorry, but this story will have to wait. I've got to get out of here. Get some sleep. I need your help tomorrow morning. There's this hole in my ceiling I haven't had time to repair."

Peter went off to find her coat. While he was gone, she whispered in my ear. "I hope you get my drift about that temptation stuff. Since Peter found himself a barber this morning, he simply reeks of masculinity. Not that he didn't before. I just never warmed toward that gang leader/street killer disguise."

"You wouldn't happen to have any voodoo dolls casting spells around me, would you?" I asked. "Men have been acting very strangely." Mattie frowned and said nothing.

Glancing one last time in Peter's direction, she shivered. "He's simply too sexy for my old bones. Oh, to be young again."

She knew what she was insinuating and so did I. Throwing the pillow at her head, she caught it. "One of these days, Mattie, I'm going to get even with you. Hush! I'll handle this in my own way and you keep your nosy butt out of it. Stop pushing me."

Peter came through the door and heard the last sentence. "Stop pushing? Do you mean to tell me sweet, demure Mattie is giving you some friendly advice? Get used to it. Trust me. It comes naturally."

I nodded my head in agreement. "Since the day I met this woman, it's been Meddlesome Mattie. She never gives up."

I got up from the floor spanking her playfully on her bottom. "Oh, well, Miss Meddlesome Mattie, I still love you. I'll see you at the end of this week. I have a grueling schedule at work. If I have a headache tomorrow, I'm blaming it on you. You're turning me into an alcoholic. Thanks for coming, and, more importantly, thank you for my table."

"You're welcome, my dear," she replied, as she headed toward the door.

I adjusted the curtain so that I could watch the two of them together. Peter helped her inside her old, beat-up pickup truck. I could tell she was saying something witty and unbecoming by the way he threw back his head and laughed.

Peter had to slam the truck door hard. The first attempt failed, but on the second attempt, it stayed shut. I didn't want him to catch me spying so I ran back to the living room, placed myself none too gently on the floor, and pretended I had been there all along. Why was I acting like a ridiculous teenager?

Peter locked the door and saw me sitting there. "Oh no, lazy bones," he scolded. "You're supposed to be cleaning up the kitchen. The rule is, whoever cooks gets to sit in front of the fire."

Obligingly, I started to get up. Peter stopped me. "No, I'm only kidding. You look tired. Go take a nice, relaxing bath. I'm on clean-up duty tonight. Just don't expect this kind of treatment every day."

"You're right. I could use a little spoiling." Peter helped me to my feet. I glanced down at Jack. "Do you suppose this child is going to sleep all night? It's my bet somewhere around midnight he's going to want to play."

Peter chuckled. I liked his laugh. It was warm, and masculine. "Go get your well-deserved bath." As he headed for the kitchen, the spoiled woman did as he suggested.

Slowly settling into the tub, my thoughts automatically shifted to my houseguest. Mattie was right. He was extremely handsome. I was glad the barber had merely trimmed his hair. I liked men with long hair and ponytails. I found them sexy. He had a sense of humor, intelligence, and could cook like a master chef. Of course, anyone who could successfully boil water without burning it was a master chef in my mind.

But who was Peter Harrison? In fact, I knew very little about him. He was a mystery man. The prudent side to my nature was sending off the warning signals. Would I listen to it or succumb to his irresistible charm?

I'd be all right. My heart was armed with protective barriers soundly secured. Who was I kidding? Even if I got hurt, the most important thing I'd learned from the horrible ordeal of divorce was my own strength. It's funny, really. I had learned a lot from failure. Maybe it was time to succeed.

Throughout the last several months, I had changed a great deal. For the first time in my life, I had stopped being afraid. I took chances on people, relying on them, even caring for them. Was it Mattie working her special kind of magic or was it Jack, a mother's natural instinct to build roots? Whatever the cause, I was actually making friends.

My spirit had always had this uncanny way of renewing itself. Oh, the fathomless depths of a human soul. I suppose life is a lot like Mattie's garden. You plant a seed and you watch it grow. Then suddenly some big frost comes along and it looks withered and you think it's dead. A rain comes, the sun shines, and it fights to live. Suddenly, a beautiful flower begins to emerge. And like everything else, eventually it dies. But it doesn't really die; instead it hibernates, sending the seeds on their way to a new birth. Maybe that's what will happen in death. Your soul begins a new birth.

Or perhaps it's what happens to you in life. That's what was happening to me. I was like one of those dormant flower bulbs. I was embarking on yet another journey, another place to call home. I laughed at my own inspirational brainstorm. Thanks to Mattie I was well on my way to alcoholism for sure. Maybe I should write a book. It's too bad I didn't have a pencil. I'd write it down and we could laugh about it later.

What do you suppose changed Mattie into this paragon of strength? When I was exposed to adversity as a child, I would scurry right out of the room and cache myself into one of my hiding places. There I would quietly remain until my brother found me or hunger drove me out.

Also, as a child, I was always daydreaming. Similar to what I was doing at this very moment. I'd put myself in a far-off land. Like most girls, inevitably, I became a kidnapped princess or a child mistakenly switched at birth. I would dream up anything to rationalize my parents' hatred. I was always somebody more important, somebody deserving of love. That had always been a large part of my problem. I never felt I deserved love.

Grow up! Don't be such a fool. This self-psychotherapy was boiling down to one thing. Peter. Couldn't I just enjoy my moments with him without getting my head mixed up with fairy-tale endings? Think excitement. Besides, what's wrong with having fun and mixing it with some delicious sex?

Maybe Mattie was right. Seize the moment. If you can't learn to love because you're afraid of being hurt, just have sex with this delicious-looking man. But where do you put the guilt?

Guilt, something my Roman Catholic upbringing liked above all else, penetrating my core of consciousness to rip those all-pervasive dirty thoughts right out of my brain, always, always leaving behind that useless sense of intractable guilt.

I was grown up enough to give up those juvenile beliefs, wasn't I? One thing was for sure. I had a knack for making mistakes where men are concerned.

As I let the warmth of the bath envelop me, I came to only one conclusion. I was a woman who needed to experience love, sex, or lust, whatever you wanted to call it. Mattie was right. Lately, I've been saying that a lot. Pretty soon, it would become an automatic part of my vocabulary. She'd dearly love to hear that. The bottom line is mortal sin was a hell of a lot more tempting than no sin at all. What was wrong with experimenting, letting loose, succumbing to the baser animal instincts flaring up within my female body? At least I was feeling them again. What was I supposed to do? Suppress them? Hogwash and propaganda.

I got up from my bath, and grabbed for a towel. Damn. It wasn't in its usual spot and all the other towels were in the linen closet outside the bathroom. All right, Miss Bravado, what do you do now? Should I get out and make a leaky trail from the bath to the linen closet? Or better yet, should I call Peter to bring me one?

I looked at my naked self through the mist on the mirror. It wasn't all bad. My stomach was flat. My hair was piled on top of my head. Loose tendrils clung to my damp neck. My breasts were firm, yet full. If I yelled, would he find me attractive? He would unquestionably check out a number of my endowments.

I decided it would be best to make the leaky trail. In my present state of mind, the alternative would be much too risky. After all, I was still up for the nunnery-life-of-the-year award and too chicken to change it.

Peter knocked on the door. Embarrassed, I jumped ten feet in the air and quickly sat back down in the tub, sloshing water all over the floor. "Annie, I'm so sorry," he said, as he called through the door. "I washed the towels this morning and I forgot to take them out of the dryer."

The tone of his voice changed to one of wicked pleasure. "Shall I come in and place it around your lovely body, or toss it in to you? It's nice and warm."

I thought to myself, well, girl, are you a chicken...or slut? Chicken or slut? My father's face contorting with anger as he yelled that word to me over and over raced through my memory banks. With a revengeful smile, I decided upon slut.

"Nothing doing, buster. Bring me that towel." Then the chicken in me responded. "Never mind. Close your eyes as you toss it in."

"That's totally unfair," he said plaintively, as he opened the door. Quickly, I shut one eye. Peter inched toward me. Lowering my body further into the tub, I turned a bright shade of red. To hide my fear, I put my head under the water and came up with a mouthful. Playfully, I spat it at him.

Retaliation was not long in coming. Peter, a little more relaxed than I, stood next to the tub and splashed the water back in my face. He wiped his wet shirt with my nice, warm towel. "Is there room for me? If you're not ready for this, I'll turn around and walk out. After all, you've known me for such a long time. It's been at least twenty-four hours, hasn't it?"

He bent down and placed his hand under my chin. "Really, I'm not trying to push. No, that's not true. Women like to hear that. Men are always pushing," he jokingly continued.

"I can't get you out of my head. I want you. As a matter of fact, I'm beginning to believe I need someone like you in my life. This isn't about sex. Well, maybe I'm a liar. It's definitely about lust. Oh, the hell with it. I want to kiss you and I'm making a mess of this."

Planting a firm kiss upon my lips, he said, "God, you take my breath away." Peter knelt down on the floor next to the tub. Our eyes locked. I caught a glimpse of pure seduction.

I was mesmerized by the sheer masculinity of him. Slowly and deliberately, he took off his shirt exposing a sleek, bronze torso. I gazed upon pure, unembellished perfection. Quite shamelessly, I beckoned him toward me.

He placed his hands in the small of my back. Without saying a word he traced his fingers upward and began to slowly massage my neck. Bending forward, he planted light, feathery kisses upon my hair and face.

He stood up and without taking his eyes off me, began to unfasten his pants. My eyes darted toward his mid section. In my half-drunken state, my senses were keenly alert. My body craved for his touch. Smiling seductively, he bent down and lifted one of my legs out of the water and began to gradually massage my foot. Thoroughly relaxed, he inched listlessly downward toward my inner thigh. There he began to rub me slowly and provocatively.

Gradually he lowered himself into the bathtub. Beginning with my shoulders, he squeezed the washcloth letting the water trickle across the nape of my neck and down my breasts. Closing my eyes, I felt his fingers along the sides of my temples. In small languid circles, he slowly began his massage of them. I raised my head and he moved his hands to the upper portion of my back.

My skin was on fire. My heart began to race. He moved methodically to my breasts, toying with them first lightly, at other times squeezing them more earnestly. Deliberately and meticulously he moved his mouth lightly upon my lips. He pressed harder. Obligingly, I opened my mouth so that his tongue could enter. It was as if he were sucking the breath out of me.

Exhilarated and slightly breathless, I wanted more. When I looked at him, I was magnetically drawn to his flesh. I moved toward him so that my breasts could touch his chest. Instantly my body was being transfixed with his, filling me with unimaginable depths. I felt myself floating, as if encountering one spirit, as if our bodies had become one soul in the universe.

A baby's cry shattered the spell. I opened my eyes as reality jolted its way back into the room. I struggled to find composure. "Are you going to get that or shall I?" I asked.

Peter's devilishly handsome grin lit his face. "I'm off duty," he replied. "As you just pointed out, he is your baby, and, lady, you've had your bath. I'll just lie back and watch that fabulous body of yours rise and exit the tub. I'll also try not to be too remorseful. I know there's a heaven after all."

Feeling a little embarrassed, but eager to play his game, I raised myself out of the tub. "For your entertainment, I'll make my exit in true Mata Hari form," I said, as I attempted to effectuate an exotic dancer. Wrapping the towel around my body, I shook my hips as I walked. Placing my hand on the door handle, I bowed, looking over at Peter to see if he was still watching. With his hands folded behind his head, his pleasure was written on his face. Smiling seductively, I did my best Mae West imitation. "See you later, lover boy."

As I closed the door, the self-effacing woman returned. My smile vanished. What on earth was I doing? Was I totally insane?

For Christ-sake, the man was a stranger, a damn gorgeous stranger at that. Annie, my dear, get a grip.

When I entered the living room, Jack stopped crying. Tonight I was lacking my usual enthusiasm toward mothering. "It's all your fault. Were it not for you, your sweet Mama would be halfway to the moon right now or at least in blissful space." As I rocked him, of all nights, he refused to fall back to sleep.

"Come on, Jack, you shouldn't be doing this to your poor mama." It took about forty-five minutes for those eyes to drop shut. Tiptoeing upstairs, I gently placed him in his crib and quietly left the room.

I took a deep breath and went to find Peter. I assumed he would be in my room. To my surprise, no one was there. Lying on the bed was a handwritten note.

I smiled as I read it. "Dear Annie: You're an intriguing woman. Perhaps you're a witch and I'm caught under your spell; at the very least a miracle. Sweetheart, whenever you're ready, you know where to find me. Please make it soon. I can't wait to thoroughly explore your stupendous body and hear you scream with pleasure. But for now, my dear, I will leave you with tonight's delicious remembrance. Your humble handyman, Peter."

For the first time in my life, I crawled into bed totally nude. Should I call him back to my room, or was the anticipation just as satisfying? 'Tomorrow is another day.' Could I endure the wait?

"Oh yes, tomorrow, my dear Peter. Beware, it is I who am captivated by you," I murmured as I relaxed, drifting into a dream-filled sleep.

C H A P T E R
XIV

Peter wasn't in my house when I got up the next morning. I didn't know whether to feel relieved or disappointed. One thing for sure, single parenting was again my fate.

I quickly fed the baby, arranged the diaper bag gear in its proper place, took a shower, washing my hair and blowing it dry. I grabbed my clothes out of the closet. Naturally, I had to iron the skirt, find my pantyhose, and throw on a little makeup. First I carried the diaper bag and my brief case with my laptop computer out to the car. I came back, wrapped Jack in a blanket and carried him to the car.

A light rain started falling. It was one of those gloomy, foggy mornings. I drove carefully hoping my tires gripped the road. They needed to be replaced, but I didn't have the money.

When I dropped Jack off at the baby-sitters, he immediately began to cry. Why was he crying? You'd think I was leaving him at a Gestapo headquarters or something. I was the one heading to work, not him, and believe me sometimes it seemed there were a lot of similarities to Gestapo headquarters.

"I'm sorry, Jack. I have to go." I blew him a kiss and waved good-bye. I have come to the conclusion that we women are an amazing breed of marathon runners. Surprise. I was late for work.

This morning I had an appointment with Lee Roberts and Joseph Gibbons. They were the two black males who Benjamin Goldstein suspected were Paula Jennings' rapists. I found them on time and sitting in the waiting room. I motioned them to follow me back.

Their suppression hearing was scheduled for that afternoon. They took a seat in the chairs next to my desk. We spent the morning going over the facts in the case and preparing for cross-examination.

Lee Roberts was the smarter of the two. He was nineteen years of age, tall and slender. As if the rest of his face had not yet received its adult growth, he had tiny black hairs on the bottom of his chin. He also had a tattoo of a star and a spider web on his right arm.

In the secret society of gangs, a tattoo usually represented status or a membership to a particular group. The one star usually meant he was not of the upper echelon. He was probably a runner or a sentry who carried out the menial tasks for the older gang members who had five stars. Five-star generals yielded extreme power and could order an execution the way the Mafia did in the early '50s. Rodney Thomas, now dead, had been such a character.

Lee Roberts had a history of drug abuse and several juvenile arrests, but so far his adult record only consisted of a couple of misdemeanors for spray painting graffiti on walls. He was lucky. Most of his family members were already serving time.

Graffiti was another way gangs communicated with each other. The symbols portrayed in the graffiti usually were written in their gang colors and could signify a number of things, turf, rivalries, the current state of gang affairs, drug supplies, and any other significant information.

Joseph Gibbons was another story entirely. He was twenty-two years old. He had on a black T-shirt and a pair of black jeans, even though I had told him to wear something conservative. He had a couple of stars tattooed on his arm. He looked like your run-of-the-mill street gang bully who carried a nine millimeter semi-automatic in his hip pocket and would kill without batting an eye.

His criminal history put him in the career offender category. He was 6'5" and extremely muscular. He had light-colored skin and brown eyes; eyes that gave me the sense he would decapitate your head and send you down river if he were instructed. He was extremely volatile, prone to fits of temper. If he wasn't yet, he would one day be a very dangerous young man.

Someone had bailed him out to the tune of $50,000. I was still puzzled why I was his counsel. Previously he had represented to the court the money had been collected from his family and the retainer fee for a lawyer could not be met. If they could afford to pay the bail, you'd think they could hire him a lawyer.

I had a job to do which was to give him the best representation in my power to provide, even if he scared the living daylights out of me and sent shivers down my spine.

That afternoon, my clients and I entered the courtroom. Benjamin Goldstein was already sitting at the prosecutor's table. He gave a pompous nod to acknowledge my presence. His face bore the usual self-righteous expression born from years of sending criminals to jail.

The judge entered the courtroom through his chamber door. The clerk hit the gavel and told us to rise. Judge Harold McNally was nicknamed "Harold the Horrible." He was an experienced trial judge with a keen knowledge of the law.

If you weren't prepared in his courtroom, he would bark and snap, then politely humiliate you in front of your clients and colleagues. I was prepared, but sweating. He seemed in good humor. Thank goodness he had eaten his noon meal.

This was my first encounter with Harold the Horrible. Despite my trepidation, I was looking forward to it. I had not prepared a scripted presentation. Other attorneys had warned me in advance that after hearing the evidence, he would fire excessive questions at you until you were exhausted. When, and if he was satisfied with the answers, he would rule from the bench.

The clerk immediately called the case. We stated our names for the court reporter. I had what lawyers call "the laboring oar," which meant I would present my evidence first.

After moving to exclude witnesses from the courtroom, I called my first witness, Robert Taylor. He approached the bench, raised his right hand, and was sworn. After he took a seat on the witness chair, the following colloquy took place:

"State your name for the record, please."

"Robert Taylor."

"Officer Taylor, what is your occupation?"

"City police officer for two years assigned to the DEA Task Force." He moved the microphone closer to his mouth and smiled at the court reporter.

"Officer Taylor, I would like to direct your attention to the evening of September 20th of last year. Were you on duty that evening?"

"Yes, I was."

"What were you driving?"

"I was driving an unmarked police car."

"Were you on patrol with another officer?"

"Yes, Officer Evans was riding patrol with me."

"I would like to direct your attention now to approximately 12:30 in the morning. Did you see two individuals leaving a convenience store?"

"Yes, I did."

"Please tell us what you saw."

"I saw two black males, recognized by Officer Evans to be gang members, exiting the convenience store and driving away in a blue Mazda."

"What happened next?"

"We followed them."

"What did you say to Officer Evans?"

"Nothing. I didn't have to say anything. He wanted to follow them, too."

"Did anything happen earlier that evening that would arouse an interest in these two black males?"

"Yes. Earlier that evening, Officer Evans and I were called to the scene via radio dispatch directing us to 1007 E. Clayburn, Apt. 3. A woman had called 911 stating she had been beaten and raped. We responded to the call, along with several other detectives. We were the first to arrive."

"What happened next?"

"We checked the building for armed suspects. We could hear the conversation through our radios. We knew the victim was alone and needed assistance. We busted the door to the apartment open. Upon entering, we observed a young woman lying face down on the floor next to the phone. She was naked and covered in blood. The flesh on her back had been torn to shreds. Her breathing was labored. We treated the wounds as best we could by applying pressure and waited for the paramedics to arrive."

"Did the woman say anything to you?"

"We tried to talk to her. She was incoherent at first. She said two men had come in through a window. She thought they were two black males."

"So she did indicate the color of their skin?"

"Yes, ma'am. She was in a lot of pain and quite hysterical. It was impossible to comprehend what else she was saying."

"What happened next?"

"Basically, the paramedics and detectives arrived and we were ordered to return to our patrol car and circle the area to check for anything unusual."

"After you saw the two black males exit the convenience store, did you have occasion to stop the blue Mazda?"

"Yes, we did."

"Why did you stop the blue Mazda?"

"We felt we had two suspects who matched the description Miss Jennings described earlier. Officer Evans and I radioed dispatch for backup."

I approached Officer Taylor and handed him an exhibit.

"Officer Taylor, I'm handing you Defendant's Exhibit 1. Will you tell the court what this is?"

"This is a copy of my police report."

"Please read it into the record."

"The driver of the vehicle rolled to a stop, inching forward across the crosswalk."

"So you were planning on stopping the vehicle before they rolled to a stop?"

"Yes, ma'am."

"What did you do next?"

"Once they failed to stop, we felt we had probable cause so we turned on the bar lights. The Mazda pulled over and stopped."

"Where did this occur? What street?"

"At Second and Monroe."

"Once you stopped the Mazda, please tell us what happened?"

"I pulled my vehicle directly behind the blue Mazda. A couple of seconds later, another patrol car positioned itself directly in front of the Mazda. Exiting my vehicle, I pulled out my revolver."

"Why did you do that?"

"It's standard procedure. I was concerned for my protection and that of the other officers."

"Did you observe the patrol officers in front of the Mazda

pull out their revolvers as well?"

"I'm not sure, but they probably did."

"Would you say immediately upon exiting the patrol car your gun was drawn?"

"Absolutely."

"Did you say anything to the occupants of the Mazda?"

"I ordered the two occupants to exit the vehicle."

"What did you say verbatim?"

" I told them to exit the car with their hands up, to lay on the ground with their legs spread."

"Did they comply with your orders?"

"No, not right away. I saw them talking to each other. Officer Douglas and Officer Lee moved closer to the vehicle. They, too, directed the occupants in the Mazda to come out with their hands up."

"What happened next?"

"Joseph Gibbons and Lee Roberts opened the car doors with their hands up. While on the ground, we asked them if they had any weapons."

"What did they respond?"

"They both said no."

"Did you then search the two individuals?"

"Yes. I patted Lee Roberts down, found no gun or contraband. Officer Douglas patted Joseph Gibbons down and found nothing."

"Did you conduct the search of the Mazda?"

"Yes. We handcuffed the defendants and placed them in the squad car. I asked Gibbons if it would be all right if I conducted a search of his vehicle. He was reluctant at first, then told us to go ahead. A couple of minutes after that, we found a nine millimeter pistol under the driver's seat and a .38 caliber pistol on the passenger side floorboard where Lee Roberts was sitting."

"Miss Stevens, I have heard enough," the judge said, sternly. "I have a few questions I would like to ask Mr. Goldstein."

"Of course, Your Honor. But I'm not finished with Officer Taylor."

"That won't be necessary." Judge McNally turned his attention toward Goldstein. "Mr. Goldstein, this motion raises a single issue: Were Gibbons and Roberts arrested without probable cause? When do you contend that Gibbons and Roberts were deprived of their freedom to leave the scene?"

Mr. Goldstein approached the podium and put down his file. "Your Honor, it is the State's position that once Gibbons failed to properly stop at the stop sign, he violated the law."

Judge McNally cleared his throat, interrupting Goldstein who had failed to answer his question. "I've also read the motions that have been proffered and the transcript from the preliminary hearing before Judge Parker. Both defendants state they made a complete stop behind the stop sign and then proceeded to make sure they were clear of traffic before making a right turn.

"Officer Taylor is not sure whether they rolled through the stop sign or stopped and moved forward. Of course, I will grant you that at one o'clock in the morning the chances of the road being busy are slim."

Goldstein wiped his brow. "That's correct, Your Honor," he said, relieved to discover the judge understood his position quite well. Goldstein glared at me and smiled. He thought he had it won. I started to pack up the file.

Judge McNally took a law book out of his revolving bookshelf behind his bench and opened it. As he quietly read, nothing was said by either party.

"It boils down to this: The facts cannot add up to probable cause unless they show the probability of criminal activity. These police officers had just come from a horrific scene. They were upset, too hasty in their pursuit to find the perpetrators of this crime. There is a fair amount of judicial precedent to be found which is directed to the question of how probable it must appear that criminal conduct is occurring. It is commonly said, 'an arrest and search based on events as consistent with innocent as with criminal activity are unlawful, so that if the observed pattern of events occurs just as frequently, or even more than frequently in innocent transactions, the pattern is too equivocal to form the basis for such a warrantless arrest."

Goldstein, realizing he was about to lose, sat down. The judge continued his reading.

"The totality of the circumstances here makes it far from likely that the subjects had committed a crime. The violation would have been a traffic violation at best, treated like a felony and this was a full-fledged arrest. There was no right of detention. It is my opinion that the warrantless arrest of Gibbons and Roberts was without probable cause." Judge McNally looked at Goldstein.

"As you know, Mr. Goldstein, an arrest is a profound and deeply resented interference with the liberty of the person, and to allow police to arrest people on anything less than a high degree of suspicion would restrict personal liberty more than has been thought justified by the needs of public security."

I turned toward my clients and gave them the thumbs-up signal underneath my desk. They both let out a sigh of relief.

"For the violation of the defendants' Fourth Amendment right to be free from unreasonable seizures, the defendants' motion to suppress is granted. Lee Roberts' statement at the time of the arrest is also suppressed. Court's in recess."

The judge quickly left the bench without giving anyone a chance to respond.

Benjamin Goldstein stood up, gave me a murderous stare, and angrily left the courtroom. My two clients had big smiles on their faces. Both put their arms around my waist and hugged me. With mixed emotions, I hugged them back.

Victory felt good, but, at the same time, there was a certain amount of remorse in knowing they would be back on the streets living among their other gang members and terrorizing someone else. I quickly dismissed the unwelcome thought.

Joseph Gibbons reached into his pocket and handed me a small plastic jar with a white bow on the top. At the same time, Lee Roberts pulled a similar bottle from his jacket pocket. I looked at them both puzzled, my face betraying my uncertainty.

"Here, Miss Stevens, do with this what you want," he said, putting the jar in my hand. "I didn't rape that Jennings girl, nor did Roberts here. I don't give a damn what that pig Goldstein thinks, but I care what you think. You're all right for a woman attorney. You've treated us like folks."

Joseph placed his hand in mine and shook it. "Don't get me wrong. I'm a bad ass, but even we got our pride. We don't rat on each other and we respect one another. Today, I respect you. I know you believe what that prosecutor says about me, but you did your job."

Joseph knelt down, as if in prayer, and placed his lips upon the floor at my feet. I turned several shades of red. "Thank you, Lord, for my freedom. It's a relief to know I'm not goin' to prison. I've been there, ya know. I'll probably still end up there, but not today, thanks to you." He got up, yanked a couple of small strands of his hair from the top of his head, placed it on the table, and slowly sauntered away.

Lee Roberts placed the jar on the table next to Joseph's. He looked me sheepishly in the eye and smiled. "Thanks." He also pulled a piece of hair from the top of his head.

"See ya, Miss Stevens," they said waving good-bye.

"I hope not, gentlemen," I replied.

They nodded their heads and silently turned and walked out the courtroom door. Collecting my books and papers, I said to myself, 'I'll be damned. They didn't do it.'

Triumphantly, I left the now quiet room and marched down the hall to the State's Attorney's Office. The receptionist, Margaret, pressed the buzzer. "May I help you?" she asked. The phone rang. I walked past her counter and ignored her. As I approached his door, Goldstein was running his hand through his hair. I could hear the clatter of the receptionist's shoes on the floor behind me. She was still trying to catch up.

"Miss Stevens, you can't just barge your way in here," she said, irritated by my lack of respect.

Goldstein could hear her petty protests which drew his attention to the doorway. He looked up just as I was entering.

He reluctantly motioned his hand to the chair in front of his desk. "It's all right, Margaret. Sit down, Anne."

"Sir, I tried to stop her," she replied in a huff. "I'm terribly sorry." She continued to mutter under her breath as she walked away.

"If you've come here to gloat, please leave. Believe me, I've had enough for one day."

Goldstein, obviously upset, pulled open his bottom desk drawer. Without waiting for my response, he placed a Jack Daniels bottle with two paper cups on top of his desk. He twisted the cap on the bottle.

"Let's celebrate, Anne, dear," he said, with bitter sarcasm. "What shall we toast to? How about the shitty jobs we both have? Or, better yet, perhaps to the next victim Gibbons and Roberts decide to knock off, or pardon me, possibly knock up."

I ignored his crude remarks and picked up the paper cup. "Oh, I don't know. Let's toast to this! I don't know why I should make you feel any better, but I have a little present for you." Placing the small plastic jars and the hair samples on his table, I downed the bitter liquid in one huge gulp.

His bushy brows raised a couple of inches in surprise. I was enjoying the puzzled look he gave me.

"For your information, they didn't rape Paula Jennings. I know I should let you wallow in your self pity, but I can't. It's my way of relieving my own conscience. You see, I thought they did it, too. This job is full of surprises, isn't it?"

Goldstein loosened his tie, unbuttoned his collar, and poured himself another cup. This time he didn't ask me to join him. He swallowed hard.

"It's a good feeling, isn't it? My first, actually. Every now and again I get to win one." I said, enjoying his discomfort. "The system works. We did our jobs. Those cops followed my two clients for one reason. Oh, don't give me that look. I know they had a couple of guns. Who wouldn't? Look at where they live and tell me you wouldn't carry a piece in your own pocket."

Goldstein shook his head, poured the amber liquid into his cup, and, once again, took another swig. "You're learning, Anne. I appreciate those little presents, too. Unfortunately, it just makes my job more difficult. They'll never find them, you know. Whoever did this will do it again. They wanted it to hurt. They meant to rip her back like it was a raw piece of meat."

Goldstein abruptly changed the subject. "Speaking of surprises, I hear you and Mattie Turner are close friends. She's a one-of-a-kind lady. I've always admired her."

"You're right" I said, surprised he'd know her. "How can a bum like you know a lady like her?"

Goldstein ignored my question. He was going to enlighten me when he was ready. He was toying with me. I attempted to change the subject.

"The people in her neighborhood are starting to listen to her, too. If you would spend more time and money on the children who desperately need help, this county wouldn't be needing new jails."

"That's not what I was referring to." He watched me closely. "You don't know, do you? I had the pleasure of meeting Miss Turner in the hospital."

I tried to conceal the surprised expression on my face. I wasn't fooling him for a minute.

"How well do you know her?" he asked, reaching for a file. "The Mattie I knew wouldn't walk out the door of her house for over two years. Even her groceries were delivered by a store clerk."

Goldstein shook his head. "Damn, you should have seen her yard. It looked like something out of a Herman Munster film. You'd think a witch lived there. The kids would walk on the other side of the street just to avoid her house. I couldn't blame them. I knocked on her door a couple of times myself. Always gave me the creeps."

I placed the Gibson file on my lap to hide my feelings and lied. "She's still unable to talk about it."

Goldstein knew he had my full attention and relished the fact. "She would never say who almost killed her. One of her neighbors reported the crime to the police. Mattie survived many stab wounds to the mid-region of her chest. It was a total miracle. One of the stab wounds collapsed a lung. You should see the pictures. It's amazing the abuse her body took. She was one of my first felony cases. I went to talk to her in the hospital. Her face was entirely black and blue. I can't imagine what the scar tissue must be like on her back today. Those bastards drew some type of vicious-looking picture up and down her entire backside. God knows what it was. Sounds familiar, doesn't it? She's stuck with that mark for the rest of her life. Incredible. You give my regards to her, will you, Anne?"

I attempted to disguise my shock. As casually as I could, I turned to leave. Before I reached the door handle, he stood up and grabbed my arm.

"Oh, one more thing. You know, the funny thing is I suspect she knows who did it, but I could never get her to say. In fact, the MO is similar to that of the Jennings girl. Hmm, very interesting. See you later."

He turned back to his desk and opened a file drawer. "Do you want to see it? I think I still have her file in here somewhere. Here it is." He pulled a picture out of the folder. I turned my back on him, refusing to look. Goldstein continued to examine the picture.

"Oh, if there is anything I can do to help, let me know. Perhaps I could take a few of those deadbeats off the street for her." Goldstein shut the file and put it on his desk.

I clenched my fist trying to hold back my temper. "Find another life. This one has thoroughly corrupted your brain," I said, holding tightly to the door handle. "Come see for yourself what kind of deadbeats these kids are. Maybe your cynical attitude would change. Of course, that's only when you find out you still have a compassionate bone in your body."

I walked down the hallway and out the door. Surely he was not talking about the same Mattie I knew? Unbelievable. She was a tower of strength. I always knew there was something driving her, some inner strength. Impossible. Mattie, I think I've finally figured you out. But why haven't you told me?

Returning to my office, I dropped the Roberts and Gibbons case on my desk. Word spread fast. My associates had already heard the good news. After a few congratulatory pats on the back, I left the office while there was still light, picked up Jack, and headed for Mattie's.

When I arrived, I found her deep in discussion with the young boy called Buddy. They were pulling vegetables from her garden. She was patiently explaining why carrots from a garden taste better than from the grocery store.

As I watched, Mattie caught a glimpse of me. Waving, she

yelled, "Oh, Annie. This is a nice surprise. I thought you were swamped at work. A little early to be getting off, isn't it? Oh, and I see you brought Jack. Good. I don't need you. I need him. I concocted this recipe with fresh herbs and vegetables from the last of my garden. Don't look so surprised. Sometimes a leopard must change its spots. This stuff looks a little like brown pea soup. I was hoping I could use Jack and a couple of the other kids as guinea pigs. The older ones like Buddy here refuse to try it."

Mattie waved, bent down to pull another green thing out of the ground. "Go on into the house. I'll be finished here in a moment. There's a fresh pitcher of lemonade in the refrigerator."

The woman never stopped talking. I turned my back on her and headed toward the house. I could still hear her giving specific instructions, something about the vegetables that are left over from the first frost. I guess carrots and potatoes last a little longer. Got me.

I placed Jack in the high chair, pulled the pitcher of lemonade from the refrigerator, and gave him a small sip. He liked the taste. He gave the grunt signal for more. After quenching his greedy thirst, I walked toward the window and glanced out.

After a cloudy morning, the weather had abruptly changed. It was one of those beautiful autumn days. I think they call it Indian summer. My adrenaline was finally slowing down and no longer pumping in high gear from my win this afternoon.

Dismayed by her lack of trust in me, I tried not to feel too betrayed. She was my best friend and I loved her. What are you afraid of, Mattie Turner?

While I was still lost in thought, she arrived in the kitchen and placed her basket of carrots and potatoes on the counter. The kitchen smelled of baking bread.

"Mattie, what's that smell coming out of your oven? Don't tell me you've finally learned to use that heretofore unnecessary appliance."

Smiling at my joke, she placed the dirty vegetables in the sink and turned on the water. "No, of course not. You know me better than that. It's Peter. I know he shouldn't be here, but you know how that goes. He's been here baking bread, canning vegetables, and cooking that roast you are now smelling. The kids will be surprised tonight."

"Oh, no, Ms. Turner." I scolded. "He is supposed to do that at *my* house. I knew we would come to fisticuffs one day. You tell Peter to march his butt right back to where he belongs."

Mattie, smiled triumphantly, quite pleased with herself. "So you're jealous, are you? Interesting development for the woman who cried wolf the other night. You kind of like having him around, do ya? Well, my dear, you're going to have to learn to share. He's mine. I found him first."

At that moment, Peter walked through the swinging door. "What's going on here? Are you two she-bears fighting over little ol' me?" he asked, as he pulled up a kitchen stool. "I'll just sit and watch. Come on, Mattie; give her a good right punch. Oh, and, Annie, since I know how your right punch feels, try and temper it a little bit," he said, as he began to rub his face.

Mattie stood there in a true boxing-style stance, moving quickly on her feet and giving me the old one-two. Responding to her enthusiasm, I pretended to punch her back with my right just as Peter had suggested.

Before I could get the punch out in full swing, Peter grabbed me around the waist and placed me on his lap. "I've got her, Mattie. Now give her a good wallop."

I unsuccessfully attempted to free myself from Peter's hold. "Be careful! Not only can she fight, but also she has this nasty way of worming her way into your heart. The choice is definitely a tough one."

I became quite self-conscious sitting on his lap so I bolted in retreat. Not fast enough for Mattie, however, to have gained a new insight into our relationship. "I see," she said with a knowing smile. "So there is a little sexual tension in the air. Well, well, well, Peter, I think the lady doth protest too much."

Peter ignored us and went to get the kids. I walked over to the high chair, where Jack was busy eating a saltine cracker. "Oh, my God, look." Fearing Jack had been hurt, Mattie walked over to the baby's chair and tried to figure out what I was worried about. Not understanding the problem, she gave me a puzzled expression.

"Jack has his first tooth," I pointed it out with concern in my voice. "Oh, no, another tragic milestone in the world of mothering. Damn. Why does he have to have teeth anyway? He looks adorably cute without them. Next he'll want to go out on a date or something. Mattie, we've got to start working on that time machine. I can't bear to see this baby growing up."

Mattie walked over to the oven. "Well, honey, let's eat and then we'll get to work on that time machine. I could sure use a few less wrinkles. Do you suppose I could turn it back thirty years? I'd give you a run for your money. Instead of looking like dear old grandmama, I could be your rotten, devious friend and steal Peter right out from under your nose."

"I like you just the way you are, thank you," I said, pretending to be shocked by her outrageous statement. "Grandmama is fine with me. God forbid you were thirty years younger. I have a hard enough time keeping up with you now."

A great roar came from the hall landing. "The children have escaped their confinement, and we are not ready for dinner," Mattie cried. "Hurry. Get to work."

Jason and Peter entered the doorway first, followed by about a half dozen other kids. "We're starved. What's for dinner?"

Mattie began to scold them. "You kids get your hands washed and get a plate. God forbid we have starving children in this house."

Jason directed them back to the bathroom. A couple of other ladies entered the kitchen to help with the preparations for the evening meal. The table had been previously set. Since it looked like I was in the way, I picked up the baby. Mattie gave me one of those you-are-not-about-to-leave looks so I stayed for dinner. After all, my cook was at her house.

Peter washed his hands at the sink and mumbled something about going somewhere with Jason. The kids ate their dinner and settled in the living room with a new videotape. While I fed the baby mashed potatoes and brown pea soup, Mattie cleaned up the dirty dishes.

"I heard some disturbing news today and I want to get it off my chest." Instinctively, Mattie sat down across the kitchen table from me. "I knew there was something bothering you the moment I set eyes on you. Okay. Lay it on me. If this is about you and Peter, stop your worrying. Believe me, he's a terrific human being, although he has one demerit: He's a man. You could look far and hard, honey, and never find a man with the goodness he has inside. Every time I look at him all I can think about is yummy."

I tried not to join in her fanciful mood, but I couldn't help myself. "Mattie, stop it. This is not about Peter. Although, your 'yummy' remark is just a little off. It's more like thoroughly delectable and incredibly enticing. He's definitely like an unlimited delicatessen. Everything in the store looks and smells seductive, but it's deadly for my constitution."

Mattie laughed. "Whoa, girl! What about all of that crap you gave me the other night?" She attempted to mimic my voice. "I don't need another man in my life. I don't need sex. Being a nun is just fine with me."

"Don't worry," I said, giving her a gentle tap on the shoulder. "I'm in control. I figure I'll keep him around as my sex slave. As long as I call the shots, he can stay with me until I'm tired of him. After that, poof, gone."

I placed my hand upon my heart. "I'm going to live that creed we discussed the other night. From here on out, this heart is made of steel. Sex, lovely delicious sex, now that I think I can handle. You're to blame, you know. You're turning me into some Jezebel."

Mattie was about to say something. I stopped her. "Don't look so surprised," I said, hitting her with the dish rag. "I'm finally coming around to your way of thinking."

Mattie stacked the wet dishes on the counter. "Yeah, you're some Jezebel all right. Methinks she speaks with big mouth. I've heard everything. Haven't you learned by now you should never listen to me. I've been full of it since the day I was born. You can say all you want about no love and just sex, but I'm here to tell you that's not the way it works. You see, we women just aren't built that way. Haven't you heard? We wear our hearts on our sleeves."

Emptying the water out of the sink, Mattie showed me her arms. "See here. I never could figure out where that old expression came from, but when you think about it, I suppose it makes sense. A woman is a natural born mother whether she has kids or not. I figure we use those sleeves everyday of our lives."

I shook my head to deny her theory. "I think it's supposed to mean we women show our emotions more readily. Anyway, I disagree with you. I had a mother, remember? She hated me."

Mattie gave me the evil eye for interrupting. "I've met your mother. She doesn't hate you. The two of you could use a psychiatrist, perhaps a trip to therapy sessions to clear out the old baggage, but she still cares about you. "

"Oh, no, she doesn't. I don't want to talk about it. Let's change the subject, shall we? Go ahead. Explain your sleeve story. It's on safer ground."

She threw another dry towel at me. Taking her subtle hint, I got up and dried a pot from the rack. "The other day Kisha came into this kitchen and said, 'Mattie, Janelle took my baby and won't give it back.' So I handed it to Kisha. Then Janelle started crying and said that she had it first and it wasn't Kisha's. So I just took the doll from both of them."

Mattie used the plate to demonstrate her behavior. "I placed the doll in my arms and pretended to rock it to sleep. Both girls put their arms around each other and cried. Puzzled by their behavior, I gave the kids a lecture on sharing. Instead of being angry with each other, they kept huddling together. It suddenly dawned on me they were afraid of me. I broke the spell by laughing and holding out my arms. Eventually they came to me.

"Those poor kids, Annie. The only thing they need in this world is someone to love them. Kisha's parents are in jail. Her seventeen-year-old sister couldn't take care of her anymore. When she arrived, she was such a quiet little thing, scared to death. Then she found out she had her own bed. You would have thought I'd given her a trip to Disneyland the way her face lit up. She told me she'd been sleeping on a blanket on the floor. The kid arrived with the filthy clothes on her back. That was it."

I put the stacked dishes in the cupboard. "Hell, Janelle wasn't much better off," Mattie said as she handed me another pot to dry. "Her mama's a dope head. Her father's in some rehab center, trying to clean up. He came by and dumped her at my front step. I never even saw his face. I guess they'd been sleeping in his car. Janelle told me her daddy was coming back. For hours, that poor little girl sat there and waited for him. It almost broke my heart to see her so hurt. He did have sense enough to call and tell me where he was. Hopefully, he'll get the help he needs to raise her properly."

"What about the sleeves? You're totally confusing me."

"I'm getting there. Back to this sleeve story. These old

sleeves went right around those two sweet girls just as they were meant to do. So, you see, it's true. Women do wear their hearts on their sleeves. It's just a common, ordinary occurrence. And what a mighty power that is, too."

I put my arms around her and gave her a squeeze. "You know what? I kind of like these old sleeves, too." I said, proudly.

"So, what's your point?" I asked, forgetting the main topic that started this long-winded story. "You're nuts. I don't know where this is leading. You have me thoroughly baffled."

"Honey, don't you see? You've taken the first step. Once those sleeves go around that man of yours, you're in for the long haul."

"You know, you're probably right. I should forget about Peter. My arms should remain solely planted around my son's where they belong. You certainly have cheered me up. I think. Now is not the time to bother you about that other topic. Besides, I'm tired. You look tired, too. Go get some sleep."

Removing Jack from the kitchen floor, I bundled him up and headed for the door. "You're not off the hook yet. We'll have that little discussion another day."

As an afterthought, I turned back to say one more thing. "You're larger than life. I think you have that one figured out, too. It's been fun. See ya."

Mattie smiled and waved good-bye. Driving home, I thought to myself. "What would I do without her?" I was right. She was larger than life. Once you thought you knew everything there was to know about her, boom, she would pop another facet right out of the stone. Perhaps she was an alien from outer space. If she is, I'm heading straight for that planet. It was too bad the world was not made up of a million Matties.

CHAPTER
XV

As soon as I put Baby Jack down for the night, Mr. Delicatessen, I mean Peter's body hovered in the doorway.

"Annie, come with me," he said, in a hoarse whisper. "I have a surprise for you."

Reaching the middle landing to the stairs, I stopped. "Please, Peter, how many more surprises do you think one can take? I'm surprised out for the week. Between the minor assault in the basement, Mattie's best-kept secrets, the new dining room table, my home changed to something like House Beautiful, warm towels, the yard work completed for the fall, I can't imagine what else could possibly be left to surprise me."

"Come. I'll race you to the living room." I pushed him aside and beat him by at least a quarter of a second. At first, I didn't see any changes. A fire was glowing in the fireplace. I gave him a puzzled look. Peter said one word. "This." As he turned on the light switch, the room underwent a complete metamorphosis.

Peter didn't use candles all around the room like something you would read in a traditional romance novel. Nor were there any flowers in sight. Instead, he had created flowers and waterfalls by reflecting the light off of natural objects around the room. The fire's amber light contrasted radiantly with the green and blue hues, transforming the room into a thousand pools of colored light.

When I say "colored light," I mean fiber optic strands twisted, flexed, and adjusted to focus in a broad and narrow band across the walls. The strands had been manipulated to accentuate the flowing beauty of waterfalls.

My mouth stopped working, and I was uncharacteristically immobile. Having paid no heed to Peter, I was startled when the music began to play. If I was being seduced, he had not chosen your regular run-of-the-mill tunes. He had chosen Bette Midler. It was actually one of my favorite songs, not what I would generally consider a romantic-seducer type. It was a plain song with a very simple message called, 'That's the Story of Love.'

Peter smiled beguilingly. He moved toward me, never taking his eyes off my face. In a motion consistent with the music, he circled his arms around my body as we danced. He was a good dancer. His strength could be felt in the muscles on his back. I rubbed my body against his, enjoying the friction. No words were spoken. I could see desire written in his eyes.

Holding me, he lowered his head and placed tiny, light kisses at the nape of my neck. Slowly and deliberately, I moved my head back to seek his lips. His tongue began to tantalize my own tongue; and, as if in unison, the smooth moistness of our lips began to merge.

The music changed to that of Kenny G and Aaron Neville, 'Even if My Heart Would Break.' His touch became firmer and the pressure on my lips more challenging.

Establishing a rhythm, I moved my hands slowly and provocatively down his chest. I wanted to feel him. Opening two or three buttons, I placed tiny kisses on the warm hairs of his muscular body. I wanted him closer. His hands found their way to the back of my blouse. I withdrew from him. With one swift motion I raised my arms above my head and pulled the blouse over my head. He sighed.

The flat of his chest against my breasts left my skin warm.

The multicolored lights radiated off our bodies. My breasts molded to his chest. I ran my fingers down his chest while he lay perfectly still on his back. His hands massaged the side of one breast.

I closed my eyes and felt him gently move me to the floor. His tongue began to trace the contours of my torso, slowly and then more swiftly, his hands moving down between my legs opening for his touch. His tongue began to probe. Inflaming sensations pulsated through my body as he began licking me, at first gently stroking and then sucking harder.

I raised my arms to reach for him. My thighs were hot. I felt a larger need for him than his tongue could provide. I couldn't breathe. Imposing myself upon him, I rolled him over so that he could come inside me. Slow, rhythmic responses burst forth at first, then the pace became more fervid.

Each stroke sent me to the edge of a precipice, only to be brought back as if unattainable, and then to the edge, again and again. Exploding in unison, it was as if the universe had spilled forth a million particles of light not unlike the waterfalls of light reflected in the room.

Content to be entwined in his arms, several minutes passed in silence. "Where did you get the lights?" I asked, as I turned on my stomach to admire the room.

He crawled over my body, kissing my neck. "My younger brother is in the business. He thinks that fiber optics will eventually be in every home come the new millennium. Surrounding us are the byproducts of his labors. Mattie kindly stored them in her basement.

"Do you really want to talk about this? Jason helped me carry the boxes here. Of course, he had no idea what was in them. I knew you would be pleasantly surprised. Besides, I couldn't afford a couple of hundred candles and dozens of flowers. So, my dear, what do you think? Should we leave them here or take them down?"

I turned my head to gaze upon the room instead of the gorgeous man next to me. "Tell your brother he's right. Elizabeth Barrett Browning once wrote, 'Light tomorrow with today.' Do you think that's what we did tonight, Peter? Will all of our tomorrows be like it was today?"

Peter kissed me on the lips and responded. "Oh, God, I hope so." Chuckling, he said, "Although I do believe I would surely die a much younger man."

* * *

Aroused by the sunlight streaming into the room, I slowly opened my eyes. The birds were chirping outside my window. A large, richly colored brown arm was draped across my body. It felt irresistibly wicked to see the contrast of dark against white skin. I thought of my question to Mattie the night of our foray into alcoholism. "Well, Mattie, you did it. Now I'm a nymphomaniac. Do you suppose I should try it on an Asian next week? Sorry, I'm not interested. He's mine and he's all I want."

A vengeful smile made its way across my face. I relished the fact that my father would roll over in his grave if he could see me now. I thought back to my life as a child. What a sanctimonious bigot he was. He would consider this wrong, a sinful act.

Unfortunately, there were too many other people in the world who would still think the same way. Most everyone in today's society still looked upon a mixed-race couple with derision.

Peter opened his eyes and caught me staring at him. When he was fully conscious, a slow smile crept across his face. "What time is it?"

"Who cares," I replied, thoroughly content. Stretching and yawning, I placed my arms around his neck and my head upon his chest. "Oh, Peter, let's spend the entire morning like we did last night. The hell with work. For the first time in my life, I want to stay home. Oh, God, I'm so happy. How many days in one's lifetime do you suppose you spend like this?"

Grinning like all smug men with their male ego still intact, he kissed me on the forehead. "Not many. I take it my lady has no complaints."

Placing a kiss upon his chest, I moaned. "Oh, yes. One – no two. I'm tired and a little too sore. I've been living like a nun. Why I must be practically a virgin." I rolled off his body and looked up at the ceiling. "Speaking of nuns, do you suppose they have sexual fantasies with God?"

Peter chuckled. "Where on earth does that mind of yours take you? I can't say. I've never known a nun."

"I'll bet you haven't," I said in total agreement. Peter ignored the comment.

"I would assume nuns and priests are just like us. We're all prone to sin. Only they get to cleanse their soul. I wish it were that simple," he said under his breath.

"So do I," I said with a complete understanding of his meaning. I wasn't ready to think about that now. "Maybe you're a warlock and you've given me a magic potion. I can't get enough of you. I'm completely insatiable."

I crawled on top, my lips following my hands. "Right now all I can think about is putting you right back where you belong. Hold me, Peter. There's only one minor detail. I've been ravaged, and I don't think my inner parts could handle the impact. Don't worry, it won't take long to be fully operational."

Peter grabbed my arm and pulled me towards him, kissing me hard upon my swollen lips. "You better be operational soon, woman.

I swell up just looking at you. If I'm a warlock, then you're a witch. You've turned me into a complete madman."

He caressed my naked back. It felt so warm and comfortable. Like a cat, I wanted to purr. Instead, I nestled closer, kissing his neck.

"No, I retract that statement," he said taking a deep breath. "You're an angel, and I think I have found the secret path to heaven."

He held me tightly in his arms for several more minutes. We were still on the makeshift bed in the living room. Breaking the bond, Peter stood up, grabbed my hands, and helped me to my feet. "I don't know about you, but I'm starving. If we're not going to do it again, I need to get away from you. Unless, of course, you need someone to wash your back. In that case, I will have my breakfast in the shower."

As tempting as it sounded, someone on the monitor made himself known to the world. Without being asked, Peter headed for the kitchen to warm a bottle. Still naked, I ran up the stairs to find my bathrobe and get Jack.

Changing the baby's diaper, I thought about last night and the question I had posed to Peter. In your lifetime, how many days do you suppose a human being gets to feel like this? For the first time in my life, I could honestly say I felt happy. I told Peter I was tired. That wasn't the truth. I was actually exhilarated. Something new and incredibly spiritual had happened.

I let my guard down and trusted someone, not just to satisfy my lust, but something more was happening, something rare. I wanted to feel this way forever. God, did it feel good to live.

Deep down I had no right to feel this way. Because of me, my brother was in a cold grave six feet under; because of me, he'd never get the chance to fall in love, to touch another person's soul as Peter had touched mine.

"I don't suppose he could use a shower, too?" Peter asked,

sneaking up behind me.   As he handed me the bottle, he saw my shoulders sag. "It's all right. If I have to share you with someone, it might as well be him," he replied misconstruing my lack of response.

Jack looked at Peter, grinned and reached for the bottle. I don't think it was the bath he was anticipating. The total opposite of what his mother was wanting.

An hour or so later, we were both fully clothed and ready for work. So much for calling in sick. Peter couldn't stay home. He had an appointment with the assistant dean of the psychology department.

Pushing the guilt to the back of my mind, I drove to the baby-sitter's house with a new perspective. The trees, the sky, and even the leaves all seemed brighter, cleaner, like I was looking through a kaleidoscope into a different world, a world with rose-colored glasses.

* * *

The morning went smoothly, but the afternoon's appointments were dull and dragging. My mind wasn't on the job. I did everything I could to keep from leaving early. As soon as the clock struck five, I was out the door.

Peter heard the car pull into the driveway. As if we couldn't wait to be near each other, he came running out the door. He picked me up, swirling me around the yard.

"Oh, Annie, what a glorious day. Do we have some celebrating to do or what? You're looking at a man with a job. Dean Edwards is some old school chum of Mattie's. He was sufficiently impressed with my transcript and wants me to start right away. What more in my life could go right?"

After kissing me a couple of times, he put me down. He held me until we reached the side of the car where Baby Jack was sitting in the back seat. After retrieving him, he danced with the baby into the kitchen.

Following close behind, I smelled that delicious aroma again. I thought to myself, "Too bad, Mattie. Tonight I'm not sharing. He's mine."

As if we were a real family, we spent the evening celebrating our newfound happiness; and, of course, the new job. When we finally put Baby Jack in his bed, we giggled as we raced to the bedroom door. I had impatiently waited all day for this moment.

As fast as we could, we ditched the clothes and got under the sheets. Feeling like a child at Christmas, I couldn't wait to get my hands on his body. We hit the bed at the same time. "Annie, I..." The words died on his lips as he watched me undress. "I hope to hell you're operational again. I've been dying to...damn, come here."

He took me into his arms and tightly squeezed my naked body. Without uttering another word, a shiver ripped through me, touching every nerve, responding to his heat. I showed him how insatiable my own appetite was. Our bodies had no trouble discovering each other again. Similar to the night before, exhausted, we fell asleep in each other's arms.

* * *

Somewhere in the middle of the night, the telephone rang. Peter groped for the phone, knocking it to the ground. It was a woman named Tamara. She was a new volunteer at Mattie's. She was incoherent and upset. From what Peter could understand of the message, there was an accident. The police were there, and it was still unclear if anyone was hurt.

Flying out of bed, we threw on a pair of sweats, grabbed Jack, and headed for the door.

Once at Mattie's, it was evident something was indeed wrong. Every light in the house was lit. An ambulance and several police cars were parked outside. Peter bolted out of the car and hit the front door about two hundred feet before I did. Walking across the porch, I noticed broken shards of glass from one of the east windows lying on the cement floor. A police officer was bending down holding a flashlight, possibly looking for bullet remains.

Taking a deep breath, I rushed into the house. Mattie was sitting on a chair with an ice pack on her ankle and a bunch of people hovering around her. Thank God she was all right. A couple of police officers had their pen and pads open.

Peter rushed to her side. Mattie seemed more frustrated than hurt. She ignored the police and looked at us. "What are you two doing here?" She asked, in a griping voice. "Out with it, who called you?" No one responded. "Snitches! You're all a bunch of snitches."

Mattie was putting on a brave face. "I'm okay. Will you people please stop making such a fuss over me? I'm getting claustrophobic. Mind the children. Everybody else out of here. Go back to bed!"

Before Jack was fully alert, I took him into the quiet room with the playpen and placed him on his side. He settled in comfortably and went back to sleep.

Thanks to Peter, most of the kids were being comforted by at least one adult, and the chaos in the room was settling down. "What the hell happened here?" Peter asked. Except for Mattie, everyone began to talk at once. Peter stopped their banter by, once again, taking control. "Hold it!" he said, pointing his finger at Mattie. "I want to hear from you."

She gave him an exasperated look and dropped the ice pack on the floor. Attempting to get up, the pain that shot through her ankle put her right back in the chair. Everyone scrambled to help her retrieve it.

"All right. I'll tell you if you'll all back off. You're suffocating me." The crowd moved back a couple of feet.

"It wasn't much really," she said, placing the ice pack back on her ankle. "I was outside walking Michelle and Buddy to the gate. Out of the corner of my eye I spotted a white van across the street. I thought it looked suspicious. They're not supposed to park there, you know. It's a no parking zone. Then it hit me. White van!"

My heart skipped a beat or two when I heard those words. Peter glanced in my direction with a concerned look on his face.

"Before the side panel door opened, I sprang across the sidewalk and knocked Buddy and Michelle to the ground. Bullets were sprayed around the three of us and across the windows in the front of the house. They took off before I got a chance to see their faces. That's it. Now, I wish you would all go back to bed," she complained.

The children, with the adults holding them, began to do what she asked. Miraculously, no one had been hurt. Whether it was intended as a scare or was an unsuccessful hit wasn't clear. However, it was without a doubt an unbelievably scary and heroic effort on Mattie's part.

I looked over at Michelle who was being treated for some superficial wounds on her elbows and knees. Her eyes caught me staring at them. Except for the fear you saw in Buddy's eyes, he appeared unscathed. He was a brave kid, this kid who asked a million questions. So brave.

Michelle smiled back, softening the hard lines around her face. A strange sense of well-being entered my subconscious. She lifted her head to give her son a comforting hand. We were kindred spirits, she and I, raising our sons alone.

One of the police officers recognized me from the Public Defender's Office. Shaking off the feeling of *deja vu*, he beckoned me toward him and whispered in my ear. "Miss Stevens, I think you need to take Miss Turner to the hospital. That ankle of hers is looking pretty swollen and there is a good possibility it's broken. I know she says she wants to be left alone, but I wouldn't listen to her. She's certainly putting on a good front for them."

I moved over to Mattie's chair and examined the ankle for myself. It was bruised and swollen. The police officer was right. She needed to see a doctor.

Peter and Jason were having their own private conversation over in the corner. I motioned for his assistance. He took the hint and approached.

"Mattie, before you say anything, shut up. You're going to the hospital," I said with authority.

Bending over her, I whispered in her ear. "Peter is going to pick you up and carry your butt out of here."

Mattie started to protest. "Not another word. It's for your own good."

She gave me a look that said, 'Get out of my life.' Placing my fingers on her lips, I stopped her. "No, don't say it. For once, don't open that mouth. You're going. Now, say good-bye." Mattie pretended to bite my finger off.

Peter picked her up and whisked her out the door. I glanced at the worried faces around the room. "It's okay, everybody. She's going to be fine. I promise. You'll see her in the morning. You all go back to bed now. There's nothing else we can do tonight."

Tamara was sitting on the couch holding a baby. "Tamara, will you take care of Jack, please? I'll be back as soon as I can."

"No problem," she said. "You go. Mattie needs you. I'll put

this one down in a little while. He's such a cuddly thing. That's why I like it here. Lots of kids to love on."

She was right. Once again approaching the kids in their little people pajamas, I bent my head to their level and whispered in their ears, "Don't worry. Mattie's going to be all right. I promise. We have to take her to the hospital because I think her ankle is broken. By tomorrow morning, she'll be hollering for her breakfast. They'll fix that leg of hers right up." I patted one of them on the head and kept talking.

"Will you guys do me a favor?" The children all nodded in unison. "Will you cook her a very special breakfast and make her a couple of get-well cards? She'll love it. Will you do that for her?" The children grudgingly shook their heads. They weren't keen on her leaving even if for a little while.

By the time I reached the door, Mattie was comfortably tucked away in the back seat. She gave me a sulking look and said nothing as I got in the car. The silence was not long enough.

Closer to the hospital, her nagging began. "I'm fine. Really. I can move my ankle. See. It's not broken. It just hurts a little." You could tell she was lying by the pain in her voice. We ignored her.

"Hello? Does anyone ever listen to me? Damn it, take me back. I don't want to go! I hate doctors."

The rest of the way to the hospital we turned a deaf ear. A couple of hours later, the doctor told us she had a fracture of the right fibula. Placing a makeshift cast on her ankle that ran up her leg, they gave her some pain medication and told us to bring her back in a couple of days. After the swelling went down, they would put her in a permanent cast.

We sat silently all the way home from the hospital. Peter carried her upstairs and placed her on her bed. After he left the room, I began to help her undress. She seemed uncomfortable and mortified at the prospect. I knew why.

To ease her embarrassment, I ignored the scars on her back. I quickly helped her put on her nightgown, then headed for the door.

Mattie, surprised that I was walking away without a comment, yelled, "Annie, are you blind? Get back here."

Trying to act nonchalantly, I was unable to mask the horror I felt. The mutilation wreaked by the brutal treatment she had received at the hands of those horrible sick monsters filled me with despair.

With tears welling in my eyes, I turned back into the room and threw my arms around her. Without saying anything more, we held each other for a very long time. When we had expended enough tears to fill her bed with water, I stood up, grabbed for the tissues on the table, and handed her one. We blew in unison and laughed at our silly behavior.

"Oh, Mattie, now I know you're from another planet. No one could have survived those wounds except for an alien," I jokingly cried.

Peter knocked on the door. Without waiting for a reply, he opened the door. "What's taking you so long? I checked on Jack, and he's still asleep. It sounds to me like you're having a party without me."

It didn't take him long to come to the conclusion this was not your ordinary party. He saw two women sitting on the bed with tears on their faces and tissues in their hands.

"What's wrong?" he asked joining us near the bed. "Damn you, Mattie. You could have been shot. Should I beat on your chest the way you beat on mine the other night?"

As he pretended to cry, Peter took the Kleenex box from my hand. We laughed. "It's not funny. This is serious," I said.

Blowing her nose, Mattie shook her head and changed the subject. "Isn't life peculiar? Do you ever wonder what crazy trick of fate brought the three of us numbskulls together? Obviously, there must be some reason! Predestined, perhaps? Can't you feel the connection?"

Mattie shook her head and waved her arms. "You guys go home. I think these pain killers are making me delusional," she said rolling over to smother her laughter with a pillow.

"Come on, Mattie, it's not funny." Peter said more seriously. He sat down and took a seat next to me. "I want you safe and sound on this earth not some hereafter. You're not a young woman. You've passed the courage test too many times. Your luck will eventually run out, you know."

Peter caught Mattie's baleful glare. "Where have I heard that before?" she asked. "Sounds like a broken record."

Peter ignored her and continued to scold. "You've been lucky. These little mishaps occur out there all the time. A broken fibula is no big deal. Next it'll be your head."

Mattie's eyes grew dark, revealing her suppressed anger. "This little thing that occurred tonight was more than a little mishap. Damn you, Peter. You men are all alike. I've been saying this to you for years. Don't worry about me. I can handle the pressure. You really don't know me, do you? You think you do, but you don't. Nobody does."

She raised her pajama top and turned her back to reveal her shame. "Take a look! Take a damn hard look at what I've faced and tell me I don't have the scars to prove it."

The knife that had torn her flesh would remain forever a prominent part of her life, a constant reminder of the insanity of people.

Mattie lowered her head as she put her top back in place. "I don't know what's gotten into me. They left more scars inside my head than on my back. Would you call that a little mishap, too?" Peter's stunned silence answered her question.

"Men and their causes," Mattie said changing the subject. "For some strange reason, it's always a contest with your species. Women are made to suffer in silence."

I didn't think that was true, but who was going to argue with her. Not me. Peter started to protest, then changed his mind heading for the door.

"Don't leave mad," she said, patting the bed indicating he should come over and sit next to her. "I'm sorry. I'm picking on you. It's just that I've been listening to your complaints for quite a while now. Your father never loved you. You raised your brother and your sisters alone with no one to help care for them and no one to care for you. It's like a broken record in self-pity. Do you know what really gets to me, Peter? You're rich! Damn you. So rich."

To demonstrate her point, Mattie picked up the phone. "At least once a week this telephone rings. It's some brother or sister calling to check on you. Like me, they worry, too. In fact, my basement is filled with your stuff, gifts from them, nieces' and nephews' pictures. There's a picture of his sister, LeAnn's graduation from Dartmouth. His other sister, Kenzie, graduated from Princeton. Did you know he has a brother who graduated from MIT with his degree in electrical engineering?" She asked, looking at me.

Of course, I knew. His fiber optics were still in my living room. Mattie missed the smile Peter gave me.

"Unbelievable, isn't it? I know it's just a bunch of worthless objects, but at the same time it's your treasure trove, and it contains volumes about you."

Mattie's demeanor changed from anger to complacency. "You ought to go down there and see it for yourself, Annie. I've spent most of my life alone in the sense of not trusting others, no family to turn to. You're a gift, Peter, my special gift. You're the one who has opened my eyes and taught me to live again, given me something to care about," she said with pride in her voice. "You're my source of strength."

Peter ignored the compliment and immediately went on the defensive. "That didn't come without driving them, Mattie, and you know it. I was only thirteen when my mother died. I pushed them to study. I made them work, and work hard. The funny thing is I would have sold my soul for their scholarships. You're right. They're successful, and damn proud I am, too."

No longer able to sit, Peter got off the bed, pacing back and forth. He stopped for a moment and grew solemn. "Isn't it funny?" he said, with regret in his voice. "It's damn hilarious when you think about it. The idiot who taught them the escape route is the one who fucked up. Hooked on my own crack. I blew it. I have to live with that fact every day of my life."

Peter leaned toward Mattie and whispered, "The same way you have to live with those scars on your back. My shame will always go a lot deeper than yours."

He came over and reached for my hand. I looked directly into his eyes. "I once had a teacher who told me 'Fall seven times, get up eight.' It's not good to beat yourself up like this, Peter. We all make mistakes."

One of his arms slipped around my shoulders as he turned back toward Mattie. "In that case, I've fallen at least a thousand times. It's true. I'm one lucky man. If I didn't know it two days ago, I do now. I want a new life, one with a roof over my head that belongs to me. There will be no self-pity from here on out, Mattie. You're right. I've got a job like the rest of my family, and a mighty fine woman to go with it," he said, kissing my cheek.

Mattie's left eye raised a notch or two above the other. She was immediately suspicious. "So I've heard about your job. Big deal. I want the scoop on your sex life. What's been going on?" Mattie asked, demanding an explanation.

Ignoring her, he whispered in my ear. "Who said anything about sex? You're not as bright as you think you are, Miss Mattie. I think I'm in love."

It was the first time I had heard him say it. A mixture of apprehension and pleasure filled my senses. Did he really mean what he'd just said? Was it possible to have a future with this complicated man?

Peter pulled the covers over Mattie's chest, then pulled me off her bed. "Now, unless you have any other nonsensical lectures to spout off, we need to go to bed."

Totally unsatisfied, Mattie shoved the covers aside. "I knew it. Well, I'll be damned. It sure didn't take you long to woo Sister Annie here. I'm damned proud of you, son."

Strictly for her benefit, Peter winked at Mattie, walked over to me, and gave me a long searing kiss. "She was an easy kill," he whispered in my ear. "One look at my body, and she was putty in my arms."

"Ignore him," I said, winking back at her. Pushing him toward the door, I muttered, "You, sir, could use some heavy duty ego-bashing."

"Who are you kidding?" he asked, quietly turning the door knob. "I've taken all the criticism I can for one day."

"Don't worry, Mattie, dear. I'll keep you in suspense at least until tomorrow, and then I'll give you all the sleazy details. See you later."

"You ingrate," Mattie yelled. "Come back here. You can't leave the word 'sleazy' hanging in the air without telling a poor old woman something."

I stuck my head back into her room. "Shh, Mattie, you'll wake the kids." I whispered as I waved good-bye.

Peter gave Mattie the thumbs up sign as he switched off the light.

CHAPTER
XVI

Between the night of insatiable lovemaking and last night's fiasco, I was exhausted. I called my office and told them I was sick. It was true. I felt like a Mack truck had hit me. Responding to Jack's lusty cry for breakfast, I gingerly moved my aching body toward his room. Halfway into the hall, Peter bumped into me carrying a warm bottle. Too tired to protest, I hobbled back to bed and slept another three hours.

It was close to noon when my eyes adjusted to the light. Still pitifully worn out, I went to the bathroom, took a couple of aspirins and showered. Peter appeared just as I stuck my head under the nozzle. Without opening my eyes, I leaned into his body. My arms went automatically around his strong back.

"Where is Jack? Did you check on Mattie? Did the police catch the guys who did this?"

Peter ignored my battery of questions and soaped my chest. "First things first." I was in love with this man's body. That's all I could think about as I abandoned myself to his hot passionate kisses.

"Jack is at the babysitter's. Mattie is sleeping like some other dead woman I know. The police haven't found the van, and, no, they haven't been caught. They probably never will. Is there anything else I can do for you? I'm available to wash your body, whatever you desire, Milady. I'm at your service."

Let's say I was languidly awakened by nature's appealing call. Still feeling heavy as lead, we went to the bedroom and fell asleep in each other's arms. I awoke with the late afternoon sun shining in my face.

I glanced at Peter who was still sound asleep. As surreptitiously as I could, I tiptoed out of the room with my clothes. Stretching, I looked at myself in the mirror. Knowing what a hopeless cause it was to look like anything other than a haunting bad dream, I dressed quickly, put my wild hair in a ponytail and left the house.

The first thing I noticed was Benjamin Goldstein's car as I pulled into Mattie's driveway. Taking two steps at a time, I headed for the kitchen door. In fact, I was in such a mad rush, I ran smack dab into the odious fellow on her back porch steps.

"Slow down, girl," he said attempting to steady us both. "We've got to stop meeting like this."

He scrutinized my face as he held me too closely. "Is that you, Anne? At least I think it's you. With no makeup and your hair pulled back, you look like a little girl. Are you sure you're old enough to play at being an attorney? When I get back, I'm going to check your license."

Not finding his sense of humor amusing, I pushed him away wishing I could take another bath. The smell of his cologne was enough to gag me. "Oh, shut up. I didn't get any sleep last night so I stayed home. Why am I telling you this? It's none of your business. What are you doing here? It's generally not your part of town."

Goldstein brushed the dust off the front of his jacket. Perhaps he was as much repulsed by my touch as I was his. Finally, he answered my question.

"I heard there was a little excitement here last night. I was worried about Mattie; so I decided to check on her."

Opening the screen door, I walked into the kitchen not buying his petty explanation for a second. "Come on, Goldstein. That's a cock-and-bull story if I've ever heard one. And from you I hear them all the time in court."

The back of Goldstein's hair raised a notch or two. He hated women with smart mouths. I, of course, knew that and loved to watch his eyebrows wrinkle with disdain. He reminded me of a bulldog.

"Why are you really here?" I asked, demanding an explanation. "Did you come to do a little investigative work on your own? I hope you're out doing the job you're paid to do. Find the jerks who did this last night, will you?"

Goldstein placed his hands on his heart and feigned innocence. "Stevens, I'm insulted. There are a couple of humane bones left in this mean prosecutor's body. If you would take the time to get to know me better, you would find that out. I'm not the big bad wolf, although it's uncanny. With a blonde wig, you could pose as Miss Goldie Locks."

Mattie hobbled into the room on her new crutches. "Annie, I was told Benjamin was here. They never said anything about you."

I helped her into the chair, pulled up another one alongside to prop her leg. She grimaced but didn't say anything as I carefully got her settled. Taking a good look at her face, I saw dark circles under her eyes. Her skin was pale and drawn. Like me, she wore no makeup, and her hair was haphazardly tied in a rubber band at the nape of her neck.

Benjamin Goldstein pulled up a chair and sat down. "You two must have had it pretty hard last night. You, Mattie, could be a witch. It's funny, Stevens. I know I made some joke about your appearance earlier, but, honestly, I've never seen the two of you look so disheveled."

With my angry eyes looking directly into his face, Goldstein cleared his throat. "You sure know how to win friends and influence people," I said, looking for a pen and a sheet of paper. Opening a kitchen drawer I came up with a couple of straight pins and some cloth. Maybe I could make a quick voodoo doll that would send this jerk on his merry way.

Mattie placed her finger in front of her nose to keep from sneezing. "You're the same nasty little prosecutor I remember, smell the same, too." We both laughed.

Goldstein fumbled with his tie and once again cleared his throat. "I apologize," he said with no remorse in his voice. "I'm only joking. You both could use some sense of humor pills. You're a brave woman, Mattie. Encountering what you did last night would have sent me into an apoplectic seizure."

With a piece of paper and a pen, I sat down to take some notes. "Say what you really came here to say, Goldstein, and leave," I said. He was right about one thing. I wasn't in the mood.

Goldstein noted my impatience and reached for his briefcase. "Stevens, where are your manners? Could I at least have a cup of coffee?"

"That goes double for me," Mattie said. "Since you so demurely judged our appearance, I think we could all use a cup."

He pulled a file from his briefcase and placed a thick manila folder in front of him. I passed him his coffee and poured cream in Mattie's. I placed her cup in front of her and settled in the chair across from Goldstein.

I caught a glimpse of the name on the folder. Puzzled, I listened as he spoke. "Mattie, I don't know if Anne said anything to you, but after our hearing in the courtroom the other day, we had a heart-to-heart talk. I knew the two of you had become good friends and felt I was on safe ground to divulge some of the facts surrounding the circumstances in your case."

Mattie was looking down at her hands. I could tell she was quite uncomfortable at the prospect of discussing this.

"Get to the point, Benjamin," she said clearing her throat. "What do you want? I've told you a thousand times I can't help you." Closing her eyes, she took a deep breath. "Get this straight. There's nothing more I can add. I couldn't see their faces. They wore masks. One was evil and sadistic, the other was obviously doing his master's bidding. Don't you think if I could identify them I would want those devils off the street as much as you do?"

Goldstein fidgeted with his pen. "Yes, Mattie," he said. "I didn't come here to rehash old memories. I'll get to the point. Since Anne's clients are no longer suspects, I pulled your file. The MOs are the same. Mattie, what I have in front of you is the Jennings file. Take a look at the scars on the victim's back.

Mattie reluctantly looked at the pictures. It was as if she had seen a ghost. Without saying a word, she handed the file back to him.

Goldstein comfortably leaned back in his chair, leaving the file exposed. He knew it would arouse our feelings of contempt. How could he so matter-of-factly toy with Mattie's emotions? The raw, red flesh of Paula Jennings' back made you want to flinch from the horror of it.

"You saw the similarities right away, didn't you? Whoever did this to you is out there again. We have to find them. Is there anything -- anything that has come back to you in the past year or so that you haven't told me about? A subtle nuance about the men, their voice inflection, the color of their eyes, anything? I could sure use your help."

Placing her hands on her forehead, Mattie took a deep breath and hesitated. She leaned closer to Goldstein's face and whispered. "I'm sorry, Ben. I can't remember."

Goldstein, at last defeated, collected the pictures and placed the file back in his briefcase. He shook his head and took a last swig of his coffee.

"Is it that you can't help me or you won't?" he asked, knowing he wasn't going to get the answers he sought.

Annoyed by what Goldstein had implied, Mattie slammed her fist on the table. "Get out! No one accuses me of lying."

"I'm sorry, Mattie. That was uncalled for," he said turning the door knob. "If you think of anything, be sure to pass it on. Oh, one other thing. I know it's a lot to ask, but before Anne throws me out of here, could you talk to Paula Jennings? She's on the fifth floor at the Presbyterian Hospital. Like you, she's too afraid to talk. The medical staff has tried everything. You'd like her. It's enough what those bastards did to her body, but what they do to the mind is an entirely different matter, isn't it?"

Goldstein finally left. Realizing I had parked behind him, I shrugged my shoulders and followed him. "You never give up, do you? Just who do you think you are? Leave her alone or I'll..."

"Do what, Stevens? Think before you open your mouth."

"Can't you stop being Mr. Prosecutor for one second and take a look at her. She's suffering. They branded her for life. If you don't stop..."

Benjamin put his finger to my mouth. "What are you going to do? Whip me? Go right ahead. I might enjoy it."

I clenched my fist and suppressed the desire to kick him in the groin. "You remind me of a tenacious little pit bull. Learn to show people respect or you'll end up a lonely miserable bastard with nothing to love in your life except for your own reflection. Sound familiar?"

Goldstein got in the car and rolled down the window. "I'm not the ass you think I am. I've got a job to do and I do it well. 'Let us have faith that right makes might; and in faith let us to the end dare to do our duty as we understand it.' Abraham Lincoln."

"'Love the sin. Hate the sinner.' Mohandes Ghandi," I retorted, trying not to kick his precious car. I backed my own out of the driveway, moving it out of his way.

Slamming the kitchen door harder than intending, I stormed over to Mattie's side. "I'm sorry. I didn't mean to shut the door so hard."

She was too engrossed in thought. "I hadn't noticed. The kids bang it shut like that all the time."

I took a sip of the now cold coffee. "That moron brings the worst out in me. I should have told you about him when I was here for supper. Goldstein told me about your – what do I call it? Unfortunate incident doesn't sound right."

"I've never been able to put it into words, so why should you?" Mattie was rubbing her swollen ankle and eyeing me with amusement. "It's one of those subjects people have trouble with. Me, in particular."

"We were having so much fun the other night it seemed a shame to spoil it; so I left without saying anything. You do believe me, don't you?"

Mattie was lost in her own world. She gave me a queer look. "What are you talking about? Why would I be mad at you? This subject isn't something you bring up at a supper table. Perhaps we should. Maybe that's been my problem. Maybe Ben's right. I think I'll go and see that Jennings girl after all."

She looked suspiciously around the room then bent over to whisper in my ear. "Annie, I need to talk to you, but I can't do it here. Damn this leg."

Thinking swiftly, I yelled for one of the volunteers. I heard Tamara's heavy footsteps coming through the dining room. As she entered the kitchen, I could tell the effort left her winded.

"Sorry I've been wrestling with the kids," she said as she wiped the sweat off her brow.

"Tamara, I need your help," I whispered. Do you think everyone could manage without Mattie for a few days? It's so noisy and chaotic around here, I think it would do her some good to come home with me. She looks awful. She's not getting any sleep."

Tamara studied Mattie's face and nodded her head. I knew Mattie would protest so I left them there, ran upstairs to pack a small bag.

I heard the children in the other room. I opened the door and sat down on one of their beds. Six scared and unhappy children stared back at me.

"Why is it every time I walk in this room, you all look at me with those beautiful brown eyes of yours and wonder what this monster woman wants now? I'm not here to hurt you. I'm your friend.. I came in to tell you I'm going to take Mattie home with me."

They started to protest. "Shh, it will be all right. Tamara and the others will take care of you."

They were not convinced, but oddly accepting. I guess they were used to loved ones going in and out of their lives.

"It'll be okay. Nothing is wrong with her that a few good nights' sleep won't cure. She'll be back on Sunday night. I promise. Until she returns, will you do me a favor? You are my big guys. Can I count on you? I'll even bring back a special treat. How about something sweet and gooey? Truly, Mattie loves you but she needs to get some rest."

One little girl started to cry. "I don't want her to leave. We can take care of her." The other children nodded in agreement.

"Really, she's going to be fine, Phoebe." I gave the little girl a hug. She was so sweet. She loved to hug people. "Will you go downstairs and give her a great big kiss and tell her you're going to miss her?"

The boys jumped up and headed for the kitchen. The girls

reluctantly followed. They beat me by a couple of seconds. Mattie was surrounded by at least a half dozen people. She was still protesting she didn't want to go. Tamara took control. What a friend she was becoming.

"You shut your mouth, Mattie. You need your rest. It's a fact you ain't goin' to be resting here. Now get on out of here and let me mind the house. We can go a couple of days without you."

No one paid any heed to Mattie's objections. They all kissed or hugged her. Jason picked her up and carried her out to the car.

As I backed down the driveway, I could see at least twenty kids waving good-bye. Mattie waved back with tears in her eyes.

"Why did you have to go and do that?" she asked, in an irritated voice. "I don't want to go to your house. I belong in my own bed. Who is going to run this place? At this moment, I would like to ring your scrawny little neck. We could have found somewhere in my house to talk."

Ignoring her, I continued to drive. "Once in a while someone has to take care of you," I replied with irritation in my voice, too. "Did you look in the mirror this morning? You look like hell. You're not a young chick anymore. Anyway, I knew you weren't going to get much sleep, and what you need most right now is some rest. Besides, it will do you some good to get out of there. Plus it's safer. What if you are the target?"

Mattie looked sullenly out the window while I changed the subject. "Hey, don't you remember what I have at home? I have this cooking mad man. Besides, you can talk all you want about my scrawny neck. You could use a little fattening up."

In my haste to leave Mattie's house, I forgot one very important aspect of my own life. Pulling into the drive, I hit my fist on the steering wheel. "Damn. I forgot Jack. Let me go in and get Peter. I don't think I'm going to win any mother-of-the-year awards. What kind of a lousy mother forgets her own son?"

"The same idiot that kidnaps her friend," Mattie replied as I got out of the car. Once inside, I hollered for Peter. The house was empty. I found a note on the kitchen table. Evidently the baby-sitter had called him, and he left to get Jack.

Sprinting back to the car, Mattie was attempting to maneuver her butt out of the passenger seat. Wasn't there anything to keep that woman down? I grabbed her arm a little too brusquely and she immediately complained.

"Let go of my arm. I'm better off doing this myself," she said, slapping my hand away.

"Can't you wait ten seconds? Are you trying to break the other leg?" I asked.

"I'm not an invalid," she barked. "I can take care of myself." Ignoring her misguided attitude, I took her arm and helped her into the house.

With difficulty, we made it to the couch. I helped her settle in by lifting her ankle. "It's cold in here," she grumbled. I quickly handed her a blanket.

"We need a fire." I noticed the paper sitting on top of the dining room table. Mattie's picture was on the front page. Surprised, I tossed it to her. "You're a celebrity. Check this out."

Mattie studied her picture. "It's definitely not my best side." It was a picture of Mattie sitting in her chair at home. I hadn't noticed the news media there last night. Several children with concerned looks on their faces were hovering around her.

I took it from her hands to examine the picture. "Well, they caught the pose I see most often. As usual, your mouth is wide open."

"That's because I'm the smartest one in the room." We both laughed.

"Why don't you read it out loud while I light the fire?" We were both shivering. It wasn't bitterly cold, but it was cold enough to leave your jacket on.

I piled the logs up around an old newspaper and found the matches on the mantel. A couple of seconds later, smoke engulfed the room.

"Damn, Annie," Mattie said, waving the newspaper back and forth choking, "What the hell are you trying to do, asphyxiate us? I'm sorry, child. I don't think I can read this article."

I took another newspaper and attempted to blow it out. Of course that made it worse.

"Stop fanning it," Mattie demanded. "Let me give you some practical advice."

She started to cough as the smoke alarm in the kitchen went off. In frustration, she yelled, "Damn it. Open a window." Frantic, I did as she asked.

"Now try to smother it. Throw another log over it or something." Again, I did what she suggested. There was still smoke, but it lessened a little. "Now, quick, open the flue."

"What's a flue?" I asked, totally confused.

"You have a graduate degree, and you're asking me what's a flue?" she muttered loudly and rolled her eyes.

"You're not helping!" I said, kicking the logs.

"I can't. I'm an invalid, remember." I ignored her smart aleck remark and headed for the kitchen, grabbing an oven mitt.

"For your information, Miss Know-it-All, I've never owned a house much less a fireplace." Then I turned on the sink and filled a water glass. I ran back into the room, throwing the water on the fire.

"That wasn't smart," Mattie grumbled, struggling to get off the couch as more smoke engulfed the room.

"At least if I'm to meet my maker, I'll die laughing." I took a hold of Mattie's arm, helping her to her feet. "A flue, my dear, is the only way the smoke can flow out of the house. It escapes up the pipe, allowing us to breathe in here.   When you are not using a chimney, you shut the flue," she said, wobbling toward the smoke.

Peter came bursting into the house obviously having heard the alarm. "What on earth is going on in here?" he asked, quickly grabbing the poker from my hand. He knocked the logs onto the hearth, bent down, and reached in back of the fireplace and opened what I could only guess was the flue.

Piling the logs back up, he relit a piece of newspaper. With the smoke heading in the direction it was supposed to go, Peter stood up. His face was covered with soot from the logs and the poker stick. Mattie and I burst into laughter.

"What the hell were you two trying to do? Burn the house down?" Peter was doing everything he could to control his temper. We fell on the couch still laughing. " I don't think it's funny."

"For your information, Peter, this is my first fire. I've never had a fireplace," I admitted somewhat embarrassed. "Since it was chilly in here, I didn't think it took an architectural engineer to figure it out. I'm sorry, but I was attempting to warm the place up, not burn it down."

Peter shook his head as he looked at Mattie. She shook her head and said, "Don't look at me. She did it. I was just sitting here minding my own business."

"Look guys. Until ten seconds ago, I had no idea something called a flue even existed," I said attempting to restore my already ruined reputation. "And we're both laughing, because, right now, Mr. Fireman, you look..."

Mattie interrupted me. "-- cute as a man can look with soot all over his face."

Peter ignored us and headed for the stairs. At the last second, he turned back. "Oh, by the way," he replied sarcastically, "if there is anyone in the room the least bit concerned about her baby, Jack is probably crying his fool head off in the back seat of my car. I just thought I might mention it because his sweet mama forgot to pick him up."

Thoroughly chastened, I ran out to the car and brought the screaming baby into the living room.

"And you think I'm supposed to get my rest in this house," Mattie complained as I soothed Jack's frazzled nerves.

"I demand to go home. My house is less chaotic than yours."

Ignoring her, I grabbed the bottle in the diaper bag. Rocking Jack, he quieted down instantly.

"Forget it, my misguided friend. You're staying here. So shut your mouth. Why am I always telling you that? You never listen," I complained, rolling my eyes.

Mattie and I could hear the shower running. She looked up at the ceiling. "Well, if you're not going to take me back, you better start spilling your guts, Miss Sleazebag. I've been patient enough. Tell me what's going on here, and maybe I'll stay for dinner."

Jack's cute little face seemed interested in the story, too.

"Okay, Miss Nosy, I'll tell you and I'll do my best to include some of the juicy parts, but a woman of class has to keep a few secrets."

"Annie, first of all, a woman of class knows about chimneys and flues. Second of all, stop stalling. Out with it already."

My voice changed dramatically, searching for the right nuance to add mystery. "Okay. It began on a cold, dark evening in mid October. The trees were dropping their colorful array of leaves onto the green carpet of the earth. At first, there was no hint to the intrigue and danger which lay ahead of my dear friend Mattie and me as we sat sipping our wine in one of the city's hottest new restaurants. But unbeknownst to the youngest of these women, this was to be a new journey, one fraught with sexual exploration and betrayal."

Then my voice changed back to its normal pitch. "You see,

that same rotten, no good friend of mine made me take the sexiest, most extremely irresistible man I've ever encountered home. Being the benevolent hostess my mother raised, I had to make my guest feel as comfortable as possible, right? So when the house guest of my dreams cooks, cleans house, interior decorates, does the yard work, and continues to carry this insatiable desire for me, it doesn't take a genius to know what will happen next. Does it?"

Mattie gave me an evil smile and her voice changed, too. "Let me tell you what really happened. You seduced poor Peter, didn't you? It happened while on one of your rare trips to the grocery store. You were wearing a low-cut dress which exposed quite nicely your coveted endowments," she said as she cleared her throat. "I need a drink of water, Miss Hostess. The smoke is still caught in my throat."

"I'm sorry. I'll be right back." I put the baby on the floor and went to the kitchen, poured another glass of water and handed it to Mattie. She drank every drop.

"Thank you. Pretending to be the sweet, demure woman you weren't, Miss Stevens...I mean Miss Sleazebag's main objective was to taunt this man, this paragon of virtue. You were a snake charmer by trade. You quickly spotted your prey and nonchalantly dropped a can of green beans."

"A can of green beans? Really, Mattie, why not a jar of baby food?" I asked.

"It's my turn. Hush. Like a true gentleman, the dear boy bends over to retrieve it. This snake charmer wanted him to get a good look at her cleavage. The timing was perfect. Her plan worked. His desire for her became insatiable. The man was quite literally frothing at the mouth."

Abruptly, Mattie changed the subject for a second. "Speaking of frothing at the mouth, I'm famished. You then took my Peter home and devoured him for supper. Isn't that how it really happened?"

"Absolutely. Except for one minor detail."

"What's that?" Mattie asked.

"I hate grocery stores. Couldn't we set this seductress scene in a more enchanting place? How about Saudi Arabia? When I grew tired of him, I would make him a eunuch for the rest of his life so he could be my slave."

Relishing the thought of Peter as a slave, I got up to find Jack a toy. He wasn't interested in our story-telling. He wanted my attention.

"If you made Peter a eunuch, it would be an utter travesty." Mattie said, with a jealous gleam in her eyes.

"You're right," I said, picking up the multitude of toys lying on the floor. "I wish every woman in America could experience half of what I've experienced in the last few days. Why, the man is diabolical."

Descending the stairs two at a time, Peter asked, "What man is diabolical?"

Attempting to come up with the most diabolical man I could think of off the top of my head, I replied, "Hitler."

Mattie unfortunately answered at the same time I did. "Mayor Donovan."

We were caught. I laughed and questioned Mattie's choice. "Mayor Donovan? You could at least think of somebody like Stalin or Sadam Hussein. Mayor Donovan?"

Mattie mimicked me. "You're not exactly up on current affairs, are you, my dear? At least I stayed in my own country. Besides, he is diabolical. It took me three years and four months to fight that man and his white supremist attitude. You're the one who nicknamed him 'Nazi man' behind his back."

"That was only in your company. Besides, I wouldn't exactly call him evil. He's just your typical -- you're right. The man is scum. You win."

Peter was not himself. For the second time in twenty minutes, he was irritated by our female banter.

"I'm sorry I asked. But you see, I don't care. Keep your little-girl secrets to yourselves." We were both surprised. Something was wrong. Mattie looked at me and I looked at her. Together we shrugged our shoulders.

Knowing he sounded petty, he quickly changed the subject. "What's for dinner?"

"What do you mean, 'what's for dinner?'" Mattie asked. "Annie dragged me over here kicking and screaming promising me a plate of your fine culinary skills. Having experienced her still undetectable achievements in the kitchen, I know we can't count on her. And, me, well, I'm a cripple, you know, so you can count me out, too. So Peter, my dear, that leaves you. You're the elected chef by a unanimous decision. So what's for dinner?"

Peter shook his head and pointed toward the kitchen. "Oh, no. It's not that easy. First of all, there has been a lack of teamwork shown by a person in this room whose name I won't mention regarding something called grocery shopping. That's why there's no food in the refrigerator."

"See, what'd I tell you? Bad place, grocery stores, " I said laughing so hard I fell into the chair. Mattie put the blanket over her head to supress her giggles.

Peter smiled, thinking he had said something funny and nodded in agreement. "Even though I admit my skills are abundant, I still haven't figured out how to turn nothing into something. So I suggest either the three of us pool our money together and order out, or we go to a restaurant. Now, which of those two options do you ladies prefer?"

"I suppose if we were to send Annie here over to the grocery she'd bring home more than supper. Green beans sound terrific."

We both cracked up laughing. Peter not understanding the joke, shook his head.

Peter decided to add his two cents worth. "She would probably get lost," he said smiling at his own joke.

"Oh, forget it," Mattie said. "I'm starving now. I'm not going to some stupid restaurant looking like a bag lady. They'd throw me out, anyway. Order out. Order out. Pizza is fine with me."

Peter found the telephone and handed it to me. "You heard the lady. Order out."

After the pizza arrived, there seemed to be a genuine lack of enthusiasm for conversation.

The doorbell rang. I opened the door to see Jason standing there in black boots, black jeans, and a black T-shirt. His muscular physique surprised me. I was used to baggy jeans and flannel shirts, not bad boy clothes radiating danger.

"Wow, where are you going?" I asked.

A boyish grin played across his face. "I've got a date. You didn't notice?" I gave him a puzzled look.

"I rang the doorbell. I didn't barge in," he said, following me into the dining room.

Mattie checked out the clothes and whistled. "Jason, my boy, young men are asking for trouble when they dress like that. Who is she? Dracula's bride?"

I went to the kitchen and grabbed him a plate. He had already taken a bite. He accepted the plate and sat down.

"Peter, I need your help. I'm supposed to pick up Katrina, except there's one problem, man. There's a leaky water pipe in the south bathroom. Water's going everywhere. Can you fix it?" Jason swallowed the pizza whole.

"Sure. I'll go out to my car and get my tools." Peter came back carrying a gray metal box.

"I hope you don't mind." Peter bent down and gave me a

peck on my cheek. "You'll have to clean off the table without me. See ya tonight, my dear." He turned and they both walked out the door.

Mattie broke the silence first. "See ya, tonight my dear, she mimicked. "Damn, I'm jealous. I don't know about you, but I'm beat. My back hurts. My muscles are sore, and I'm desperate for a bath. Annie, do you suppose you could help me up the stairs and into the tub? I know I'm not supposed to get this thing wet, but what if I just kind of draped it over the side?"

"Well, there is only one way to find out," I said helping her to her feet. "Let's give it a try."

Mattie put her arm around me and we hobbled up the stairs. I ran the tap water and then glanced at her cast.

"Let me run downstairs for a garbage bag," I suggested. "You can put your leg in the sack and we'll tie it up so it won't get wet."

"I have a better idea," Mattie suggested. "Let's just take the thing off. It's only an ace bandage and some plastic. That way I can soak the foot as well."

I helped Mattie unwrap the leg, took a look at her gruesome blue and purple ankle, shook my head, and left her soaking in the tub.

The next several minutes were spent with Jack. He was becoming a nuisance. If you turned your back on him for a second, there was no telling where you would find him. So far he was imprisoned in the playpen and could not escape. I figured it was only a matter of time.

I picked up the newspaper. Worried kids stood around Mattie's chair. The headline read, "Female Philanthropist, Mattie Turner Narrowly Escapes Death."

Just as I was about to read the article, Jack decided he was hungry and lost his temper. Reaching the refrigerator door, I noticed I was perilously close to no baby food and formula. Grabbing what was left out of the diaper bag, I walked over to him and placed him in his high chair. Placing a bib around his neck, I spoon fed him a jar of apricots. He must've been hungry. He ate half a bowl of warm cereal, too.

I picked up the phone and dialed Mattie's house. I was hoping to talk Peter into a little grocery shopping.

"Hello, Mattie's House," a voice answered on the other end.

"Tamara, is that you? This is Anne Stevens, may I speak to Peter?"

"Peter's not here. I haven't seen him all night. How's Mattie doing?" she asked.

"She's doing fine. She's upstairs soaking in the tub. I'm going to put her to bed here in a minute. Have you had any problems with the water pipes in the house?"

"No, ma'am. Everything is fine. We're just about to put the kids to sleep, too I've got to run. You know how it is around here. Gotta go."

After I finished feeding Jack, I kissed him good night, placed him in his bed, and headed for the bathroom to see if I could assist Mattie.

She was already in her pajama shirt. Without saying anything, I bent down and carefully wrapped the bandage around her swollen foot. I did my best not to make any sudden moves.

"Mattie, there's something strange going on here. I just talked to Tamara, and she told me there was no such thing as a leaky faucet. What do you suppose they're up to? Here, let me help you."

Rising to a standing position, Mattie contemplated my question. "Well, I'm not surprised. Don't you remember? A year ago the city made me replace every pipe in the house because of lead poisoning. I don't like this, Annie. This is not a good sign. They were both lying and acting very strangely."

Placing my arms around Mattie's waist, she leaned into my body as I helped her to bed. "Come to think of it, Jason and Peter have been leaving the house several times during the day and coming back with worried looks on their faces.   What do you suppose they're up to?"

"Trouble, since they're not telling us," I said, tucking the bed sheets carefully around her sore ankle. She was deep in thought. The concern written on both our faces.

"We'll get to the bottom of this tomorrow. They're up to something. That's for sure." Mattie said, taking her time settling in.

"Let's change the subject and talk about why I kidnapped you," I said, pulling up a chair. "What did you want to tell me?"

Mattie stretched her arms over her head and yawned. "Oh, that, I'm too tired. It was nothing. If it weren't for you, I'd be home in my own bed. When you get an idea in your head, there's no stopping you."

"I know. I'm sorry. It's Mr. Peacock Goldstein's fault. He had me almost convinced--"

"Convinced that I know more than I'm telling him. It's not exactly a lie. Something has been nagging at me. I can't put my finger on it, but I will. Damn Goldstein.   He has me going crazy, too."

"The man's a lunatic," I said. "Don't worry about it. It'll come back to you if it's supposed to."

"I'm getting old and feeble," Mattie said as she tucked her arms under her pillow.

"Here take these aspirins. I hope you can sleep through the night. Jack is off schedule. Thinks he deserves companionship in the middle of the night."

"He's not the problem," Mattie said. "Damn Peter. I'll be listening for his footsteps."

I tried not to feel too disturbed by their betrayal. "Oh, well, let's not worry about it now. Whatever it is can wait until morning."

Placing a kiss on Mattie's cheek, I turned off the light.

"You're right. Good night, Annie."

"Good night, Mattie," I replied. "We're making a habit of this, you know."

"It's all your fault. My bed's more comfortable." I stopped listening to her and closed the door.

Straightening up the house, I remembered I still had to get baby formula. I grabbed a pair of sweatpants from the drawer and jogged down to the corner convenience store.

Just as I was about to pay, I saw Peter getting out of a car in front of the bank across the street. With the bags in my arms, I stopped to watch. He and three or four guys in the car were exchanging small talk. Whatever was said, they were laughing. Peter smiled and waved good-bye. The driver floored the car and quickly left.

Peter glanced up and saw me standing there. With the smile still on his face, he ran over, greeted me with a peck on the cheek, and grabbed for my grocery sacks. "I'm impressed," he said. "I didn't know it was possible. The lady of the house can truly find a grocery store when she wants to."

Not happy with what I had witnessed, I turned a hurt expression toward him. "Stop kidding around," I demanded, with more anger than I had intended. "You're not a week into this relationship and you're already lying to me. You weren't at Mattie's tonight because I called there. What are you and Jason up to? And who were those people in that car?"

"Before I answer any of your questions, we need to keep walking. Someone might hear us." I looked around the parking lot. Nothing seemed out of the ordinary.

Peter was making me nervous. I half expected the bogey man to jump out of the bushes. After a couple minutes, he turned to speak. "First of all, you're overreacting. Jason and I were out having a little fun."

"Peter, stop it! Credit me with some common sense. Less than a week ago, you were almost killed."

Resigned, Peter took a breath and told the truth. "Jason and I are doing what you might call flushing out the stool pigeons. The gangs are turning on each other. There's trouble brewing. Ever since Rodney Thomas' throat was slashed, the upper classmen have been attempting to step into his position of power. I hate to tell you this, but there's going to be several more fatal shootings if someone doesn't try to stop them."

Upset at what Peter was suggesting, I kept my voice calm. "Please don't tell me the two of you are plotting to stop the assault before it begins. If so, you're right. I don't want to know. You're not in this anymore, remember? You said you wanted to lead a respectable life."

Peter's reaction was strangely distant. It wasn't anything he was doing. He just stood there with a guilty look on his face. I had been receiving mixed signals all night.

"What you'll succeed in doing is spreading your own carcasses right next to the two boys you were attempting to save the other night. Damn it, Peter. Can't you leave it alone?"

Peter refused to answer the question. We walked a couple more blocks in silence.

"For the first time in my life, I'm happy. Damn you. I'm in love with you, you creep." There I said it. "You're not about to blow this, are you?" Peter dropped the groceries.

Trying not to sound too weak and vulnerable, I leaned into his chest. "This is ridiculous. I don't know what to do."

Peter smiled and moved my head closer to his face. "I don't know what to say. I want to be with you," he said, squeezing me.

"I've been touched by your heart, your compassion, your kindness, not to mention your damn gorgeous body," he said kissing my nose. His artless endeavor at humor made me laugh.

"Because of you, I've found some redeeming qualities in your species," I said as I planted a kiss on his lips.

He kissed me long and hard. Holding my face in his hands, he smiled. "It's going to be all right." Peter said reassuring me. "You'll see. But you have to understand, I can't turn my back on this. I'm not giving up."

The wind blew my hair into Peter's face. He pulled it back and held it in his hand. "It feels like silk and smells like baby lotion. Women are men's debilitation. I'm trying to be serious, and all I want to do is crawl into your sweatpants. Think we'd fit?"

"I don't know. They're a man's large. Tell me what you were going to say, then maybe we can give it a try." Peter moved away from me, almost as if he didn't have the courage to look me in the eyes.

"Do you have any idea what it feels like to be a black man, to be a man's target? That's what I am. I'll always be a hood. It doesn't wash off."

I didn't want to hear it. I knew what he was about to say.

"It's not the whites who are killing them off," I said, picking up a bag. "There's no white conspiracy here. They're targeting each other for a massacre."

Peter was unconvinced. He picked up one of the bags, said nothing, and headed toward the house. We walked in silence for another block.

"You don't understand," he said. "Who is going to stop them? Who will care? Just watch T.V."

"I hate T.V. It wasn't until I was pregnant with Jack that I bought a telephone. I don't like technology."

Peter did not laugh. He was too busy making his point. "Well, you read the paper every day, don't you? You read about genocide occurring in other countries; you see refugees on the run; you see their babies dying of dysentery. And while you're sitting in your warm little house, you think to yourself, 'Thank God I live in this country.' That's what you think, isn't it, Annie?"

Peter was so upset he put his bag back on the ground. "As long as it's in Kosovo, Croatia, Iraq, Somalia, you're not touched by it. You're not interested. Until are troops are sent there, of course!"

I started to disagree with him, but he tightened his grip on my hand to demonstrate how strongly he felt. "But that's what really irks me. It's happening in our own backyard. When a young black kid gets shot in the head by a rival gang member in Mattie's neighborhood, who stops to care? If you were shot by a black man, it would make an outrage that would spread across at least a couple of states. The FBI would conduct an investigation. Don't you see? You can't keep turning your back on the truth. The truth is, no one gives a damn because it's a bunch of black asses, and it's happening in 'Our America,' too." You said it yourself the other day."

What did I say? I couldn't remember.

"We're placed behind bars with mandatory sentences for selling crack. Ironically, it's the white man who put the crack in the black man's hands. You're wrong. There is a white conspiracy. I know. I've met them. My deals were made with white businessmen in gray suits. They were not Hispanics or other African Americans. Some of them even worked in banks."

Peter's voice could not hide the betrayal and anger he felt. "I'm sorry. I can't do what you're asking me to do. I won't. No matter how much I may want to give up, we're not animals. We're flesh and blood, too. I can't stand by and watch us kill each other. If it's in my power to stop them, I will."

Peter shook his head and shrugged. "Annie, I know I'm not making much sense. I'm tired. Let's change the subject, shall we? Let's go back to those sweatpants. For the first time in my life, I'm afraid. I'm afraid because I love you. Let's put these groceries away," he said opening the front door.

Peeking into the bag, Peter held up a box and attempted to smile. "All right. We can have pancakes and eggs for breakfast."

After the groceries were put away, we went to my room. I suppose it wasn't *our* room yet. Instinctively, I knew I had to make every moment count.

Peter was taking off his shirt in the hallway. I started to do the same. "Shh, get in here. I'm crawling into your sweat pants, remember?" I looked dubiously at my clothes.

I didn't think his six-and-a-half-foot body would fit. I was wrong. It worked in the pants, but the shirt had to come off. It was a tight squeeze, but utterly satisfying. He picked me up and we fell on the bed. I made love to him ferociously tearing into the soft warmth of his neck. This time it was different. I was on fire and madly in love.

Afterwards, I was tightly cradled in Peter's arms. Even in sleep, he was afraid to let me go. Did my man have misplaced priorities? I knew I mattered to him. Was it enough to hold him? If I held him, could he live the life Jack and I needed? I wanted a family. Did he?

Indisputable doubts nagged at my conscience. Was it possible to change what you were? Changes can't be touched. They can only be felt. I wished I could take a magic wand and make him forget who he was. Did I really want that? I didn't know what I wanted. Yes, I did. I wanted him safe with me. Like my brother, would Peter be killed, too? One thing was for sure. I couldn't take it again.

Through passion-dimmed eyes, I could see his shadowed face in the moonlight. I caressed his cheek. His scars went far deeper than the ones on Mattie's back. I believed in this man's spirit. Maybe if others believed in it too, they would follow his change. Centuries ago, a man had walked this earth with an extraordinary gift, a gift that changed the world forever.

Here I was doing it again. Whenever I was too tired, my mind

would not rest. I called it my nights of psycho-schizoidism. I
decided to think positively. My last thoughts before drifting off were
warm. The man I was holding was real. He was special. His touch
made me feel special, too.

C H A P T E R
XVII

Peter awoke, showered, and started cooking breakfast. I could smell the heavenly aroma of coffee brewing. The phone rang just as I was heading to Jack's room. It was Kevin calling to tell me my calendar was empty. The judge was home sick. I looked out the window and realized the sun was shining. What a break! I'd take the morning off and show up at noon.

Mattie failed to see these things as I helped her get dressed and down the stairs. She was in a sour mood. Peter's deceit had put a kink in her otherwise good nature. I couldn't help her with that one. I felt it, too. I dropped the cordless telephone in her hand.

"Here, ET," attempting to be funny. "I know you're dying to find out whether or not the house survived without you. While you're talking, Jack and I are going for a walk around the block. We could use some exercise."

Mattie waved me off. "If you had a wheelchair instead of that stroller, I'd go with you," she said, dialing her number. "Forget it. I'll just phone home and sit here and watch Peter cook."

Several of my neighbors were raking the leaves off their landscaped lawns. I probably should be doing that, too. There were kids on bikes, dogs being walked by their owners. When I passed them, they greeted me with a friendly smile.

I couldn't help but think of the previous night's conversation with Peter. I'll be damned if I was just going to sit back and let the man kill himself. If he didn't care about his life, Mattie and I did. Two intelligent women could come up with a plan to save his scrawny ass.

A couple of leaves fell in Baby Jack's stroller. He picked one up and examined it. Of course, the next place it went was into his mouth. When I bent down to take it, Jack puckered up his face and let out a loud protest.

"Well, Jack, if you would hold on to it instead of putting it in your mouth, you could keep it. It's not food."

As if he sensed what I was telling him, he snatched it back from my hand and studied it. With a determined smile and knowing it would please me, he handed it back. Changing his mind, once again he snatched it back. We played this game all the way home.

Mattie and Peter were sitting at the dining room table when we arrived. Mattie jumped as I came in the door. I caught her not too subtly wiping tears off her cheeks. Obviously, I had interrupted a very unpleasant discussion.

Peter finished setting the table. I placed Jack in his high chair and sat down to eat. The humorous banter was missing. I was the first to break the silence.

"I've been out walking and thinking. Fresh air clears your head of cobwebs. It's time the two of you level with me and tell me everything." I glanced at Peter. Warmth traveled up his cheeks.

"There's more to you than meets the eye. You need to let me in on your little secrets. Who are you, Peter Harrison?"

He ignored me and quietly put the food on the table. I tried to hold back my anger as I buttered my toast. Drawing a deep breath, I glared at Peter who was busy putting pancakes in front of Mattie's plate. I wasn't going to get an answer from him; so I might as well start with her.

Mattie poured syrup on her pancakes and placed a large sized piece of butter in the center ring to melt. After accomplishing this feat, her attention shifted toward me.

"I knew it wouldn't take you long, Annie," she said with a curt nod in my direction. "You're right. You deserve to know. We haven't been entirely up front with you. Not because we're intentionally deceitful."

I gave her a look that questioned her credibility thus far.

"Okay. So I've told a few half truths. Big deal. I've known Peter for a long time. I wrote to him in Los Angeles and asked for his help. Shall I continue, or are you going to tell her?"

Peter took a seat at the table. They looked resentfully at each other, trying to make up their minds who was to go first.

"You win, Mattie," Peter said, passing me a bowl of scrambled eggs. I put a little on Jack's plate. "You do it. I'll try to keep the utensils at a safe distance from her hand. I'm not convinced this is a good idea."

Mattie smiled. This wasn't a joking matter, so I refused to follow her lead. Taking a sip of her coffee, she placed the cup back on the saucer. She let out a heavy sigh and looked longingly at her plate.

"First, let's eat. We don't want to waste this delicious-smelling food." She picked up her fork and cut into the pancakes. "If I'm going to spill my guts, I'd rather do it on a full stomach. Trust me. It's a long story."

It was the second meal in twenty-four hours spent in silence. Jack kept us mildly entertained. Even his antics could not dispel the awkwardness in the room.

After breakfast, Peter and I got up and removed the dirty dishes. We then replenished our coffee, pulled the chairs out and sat back down.

"It's hard to know where to begin. I guess I'll start by telling my story first. This is my past, not Peter's. Oh, dear, I'll have to go back fifty years. Has it been that long ago? It seems like yesterday."

She was not teasing. She lowered her eyes and examined the wood grain on the table. "I was sixteen years old when I found out I was pregnant. My parents didn't want my baby. They told me if I kept it against their wishes, they would throw me out of the house and never speak to me again. I was an only child, a lonely child really. Much like you, Annie, I lived life vicariously through the fantasies I read in books. I was an awkward teenager with not a lot of self-confidence. The father was a neighbor kid who lived around the corner. I never told him.

"Education meant the world to me. There would be no college if I kept the baby. You have to understand. My bull-headed father gave me few alternatives. This was close to fifty years ago. My parents' humiliation was such that they couldn't bear to have a baby born out of wedlock.

"For the next several months, my parents paid for my room and board in an unwed mother's home. Our friends and family were told I had to leave town to help out a sick aunt. I always loved those sick-relative conspiracies. It never fooled anyone.

I smiled, then Mattie smiled back. "On June 3rd, 1947, I gave birth to a tiny baby girl. Sadly, I never got to see her. To this day I can still hear her lusty cry when she entered this world. It was the toughest decision of my life. I signed the adoption papers, knowing full well it was a stupid thing to do. I did my best to put the guilt aside and go on with my life. You rationalize things in different ways. I used to imagine my baby with some fairy-tale parents happy and content in a fancy big home living the life of the rich and famous.

Mattie nervously twirled the beads on her head and gave Peter a guilty look. "Several years later, my mother contracted pneumonia.

The doctors gave us little hope. Before my mother died, she gave me a slip of paper with my baby's name on it. She told me she had never agreed with my father's opinions concerning her grandchild. She hired a private detective to track down her whereabouts. As it turns out, my daughter's adoptive parents had died in an automobile accident. Since these people had no other living relatives, my child was made a ward of the state. That state was California.

"Several months before my mother's illness, this private detective found my daughter. He discovered her in an orphanage living outside of Los Angeles, California. The detective and my mother secretly corresponded. On special occasions, my mother sent my daughter presents. She told me my baby's name was Ruth Ann. She was twelve years old. On her deathbed, my mother told me to find her and bring her home. She died before I could leave.

"I helped my father bury my mother and left him standing on the front porch. That day I said many things I regret now. It was the last time I would ever see my father alive. Three years later, he died of liver cancer.

"I was not as tough as I am today. I was still living with my parents at the ripe old age of twenty-eight years. As you know, I received a bachelor's degree in elementary education. I started out in an all white school. I thoroughly enjoyed teaching my classes, but I was also a shy, unassuming young woman. My father's criticisms of me kept me believing I wasn't worth much. Like the kids I see today, I had no self-esteem.

"That afternoon, I went to the bank, took out my entire life savings, and headed for the bus station. I flagged down a taxi in Los Angeles and gave him the address to what he called the 'colored children's orphanage.'

"After paying the man his fare, I observed a run-down house with peeling white paint, rusted cars and rotten bed frames lying discarded around the yard.

"Several of the children were outside playing, jumping up and down on moldy mattresses. So appalled, I was sick to my stomach. I asked one of the little girls if she had seen Ruth Ann. She pointed to a house across the street and said Ruth Ann had run away.

"Confused, I gazed in the direction she pointed. It was a freshly painted, nicely kept, wooden-framed home. Watching from that distance, it took only a few seconds to discover what it was. There were men and glittery-dressed women sitting on the porch. It was a brothel.

"Still carrying my bags, I walked up the uneven steps to the front porch and knocked. A heavy-set, unkempt young man answered the door. I gave him my name and asked to speak to the person who ran the place. A couple of minutes later a sour old woman with rotten teeth came to greet me. She directed me to the living room and asked me to take a seat. I told her I was Ruth Ann's natural mother, and I wanted to take my child home. She informed me a couple of months before Ruth Ann had run away. They hadn't seen or heard from her since.

"Angry, I repeated what the little girl had told me outside. The old woman grew vindictive and asked me to leave. I responded by telling her I would notify the police. She became belligerent. She called for the young man and he grabbed me by the arm and threw me out.

"As I left, I stopped and talked to the little girl outside. She told me Ruth Ann had told her they do bad things over there and she was to never cross the street. To make a long story short, Ruth Ann had been sold by the abhorrent woman who ran the orphanage.

"I stayed in Los Angeles and notified the police. The state took action, and the orphanage was closed. The proprietor was arrested and sentenced to prison. For years, the detectives and I tried to find my daughter. I was always met with another dead end.

"From 1958 through 1969, I continued living in Los Angeles.

I taught school, and in my spare time I searched for her. When I received the news my father died, I hired a caretaker to close up the house. Throughout the years, I paid the taxes so I wouldn't lose it, but without anyone there it had fallen into disrepair.

"Los Angeles in the '60s taught me a lot about drugs and free living. The hippie generation was at its peak. I took night classes to get my master's degree, and in my free time I became interested in my ancestors. There was a man, a professor from the University of Southern California, who taught me my heritage. He taught many students their African history and set up an organization called the Black Reformation Movement. His name was Daniel Fields."

Mattie's face lit up at the mention of his name. "Annie, he was the love of my life. We lived together for five years. At that time, everyone was living in sin so it was no big deal. That's where Mattie changed and found her courage. That's where my radical behavior first began. It's funny. They were the happiest times in my life.

"For a while, I even left this country with Daniel and spent a year or so in South Africa. At that time, the policy of separate government of races, or the apartheid first began to exist officially. Before that, there were separate developments, separate residential areas, and political independence for the whites. Not unlike this country only white folks could vote or run for office."

Mattie took a sip of coffee and looked for a piece of paper. She drew the shape of the African continent. "I need to deviate for a moment and tell you a little bit about its history. Ten years earlier, the government passed acts providing for the eventual creation of several Bantu nations. This is where I lived," Mattie said pointing to her map.

"Most black leaders opposed the plan. The Coloured People's Representative Council was created in 1969. Fighting and riots broke out daily. Frightened and alone in a country I could not call my own,

I decided to leave.

"Daniel, who found his home there, tried to get me to stay. He had a cause to fight for. He kept telling me our people needed us. I didn't feel the way he did. My home was here. I was born an African American and I'll die an African American. I said a sorrowful good-bye to the love of my life and walked out. I missed him terribly. For a number of years, we stayed in touch. Tragically, my Daniel was killed in the 1976 riots protesting the apartheid. My Daniel was a hero. He died alone in a country fighting for a cause that was not really his."

Mattie turned toward Peter hoping she was conveying the same message to him. He said nothing, not responding to her innuendo. "In 1970, I moved back here and went back to teaching. I had enough money saved to repair the old place, but that was about it. I never gave up hope. I truly believed someday I would find my daughter. The private investigator continued to search. As you probably figured out by now, the biggest disappointment of my life was never having met my daughter. Ruth Ann died of a heroin overdose in 1977. She was thirty-two years old."

Mattie stopped talking and wiped her eyes. I could sense the guilt she still felt. What a waste. Their lives would've been so blessed if only she had found her. She reached into her pocket to find a tissue. I got up and handed her one. She blew her nose and rubbed her eyes.

"Oh, Mattie, I'm so sorry," I said, catching a look from Peter which was not at all comforting. Refusing to participate in this conversation, he walked into the kitchen and brewed a fresh pot of coffee.

"Perhaps we should put something stronger in this pot," I suggested. Mattie smiled and nodded her head in agreement. "I'll be all right, Annie. It's only history now. It's the suffering that brought me here and molded me into the woman I am today. To tell you the truth, I've been a lucky lady."

With a knowing smile, she raised her coffee cup and with pride in her voice said, "I'm truly blessed. After all, Peter is Ruth Ann's son and you haven't even met the other three. Thanks to my grandson here, our family has a lot to be proud of." Peter refused to look at me saying nothing.

"When we do get together, it's some of the best days of my life. Can you believe it? I have four grandchildren and two great grandkids, oh, and one more on the way."

I was too stunned to say anything. Why hadn't she told me this in the first place? "Well, the rest you know, Annie. I'm done. I think it's time for Peter to spill his guts about the rest of the Turner story. You see, it was my dear sweet Peter who found me."

Peter looked into Mattie's face and rolled his eyes. Then as if caught in a secret known only to them, he smiled at her warmly.

"Enough surprises for one day. Can't we stop?" Peter asked.

"Sure," Mattie snapped. "It's totally up to you. It's time she knew the truth about you and me. I'll give her my version, of course."

Reluctantly, Peter must have decided it was better to give his version than hers. "Hopefully, this tale won't be as long as Mattie's, he said, finally taking a seat in his chair.

"Part of this story you know. I was born in 1963. My mother was seventeen years old when she had me. From the beginning, she hated the name Ruth Ann. When she escaped from the orphanage, she was twelve years old. My mother changed her name from Ruth Ann to Lola Elizabeth Barnes. For about five years, she found odd jobs and ran around with a bunch of other street kids. In 1962, she met my father and was married.

"A year after they met, I was born. Early childhood was uneventful. Dad had a job in a warehouse and Mom stayed home. Two years later, my brother, Mark, was born, and soon after that my twin sisters arrived, Kenzie and LaTisha.   When I was about six, my father's younger brothers were sent to Vietnam. In 1969, he received a letter from the U.S. Marines informing him my uncle was missing in action."

Peter was telling the story of his life, yet, unlike Mattie, his was free of emotions. It was like he was reading his biography from a book. His pain went far deeper that the forced smile on his face.

"This is where our troubles began. Fearing the worst, my father went to Washington along with some 250,000 demonstrators protesting the Vietnam War. There he took up with another woman protester. Not long after, he sent a letter to my mother asking for a divorce. I never saw my father again. My mother found a job and became a very bitter woman. She started messing around with bad people. I kept my brothers and sisters out of her way. We were frightened by our live-in stepfathers and constantly hungry. Eventually, my mother became a heroin addict.

"Those were the worst years. In order to keep from starving to death, my brother and I raided soup kitchens, burglarized homes, shoplifted, you name it. We did what we had to do to keep our family together. I was thirteen when my mother died. It's sad, but she was hardly missed. By that time, we had been surviving by our wits anyway."

Peter cleared his throat and looked up to see the sympathy in my eyes. He ignored the signals and cut his eyes toward Mattie. She had heard it before. The sadness of not finding them until it was too late was written on her face.

"Annie, are you sure you want to hear the rest?" He asked. "It's not a story I'm very proud of, nor one I enjoy telling."

The chair creaked as he uncomfortably shifted his weight. I reached my hand out to comfort him. He was embarrassed. He rejected my hand, leaving the room. Pretending a nonexistent chore, he looked out the kitchen window and said nothing for several minutes.

"We've all done things we'll never be proud of, Peter. You did what you had to do in order to survive," I said not really knowing how to comfort him.

This did not seem to reassure him. "Well, let's put it this way. There weren't a whole lot of answers out there for my family and me. I was the man in charge. Before my mother passed away, I was already involved with the gangs. The gangs back then were called the Slausons, the Avenues, and the Businessmen. These guys weren't interested in us; so we started up our own gang. I'm sure you've heard of them. We were called the Crips."

I had indeed heard of them. They were one of the first notorious gangs established and organized on the streets of L.A.

"In the beginning it was stealing somebody else's leather jacket. Later on we started wearing clothes which identified you as a Crip. Back then it was just a fighting kind of thing. We would jump on a couple of guys and start smashing their faces in. Nothing much."

"What do you mean nothing much?" Mattie asked testily.

"That's what I meant. We were kids. We lived our lives on the street. Fighting was just part of the system, proof of your manhood. Everyone in the family continued to have good grades, including me. I was also quite the athlete. I made a deal with a college basketball coach from USC. If they gave me and my family a place to live, I would play basketball. My brother and sisters were still in high school. The coach took us under his wing and provided us with a nice home. I broke away from the Crips, started studying and attended college.

"Two years later, it all fell apart. My knee was injured. I suffered from some bone condition that developed in early childhood. Ironically, it wasn't my knee that suffers this pain, but my foot. Anyway, the whole ridiculous thing ended my basketball career.

"The coach was a decent guy. He tried to find me a job, but it didn't pay enough to support my family. Mark was ready to start college. He had received a scholarship to MIT in Cambridge, Massachusetts. My brainy brother wanted to become an electrical engineer. Unfortunately, the scholarship did not cover room and board. What else was I supposed to do? Where else could I get hold of that kind of money? I went back to gang banging. I became a soldier or foot runner for the hood. I was barely paying for my brother's room and board, much less my sisters. They helped out by getting odd jobs. Unfortunately, the street wars started getting heavy. This was 1980. I was twenty years old. A lot of the guys went to jail. I knew what I was doing and moved up in rank. It was mighty ugly. To hide my shame, I started wrapping the weed in cocaine."

Peter lowered his head to the ground, then looked me in the eye. "You're looking at an evil man. I never actually pulled the trigger on another human being, but I used my brain and my gun to control the others. I ordered hits on other gangs because they killed my own. I was hooked, and there was no way out."

Peter rubbed his eyes and, like Mattie, studied the grain of wood on the dining room table. "My family became educated on the proceeds from narcotics trafficking. Amazingly, I never spent a day in jail. I'm a man with many names. None I would want to give my own children. It's the side to my life which gives me very little joy and a lot of guilt."

His fingers touched the side of my face. "I'll say nothing more," he whispered. "I'm shifting gears. There are brighter aspects to my life."

Peter looked at Mattie and smiled. "Sometimes there is salvation in sin. I met up with a woman in the 'hood who'd been my mother's friend. She was poor and desperate. A couple of weeks before, she had approached me to buy some crack. She thought because she was my mother's friend I'd give her some dope. She told me about this private eye who'd talked to her several years back. She couldn't remember his name, said something about a woman looking for Ruth Ann. I'd forgotten Ruth Ann had been my mother's name. I gave the woman what she wanted and sent her away. After that, I did a little research on my own. It sounds crazy, but it didn't take me long to track down Mattie."

"My grandson is quite the genius," she said squeezing his hand. "Some other time I'll tell you what he did in order to find me."

Peter ignored her and continued. "At first I was going to send Mattie a letter. Instead, I sent her an airline ticket. She flew to L.A. Let's just say she didn't find the grandson of her dreams. It took her months to straighten me out. She and my coach, whose name, by the way, is Peter Harrison, put me in a rehab center. My sisters came home and used their influence to do a little brow-beating of their own. That year was my hell on earth. Once my head cleared of crack, I could think again."

"Come on, Peter," Mattie said scolding him as if he were a naughty child. "You can't end it there. You're not getting off that easily. Are you going to finish it or shall I? I told you we would tell Annie everything and I mean every word I say. Whatever she thinks about us is totally up to her. I'm sorry. He's my grandson, but sometimes he still needs his ears boxed."

Mattie took an exasperated breath. "Here's the part Peter wants to leave out. He's right. I used that ticket to find my grandson. It was a hellish year for him, but the rehab and counseling changed his life. I got a job as a sixth grade teacher, and Peter lived with me while he finished his degree in social work. He graduated Phi Beta Kappa from the University of Southern California."

"Mattie, stop bragging," he said, embarrassed by her loving attention. Peter walked back to the kitchen and turned on the faucet to wash dishes.

"Okay.   Okay.   What do you expect from your proud

Grandma?" she asked. Peter shrugged his shoulders and didn't respond. Mattie, knowing she had my undivided attention, continued with her story.

"L.A. has never been my favorite city. To my way of thinking, it's too fast, too crowded, and too unstable, both its people and its land. Coming from the Midwest, especially where I can breathe a modicum of fresh air, I'm at home. It's kind of like Mother Nature's mental telepathy. I kept yearning for the seasons to change and longing to plant my garden in the only dirt that can feed the world, God's soil. So, Grandma left Peter in L.A. and moved back here."

"Don't believe a thing she says," Peter said as he dried a plate and placed it in the cupboard. "She stayed long enough to make sure I'd stay out of trouble, and, poof, she was gone."

"Peter," Mattie admonished him, "mind your own business and stay in the kitchen. Anyway, you talked to Goldstein so I will not bore you with the gory details. Ironic, isn't it? I left the rabid streets of L.A. and was then almost murdered. There's something about meeting your Maker that changes a person. You can say there isn't a God if you want to, but I saw him. My mother and Ruth Ann were there, too."

Did I believe in Him? Not really. If I did when I was younger, He had pushed me away by taking Jack. The truth was I didn't know what to believe.

"For a little while, I was ashamed. I really had a hard time walking outside my door. Agoraphobia is what the nut doctors called it. I never told anyone, not even you, Peter. I quit living. I quit teaching. I had no self-respect left."

Peter, glad the subject had changed from him returned to the table and sat down in his chair.

"He doesn't know this either," she said with pride and turning to whisper in my ear. "He was my salvation. Thanks to Peter, I was able to regain my life again. Not knowing how I suffered that year, he called me with an intriguing solution to save America's youth. It only took a computer, a modem, and, more importantly, a list of names and addresses of families willing to accept a child. There's a little more to it than that, but we're a network now. I'm not the only base of operation. There are dozens of them around. Thanks to anonymous volunteers, these computers are set up all over the country."

Mattie saw the shock registering my face. "Quite a coup, isn't it, Annie? We have volunteers in the white community, as well as the black. It's really happening. We're saving children on a small scale, of course. You see, it's what I'm always preaching. People can make a difference."

At first I couldn't respond. I was too overwhelmed. The ramifications were astounding. Jack's head dropped to one side. He'd fallen asleep in his high chair. It occurred to me if change was to take place it had to happen to them, the ones now sitting in high chairs. Many years ago, we had desegregated our public school systems, unfortunately you couldn't desegregate an individual's heart. Sometimes change was slow in coming, but I believed it was possible. I got a peculiar picture of many children around the world in their high chairs.

"Look at that face," Mattie replied. "Our future lies within their grasp. They can make a difference. Teach them well, Annie and Peter. Teach them to care. There lies your answer."

At that moment, the future generation was sleeping in a plate of scrambled eggs.

CHAPTER XVIII

The phone rang before Mattie had a chance to wrap up her act of contrition. It was Tamara. The police were there again. Only this time they were interested in the whereabouts of Buddy. Tamara told them Mattie was staying at my house, and she warned us they were on their way.

I headed for the kitchen and grabbed a rag to wipe the egg from Jack's face. I carried him up the stairs and put him to bed. As I returned to the living room, I heard Peter say to Mattie, "What if they're after Reggie Parks?"

"I don't think it has anything to do with Reggie Parks," I said with irritation in my voice. "Since you've been so sneaky lately, perhaps it's Peter Harrison they're looking for."

He clenched his fists in anger at my accusation. "Peter Harrison has done nothing against the law. Yes, I've been out, but basically I've been doing what cops do best, spying. Don't start accusing me of anything until you know the facts."

Peter walked over to the hallway where I was standing and reluctantly placed a haphazard kiss on my cheek. "We'll hash this out later," he said, heading toward the door. "Good-bye, Mattie. I'll meet you back at your house. I know you're dying to go home."

A few minutes later, the police knocked on the door. I directed two uniformed officers toward the living room. The first one was Investigator Robert Morris, a middle-aged veteran cop who had worked for the Drug Enforcement Administration when it used to be called MEG.

The other one was a young man who approached the couch with a nervousness only associated with those who had not reached the rank of officer, probably a cadet. He was fidgeting with his hat and still had pimples on his face.

"Take a seat, gentlemen. This is Mattie Turner. She runs the youth home on Holloway Street." Everyone sat down uncomfortably. "What can we do for you?"

"I don't know if you remember me, Miss Stevens," Morris began, pulling out his identification. "We met briefly. You cross-examined me on the Karo syrup case."

Of course, I remembered the sanctimonious asshole very well. "Oh, yes, sir, I thought I recognized you."

Morris pointed to the young man sitting next to him. "This here is Eugene Wendell. He's here as an observer, still learning the ropes." The poor young man squirmed in his chair.

Mattie had her leg propped up on a stool across from them, eyeing them suspiciously.

"We've been told you wanted to speak to Mattie," I said, in a calm voice.

Investigator Morris, remembering his manners, removed his hat and shook Mattie's hand. "That's right, Miss Stevens. We don't want to take up much of your time. I've read the police reports on the incident you had in front of your home the other night. You're a damn lucky woman, if you don't mind my saying so."

"You're right," Mattie politely responded. "It's one of the worst scares I've had in a long time. What can I do for you, gentlemen? I gave my statement to the police the other night. There isn't much I can add. As I said, I never saw who did it. My face was buried in the grass next to the sidewalk, a most uncomfortable position to be sure."

The investigator chuckled and cleared his throat. "Well, this concerns the young woman you knocked to the ground. Michelle Jacobs was killed in her home last night. Whoever was trying to kill her succeeded. Michelle Jacobs worked for you, didn't she?"

For a moment, Mattie sat in stunned silence. She covered her face with her hands. "Oh, my God, that poor, poor little boy. How is Buddy? Is he all right?"

Morris glanced at Wendell. "Yes, ma'am, at least we think so. Wendell here turned his back on him and the kid got away," he said bitterly.

Noting our apparent confusion, Morris sighed. "Perhaps I should start at the beginning. Michelle Jacobs is married to Darrell Jacobs. He's being held without bond at the county jail. A month ago, Darrell was found in a hotel room distributing a kilo of crack. It was an undercover drug bust. Darrell Jacobs is facing a life sentence. He was showing some interest in cooperating to reduce his sentence. We are interested in a gang leader by the name of Edward Leon. The other young men involved in the bust are out on bond."

"So what you're trying to tell us is Michelle was killed to shut Jacobs up," I intervened, knowing what a screw-up this whole thing was.

"Precisely," Morris agreed. "Last night, the thugs who entered Michelle Jacobs' house shot her in the head at point-blank range. She died instantly. The kid's mother must've told Buddy to hide upstairs. He called 911."

Edward Leon was the leader of one of the most notorious gangs in the city. For many years, the cops had wanted him behind bars. So far he had successfully alluded them. His street name was "Scab." Once you attached yourself to him, he became an ugly part of you. There was no walking away. He was like a chameleon. His bodyguards protected him around the clock.

Morris cleared his throat and continued to tell us what we didn't want to hear.

"The poor kid was hysterical. He was hanging on to his mother when the ambulance arrived. He took off before we had a chance to question the kid. Search teams and canine units have been out looking for him all night. That's why I'm here. If you see Buddy, will you notify the police immediately? It's for his own protection."

Investigator Morris and Mr. Wendell stood up to leave. "We can count on your help, can't we, Miss Turner? We don't want to harm the boy. If he saw the men who did this to his mother, perhaps he can help us put them away. It's imperative we talk to him."

Mattie could not respond. She shook her head still in shock. Investigator Morris turned toward me. "Well, I guess that's all I have to say. My apologies for being the bearer of bad news. I'm afraid that's one of the drawbacks to being a police officer." Morris tipped his hat. "If you see Buddy, please let us know."

When they left, Mattie's tears were already rolling down her cheeks. Her body began to quiver. At first she said nothing. She kept staring out the window.

"Oh, Annie, that poor, poor child." She put her head in her lap. "We've got to find him. Don't you remember how that sweet kid huddled around his mother the other night? " I closed my eyes remembering the moment all too well.

"Damn it," she continued, "Michelle was devoted to her son. She was awfully tough on him; but, unlike most of these kids, Buddy had someone who loved him."

Reaching for her crutches, Mattie attempted to get out of her chair. "Well, don't just stand there! Help me up. We've got some searching to do. That boy can't spend another night out there hiding in the dark. Let's go!"

I helped Mattie out of her chair. Immediately, she started heading for the door.

"Hold your horses," I demanded. "Don't forget I have a baby sleeping upstairs. Let me see if I can get Hannah next door to take care of him."

Hannah was happy to earn a little extra money, and in no time at all we were ready to leave. I backed out the driveway, then turned to Mattie for directions. "Well, where to?"

"Home. There's only one place Buddy would go. He's in my greenhouse. Whenever Michelle couldn't find him, I knew where he was. Don't you remember? You saw us there the other day. He loves my vegetable garden. That's his special place. It's a fair bet Buddy will be there."

Mattie was clenching her hands. As hard as she tried, she couldn't hold back the tears. "Oh, God, what will he do without her?"

With tears welling up in my eyes too, I swallowed hard and headed toward Mattie's. Pulling into the driveway, I observed several kids playing on the front steps. When they spotted the car, they all came running. Soon enough, she was surrounded by jubilant children. It was obvious she was missed.

I picked up her suitcase and followed the children into the house. Mattie assured everyone she was all right and well rested. It took twenty minutes before we were able to get away. Hoping Buddy would be hungry, I made a couple of peanut butter and jelly sandwiches and grabbed a bottle of water out of the refrigerator.

We went directly to the hothouse which smelled of earth, moss, and sweet fragrant flowers. It didn't take Mattie long to find him. He was huddled in a corner under a piece of plastic tarp. Speaking soothingly, she urged him out of his hiding place. "Buddy, come here, baby. Ol' Mattie's here now. I'll take good care of you."

Buddy slowly crawled out from under the tarp. Mattie sat down with her back to one of the tables. He quietly came forward and placed his head in her lap.

Mattie's lump in her throat would not allow her to speak. She closed her eyes to allow the tears to fall freely down her face. For several minutes, Buddy laid there saying nothing. Mattie held him while stroking his head.

His jeans and shirt were covered with dark brown stains. There were streaks of dried tears still on his face. His body quivered from an ordeal no child should ever have to experience.

Buddy was the first to speak. "Mattie, where have you been? I've been hiding out here all night. Why did it take you so long?"

I understood Buddy's loss. Another time, on another day many years ago, the memories came flooding back. I was a little older than Buddy when my brother died. I was so overwhelmed with emotion I turned to leave.

Mattie motioned me back. "Annie, come here. Buddy, you remember Annie, don't you?"

Buddy turned his wet face toward me and nodded. I tried to find the words to comfort him. There was nothing I could say.

"What am I going to do?" Buddy asked, pleading for answers. "My mom's dead. It's all my fault. I was too afraid. I couldn't move. I should've been there for her, but I wasn't."

"It's okay, honey. Mattie will take care of you, she said, squeezing him hard. He abruptly pulled away from her, kicking the ground.

"We heard footsteps on our back porch. She whispered and told me to run upstairs and hide. I'm pretty sure she ran toward the phone. I heard them come through the door. They didn't even let her speak," he whispered totally out of control.

For a few seconds nothing else was said. "I think they went looking for me. One of the guys came in and said to the other, 'The kid's not here.' I was hiding in the closet."

Buddy's voice thinned to a whisper. Mattie had no words of comfort. She seemed beaten, paralyzed of speech.

"After that, I couldn't hear anything. I was so afraid. I snuck out of the closet and went downstairs. My mom's blood was all over the floor. Oh, God, I tried to wake her up! Why, Mattie, why couldn't she wake up? I didn't even get to say good-bye."

Buddy choked and couldn't continue. Mattie held him, knowing that was the only thing she could do.

"She's in a place where no one can hurt her now, child   Your dear mama is in heaven with God. It's not your fault. You did the right thing. You did what you were told. She saved your life."

"That's fuckin' bullshit," Buddy said, angrily. "She hates to be alone. Can't you understand? I need her. I don't know how to go on without her. I have nowhere to go."

Buddy stood up, walked toward the tarp, and kicked it hard. "Tell me how I can get her back, Mattie. If she's in heaven, then God knows she wants to be here with me. Tell Him to bring her back!"

Buddy fell to the ground, pounding his fist in the dirt. I understood too well Buddy's anger. Reaching out to him, I bent down and tried to take his hand. He was not quite comfortable with me. He snapped his hand away from my touch, looking at me with suspicion.

"You're right, Buddy," I said soothingly. "I know exactly how you feel. Scream. Do whatever you want. Kick this place apart. Let the anger out!"

Buddy, startled, wiped the tears from his face with the back of his hand. "I want to kill those creeps!"

Buddy paced back and forth, throwing a potted flower to the ground. He picked it back up, gently putting it back into place. Eventually, he calmed down and sat down next to Mattie.

"I can't be brave anymore. I'm so scared. Last night, I ran away and kept on running. When I stopped, I threw up. It's weird but when my supper was on the ground, I heard my mom's voice telling me where to go. I came here and found my hiding spot. Will you take care of me, at least until my dad's out of jail?"

Mattie nodded her head. "You can count on it, Sweetie. We're going to take good care of you."

Pulling out the lunch bag, I handed him the bottle of water and peanut butter and jelly sandwiches. "I don't know if you're hungry, but I know you could sure use the water. Drink it slowly. We don't want you getting sick on us again."

Buddy drank the water and ate one of the sandwiches. When he couldn't eat any longer, I took his hands and helped him to his feet. "Right now let's get out of here and find you some clean clothes and a nice, warm shower."

Buddy was reluctant to move. "What about the police?" he asked.

"Ah, forget about the police," Mattie said. "Let's take care of you first. Hopefully, you can help them find your mother's killers."

Buddy and I took Mattie's hands and helped her to her feet. "I'm gonna kill them myself," he whispered. "They hung with my father, smoking weed and drinking beer. When my mom made me run upstairs, I looked out the window. I saw them putting on their hoods as they busted in the door."

Mattie, not liking what she heard, shook her head. "Enough of this kind of talk. Revenge will not bring your mother back."

"You listen to me and you listen good!" she said, grabbing him by the shirt. Her voice was tight with anger. "None of this talk about killing. The last thing your dear mama would've wanted was for you to end up like them. Let the police do their jobs. Do you hear me, boy?"

Buddy shoved away from her and turned his back. I intervened trying to reassure him. "They'll be punished, Buddy. They'll get what they deserve," I said with more conviction than I felt.

Buddy seemed unconvinced. He brushed the dirt off his shirt and walked away leaving Mattie and me alone. While she wobbled along, he stopped and waited for her to catch up.

"You're right. That's exactly what she would've said. My mom would kill me if I ended up in jail. As much as she loved my father, she did everything she could to keep us off the streets. That's why she made me stay here after school, to keep me out of trouble. My mom was glad you came into our lives. She said you were the bravest woman she'd ever known."

Buddy's eyes rested on Mattie's kind face. "She wanted me to be good. I sure hated her nagging. She never understood how much I worked for those B's."

"You are a good boy, Buddy, lucky too, and so was she." Mattie caught up with him and took his hand.

"Yeah, right. Lucky me," Buddy said, sarcastically.

"Your mother was a fine woman. She gave you a very precious gift."

Buddy shook his head. Mattie patted his arm. "You do know, don't you?" For the first time, Buddy smiled, as if knowing what she meant. "She gave you her love. Treasure it always. I loved her. And I'll miss her, too. She was my friend. We were both lucky. The best thing you could do for her now is to see to it she gets her wish. You become the man she wanted. If you don't, I'll beat you into submission."

"I bet you will, too," he agreed. Arm and arm the two of them walked away.

Still not fully recovered from the intrusions of the past, I stayed behind. Like Buddy, I found its smell comforting. It was the aroma of growing life. The flowers were so fragile, yet so beautiful. Wiping the tears from my eyes, I took another deep breath.

For years I asked for nothing and expected nothing. It wasn't hard when you wished your life away. My brother should not have saved me. I was convinced it was tougher to live with the loss of someone you loved than to live in a world with shame and doubt.

Sighing to myself, I sadly watched the woman and this sad, sweet boy enter the house.

* * *

Knowing the stairs were a chore for Mattie, I caught up with them and took charge of Buddy. Tamara was in the kitchen attempting to kick the stove to death.

"Mattie, where's your fuse box? This darn thing won't light." Tamara cried.

"Well, kicking it isn't going to do any good. Let's get a pick ax. I hate these contraptions," Mattie replied, then changed the subject.

"Ignore the stove, Tamara. Do you think you could find some clean clothes around here?" She frowned at Buddy.

I signaled her with my hand to say nothing. We walked up the stairs to the bathroom.

"Here, take this." I pulled a clean towel out of the linen closet and handed it to him. "Tamara will find you some clothes. When you're done, meet me in Mattie's room. We'll figure out this police business."

Gently pushing him into the bathroom, I walked down the hall to Mattie's room. Once there, I picked up the telephone and called the city police department.   After I was put on hold for a couple of minutes, Morris answered. "Ah, Miss Stevens, did you find the kid?"

Angered by his tone and the fact that Buddy had a name, I lied. "No, not yet. Mattie and I drove around the neighborhood. We still have a couple of places to check. Why don't you drop by, let's say in a couple of hours. If we find him, what do you plan on doing with him?"

Morris was a despicable human being, and I didn't trust him. I knew full well Buddy's fate was in our hands.

"The way I see it, there's not much choice in the matter. We've notified the Department of Children and Family Services. There's also police protection if he knows who shot his mother. It's my understanding the kid has no other living relatives except the father in jail. Am I right? No uncles or aunts anywhere?"

I didn't know Buddy's background.   Perhaps there was someone.   We'd have to discuss that later.   "If his father was cooperating, why wasn't there any police protection on his family?"

Morris cleared his throat and did not answer me.

"He'll probably be placed in foster care," he added. "With a kid his age, it'll be hard to find a home. Not many families are interested in taking on the responsibility of a kid from his neck of the woods. It's a tough situation."

I was not really surprised by Morris's statement. Nevertheless, it painted a bleak picture for Buddy. Fearful that my voice would give too much away, I was quick to dismiss him.

"Well, thank you for the information, sir. If we see the boy, we'll certainly call."

As I hung up, Mattie was standing in the hallway. "Oh, what are we going to do," I asked falling back on her bed. She came in and plopped herself down in the same way, although a little less gracefully with the cast on her leg. I told Mattie what Morris had in mind.

-301-

"The way I see it, we have two alternatives," I said looking up at her ceiling. "Either we let Morris take him into protective custody and place him in some foster home, or you get on that damn computer and find him a safe place to stay. I'm sorry, but that means he has to leave."

"You're right. I wish you weren't." Mattie shook her head. "What about his mother's funeral? Surely we can keep him until then."

"They won't release her body until after the autopsy," I said. "Someone's going to have to be in charge to make the necessary arrangements. I'm afraid when Buddy gives his statement to the police, the information will leak to Leon's gang."

Mattie sighed, understanding her role and the overwhelming responsibilities placed upon her. "There is no alternative," she sighed. "Tonight we won't tell Morris anything, or better yet Buddy can lie and tell him he doesn't know anything. That way Buddy can stay here until after the funeral. Once Michelle is buried, then we give Morris a written statement."

"It sounds plausible, but it won't work," I said, tapping my finger on the bedpost. "Once Morris learns that Buddy was lying, he can charge him with perjury. His first statement will be admissible in court, which will put the defendants in a better position for acquittal. Buddy's credibility as a witness would be ruined. Any defense lawyer could imply that since Buddy lied then, he is lying now. Not only that, if you hide Buddy, Morris could slap you with obstruction of justice. What's new? We could both go to jail for that one." I said, shaking my head.

"If we're going to make a deal with him, it will have to be tonight. Somehow we must convince him to wait until after the funeral to question him."

A knock sounded at the door. Alarmed, we both jumped. It was Peter. "What are you two conspiring about now? Did you give

Annie the low down on the rest of your life's story?"

"To tell you the truth, Peter, we haven't had the time. We've got bigger troubles."

Mattie filled Peter in on the details. Before she had a chance to finish, Buddy walked into the room. He carried his dirty clothes in his arms, neatly piling them on Mattie's dresser.

"I don't know what to say. I'm sorry, Buddy," Peter said patting him on the arm.

Buddy said nothing. I noticed Peter had left the bedroom door open. I closed it and took hold of Buddy and maneuvered him next to Mattie on her bed. Peter grabbed a chair for me, then grabbed another one for him. We sat down to discuss a plan. No one wanted to speak first.

Finally, I broke the silence. "Buddy, I talked to the police. It doesn't look good. If you tell them who did this, they'll put you in a safe place until they can get your mother's killers to trial."

Buddy seemed so lost. In many ways, he had aged a thousand years. Sorrowfully, I put my hand in his. "I know your choices seem pretty hopeless. On the one hand, you want to see her killers get what they deserve. On the other, if you do, you can't stay here. Those men that did this to your mother will come after you."

I hated to be so frank. Buddy's hands were folded in his lap. He studied them, not wanting to listen.

"Peter and Mattie know a way to hide people so they won't be found."

Buddy, confused, looked at Mattie. "We'll find you a good home away from here, somewhere safe." Her voice lacked the encouragement she needed to convey. "I promise. It won't be a prison. It's totally up to you. You have to make the choice."

Buddy was too overwhelmed. "What choice do I have?" he asked.

With little hope in my heart, I continued to talk. "This is

going to be tough, but it's the only way we see it. You and Mattie need to decide on the plans for your mother's funeral. The best way to avoid Morris is for Peter and me to take you to my house. We'll hide you there until the funeral. The police will show up hoping to find you. Even they won't interfere with you until after the ceremony."

Buddy seemed totally confused but willing to do whatever he was told. "By that time, Mattie will have set up a small reception for the guests. Then the tough part. In order to distract Morris, I'll hand him your statement. That should give him the probable cause he needs to get a warrant for your mother's killers."

"While I'm distracting Morris, Peter or Mattie will put you in their special hiding place. It's in the basement. Don't worry. You will be safe. If you guys can think of any other ideas, I'm open."

Peter spoke first. "For right now, the best thing we can do is get Buddy out of here. With a couple of more days to think about it, perhaps we could make the plan a little more foolproof."

Disheartened by the events that had occurred in the past few hours, Mattie looked drained. "Buddy, is there anyone to call, anyone special you want at your mother's funeral, anything specific you want said or done?" Mattie asked.

Buddy held back the tears. His sorrowful face slowly dropped to the bed covers. "I want my mom buried in her favorite beige-colored dress with this lace at the collar. It's hanging in her closet. She wore it only to church or special occasions. There's also a string of pearls in her jewelry box. My dad gave them to her a long time ago. I bought her a butterfly ring with my own money when I was eight. She told me it was the best gift she ever got. Its wings flutter when she moves her hand."

Buddy choked. Tears welled up in his eyes and fell down his face. "Can you put that on her finger? When I was little, she would dance around the room making the wings flutter. I'll never see the butterfly wings move again, will I?"

No one stopped Buddy. He needed time for grieving. After a couple of minutes, he wiped his face and took another deep breath. I handed him a tissue.

"I'm sorry, guys," he said, trying to regain his composure. "I'll be all right. If I'm supposed to get out of here, let's get going."

Mattie walked up to him and wiped away his tears. "We'll get through this together." Mattie hugged him and watched him walk away like he was carrying the weight of the world on his shoulders.

"When will it ever end?" Mattie asked in a hushed whisper.

"When we're dead, too," Peter whispered, squeezing her shoulders.

***

While I drove Buddy to my house, Peter and Mattie stayed behind to meet Morris. The drive was one of silence. We were too worn out to talk. There were no comforting words for moments like this.

When we walked into the house, Hannah was attempting to feed Jack his baby food. Bottled carrots were not one of his favorite meals. He was holding his mouth tightly shut, and the orange gunk was spread all over his face.

I introduced Buddy to Hannah and handed her the baby-sitting money. She smiled and was out of the house in a flash.

Buddy picked up the spoon and attempted to feed him. I went to the kitchen to find a jar of bananas. I figured Buddy would have better success feeding Jack what he really enjoyed.

"Meet Baby Jack. This here is Buddy. He's going to stay with us for a while. He also has your favorite. Bananas."

My son was getting used to strangers in the house. He smiled reaching out for the jar. I needed to change my clothes.

"Now that you two have become friends, feed him," I said, passing the jar to Buddy. He wiped Jack's face, which he hated, giving him one of those unhappy looks. He opened his mouth for the bananas. Pleased with the food, he began to eat with more enthusiasm..

Knowing Buddy had it under control, I ran upstairs to change my clothes. We spent the next hour playing with Jack. There wasn't much to say. The room was not cold, but the sun was beginning to set. This time I opened the flue and was attempting to light the logs. In true male form, Buddy took the matches from my hand and crumpling a newspaper lit it himself.

After we settled ourselves down in front of the fire, Buddy was the first to speak. "Can I call you Annie? The kids at Mattie's call you Miss Stevens or Anne. I like Annie."

I gave him a reassuring smile. "Of course. Mattie is the one who insists on that polite stuff. If you want to know the truth, I hate to be called Miss Stevens. I always feel like I'm someone's teacher or some old lady. You and I both know she's also the first one to break her own rule."

Buddy smiled in agreement. "How old is Jack?"

"Well, let's see. He's ten months old last week. He can talk a mixture of Japanese and Russian. It's amazing how smart he's becoming. You turn your back on him, and he crawls out of the room. He adores the stairs. He and Hannah must spend a lot of time there because every time she comes over to babysit, Jack is zonked. Mark my word, it won't take him long to fall asleep."

Buddy grabbed a toy out of the playpen and began teasing him. "Can I ask you a couple personal questions, Annie?"

Sitting on the couch, I pulled a pillow up over my legs. "Shoot."

"Do you love Peter?" Buddy asked.

Surprised by the question, it took me a few minutes to answer. "To tell you the truth, I haven't known Peter very long. When I'm with him, it's like I've been hit with a blast of warm sunshine."

Pointing to the fire I said, "Maybe it's like that warmth over there. I know the man and then the room gets chilled and I don't know him. It's difficult to explain. Why do you ask?"

Buddy did not answer. Instead, he tickled Jack's neck. Smiles and giggles took the place of any more intrusions into my love life.

For the next several minutes, he seemed content to sit and play. Thanks to Hannah's having paid heed to Jack's every whim, his eyes began to droop. Buddy went over to the rocker. I handed him a warm bottle. He placed it in Jack's mouth and rocked him to sleep.

I started to get up to take him to his bed. Buddy shook his head and continued to rock. He readjusted his head and put him, more comfortably, in the crook of his arm.

"I always wanted a baby brother or sister," he said sincerely. "Mom didn't want any more kids. After me, she had her tubes tied. She always told me if Dad got a decent job she'd think about having a brother or sister for me. She had no family of her own. She grew up in foster homes. Of course, I knew Dad would never get a decent job. Mom always said he was a lost soul."

"It sounds to me like your mother was a very intelligent woman."

"Annie, why aren't you married? Where is Jack's father?"

"We are divorced. He left me quite a while ago." I grabbed for the poker and placed another log on the fire.

"When I was your age, I was what you'd call a loner. Nick, my ex-husband, was just the opposite. He was quite handsome, and I think I loved him from the time I was six. He was one of those guys who didn't have to speak. When he smiled, oh, it would melt your heart. We got married, put ourselves through college by taking turns working. Basically, that's the story. After that, I got pregnant and he left. Why all the questions?" Then it hit me. He wanted to talk about anything so that he didn't have to think about his own troubles.

Buddy was not going to let me off the hook. He continued to pry. "What about your parents? Didn't you get help from them?"

"No. I was a little older than you when I ran away from home. My grades in school were always good. In fact, I was what my teachers called a child prodigy. They were always putting me in accelerated classes. Finally, I became so bored they let me skip a couple of grades. I was sixteen when I graduated from high school. At seventeen, I went to work as a waitress and took college courses during the day."

"Where'd you and your husband meet?" he asked.

"We grew up together. He was my next-door neighbor. Like I said, I think I had a crush on him my entire life. He and my brother were friends. When I'd hear his basketball, I'd sneak upstairs to my brother's bedroom to watch them play. I'd sit and daydream about him for hours. Eventually, I grew breasts, and that's when he finally took an interest in me."

Like most young men, Buddy warmed to the idea of breasts.

"Nick and I were having troubles at home. His were mainly due to not studying and wanting to have a good time. My troubles started when I was born. My mother and father didn't like me much."

Buddy got up and placed Jack in my arms. "He gets heavy after a while. I'll put him to bed. Would you like to see the rest of the house?" He followed me to the baby's room. I kissed Jack covering him with a blanket.

The house was small so it didn't take long to finish the tour.

"You want a drink? I think there's a couple of sodas in here somewhere. I handed him a can of pop and he walked back to the rocking chair. I was hoping the interrogation was over.

"You said something to me today about knowing how I felt. Do you think you could tell me about that?"

Buddy noted my reluctance. The pain was plainly written on my face. "If you would rather not, it's okay."

At that moment, the front door opened. Buddy and I jumped at the same time. "Peter, that better be you; otherwise, Buddy and I are going to have to hunt for some kitchen knives."

Peter entered the room sniffing the air. "I was hoping to smell kitchen food. Why am I not surprised?" Peter came over and sat next to me on the couch. "Buddy, when you go off into the world to seek a woman, please find one that likes to cook."

Peter tickled me in the stomach and playfully punched my arm. "Although I must admit, this lovely woman is blessed with a few other redeeming attributes. However, if your interests are in your stomach, forget it."

"Stop being such a brat," I said as I smacked him. "Buddy, he's right. I am a lousy hostess. Supper never even occurred to me. What would you prefer, home cooking or a little fast food?"

Buddy contemplated the question. "If you guys don't mind, a pizza sounds great."

Peter and I looked at each other. Pizza for the second night in a row. "Pizza sounds fine with us," I said, hiding my lack of enthusiasm. "Why don't you go and phone it in. I believe it's your turn."

Peter left without saying a word; however, it wasn't long before he returned. "I'm about to order the works. Is there anything you can't stand, Buddy, anchovies, pineapple?"

Buddy wrinkled his nose and stuck his tongue out. "Pepperoni is fine."

"Boring guy, huh. Okay. Pepperoni it is." Peter turned back toward the kitchen and placed the call.

A couple of seconds later, he returned. Putting my legs on his lap, he massaged my feet. After a brief moment of silence, the three of us started to speak at once. "No, you go ahead, Buddy. What were you about to say?"

"It's not what I was about to say. It's what Annie was about to tell me. We were talking about her when you walked in."

Peter looked at me and could see the uncertainty in my face. He started to get up. My past was something we'd never talked about. I suppose it was my turn to spill my guts.

"You two stay and talk," he suggested. "I'll go upstairs and get some laundry. That's another thing, Buddy. She hates doing laundry."

I stopped him by putting my hand on his leg. "It's okay, Peter, you don't have to make excuses. Stay put. After this morning, I'm beginning to realize how little we know of each other. Talking is wiser than keeping all these secrets, don't you think? I'd like to get it off my chest."

Two sets of eyes in the room were fixed on me. I looked at Buddy. "Oh, all right. I don't think this is a good idea. It's not a pleasant story."

"It beats talking about funerals." Buddy was right. Except eventually that's just where this story was headed. "Let me start out by saying most everyone has something bad happening to them at one time or another in their life. I see it in my work every day. We are not exceptional people. In fact, Mattie, Peter, and I are all products of what we call nowadays 'dysfunctional families.' What family isn't?"

I wrapped my arms around myself and cleared my throat. "It's not easy. I've been foolishly tucking it all away for years. If only it was a bad dream. I think the psychiatric term for this is 'denial.' I'm sure they'd tell me facing reality, accepting it, is the only way I'm going to put the past behind me. It's a lie, Buddy. You can never put the past behind you."

Buddy saw how uncomfortable I was. He picked up one of the pillows and threw it toward me. I caught it and put it over my lap. "Thank you. It's the truth. I don't know when you'll stop feeling the pain of your mother's loss. At least, that's the way it has been for me."

I hated telling him that. Me and my big mouth. At a time like this, maybe honesty wasn't the best approach. He wiped his nose with his fingers and looked out the window.

"It's not all grim. You'll be able to make a new life. In time, you'll become the man your mother wanted you to be. In fact, if she were here, she would be very proud of you. I guess what I'm suggesting to you is that you use what you feel now to become a stronger person. It's not easy to explain."

Immediately Buddy interrupted. "It's funny, but I think I know what you mean. It's like I feel disconnected but at the same time whole. It's true. I'm all torn up inside. Yet I know what Mom would have wanted, and I don't want to fight her anymore. I want to do what's right. Does that sound silly?"

I understood all too well what he meant. Peter turned and studied my face. He opened his mouth to reply but closed it without speaking.

"In a way, that's exactly what happened to me. You see. I grew up in a small town on the border between Illinois and Indiana. We weren't rich, mostly middle class. My father was a deputy sheriff. He spent most of his days in his squad car covering the county. Unfortunately, in the various towns he traveled, he was a friendly guy. I used to call him my father of many faces. He drank."

As if that explanation would explain away my father's lack of control. Nothing explained away evil. It was merely an excuse and I knew it.

Peter got up and put another log on the fire. I went to the

kitchen and poured us some water. "Here. You need to drink. Shedding tears has a way of making you thirsty."

"Thanks." Buddy took the glass from my hand and drank the entire contents in one big gulp.

"My father was a tall, slender man who was very quick with his fists. In fact, men came to these taverns for the sole purpose of fighting him. He had been a boxer in college and seldom lost a fight. Whether it was the bottle that made him this way or the lack of my mother's love, he was a very cruel man. When I was little, I was so proud of her, so proud to be her daughter. She wasn't like the rest of the mothers. She was beautiful. Behind her back, I'd call her the 'Ice Queen.' Oh, how I tried to make her love me. There was no real explanation of her hatred for me. She loved my brother Jack, maybe there wasn't enough room for me. Anyway, after he left for college, she spent most of her time in the bedroom watching T.V. That's why I hate T.V.'s. Instead of facing reality, she grew depressed and hid from the world.

"What my father failed to understand was my mother had eyes only for my brother, Jack. Unlike me, he was spoiled and loved. Even Dad would take him on his camping trips. Every now and again I got the privilege to tag along. Those were the fun times with my father. Nature brought out the best in him. He'd seem a different person.

"Jack was six years older than me. Like my parents, I, too, loved him. He was the sunshine in my otherwise darkened life. He made me feel important. I was an awkward kid with long skinny legs and a brain none of them could match."

Peter took my hand and kissed my palm. "They might still be skinny but they're gorgeous. The woman I see today has a lot to be proud of. Look in the mirror, Annie. What do you think, Buddy?"

He smiled and eyed my legs. "She's kind of cute. A little too old for me."

"Thank you, Buddy." I tried not to turn red but could feel my blood pressure rise to my face. I gave him an embarrassed grin.

"You two, on the other hand, do wonders for my self esteem," I said, squeezing Peter's hand.

"Do you want to hear this or not?" I asked. They both nodded their heads. "When I was a freshman in high school, Nick finally paid attention to me. I was telling Buddy it probably had more to do with my wholesome figure; but, at any rate, he noticed me. I was delighted. For the first time in my life, the boy I adored loved me back.

"When my brother went away to college, everything fell apart. My mother was a perfectionist, not a hair out of place or a wrinkle on her dress. The house was immaculately clean, and the yard had always been full of flower beds. When Jack left, it was as if he took her spirit with him. Just when he was about to graduate with honors, Jack wrote a letter informing my parents he was interested in joining the ministry. He wanted to study theology. Jack wasn't coming home and getting a job like she'd planned. My parents were furious. Unlike the rest of my family, my brother had always been a warm and giving person. He wanted to save the world and loved helping others. I had always understood that about him. He was a lot like you, Peter. He believed he could make a difference, make this a better world."

Holding the pillow tightly, I took a deep breath and watched Peter as he stared at the rug pattern on the floor. He looked up and caught me staring. He smiled. Perhaps that's why I was beginning to love Peter, too. It was like having a piece of Jack in my life again.

"Now, for the tough part. I was sixteen years old and very independent for that age. I'd been working nights as a waitress and attending the local junior college during the day. I came home a little later than usual. There was no one there. It wasn't like my mother to leave the house in the daytime, let alone the evening.

"Fearing for her safety, I tried to call my dad, but he wasn't at the sheriff's department. I was certain something had gone wrong. I didn't know what to do. It was two o'clock in the morning when I finally called Jack. He was concerned enough to drive the four hours it took to get home.

"Nick had been there earlier, but he had gone home. He called me from his house in the middle of the night. I was still alone and upset. He came back over, and together we sat waiting for my brother to show up.

"About six o'clock in the morning, my father finally appeared in the doorway. Nick and I were asleep on the couch. I could smell the alcohol on his breath. He staggered over to us, gave me this dirty look, and walked away. 'Where's Mom?' I asked. He kept mumbling to himself.

"Nick wanted to stay, but I told him to leave. We assumed Dad had gone to bed. A few minutes later, he returned with his gun in his hand. He kept calling me names. 'You're a whore, a slut,' mumbling something about Mom. He broke down and started to cry. He raised his head, looked me in the eye and said, 'You're like her, you know. Just a no-good slut. You think you're too good for the likes of me, don't you?'

"We weren't really afraid. Nick tried to reason with him, but he shoved him aside, knocking him against the wall. He kept calling me names. I tried pleading with him. I said, 'Dad, listen to me. It's not what you think. Nick is trying to tell you Mom's missing. Do you know where she is? She could be hurt.' All the while, his gun was still in his hand.

"My father said, 'There's nothing wrong with that bitch. She's not coming back. The whore left me for good. Did you hear me, girl? You're a slut just like her, nothing but a damn slut.'

"He went to the refrigerator and got another bottle of beer. Jack walked through the back door. He said, 'Dad, why don't you go to bed. Get some rest.' He tried to take the gun out of his hand. My father pulled it away from his grasp."

I buried my head in the pillow. I tried to hold the tears back but it wasn't working. I saw my brother's face as he held the gun. "My father shoved Jack against the kitchen sink, snatching the gun back from my brother's hand. He tripped on the rug. The gun went off. My brother staggered and fell forward. I grabbed him. He was so heavy. I couldn't support his weight. We fell to the floor. It had happened so fast. At first I was confused. I hadn't realized he'd been shot. A few seconds later, my father said, 'Oh, God, what have I done. I'm so sorry, Son. I'm so sorry. Oh, God, please forgive me.' A couple of seconds later, I heard another shot."

Peter took the pillow I was gripping and pulled me to his chest. "Sometimes I get these nightmares. Blood was everywhere. Nick pulled me away from Jack's body. I couldn't move. I started screaming. I couldn't stop. The blood, oh God, the blood was everywhere."

The words caught in my throat as I cried. Peter held me until the shivering stopped. I buried my face in his chest. For a while, nothing was said. I stopped thinking about myself, realizing what my words must've done to Buddy. His nightmare was still too new. Why after all these years did I speak of it now?

I left Peter's side and approached Buddy. He was sitting quietly lost in thought. I caught one of his hands in mine and squeezed. With the light behind him, I could not see his face. I knew I didn't have to.

"Like you, Buddy, I held my brother until they took him away."

There was no answer, nor was one expected. The room was silent except for the occasional crackling sound from the fireplace. I was unable to speak. With my hand still holding Buddy's, I turned to stare into the blue amber flames. I was at peace. In a peculiar way, I felt purged, much like the feeling after leaving the confessional. Here there was no priest to give me my penance. I had punished myself many times over.

Buddy's voice broke the spell. "You weren't alone. What about your mother?" he asked.

"The police found my mother and brought her home. She refused to speak to me. I am sure she blamed me for Jack's death. After the funeral, she sold the house leaving me to fend for myself. Nick and I ran away and got married. I left and never returned. The rest you know. We graduated from college and divorced. End of story."

Buddy swallowed hard. When I looked at him, I no longer saw a boy. I saw a man.

"I'm glad you told me," he said softly, putting his arms around me. He was comforting me.

"I shouldn't have," I said, rubbing my hand across my wet cheek.

"Don't you see? You did all right. You're a lawyer now. You got through it all and survived," he said finding a way to comfort me. I couldn't talk about the many nights I wanted to die, too.

"Everyone will be talking about me behind my back. I don't want to leave. Oh, God, I want my mom back!"

Buddy got out of his chair and sat on the floor next to me. He eased himself down beside me, leaned forward, and cried in my lap. I caressed his hair and cheek. After a little while, he moved and wiped away the tears.

."You told me somehow you found the strength to go on. Nick helped you get through it, didn't he? Look at me. I don't have anyone. My father's in jail. Like you, I have to run away from everything I know. There's no one who'll know who I am. Maybe that's better. Maybe I don't want them to know who I am."

How could I reassure him, convince him he wouldn't be

alone. I wiped a tear from my cheek then reached over wiping the tears from his; as if mingling our tears we could share each other's pain. He understood and smiled.

"This may sound silly, but you have to go on for them. I couldn't let the sacrifice Jack made for me go for nothing. There had to be a good reason he saved my life, just as your mother saved yours."

I raised his chin with my hand. "Listen. Don't you see? That's your special connection with her. Only you have the power to do what is right, prove to your mother that you were worth saving."

I could feel the fear I saw in Buddy's eyes. I knew all too well the emptiness he felt. I cast a helpless glance at Peter. His face was cast in the shadows of the firelight. For a second, I saw my brother's face instead of Peter's and understood what I had to say.

"You see this hand, Buddy. Touch it." He looked at me oddly but did as I suggested. "Now, close your eyes." Buddy did what I asked.

"Now think of your mother, her special scent, the way she walked, the sound of her voice."

He held my hands so tightly they throbbed. "Can you see her? She's there, isn't she? Feel the warmth of her spirit."

Time stood still. Minutes passed and not a sound was heard. Buddy opened his eyes and stared fixedly into my face. His smile told me what words could not convey.

"She was there, wasn't she? She's not a ghost." I said, hugging him around the neck. He took me in his arms and squeezed hard. Releasing me, he smiled. He understood. You see, she'll always be a part of you. It's her special legacy," I whispered, "everlasting life."

The doorbell rang. Buddy let go of me and glanced at Peter. I patted him on the knee and helped him off the ground "Come on. Let's eat. We'll get through this together. You've got a new family now." Peter got off the couch and approached us. He took us both in his arms.

"You'll never be alone," Peter whispered.

* * *

The rest of the evening was spent eating pizza and playing with Jack. We were all emotionally and physically drained. Calling it an early night, I settled Buddy in the guest bedroom and went to the bathroom to retrieve a nightgown.

"Annie, what are you doing?" Peter asked.

"Shh, if Buddy needs me in the middle of the night, I don't want him to catch me naked." I whispered.

"He'd think he'd died and gone to heaven." Peter pulled me to him. His naked flesh was too irresistible. Dropping the garment to the floor, I crawled in next to him. Our lips met and the day's memories were washed away by the sheer force of our need for each other.

It was as if we sensed time was running out. I made love to him not with just the desire for pleasure, but with a new kind of love, a love that made my heart ache for more. I wrapped myself around him wishing I could meld my body into his, to become one person forever in a world that could never pry us apart. Alas, reality was a heavy burden to ignore.

CHAPTER
XIX

When the alarm went off the next morning, we were greeted by a brilliant sun. I dragged myself out of bed and headed for the bathroom. Peter was still sleeping. After showering, I returned to my room and gave him a shake.

"Wake up, you lazy bones! I've been missing too many days of work. And now you've got a job to do, too."

Peter spoke incoherently. At first I didn't think I heard him correctly. He was half awake and mumbling.

"I forgot to tell you," he sighed. "I called Professor Edwards and told him I'd decided not to accept the position."

Fully awake now, he propped himself up in bed. "Annie, I'm sorry. It slipped my mind. That's why Mattie and I were fighting yesterdaymorning."

Peter pulled me down next to him. "How am I supposed to help these kids? It doesn't make any sense. They are my job. I wanted to do it, for you, but I can't."

What he was trying to tell me was perfectly clear. If I wanted him, it had to be on his terms, not ours. I felt betrayed.

"While we were out walking the other night, I came to a few simple truths. How do I make you understand? I've the power to make a difference, to make this world a better place for these kids.

I know that sounds corny, but I've seen it work. And, as much as I love you, that will always come first. I can't be anything but who I am, not even for you."

Jerking away from his grasp, I was too stunned to say anything. "Don't turn your back on me, Annie," he demanded. "I can't blame you for being upset."

"Do you call what I am upset?" I asked, pacing the floor. "I'm not upset. I'm furious! What am I supposed to be to you? Where am I supposed to fit in with your little plan? Damn you! How could you be such a callous, such a callous son-of-a-bitch?"

"How do I make you understand?" Then he answered his own question. "You'll never understand. I'll take care of Buddy and Jack. We'll talk more about this tonight."

"Oh, but Buddy and Jack might get in your way," I sarcastically replied. "When you take care of them, you're also taking on responsibility. Are you sure you have your priorities figured out? Because they sure as hell seem incredibly selfish to me. It's pretty clear. You can't save the world and care for the people you love, too. You won't let it!" I pulled open the dresser drawer hunting for some clothes.

"Now, if you'll excuse me, I have to get dressed. I have a job. I don't want to talk to you tonight or any other night. Why didn't I see the writing on the wall? What an idiot I've been!"

Scrambling for my clothes, I made my way to the bathroom and slammed the door. After changing, I went to Jack's room. I wasn't about to let Peter take care of him. Then I thought of Buddy and how Jack had the uncanny ability to cheer him up. I kissed my sleeping child on his cheek and left him in his room. Finding my briefcase in the hall closet, I quickly left the house.

My mind was not functioning on my work. Having checked the schedule, I was fortunate to discover I only had what I call "lobotomy work." It was just the morning's arraignment call. And, thank goodness, I could do that in my sleep.

It was close to noon before I went back to my office. Mattie was sitting in the waiting room reading a magazine. She looked up and gave me a sheepish grin. If she was coming to ply me with sympathy, now was not the time. Unaffected by my lack of enthusiasm at finding her there, she stood up.

"Don't give me that look, Annie. I might think you're mad at me, too."

"I suppose Peter called you," I replied.

Mattie nodded. "Of course, but that's not the only reason I'm here. I made the arrangements for Michelle's funeral. I figured as long as I felt so miserable you could take me over to the hospital so I could visit Paula Jennings."

I shook my head in bitter annoyance. "Is there no end to your sacrifices?" I asked sarcastically. "It must run in the family. Don't you ever want to crawl in a corner somewhere and hide?"

There wasn't anyone in the waiting room, but I felt a need to speak privately. Frustrated, I motioned for Mattie to follow me down the hall. She limped along trying to keep pace with me.

"Have a seat," I said in an angry voice, reaching for the door handle to shut it.

"In answer to your question, no, I don't want to go with you to speak to Paula Jennings. You two 'saviors of the world' can count me out."

I folded my arms and stared out the window. A couple of seconds had passed in silence. Giving me that disapproving look without saying a word, Mattie pulled a handkerchief out of her purse and dabbed at her eyes.

I knew I was being repetitive but I couldn't help myself. "When will it all end? Where on earth do you find the strength to keep going every day? Do you two get off on personal tragedy or something?"

"Look at me," pointing to myself, "I'm exhausted. In the last few weeks, I've shed enough tears to fill a fish tank."

The woman whose mouth had never shut up since the day I had known her said nothing.

"Why haven't you been honest with me? I'm supposed to mean something to you. Why didn't you warn me? You practically pushed him at me."

Mattie sat uncomfortably in her chair. "I'm sorry. I thought he would change. When I saw the two of you together, I was happy for Peter. He deserves somebody like you. I hoped he would stop taking risks and settle down, give me some more grandchildren. You have no idea how much I worry about him. It scares me so to see him risk his life day in and day out."

I gave her a look of disdain and anger.

"I know how you feel. There's no redeeming myself to you."

"More grandchildren, you say." I mocked her voice. "It wasn't until yesterday morning -- how long have we known each other? Two years. You've been a mother and now you're a grandmother, and a great grandmother to boot. You're right. I feel betrayed. And you know something else, I feel sorry for you."

I put my hands on my hips and started pacing the floor. "My God, what does it take for you to trust someone? I thought I was a head case, but you people have me beat. I helped you build your dream when everyone else thought you were nuts. I'm the one who's nuts!"

My voice grew tighter as the tears spilled down my face. "I've risked my career, harbored a gang leader who happens to be your grandson and why? I'm the only white person within ten miles of your place. I certainly found out the hard way how it feels to be a minority. But I took it all, and for what? For you, Mattie. Damn it. For you." I put my head in my hands and tried to stop shaking.

Turning back toward her, I opened the door. "I gave you each a piece of my heart, and I stupidly thought in return I had found a place to belong," I whispered. You can tell that no-good grandson of yours to stay away from me. Frankly, I don't want to listen to any more of his lies or yours."

Mattie, defeated, rose from her chair. "I have no excuse. I should have told you. I apologize for that. But as far as Peter and Buddy and those tears you've been shedding, that's a part of life, Annie. It's what I call 'The College of Hard Knocks and Deep Bruises.' Get used to it. It's acquiring life's lessons by learning from our mistakes and, by golly, that's the only way to live."

Mattie moved closer to me. "Take a good look at yourself. You're not the woman I first met. She was a cold and confused woman who was too afraid to live. For Christsake, you wanted to hide in a library. When you tell me it hasn't been worth it, I'll leave you alone. And, as for belonging, that can only come from you. It's simply a state of mind. See you at the funeral."

She leaned on her cane and sadly limped away. When I closed the door, I burst into a new round of tears.

* * *

Arriving home, I found Buddy and Jack playing hide and seek. Both of them looked up when I came through the door.

Placing my briefcase on the dining room table, I gave them each a smile I didn't feel and a kiss on the cheek. Buddy noticed me looking around the room for Peter. "He's not here, Annie. He left about an hour ago. He spent the afternoon loading up his car. There's a note for you on the table. What happened? Did you two get in a fight or something?"

I turned my back on Buddy and walked toward the kitchen. "Yeah, something like that. Let's just say we had differing opinions."

"Did I do something wrong?" Buddy asked.

"No, honey, absolutely not. It has nothing to do with you."

Buddy gave Jack a teething ring. "I asked Peter the same question and got the same answer. Do you want my opinion here? Since you've been so good about helping me, I'll give you some advice. You can take it or leave it. Life's too short for these kinds of things."

I opened the refrigerator and poured a glass of Kool-Aid. "What kind of things?"

"Well, you two have had some sort of a fight. So it's easy, stop fighting. You never know when the person you love will be gone for good. My mom always said, 'It's an empty house without anyone to love.' And sure enough now I'm alone I'd do anything to have someone to love. It scares me to death."

I was astounded by his level of maturity. "Are you forgetting our pact?" I asked. "You, young man, will never be alone in an empty house." Reluctantly, I walked over to the kitchen counter and picked up Peter's note.

It read: "Dear Annie, It was never my intention to hurt you. I can be nothing more than what I am. I will forever cherish the days and nights we spent together. It was a small piece of heaven. Please forgive me. I love you, Peter."

Without tears, I placed the note back in its envelope and turned toward Buddy and Jack. "Are you two hungry? What fast food shall we pick up tonight? Of course, if you want me to cook, I'm sure I can scramble an egg or something."

Buddy turned his nose up and gagged. "I know where there is a great drive-thru called McDonald's. Ever hear of it?"

I picked Jack up from around my legs, and gave him a kiss.

He said something in baby talk. Smiling at Buddy, I grabbed my purse. "That's Portuguese for, let's go to McDonald's." Buddy's laughter was a welcoming sound.

As we were carrying our drive-thru feast into the house, the phone rang. Buddy picked it up and had a brief conversation with Mattie. Then he handed the phone to me.

"Michelle's funeral has been set for two o'clock. Reverend Miles will officiate. Family members are expected a half hour early," she said, in a toneless voice. "I'll see you there." It was an obligatory call, devoid of Mattie humor.

Buddy and I spent the rest of the evening playing cards. My mind was not on the game. I was down a couple of bucks before I called it quits.

The next morning I called my secretary to cancel the day's appointments and typed Buddy's statement on my laptop computer.

Early afternoon, I called the police station and informed Investigator Morris that Buddy would be at the funeral. He didn't accuse me of deceiving him, but I could hear the insinuation in his voice. He, in turn, told me Buddy's father was being temporarily released under police surveillance.

When I told Buddy, he seemed pleased his father would be there. Jason came by and dropped off the only suit Buddy possessed. He tried it on, and it was a couple sizes too small.

"I haven't worn this suit since one of mom's friends got married," he complained. "I've always hated it. Do I have to wear it, Annie?"

I wasn't quite sure how to answer. "What would your mother want you to do?" I asked, avoiding the decision.

Buddy smiled. "If you want to know the truth, my mother would probably make me wear it. I don't suppose you know how to let the hem down. Your sewing is probably as bad as your cooking, right?"

Lightly punching him in his chin, I responded to his boyish charm by walking around his body. "Of course. If you're asking me, I would say be yourself. Wear your jeans and the jacket. The pants are definitely high waters, but the jacket you can roll up the sleeves and no one will know the difference."

Liking my suggestion, Buddy grabbed his lapels and smiled. "This hideous suit is definitely not my style."

"You're right. Don't wear it. She'll be proud of you no matter what you have on. You're a great kid. But you know that, don't you?"

Buddy took the compliment like any fourteen-year-old would; with his head held high.

"Now give me a chance to get dressed."

After changing my clothes, I ran across the street and left Jack in the care of Hannah and her mother. Then Buddy and I got in my car and left.

When we arrived at the funeral home, Buddy spotted his father and ran into his arms. Trying to hold back the tears, I uncomfortably sat down in one of the chairs toward the back.

I noticed there were two uniformed policemen at the two doors leading to the foyer. The mourners arrived in single file, giving their condolences to Buddy and his father. Peter and Mattie were nowhere in sight. Investigator Morris startled me as he sat down in the chair next to mine.

"So, Miss Stevens, you've known where the kid has been all along, haven't you?"

"Give me a break, Morris. I'm not stupid. You'd get a kick out of arresting me for harboring a material witness, wouldn't you?"

"I could have arrested you in the parking lot when I saw you getting out of the car. Don't push me, Miss Stevens I'm not stupid either."

His breath smelled of coffee. The expression in his eyes were hostile. "Did you at least bring the boy's statement with you?"

"You'll get it when I'm damn good and ready to give it to you. Now is definitely not the time. I suggest you walk away and leave me alone, and don't you dare talk to Buddy. People have eyes and someone may suspect he is cooperating with you. You've done enough damage to this investigation." I leaned my head in the direction of Michelle's casket.

Morris turned a deep shade of red completely understanding the message.

"You'll get your statement at the proper time and in the proper place, and, please, outside of public scrutiny. Do I make myself clear?"

He shrugged his shoulders. I was getting under his skin. I was glad.

"I'm not a patient man, Miss Stevens. See ya around," Morris threatened, as he got out of his chair and walked away.

A few seconds later, Mattie and Peter walked through the door. Uncomfortable at the prospect of facing them, I swallowed hard and prepared for the worst. Seconds later, Peter sat down in the chair previously occupied by Morris.

He tried to reach for my hand, but I drew back. "Leave me alone. I have a lot of thinking to do, and I'm not up to this right now. My only concern at this moment is Buddy's safety. Have you and Mattie made all the arrangements? I told Morris he gets the statement when I'm good and ready to give it to him. I'll find a quiet room at Mattie's, shut the door, and keep him busy for a while. If you have a better plan, tell me now. Buddy knows what to do."

To hide my feelings, I was speaking too fast. Peter nodded affirmatively. "We have the distractions planned if Buddy is tailed by any police officers. Let's hope for the best. All the other arrangements have been made. Once we get him out, he's going to a terrific home. My sister is looking forward to it. He'll love playing with my niece and nephew."

He'd surprised me again. "You didn't think I would pass him along to just anybody, did you? We made a pact. She's the best. She'll take good care of him. Mattie has written down the code he is to follow in case they put taps on our telephones. She makes an awesome spy."

"Apparently it runs in the family," I replied with sarcasm.

Peter touched his heart as if I had struck him a blow. "Touche, my dear. I take it I've not been forgiven. Frankly, I don't blame you."

Nevertheless, he looked disappointed. "If it makes you feel any better, you're not the only one hurting here. This has not been an easy decision. I'll suffer without you for the rest of my life," he whispered, looking at the floor.

I didn't want to listen to him, but he persisted.

"Try to understand. What happened to Michelle I don't want happening to you. Before this is all over, a lot of people may get killed. I would never forgive myself if I turned my back and allowed this tragedy to happen to you or Jack."

"If you had any respect for me at all, Peter, you would have confided in me." I looked him straight in the eye and instead of whispering my voice came out louder than I had intended. "Like the egotistical male you undoubtedly are, you made the decision to leave and allowed me no voice. Go ahead and destroy yourself, Peter. Alone is a good thing for a man like you."

People were beginning to stare. I gave him a look of scorn and didn't care. I directed my gaze toward Mattie who was sitting in a chair a couple of yards away talking to Reverend Miles. I tried to control my anger, but the hurt returned, making it difficult to talk.

"You two can keep your little secrets to yourselves. I'm through! You do what a man's got to do. Relationships are built on trust and mutual understanding. We didn't have it; therefore, we had nothing."

Without saying another word, he got to his feet. I sat in the chair for a long time before my breathing returned to normal. Trying to compose myself, I saw Buddy coming over with his father.

"This is Annie, Dad," Buddy said, with a hint of pride in his voice.

Buddy's father sat down and shook my hand. "Hi, I'm Darrell Jacobs. My son tells me you've been taking care of him. I thank you from the bottom of my heart. He's the only thing I've left in this world, ma'am. If something happens to him, there'd be nothin' left to live for."

I leaned over and whispered in Mr. Jacobs' ear. "I understand how you feel. Don't worry. I'll keep Buddy safe. Give me a couple of days and I'll come to see you. I won't tell you where he is. In fact, I won't know myself. But you will be able to communicate. We'll work out something."

It was too dangerous for us to be seen talking to each other. I looked at Buddy and gave him a wink.

"You should be proud of your son. Michelle has raised him up to be a fine young man."

Catching my implication, Buddy's father nodded. "You're right, Miss Stevens. I deserved that. She was a fine woman. I don't know how to live without her. I wish I could turn back the clock, but I'll do right by Buddy. You wait and see."

Not really believing him, I kept the thought to myself. The truth was it really didn't matter. Buddy would become a wonderful human being without his help. Thanks to his mother, he was more than already there.

"I hope you'll change for Buddy's sake; but, even if you don't, he has a lot of friends who will take care of him."

Embarrassed by my frank remarks, he rose from his seat. What was wrong with me? I was being rude to everyone.

"Thanks, Miss Stevens. You are being more than fair."

Mr. Jacobs' chin lowered a notch or two as he walked away. Buddy quickly sat down in the chair his father vacated. You couldn't help but notice all the security. Buddy was terribly uncomfortable.

"I sure hope your plan works, Annie," he whispered. "I have to tell you I'm scared."

I placed my arms around him and gave him a squeeze. "Haven't I promised you everything will turn out all right? Now, give me another hug. Who knows if we'll get the opportunity later. Good-bye, my friend. I'm going to miss you. Just hang in there and be brave."

Buddy took a deep breath and smiled. Mattie appeared casting a shadow in my eyes. "Don't you run off yet, young man," she snapped. "Here. Give me a hug, too." Buddy stood up and did what she asked. "Here. I have something for you. It's a gift."

Mattie pulled a small tissue-wrapped package out of her pocket. Buddy enthusiastically looked at it, unsure whether to open it now or later. "We don't have all day. Open it." Buddy tore the wrapping off the box, reached in and came out with a blue plastic card. He seemed puzzled by its contents.

A sly smile played across Mattie's face as she took the card from his hand. "This here is what Mattie calls the gold card. Don't look at me like that. It's not Visa. Put it in your wallet. When you get to your new home, you better be using it."

Buddy and I were both confused. "It's a library card, silly." Mattie whispered. "It's the best card no money can buy, absolutely priceless."

Buddy smiled and shook his head. "Thanks, I think." He slid it into his pocket conscious of the many stares.

"I better get back to my dad," he said with concern in his voice. We watched him walk back to the front where his father was standing by the casket. He knelt down, closed his eyes, and silently prayed for his mother.

The Reverend Miles stood calmly at the podium ready to conduct the service. Michelle had a lot of friends. I saw handkerchiefs and wet eyes all around the room. Mattie didn't say a word. She walked away to sit with Peter two aisles over.

* * *

The wind was whipping the coats of the mourners away from their bodies. You could hear the rumble of the thunder in the distance as the sun was dipping into the dark gray clouds. I hoped for Buddy's sake the rain would wait until after the burial service. Reverend Miles opened his book.

"No matter how well we think we have prepared ourselves for the troubles we know will be ahead, it's times like these the answers seem so far away. We are never fully equipped outside of the grace of God, which comes to us moment by moment, just when we need it. Please bow your heads."

I watched the others as they closed their eyes and bowed their heads. Could I believe Michelle was in a happier place, away from the only person she loved? I wasn't convinced.

" Dear Lord, sometimes life takes our breath away. May we always have enough left to praise you when your work takes a beautiful woman like Michelle away from her son who loves her, a husband who always believed in her, and her friends she blessed with her presence. She will be missed. Thank you for allowing us to love this remarkable woman. "

I wiped the tears from my eyes, sorry I never knew her. Although in a way I did. I would know her son. I could thank her for that. Everyone said their condolences and got in their cars. Some of them would be attending the small reception at Mattie's.

Buddy's father looked into his son's eyes and said something I couldn't hear. Whatever it was Buddy seemed pleased. I kept my distance knowing he needed this opportunity to say his final good-bye alone. Sadly, Buddy was leaving both of his parents. Hopefully, his father's good-bye would not be forever.

Buddy leaned down and kissed her coffin. Wiping the tears from his eyes, he reluctantly turned to leave. Mattie approached, putting her hand on his arm and guiding him to the car. He needed her special kind of support. More importantly, he needed to know where he was going, who he would meet. I felt a slight stab of jealousy.

Jason opened the door to the back seat, and Peter got behind the wheel. With a quiet dignity, they left the cemetery.

I was standing alone under a large maple tree. I could see Mr. Jacobs' face. His shoulders were hunched like that of an old man; shoulders that spoke of guilt and long-forgotten promises from the woman he loved. Although he had left her many times before, he didn't want to leave her now. He, too, bent down and kissed the gleaming metal surface of her coffin. A solitary rose was lying on the ground. He picked it up, breathing in it's special scent.

Before he had a chance to put it back on her coffin, a corrections officer grabbed his wrists, placed them behind his back, handcuffing him. The rose fell discarded to the ground.

He was escorted to a large blue van discreetly parked at the curb. It took them a couple of seconds to load him into the caged-in area of the back seat. Once safely secured, the two officers got in the front seat and drove away. Buddy's father used the sleeve of his jacket to wipe away his tears.

Alone, I walked down the hill through the slippery wet grass. Across the field I could see two men with their shovels waiting for me to leave. They were going to have to wait. I had something to say to her.

I picked up the rose and smelled its sweet aroma. It joined the rest of them lying on the top of her casket. On the pink tag it read: 'To my dear sweet mother.' Tears welled up in my eyes as I thought of her son. I remembered the strange way Michelle looked at me the night Mattie had saved their lives. Her silent message was now quite clear.

"Michelle, Buddy's going to be all right. He is going to make you proud, proud to have been the mother of such a child. He'll always have a place to belong, a place to call home. That's my promise to you. I love your son."

I put my right hand to my lips and touched her coffin. The metal had been warmed by the sun.

CHAPTER
XX

I found a parking place a couple blocks from Mattie's. The rain had stopped falling but a peculiar shift in the clouds turned the afternoon cold. I glanced down at my black pumps wishing for my leather boots. Locking the car door, I started walking. Rows of wooden houses were linked together crowding the narrow street.

These houses were unlike the ones where I grew up. There were bars on the windows. Nothing was growing except for the weeds around the rusted old cars which had been abandoned by their owners. I thought of those cars, and I thought of the people who lived here. Did we abandon them the same way they abandoned their cars? The horrible appearance of the sky and the rumbling thunder seemed to answer my question.

I shivered, buttoning my trench coat tightly around my black wool dress as the wind whipped the hair from around my neck. The sidewalks were so cracked they jutted out from the ground causing me to slow my pace. I thought of the many times I had taken Jack for a walk in my own neighborhood. A mother could never do that here.

Poor wretched dogs were tied to the trees barking at my intrusion. Something cracked under my shoe. It was a dirty syringe. Grimacing, I walked a little faster appreciating the fact I had been a sheltered kid growing up in rural white America.

When I arrived at her door, the first person I saw was Mattie. With a frown on her face, she shook my hand. "Glad you could make it, Annie." Taking me by the arm, she dragged me to the dining room. We both ignored the men in uniform.

"I have someone here I want you to meet," she said, looking around. "Paula, Paula dear, come over here."

I noticed a young white woman with a petite shape coming toward us. She was probably in her early twenties, dark brown hair, and a prominent nose. There were dark circles around her large expressive eyes. She had spectacular looking skin, pale but flawless. I could sense how uncomfortable she felt around so many people. I watched as Mattie placed her arm around her shoulder offering comfort.

"You must be Annie," Paula said. "Thanks to Mattie, I feel I know you. I would like to be your friend."

"I'm sorry. I didn't catch your name." The noise in the room died down.

Confused, but still quite amicable, she replied, "Oh, I thought you knew who I was. My name is Paula Jennings. I checked myself out of the hospital yesterday afternoon. Mattie calls this place her therapy center. Although I'm still intimidated by the crowd, it's the first time in months I've gone somewhere and cared about somebody other than myself. Does that make sense?"

Understanding her meaning quite well, I smiled, giving Mattie the evil eye. She gave me back one of those I-told-you-so looks.

"Yes, Paula." I said, patting her hand. "I'm sure we can be friends. Trust me. Mattie's therapy center works. You should have seen me when I first started my treatment. How long has it been now? It feels like at least a couple of centuries. While you're getting this so-called treatment, be sure to bring lots of tissues."

Mattie shrugged her shoulders, pretending ignorance. Paula, puzzled, exchanged a few more social pleasantries, then turned toward the refreshment line and left.

"Na, Na, Na, Na, Na, Na, now you're not the only white woman here," Mattie said, singing that obnoxious song in my ear.

I couldn't help myself. I burst out laughing. Mattie smiled and hit me in the arm. "A beautiful thing it is, that laugh of yours."

"It sure beats your singing," I jokingly responded.

"Don't think I'm going to let you feel sorry for yourself for long, young lady. You're my friend, and I intend to keep you. Oh, I'll give you a few days to cool off. Here, take this."

I looked at my hand to see what she'd placed in it. Money. I knew what she wanted. I played her game anyway. "What's this for?" I asked.

"I'll give you two nights. After that I'm coming over for dinner. See to it you pick up one of those roasted chickens at the grocery store," she yelled, as she started to walk away. Someone else was in need of her attention. She turned back and raised her hand. "Oh, and don't forget the wine. You get to buy that. I'm broke."

Singing, "Na, Na, Na, Na, Na, Na, you're not the only white woman here," Mattie headed for the kitchen.

I could still hear the incorrigible woman's discourse, as she shut the door. I put her money in my pocket and smelled the food. I was hungry. Heading for the refreshment table, Investigator Morris bumped into my hip.

Keeping my voice as calm as I could, I took the man's outstretched hand. "Ah, Investigator Morris, what a pleasant surprise. It didn't take you long to find me. Isn't it a coincidence? I was just about to look for you."

Morris loosened his tie and suspiciously looked around the room. The guests were enjoying Mattie's feast.

"Stop toying with me, Miss Stevens," he said angrily. "I'm

not a patient man. Do you have the statement or not? If this is your idea of some practical joke, tonight you'll find yourself in jail."

We entered the foyer and walked down the hall. "Morris, I don't joke with a little boy's life," I said, trying to keep the animosity from my voice.

"My informants tell me you like hanging around all these black people. Why is that, Miss Stevens? You're pretty close to some black stud I've been told."

"Morris, let's get our business over so you can take the bigotry back to the station, shall we?"

Morris pulled off the tie and put it in his coat pocket. "Sounds like a good idea to me. Hanging around here makes me feel like vomiting, a little too close to them, if you know what I mean."

Funny he should mention vomit. That's just what he was, the wretched creature.

"Why are you so interested in this statement?" I asked. "It surely can't be your altruistic dedication to your work. Since it's obvious to me you don't care about the boy, why care about his mother's killers?"

Even though he should have been mindful of the fact he was speaking to me, his words were not chosen carefully. I must have been getting under the man's skin.

"Oh, come now. You're an intelligent woman. If I can get Michelle Jacobs' killers, that's three more African Americans off the street. And, of course, that'll makes my job a lot easier. It's my duty to uphold the law."

He reminded me of my father. I wanted to say, "Why don't you just call them niggers you piece of shit?" But I didn't. It'd sure make my job easier. Oh, where was a tape recorder when I needed one? Knowing I was talking to a moron, I tried to keep my temper in check.

"I think we understand each other quite well," I replied. "It's my duty to protect my client from cops like you!" We were nearing Mattie's office. "Please don't make a scene."

I opened the door allowing him to enter. As I quietly closed the door behind me, I glanced around the room. It was the first time I had been in her office. Prior to today, it had been off limits, her private place for quiet reflection. It was lovely. There was an extraordinary mahogany desk in the center of the room. Several glass-beveled bookshelves lined the walls to the ceiling.

I placed my briefcase on the shiny glass top. There were picture frames of, I could only suppose, Mattie's secret family. I was not surprised to see the state-of-the-art computer equipment on top of her desk.

I opened my briefcase and handed Morris the statement. He took it from my outstretched hand and sat down to read it. Seemingly impressed, he folded it in his pocket and stood to leave.

"Not so fast," I said, putting my arm on his sleeve. "We have some unfinished business to conduct."

Morris's face seemed puzzled.

"The boy. What are your plans for him?"

With his hand on the knob, he turned and opened the door. "To tell you the truth, I was just on my way to get him. Don't worry. We'll put the kid into protective custody. Anything else?"

I walked over to him and slammed the door. "Yes. The kid has a name. Perhaps we could work out a deal. Give me a chance to protect him."

Morris chuckled. "You have to be kidding, Stevens. You'd get yourself killed. These men are dangerous. The kid is my responsibility. He stays with me, and that's final."

Morris removed my hand from the door and gave me a disdainful stare. Hoping that I had stalled him long enough, we left Mattie's office.

A police officer immediately approached Morris and

whispered in his ear. He turned back and gave me a scowl. In several angry strides, he stood next to me.

"It seems the boy has disappeared. Where is he?" he asked menacingly close to my face.

People were beginning to notice our exchange. "I haven't the slightest idea, sir." I said shrugging my shoulders. "You and I've been together since I arrived."

He walked toward the foyer looking for his men. The guests were still mingling around the refreshment table, balancing their food on paper plates. I grabbed a plate and started eating a few snacks.

"I'll turn this house inside out," Morris yelled. "Where's the kid? What have you people done with him?"

The guests gave him a confused look and whispered among themselves. "What kid are you looking for?" one guest asked.

"If we don't find him, you're all going to jail!"

Letting out a sigh of relief, I knew Buddy was safe. I leaned against the wall and enjoyed Morris's theatrics. It wasn't long before the creep came back to me.

"You're involved in this, aren't you, Stevens?" he asked, with a clenched fist at my face. "You're being a very foolish woman. No one's to leave this house. I want the doors locked and the adults and kids in the foyer. Stay put, or you'll be arrested."

The other officers secured the door and corralled the rest of us in the living room.

He grabbed Mattie by the arm. "It's your house. You come with me." She did not look in my direction. They left the room, heading for the basement stairs.

Approximately twenty minutes later, Morris had failed to find Buddy. I took a couple more bites of potato salad and put my plate on the table. I knew it was my turn as he stomped toward me.

"Miss Stevens, you are under arrest. You have the right to

remain silent. Anything you say, can and will be used against you in a court of law. If you cannot afford an attorney, one will be appointed for you."

I turned toward him trying to control my anger. "I'm well aware of my Miranda rights, sir. I have done nothing. Let go of me!" I demanded, jerking my arm out of his hold.

With one hand on my arm and the other in his pocket, he pulled the handcuffs off his belt.

"I'd watch my step if I were you, sir," I said calmly.

Quite comfortable with my own abilities to represent myself, I extended my hands.

"Up against the wall!" He yelled.

I did as he asked, turning my face to the wall. "Go ahead and do your job! Arrest me on your phony charges!"

Morris roughly used his elbow to pin my body to the wall, handcuffing me from behind.   Mattie entered the room with a confused look on her face.

"What's going on here?" she asked, confronting Morris while the rest of the guests stood protectively behind her. He paid no heed to her question, pushing her aside. Surprised by his bullying, she clinched her fist to throw a punch. Morris grabbed her hand.

"I wouldn't do that if I were you, Miss Turner." The crowd moved forward blocking Morris's exit.

"You let her go or I'll..."

"Or you'll what? You threaten me and your ass will go to jail with hers." Morris was hurting my arm. I was sure to have a bruise in the morning. It would make a terrific picture of police brutality.

"I'll report you to the police commissioner and his board. I know him personally," Mattie said with her finger close to his face.

"Go ahead! You're the ones harboring my material witness."

The last thing we needed was a small riot. Moving between the two of them, I whispered in Mattie's ear.

"It's all right. Quick! Go get your video camera. Don't worry about me. I'll sue him in civil court." Mattie immediately understood, heading quickly for her office.

Morris shoved me into another officer who was standing by the stairway. "You stay put. Mike, see that she doesn't go anywhere." Mike took me gently by the arm. Another officer came forward and stood on the other side of me.

Two other uniformed police officers approached Morris. Huddling together, I heard one of them say they'd looked everywhere and there was no way the kid was in the house. With an evil expression on his face, Morris returned to me.

"What did you do with the boy, Stevens?" he asked, in a threatening tone.

"What would I know about hiding kids? I'm just a stupid female who likes black people, remember?" That wasn't a smart thing to say. The people in the room began to surround the police.

Mattie came running down the hall holding the camera. My voice changed back to its normal pitch. "I had nothing to do with the boy's disappearance. I haven't the faintest idea where he is."

Mattie maneuvered the camera to get Morris's response. "Smile, honey. Remember what they did to Rodney King?" she mocked as she waved to him with her eye focusing on the lens.

Morris flung his fists in Mattie's direction. "Turn that thing off," he yelled. Mattie backed away from him and continued filming. He roughly grabbed me by the arm and pulled me in the direction of the front door. The guests in the house were getting extremely agitated.

Peter came out of nowhere and stopped short of the door, blocking his escape.

"You're not going anywhere with her, sir," Peter said. "She's done nothing wrong." His feet were firmly planted on the floor. His arms were at his chest ready to push him back into the foyer area of the house, if necessary.

"Get out of my way!" Morris demanded.

Mattie walked over to Peter and whispered in his ear. He reluctantly moved aside. Fearing a riot, Morris quickly shoved me down the steps. Two uniformed police officers did not like what they saw and came forward getting between the two of us. They said something to Morris I could not hear then gently took me by the arm and escorted me through the gate onto the sidewalk. Like Buddy's father, they placed me into the back seat. It was cold and my coat was still in the house. While they peeled rubber, I turned to look at the crowd congregating outside.

Jason was standing next to Peter with a troubled look on his face. Peter was visibly upset. Mattie had her camera pointed directly at the squad car. They all waved good-bye.

Arriving at the station, I went through the standard booking procedures. First, they took my fingerprints, then they questioned me concerning my background. Several Polaroid pictures were taken of my profile.

Later, a female officer led me to a room with a shower stall and told me to strip. She seemed quite chagrined. It wasn't every day she had a lawyer to abase. I took off my dress and placed it on the cold steel chair. I knew the procedure, but I never thought I'd have to experience it.

"Open your mouth," she said. I did as she asked.

"Now bend over and spread your cheeks," the woman ordered.

Thoroughly humiliated but courageously driven by my anger, I bent over so that she could conduct a body cavity search. Then she turned on the water and told me to take a shower.

"Do I have to wash my hair?" The woman glanced at my long thick hair and shook her head. Then she left me while I soaped myself down. A couple of seconds later, she returned with some clothes and told me to get dressed. I had seen these orange suits on people a hundred times in the courtroom. I was freezing. Anything was better than nothing. I quickly donned the warm jumpsuit.

Trying to remain strong, I thought of Mattie and that camera. Hadn't she taught me to find humor in every situation. At least, orange was somewhat my color. The slippers were a lovely shade of pink. Finally dressed, I looked at myself in the mirror and laughed.

The woman deputy shook her head and gave me a queer look. I shrugged my shoulders and turned my back to her.

Ready to leave, the woman placed the handcuffs on my wrists and escorted me to a cell. Finally alone and happy to be away from them, I sat down on my bunk. Closing my eyes, I discovered I was tired. Hopefully, Mattie would come up with some bail and this would be over soon.

Several hours later, Benjamin Goldstein came to my cell. I yawned nonchalantly, disturbed from my sleep. A uniformed guard placed the key in the lock. Goldstein stood silently watching. He said nothing. I was surprised. I thought he'd get some type of smug satisfaction in seeing me here. Maybe there was human compassion in him after all.

The guard started to place the handcuffs on my wrist. "We're only going across the hall, officer. Leave them off," Goldstein requested.

The guard shook his head and placed them on my wrists anyway. "Sorry, sir, but it's standard procedure."

As we entered the conference room, he was obviously upset.

"What the hell do you think you're doing?" he yelled, flinging his arms in an agitated manner and slamming his file on the table. "Are you insane?"

"Bullshit!" I yelled back. "If you know what's good for you, you'll back off. Leave me alone." I was sick of the whole mess. He was toying with me, and I wasn't going to play his game. I'd been through enough degradation for one day.

"You're talking to me, not some poor schmuck who doesn't know his rights. Morris had no grounds to arrest me, and you know it!"

Goldstein did not reply. He took a seat, letting out a long exasperated sigh.

"Look! Take a good look!" I screamed, lifting my arms and pointing to the bruises Morris had left. My wrists were red and swollen from the handcuffs.

"That bigoted piece of shit is going to lose his job and if you're on his side, I'll sue your ass, too."

I was unable to control my temper. "Do your job, Mr. Goldstein. File your phony ass charges, and I'll be delighted to see you in court. As soon as I'm bailed out, I'm going to slap this city with the biggest civil case it has ever seen. I have nothing else to say to you. Now, damn it, put me back in my cell!"

Not responding to my orders, Goldstein rubbed his chin. "You're actually relishing every minute of this, aren't you?" He asked.

Goldstein reached in his pocket for his eye glasses and opened the file. "You're forgetting the fact the city pays your paycheck, too. We're friends, remember. I'm on your side."

He caught the surprise on my face and politely extended his hand for me to sit down. "Calm down. I'll make you a deal. Tomorrow morning I'll file disciplinary charges against Inspector Morris. Hopefully, the board will agree with me, and he'll lose his job. But you know how long those things can take."

Was I hearing him right? The honorable prosecutor was agreeing with me? A puzzled expression was still on my face.

"Caught you off guard, didn't I? If I wasn't working in the State's Attorney's Office, I'd ask you to be my client. A prosecutor's job not only pursues the guilty; it should also protect the innocent.

-344-

I'm not saying you're completely Miss Innocent, but you've every right to be upset."

He leaned into me and whispered, "Now, can we talk like two civil human beings? Cut me some slack here."

Placated by the fact that he understood the seriousness of the situation, I sat more comfortably in my chair.

"You're still a sneaky, annoying, self-centered jerk, but if you're going to help me get out of here, I'll end it there."

Goldstein gave me a nefarious smile and pulled out his pen and paper.

"You have no idea what a horrible experience this has been. Furthermore, I'm not harboring a material witness. I have no idea where Buddy is, and I don't want to know."

Goldstein was unconvinced and shook his head. "You're a good liar. Wait! Before you start on me again, listen to what I'm trying to say to you. As long as you can communicate with the kid, we'll do it your way. If you'd come to me in the first place, you wouldn't be in this mess."

For the second time in one sitting, Goldstein was on my side. "Morris is an idiot, not to mention the worst kind of cop. I've been wanting to strip him of that badge for years. If you tell me Buddy will testify, we'll do this your way."

I was surprised to hear him tell me this, but I didn't want to fall into a trap; his trap could keep me in this cell, and I wanted out.

"You have my word he'll testify against the creeps who killed Michelle," I said, assuring myself as well as him. "Buddy knows his mother's killers. I don't want him to end up dead just like she did. Speaking of which, if you were so keen on getting Darrell Jacobs to cooperate, why weren't you protecting his family?"

Goldstein was not going to admit that he screwed up, nor did I expect him to. "It's a tragedy that will not happen again. You may want to quit your job and sue the city for that, too. I wouldn't blame you. It's my fault. Apparently, the gangs have moles everywhere."

"Could you put that on tape?" I asked. Goldstein frowned and shook his head. For the first time that day, I smiled. He smiled back.

"Too bad," I said. "It'd make my job a little easier. Get a nice college education for Buddy and my son, I'm sure. You should have heard the things Morris said to me privately. Darn it. Not a word was said on tape."

"I want him gone as badly as you do." He seemed sincere. Perhaps I could trust him.

"Thanks, Ben," I said meaning it.

"What, we're friends now?" Goldstein asked. "That's the first time you've called me by my first name."

"Don't push your luck. For now, we might be on the same side. Don't worry. It won't last. Morris told me all he was interested in was using Buddy to get more African Americans off the street. Do you think I could get it in as hearsay? I'll have to do my research, excited utterance or something."

Goldstein did not seem surprised. "I know what kind of man Morris is," he replied shaking his head. "I'll promise you I'll do what I can."

"In that case, you have my word Buddy will appear when you direct him," I said gratefully. "If there are any questions you wish to ask him, write them out. I'll see to it he receives them. Now, if you can get me out of this hellhole, I want to go home to my son. I've been a lousy mother and I have a lot of making up to do. And, as for that lawsuit, I have two years to file it, so, you better watch your step."

Goldstein chuckled, stood up, and motioned the guard forward. "Let us out, George. This obstinate woman may change her mind. See to it Miss Stevens gets the clothes Miss Turner left at the front door. I'm releasing her and dropping the charges against her for lack of probable cause."

"Yes, sir," George said, opening the cell to let me out.

Goldstein took my hand and shook it. Turning toward George, he said, "Oh, and see to it she gets the privacy she needs to get dressed. We don't need to give Miss Stevens any more counts to that lawsuit she intends to file."

He once again looked at me and nodded. "I can't say it's been a pleasure, Anne. Foes can be friends as well as enemies. See you around, my dear."

He lifted my hand and kissed it. "Oh, by the way," he said, walking back to the table to pick up his file. "I almost forgot. You've got a ride home. She's ranting and raving out in the waiting room. Has been for hours. Give Mattie my regards, please. I was told she took Paula Jennings home. Thank her for me, will you? I'd do it myself, but I treasure my profile. One more thing, orange is not your color."

Goldstein walked away whistling. Trying to get the last word in, was he? I began yelling at his ugly back. "That nose of yours could use a little plastic surgery."

Without turning around, he waved a farewell. After dressing privately, I was escorted out the door. When they pushed the buzzer to exit the Sheriff's Office, Mattie was frantically standing by the door.

"Are you all right? I've been here two hours trying to post bail. They're all a bunch of jerks!"

Mattie started tormenting the poor officer in the window.

"We're going to sue each and every one of you. No one seizes my friend and gets away with it. As citizens in this country, we have our rights to be free from unlawful search and seizure." She conspiratorially whispered in my ear, "How am I doing?"

"They're going to arrest you. That's how you're doing. Let's get out of here!" I grabbed her by the arm. She jerked it away and went back to the window.

"We're going to be rich! We'll see you in court."

The officer at the window smiled and waved good-bye. She headed for one of the plastic gray chairs in the corner and picked up her video camera. Mattie placed it over her shoulder and limped proudly to the metal doors.

"Come on, my dear friend," she said, taking me by the arm. "I hope the city is well insured," she yelled before the door shut.

Reaching the car, I held out my hand. "Give me the car keys! How on earth did you drive? No, don't answer me." Mattie did what I asked, handing me her keys.

"It's safer if I drive. Besides, I've had a very bad day and all I want is to get home in one piece." I started the engine while Mattie took her time adjusting her leg. It wasn't long before she spoke.

"You call this a bad day?" Placing the camcorder between her legs, she turned to face me. "No way! This is your lucky day. You're going to be a rich woman."

Pulling into the turning lane, I hated to disappoint her. "Sorry. I'll have a hell of a lot more fun hanging the city's mistakes over Benjamin Goldstein's head."

A surprised Mattie began to protest. Placing my hand on her lips, I said, "Don't say it! You're the one who's always telling me money isn't everything."

Mattie shook her head ready to deny it. "When did I say that? Oh, well, money may not be everything, but revenge is absolutely orgasmic. Oh baby! Oh baby! When I think of all the trouble the city council gave me, I mean us."

She couldn't stop rubbing her hands together. "Those lousy politicians and their stupid rules. We'll show them."

"I hate to burst your bubble, but I mean it. I'm not filing a lawsuit."

"I think I've gone deaf." Mattie stuck her finger in her ear.

"I don't think I'm hearing you."

"Look, I didn't pay for nineteen years of schooling to sit at home. I'm a practicing attorney. I don't care about revenge. All I want is Morris's job. If I can take that bastard off the police force, I'm a happy woman."

Mattie was unable to mask her disappointment. She looked out the window and for a few seconds remained silent. "That's all you want? Who am I anyway? You're still pissed at me. You wouldn't want to take revenge on me, would you? If you do, I wouldn't blame you. What do guilty parties plead to?"

"It's *nollo contendere*. It means 'no contest,'" I replied.

"Then I plead *'nollo contendere,'* she said as she wiped her brow. "Oh, God, when they put you in that police car, I was ready to have a heart attack. Poor ol' Mattie was almost on her deathbed."

"Deathbed my ass. I saw you limping out there with that camera on your shoulder. Be honest, you were having the time of your life."

She picked up the camcorder and started filming me. "I must say I was a pretty good camera woman. Maybe we should move to Hollywood."

As we pulled into the driveway, we saw three kids out in the backyard smashing one kid on the bottom of the heap. "What?" I replied sarcastically. "And give up all of this?"

Too exhausted to break it up, we sat taking in the scene. When the children saw Mattie exit the car, all four of them scrambled into the house.

"See you later, dear. I have some children to kill. By the way, don't forget about that dinner. See you at your house in a couple of days."

I waved good-bye. Remembering where my own car was parked, I turned to go in the house. Oh, the heck with it. I was in a hurry to get home. Jack needed me.

If I thought this afternoon's walk down this street gave me the creeps, nighttime was worse. It took me a couple of minutes to reach my car. Shivering, I quickly turned the key. I was struck from behind. The last coherent sound I heard was Peter's voice.

* * *

I was cold and the air smelled of smoke. Slowly my senses became more alert. My hands were tied behind my back, but my feet were free. I could feel the damp grass at my face. Pretending I was still unconscious, I tried to listen. There were several male voices. I, of course, was the topic of their discussion.

"Kill the bitch now and be done with it," someone said. The more authoritative male voice was calming the rest of them down.

"We have to find the kid. She must've had a hand in his vanishing act; otherwise, why would they have arrested her?"

Another voice from behind began to speak. "Let's say we put this tire iron in that fire and burn her face with it. That ought to make her talk."

Another voice, one I thought I recognized, spoke up. "Come on, Leon. I like this lady, and I owe her, man. Let me talk to her. If she's scared, she'll tell me where the kid is. God damn it! She's the fucking law. We don't want no trouble. The heat will come crawlin' asking a lot of questions."

I recognized the voice. It was Joseph Gibbons. Maybe I had at least one ally. I rather doubted he would go against the homies.

"Ain't no way," one male voice yelled. "Two-faced, ain't ya, Gib baby? You gots to be kicking back, man. Listen to the boss. We do what he says."

His idea was not the popular opinion. I was so afraid. I had to think of a way out of here. These men were Michelle's killers.

"We'll douse her in fuel oil and throw her in the fire. That way they ain't never gonna find a body," one of them suggested.

As I lay feigning unconsciousness, suddenly someone grabbed me by the wrists and dragged me toward the group. I could feel its welcoming warmth. Rather ironic if they were going to burn me in it. Cold water was thrown in my face while someone else kicked me in the stomach. I had not eaten anything. I began to choke. The nausea in my stomach produced some bile in my throat. I swallowed hard trying not to whimper.

A man in a black leather jacket with a blue knit hat stuck his face into mine. "So you're finally awake. Sit up!" he demanded. I raised my body without my hands. Someone shoved me closer to him from behind. "We've some violatin' to do, girl. You gonna find out the hard way what that is."

I was so sick I didn't want to move. Opening my eyes a little further, I looked around the crowd. There were at least twenty pairs of formidable black men with gold teeth staring down at me from across the bonfire. I was frightened. These men were used to this type of cruel treatment. These were men who had been subjected to more atrocities than a human being could ever imagine.

The men were talking casually as if they did this type of thing every day. They did. I cleared my throat. At first I couldn't find my voice.

The one I guessed was their leader came forward. Bending down, he yanked on my hair and pulled me to my feet. I knew I was looking into the face of evil.

Edward Leon, the Scab, was 5'9" and weighed approximately 280 pounds. He had an extremely large neck and no chin. His physical presence reflected his strength and the power he held over his men.

He wore a pair of black sweatpants, and a black leather vest with no shirt. Once he had you, it was all over. I could see the heat floating out of his nostrils. His eyes bore into mine, reminding me of a bull as it spotted the matador. There was no escape.

I could smell his nauseating breath. Pleased by the fear he saw in my eyes, he slapped me hard across the face. I moaned and fell to the ground. Covering my head with my arms, I lay there with the taste of blood and dirt in my mouth waiting for the next blow.

A rusty metal folding chair was pulled up in front of the fire. Behind me, a man I could not see, picked me up under my armpits and planted me firmly in the seat. A sharp snapping sound and tiny flames shot up in the air. Hoping to concentrate on something other than my fear, I tried to remember the times I had looked at such a fire while camping with my brother. The memory was short-lived.

A younger man moved into the ring and stood next to Leon. The crowd kept taunting him, urging him forward.

"Go for it, Roundy. She ain't nothing but a scared, spoiled cracker. Violate her," another voice yelled from behind. I'd heard of this expression, but I didn't have time to think about the consequences.

Roundy was smaller in build, possibly sixteen or seventeen. He reached down and pulled a long stick out from the burning logs. I caught the look of satisfaction in his eyes as he walked around my chair, taunting me. He ripped my shirt sleeve, and without a second's hesitation, placed the burning red stick across my right forearm.

The more I screamed the more the crowd applauded. I tried not to think about the agonizing pain of my burning flesh. Its acrid smell filled my nostrils. Terrified, I watched Leon approach. For the second time, he slapped me hard across my face.

"Are you ready to talk, you lousy bitch?"

Grabbing the smoldering stick from the boy's hand, he leered it at me, pressing it closer to my face. Instantly I tried to back away, but I was firmly held by the man behind me.

"Remember this here stick, Lady," he said as it almost touched my cheek. "It'd be a shame now, wouldn't it? Ruin your pretty little face. Just tell us where your friend Buddy is and Leon here will let ya go."

Frightened but unable to control my anger, I struggled with the man that held me. Glaring at Leon, I attempted to spit in his face. It hit the ground, missing its mark. The young man who had burned me with the poker moved in closer and said, "You shouldn't have done that. You're in big trouble now."

"Please, I don't know where Buddy is! Honest. I haven't done anything. I have a baby at home who needs his mother," I said pleading with them.

There were a few faces in the crowd who were not enjoying this. I tried to find Joseph Gibbons, but I didn't see him. None of them would have the guts to go against a guy like Leon. He was like the black-robed reaper. It would mean death for them. It was hopeless to try.

He approached me and held the stick above my head. "Feisty little bitch, isn't she, guys?" Guided by Leon's joke, they all laughed in unison. Leon moved closer and took the poker from Roundy. He placed it on the previously burnt part of my right arm and ran the smoldering stick down to my wrist.

Once again the excruciating pain caused me to scream. "Now, little lady, doesn't that feel good?" Bending down, he blew off the smoke from my cauterized arm. I could smell my skin and his odious breath. I wanted to gag.

"Please," I begged, "I'll do what you ask. Just let me go."

"I'm losing my patience," Leon said, poking the stick at my face again. "You're wasting my time. If you don't talk, I'm going to start with both arms and move to your nipples." He ripped the sleeve of my left arm. He didn't give me a chance to say anything. Leon stuck the burning stick down my left arm and set fire to it.

"Just kill me and be done with it!" I screamed, anguished by the pain. Then he pointed to the gun stuck in his belt.

"You're right about dead, lady. Do you see this?" It was a silver-chromed revolver tucked into his pants. "You tell us where Buddy is, and I'll shoot you in the head. I'll give you my word I won't scorch your little body no more. What do you say, guys? Might feel mighty fine between the legs, wouldn't it?"

He grabbed hold of my chin and put the stick next to my eyes. "Of course, if you prefer a nice slow death, I'll be happy to fry your face first, and then we can hit the private parts."

The wind suddenly changed direction causing the cinders and smoke to shift in his face. Leon moved away from its path. Tears filled my eyes and I started to choke. Then it suddenly occurred to me. A smile of triumph curved at my lips. I don't know why. I just knew. Not a trace of fear remained. I began to howl with laughter. Leon gave me an absurd frown. "What's so funny?" he asked.

"For years, I wanted somebody to do this to me. I wanted to die. I prayed to die. I'm like a cat with nine lives. I'm a human cat. That's what I am. You're all looking at a human cat. I'm not going to die, you are, " I said, laughing harder.

The men looked at me like I was nuts. Leon stood apart, not finding it the least bit funny.

"Don't think I'll fall for your tricks. You're going to be dead, Miss Cat Woman." He moved closer to my face.

I looked him straight in the eye. "No, Leon, I'm not. That's one thing I'm sure of. I wasn't brought to this point in my life to die, not while I've only just discovered how to live!"

As if confirming what I said, a voice was heard further out in the field. After a few seconds, another voice yelled, "Let her go!"

Leon, startled, turned to face the sounds in the distance. His men turned too, but were momentarily blinded by the light from the fire.   Their bodies instinctively moved in front of their leader to protect him.

"Who is out there?" Leon asked.

A familiar voice replied, "We have you surrounded. Let the woman go." The voice was Jason's. I tried to get up from the chair. Another man grabbed me by the hair and threw me to the ground.

My arms were numb.   I couldn't feel anything.   As I lay there, I tried to gather my bearings. I could see silhouettes in the distance. A hundred or so men were carrying weapons and moving closer. When they came within fifty feet, they stopped. Jason came out from among the crowd.

"We outnumber you, Scab, my man. What will it be? Are you gonna let this lady go? It's your choice." Jason waited.

As Leon came forward, his men moved aside. He stood tall and erect, facing Jason and his followers without fear. Guns were raised, pointing directly at Leon's heart.

"Killings!" Jason yelled. "That's what will happen here. It's not a funny thing, is it? Let the woman go, Scab. We don't want no trouble. You can do your business without her."

Leon turned his back and walked toward the middle of the fire. "You ain't nothin' without your daddy, boy. These men aren't gonna kill me. They ain't gonna follow you none either. You ain't nothin, man. Nothin! I'm the boss man. They know me too well."

He was right. His men seemed to know instinctively what to do. Leon raised his gun and yelled for the others to do the same. He quickly dropped to the ground pointing his gun at Jason. In the cross fire, he suddenly changed his mind and pointed it at me, pulling the trigger.

During those seconds, my peripheral vision picked up a shape running from behind Leon's men. Recognizing it as Peter's, I tried to struggle to my feet. "Not again," I yelled. In a flash, he was on top of me. Instantly, I felt a dull hard thud as my head hit the dirt.

Shots were being fired all around us. Peter continued to act as a barricade. Fearing the worst, I kept my eyes closed. I was too afraid to move. As if transported to another time, I began to scream. I was still screaming when the guns stopped firing.

"It's all right, Annie. You're safe." Peter quickly moved off me as someone helped him to his feet. Once again, I was lying in a pool of blood. Most of it was coming out of the bodies that had held me fixed to the chair. Death was all around me. An odd sort of quiet descended over the rest of us.

Peter picked me up like I was a child and sat me gently down on his lap. Carefully he placed his arms around me. I cried into his chest. "Shh, shh, it's over," he said, checking for wounds.

"Thank God, you're alive! You're going to be all right."

Someone came forward with a blanket and pulled out a large handkerchief. Peter wiped the blood off my chin. Wanting to sound brave, I tried to think of something clever to say. "Well, I guess I have seven more lives."

Placing my head once again in Peter's chest, I cried, happy he was alive, too.

"She's going to be all right," he said to the crowd. "You're a fine bunch of soldiers." Peter bent down to whisper in my ear. "Forgive me, Annie, but I have to talk to them."

Peter stood up, placed me back on the chair, and raised his hands. "Who wants to take Leon's place? Any of you brave enough to join him?" His men were still being held at gun point by Jason's gang.

"Lower your weapons." Jason said, directing this toward his men.

"You're all free to leave," Peter said. Leon's men seemed confused.

"Before you go, I want to say something. You all know Jason and respect him. For years, he has stood side by side, has been your brother. His father, Rodney Thomas, was once your leader."

Peter pointed to where Leon's dead body lay. "Let us give the brothers and sisters in the black community a chance to come together and realize that we are not to be feared. We are not your enemies. The evil ones are dead. We must call a halt to the killings."

Jason moved toward the fire. The men seemed unaffected by Peter's words. Jason's gun was still in his right hand. It was his turn to speak to the crowd. These were his men. Peter was a stranger.

He raised his gun toward the black sky.

"You men see this pistol here. Some of you know it well. I've probably shot you with it. For that matter, you've shot me back."

Some of the men laughed. For proof, Jason took off his sweatshirt and displayed the scars on his body. "Brothers, I know I'm young. Maybe I haven't earned my right to speak. My message is a simple one. Put the pistols down. You won't be violated for turning your back on me. Your hood will be your hood. I don't want power. I want my freedom."

Jason walked over to Leon's grotesque body lying on the ground. The rest of his dead comrades had been piled next to him. All that remained were shapeless masses of bones and flesh. Their spirits were gone and could no longer harm anyone, although Leon's rules were still a threat to all of us.

"Scab is dead. He can no longer hurt you. My dad had no right to teach his sons to be trained killers. He taught us well, didn't he? I'm the one who took my knife out of my pocket and slit his throat. I watched him choke on his blood, blood that was my blood, too. And I'm the one who smiled when he took his last breath."

The crowd grew unsettled, whispering among themselves.

"If you want to punish me, then do it. I don't want to live with the fear of what's behind me." No one moved.

"We must believe we are capable of change. Put the pistols down. Put the pistols down."

Jason approached me and put his hand on my shoulder. "This woman gave me a life. I was a spy in Mattie Turner's house. At first, I went along with my dad's game. Little by little, thanks to them, I began to change."

Jason bent down to look me in the face and then gave me a hug.

"Thank you," I said with tears in my eyes.

"Annie here taught me about something more precious than power. It's a form of power. It's the power of respect, not for your governors, assistant governors, or the upper echelon of gang command, but for yourself."

Jason moved toward the fire and knelt down next to Leon's body. "Don't you see? It's over! It's over!" he yelled. " If you follow me, there won't be head shots or mouth shots for disobedience. There won't be codes or violations. There won't be any killings! They're dead, and they can't harm us. Let them lie in the grave of hell. If you want out, then put your guns down in front of Leon and walk away. Please, I'm begging you. Put them down."

I looked in the eyes of what I could only call young boys. Young boys with gold teeth that gleamed in the fire light. The real ones had been knocked out a long time ago. I knew what Jason meant. Fear was a part of living. Pain was commonplace. They lived that life every day, expecting very little. For what? To belong somewhere, to belong anywhere.

What could they possibly know about self respect, about freedom? They were only words, not experiences. If they followed Jason, it meant death, not freedom.

"I've got my father's blood money. We'll take Leon's too. We can start over, build a new life. There's more than enough for all of us."

Jason threw his gun in the flames. "The jailers are dead, and we are free. I'll never pick it up again. If you can't do this, then go home and think about it. You'll not be forced. Freedom is a scary thing."

The men came forward and circled Leon's body. One by one, they dropped their guns on his bulging stomach. Peter smiled at Jason.

"Tomorrow we'll talk of uniting the brothers and sisters. Black power will rise to a new level," Jason said, raising his hand and displaying its symbol. One by one his men came forward to shake his hand.

When it was over, I reached out for Jason's hand. I could see his kindness, his gentleness. His bright brown eyes filled me with warmth.

"Thanks for saving my life."

"Your life was worth saving," he said matter of factly. He jerked his head toward his men. "And so are theirs," he whispered. "Tell that to the world, Annie. Maybe they'll listen to you."

I saw the guns piled on Leon's chest and the young mens' faces filled with a combination of fear and hope. Could Jason pull it off? What would it take to inspire a new generation of leaders? With a fulfilled sense of dignity and destiny, I prayed the suffering was over.

* * *

Peter picked me up and carried me across the field. When he put me in the car, I realized I was too weak to move. I laid my aching head back on the headrest and tried not to cry. We drove in silence to the hospital.

Immediately, the emergency team took control. They ran an IV and ordered a CAT scan. After examining my white charred skin, they told me I had third degree burns on both arms.

For quite a while, they flushed them with cold water and then applied a Betadine solution. Sometime in the near future there was the possibility of skin grafting and plastic surgery.

The CAT scan revealed a concussion but no apparent fractures. After gently wrapping my arms in thick gauze pads, they found me a room.

"Mattie, she'll be fine," Peter assured her over the telephone. "She's calling from your house. She's taking care of Jack."

I gave him the signal I didn't want to talk. I didn't feel fine. Between the bruises, cuts, abrasions, burns, and the pounding headache, I felt like a freight train had hit me.

"No, you don't need to come and see for yourself. She needs some peace and quiet." Before Peter could get off the phone, the nurse handed me some pain pills and told me to get some rest. Rest in a hospital? Rest, my eye. The doctor told me the standard procedure for people with concussions was to wake them every two hours. If I didn't know my name, I was in trouble.

"She'll see you tomorrow. Bye, Mattie." Peter hung up the phone. "I did what I could. She'll probably come anyway." Before I drifted off to sleep, I wanted some answers.

"How did you find me?" I asked, in my incoherent state.

"I didn't. Joseph Gibbons crept away from the fire and was going to call the police."

I tried not to close my eyes. Peter understood and smiled.

"Well, if you can stay awake long enough, I'll start at the beginning. When Mattie came into the house, I realized that you had stupidly gone to your car. I was in the process of catching up with you when you were hit on the head. They shoved you in the van and drove away.

"I started running after it and yelling for help. Then realizing I couldn't run as fast as the van, I ran back to the house. Jason and I drove around checking out what we knew of Leon's hiding spots. It seemed like ages. Then we saw Gibbons heading toward a gas station. He told us where you were and we followed him. The rest you know. Jason rounded up his father's gang. When we got closer to the field, I heard you scream."

No longer able to listen, I allowed one last thought to enter my head. What a lousy mother I was turning out to be.

CHAPTER
XXI

The big problem with hospitals is getting unwanted guests paying you unwanted visits. The first two people I saw when I opened my eyes were my old friends, Benjamin Goldstein and Sergeant John Murphy. I was stuck there, and they knew it.

Sergeant Murphy was an honest cop. I knew him well. When Mattie's House was only a dream, he was one of the few men who'd used his influence over the board to convince them we needed zoning. He was also instrumental in convincing a couple of judges to let Mattie take custody of these kids before juvenile hall. Genuine human beings were hard to find.

The nurse came in and stuck a thermometer in my ear, checking my vital signs. "Go away. I have nothing to say to either of you."

"Oh, come now, Anne," Goldstein replied. "We're your friends. Did that bump on your head cause you amnesia? Remember, I'm the stupid schmuck who released you from jail last night. Jail would have been preferable. Now we find you half dead in this hospital. Again, it's all my fault. I should have warned you. I didn't expect you'd be a target so quickly."

I was getting used to giving people confused looks.

Goldstein came forward and rubbed his jaw. "Last night, I was smart enough to put an unmarked squad car in front of your house. I was told you never showed. A few hours later, you were brought to the emergency room. We found several dead bodies in a remote field. Sound familiar?"

Grimacing from the pain, I slowly pointed my finger at Murphy. "If I have to talk to one of you, I would prefer him. The other guy can wait in the hallway."

Goldstein ignored me. Murphy smiled and moved forward.

"How are you doing, Miss Stevens? I haven't seen you for a while. They gave me a desk job, you know."

"How's your leg?" I asked. Murphy had been shot by a fellow cop who was cleaning his gun. He'd been on restrictive duty for the past several months.

"Oh, it still hurts, but I'll be back. I'm glad to see your temper is still as nasty as ever. At least I'll be able to reassure Mattie you're all right."

Watching me struggle to a sitting position, Murphy quickly came to my assistance. "If there's anything I can do to make you more comfortable, name it. Mr. Goldstein and I are actually here to apologize and do a little groveling."

Murphy was beginning to annoy me. He kept patting me on the leg.

"Relax. We know what happened, Miss Stevens. Peter Harrison and Jason Reed came to the station last night and gave us their statements. It's appalling what they did to you. All that commotion and no one called it in. I guess it's that hear-no-evil, see-no-evil mentality. Unfortunately, Goldstein is right. We need to ask you a couple of questions."

Suddenly, I started aching all over. "I know you two won't believe this, but I was hit on the head and I can't remember a thing. I have a concussion. You said it yourself. It's amnesia. Besides, most of the time I had my eyes closed. I was petrified."

Goldstein shook his head and gave me a skeptical look.

"That's the honest to God's truth. Thanks to Jason and Peter I'm still on this earth."

I tried to gently put my head back on the pillow. This time I wasn't faking it. They were giving me a severe headache. Hoping they would take the hint and leave, I moaned louder. They looked at each other and shrugged their shoulders.

Goldstein put his glasses on and bent down to take a good look at my face. "You look like hell, Stevens. It's no surprise to me someone would want to snuff you out. I can understand the urge," he said, pulling up one of my blankets to observe the bruises.

I gave him a dirty look. Like Murphy, he, too, gave me a pat on the leg. "Believe it or not, I'm not interested in solving Leon's murder. However, I do have my problems. I have seven dead bodies and enough ammunition to fill an arsenal. The news media are having a field day with this. What do I tell them, Anne?"

I took a deep, frustrated breath and decided to explain the unexplainable. "What if I were to say that there is a good chance the turf wars are over? Would you believe me? Now, I'm not saying there won't be crimes committed. I'm simply asking you a question. What if the gangs united and became one power?"

"Personally it would scare me to drink, and I'm already an alcoholic," Goldstein said as he placed a surprised hand on his heart.

Any slight movement on my part was still too painful. Piqued by their disbelief, I tried to give them a mental grasp of the entire picture.

"You don't understand. Why should you? A miracle happened last night. I suspect a change is about to occur. Gang-banging may be on a different level. If you guys can remember your history, think twenty years back. It wasn't the concept of gangs that was wrong. When the guns and the crack entered the picture, they lost their sense of family."

Goldstein looked skeptically at Murphy and rolled his eyes.

"I'm told it used to be one brother would die for another. Instead, brother shoots brother. Utter chaos. Just for a moment imagine a new beginning, the guns are dropped, and the brothers unite. Do you find that prospect particularly chilling?"

Goldstein started to open his mouth, but Murphy stopped him by speaking first. "You're kidding. It's on account of that bump on your head, right? You really believe that can happen?"

In their stunned silence, you could see their minds at work. They were beginning to comprehend the enormity of my words.

"I have to admit, I myself observed those guns lying on the ground, and judging by the foot tracks, there were a lot of people out there last night."

Murphy was still thinking it through when Goldstein walked over to the window still contemplating my words. I didn't care whether they believed me or not. What I wanted was peace and quiet and the unwanted visitors out of my room.

"Well, that's my explanation. Take it or leave it. Now, if you gentlemen will excuse me, I have to figure out how to go to the bathroom with this IV in my arm."

Goldstein was too taken aback to say anything. The impact of my words must have hit him hard. Without saying good-bye, he opened the door and left without getting the last word.

"Here, let me help you." Murphy gave me his hand. After a couple of seconds, a nurse came in and discovered I was out of bed.

"Sorry, young lady," she said scolding me. She reached under the bed and came up with a cold metal bedpan. "Doctor's orders. You're to stay right where you are."

Murphy, realizing he was no longer needed, made a hasty retreat. After a wet and humiliating experience, bedpans went high on my list of my least favorite things.

* * *

That afternoon Jason and Mattie brought Jack and what seemed like a couple of hundred get-well cards to the hospital. My baby didn't seem to care his mother was all bandaged up. He was more interested in the IV tube and the flashing buttons.

Mattie placed him gently on my lap. I kissed him with my arms outstretched.

"Well, Mattie, so much for wearing my heart on my sleeves. I think it'll be a while before I can pick Jack up." Glancing up at her, I caught the guilty look on her face. "If you look like that again, you can't come in here. It's not your fault!"

"Honey, you don't need those sleeves." With tears welling up in her eyes, she whispered, "You've got a heart of gold, and the courage of at least sixteen lions."

"Sixteen, Mattie? Sixteen you say. Wow." Trying to hold back the tears myself, I spotted Jason hovering in the background.

"Jason, get over here." Tenderly, I took a hold of his hand and kissed his cheek. "Thank you for saving my life."

"You've already thanked me. We were almost too late," he said in a hushed voice. "I'm sorry about your arms, Annie." He, too, patted me on the leg. What was it with these men?

"I think I'm going to need some help at home. You wouldn't care to be my nursemaid, would you, Jason?"

"Did I hear the word 'nursemaid?' Don't you give my job away. That's what I've been doing since the day I laid eyes on you," Fred said, rounding the corner and walking to my bedside.

"Like always, I'm here to keep your ass out of trouble, I mean, your subnormal retarded butt out of trouble. What kind of harebrained, empty-headed scheme ended you here, my dear?"

Jack was getting too rambunctious so Mattie took him from my lap. Fred gave me a hug and kissed my bandaged forehead. I was thrilled and utterly surprised to see him.

"Oh, dear friend, I didn't realize how much I'd missed you," I said as tears saturated my cheekbones. "Oh, God, it's good to see you. How did you find out I was in the hospital?"

He motioned toward Mattie, who omnisciently smiled back. For about twenty minutes, Jason caught Fred up on what had happened. The whole incident was still too fresh in my mind and gave me stomach cramps.

"Can you guys talk about something else?" I pleaded. Fred took the hint and thoroughly entertained us with tales from Chicago. A nurse came in, threw my friends out, and gave me a sedative. For about six hours, I slept like a dead person.

When I opened my eyes, I saw Peter asleep on the chair. He looked so peaceful. What a word for a man like him, a man who would never know peace. Unlike him, could I finally put the past behind me? I had been forever trapped in that essence called guilt. It was the one thing we had in common.

Mattie was wrong. My heart was not made of gold. It was made of muscle and blood; and right now it was hurting like hell. Tears rolled down my cheeks for the umpteenth time that week. I would never forget him. I wanted to memorize each impeccable line of his arresting face.

Peter opened his eyes and stretched. He caught me staring at him. Those beautiful brown eyes became alert and turned their attention on me. For several seconds, no words were spoken. It was as if we were saying a silent good-bye.

Peter broke the spell by pushing his chair closer to my bedside. He opened his mouth. As difficult as it was, I placed my finger on his lips. He caressed my cheek and slowly wiped the tears off my face.

"Don't spoil it," I whispered. "There's no need for any more explanations. It's okay. I understand."

He kissed me long and hard as our tears flowed freely, its wetness forever a part of a lasting bond, a bond of eternal friendship that would transcend time.

Peter rose from his chair and looked out the window. His body language conveyed his torment.

"Annie, I'm sorry," he said in a defeated voice. He came back to my bedside and smiled. "Haven't you noticed? Those are the two words I'm constantly saying to you. Whether you want to hear it or not, I owe you a proper explanation for my despicable behavior."

Blame was another wasted emotion. I was glad to have opened my heart, proud to have had his love. "Don't turn your back on me, Peter. Stay here. You'll find out soon enough what's out that window."

"No, Annie," he said, putting his finger to my mouth. "I need to get this off my chest." I started to protest.

He placed a gentle kiss in the palm of my hand, sending shivers down my spine. I wanted to listen, but my mind wasn't on him and his stupid explanation. It was on the curve of his mouth, the touch of his fingers, the tongue I was dying to meet with my own as I wished for more.

"Stop it! I want to tell you this." I started to pout. He held my hand. "When I was a little boy, I idolized my father. I loved him like all boys should. For years, my mother and I waited for the door to open, hoping to see his face, needing to see his face. He never came back.

"When I graduated from high school, I ran into one of his old friends. He gave me my father's address. I stole a car and drove to Portland."

I could see where this story was headed. I didn't want him to continue.

"Peter, you don't have to talk about this. It's not important."

"But that's where you're wrong. It's very important. My father taught me the importance of love, knowledge, and family, yet turned his back on his obligations. When I found his house, I saw him playing with his wife's children. He had a good job. We were stealing food, wearing hand-me-down clothes from the Salvation Army. He was a well-respected man living in a middle-class neighborhood."

I understood Peter's loss. I understood too well what rejection meant to him.

"My father was sitting on the porch of his nice brick home reading the paper. He had manicured lawns. I was used to concrete parks and boarded-up housing developments. He had a wife who cooked his meals. I was used to people's scraps and their eyes that said, 'I feel sorry for you kids.'"

A dull silence filled the room. He was lost in the pain of his father's betrayal. "This man had it all," he said muttering under his breath.

"I wanted to confront him, but I never did. Instead, I despised and hated him for what he did to us. I vowed to be a better man. I failed that vow once. That's why I won't turn my back on these kids. I'm not a hero. They're living in the same hell I know so well. Don't you see? They need me more than you'll ever need me."

Peter took the palm of my hand and held it against his face, asking for a silent forgiveness.

"Only God knows how hard it is to turn my back on you, and only God knows the strength it's going to take to walk out of your life. I love you. Now stop crying and let me see a smile."

Reluctantly, I did as he asked. Peter's watery gaze rested on my face. Gently he took me in his arms and caressed my cheek. One of his tears fell upon my neck and trickled its way toward the cleft of my breast. As if to prolong the inevitable, I leaned forward wishing to forever stamp upon his lips the fact that he was mine. He would always be mine.

All too soon he carefully laid me back down on the pillow. "You told me to smile. Now you take that tortured expression off your face and get out of here. I love you. I don't care how much it hurts, damn it. I love you, too. Now, smile."

Peter wiped a tear off his face, took a deep breath, and smiled.

"Thank you, Annie." He blew me a kiss and walked out the door. I knew exactly what he was thanking me for. I, too, would treasure these memories every single day of my life.

Tolerating the pain in my arm, I struggled out of bed and pushed the IV machine over to the window. A couple of seconds later, I spotted him walking toward his car. He glanced up at the window, as if sensing my presence. When he saw me there, he paused for a couple of seconds. With the tears flowing down my face, I waved a silent good-bye.

I'd been here before. Only this time, there was no hate, no sense of betrayal. Closing my eyes, I could feel his touch, a touch I would never have again except for the private times I chanced to dream, a dream that would never be ours.

As I watched his car pull out of the parking lot, I said to myself, "Have a nice life, you lovely man, my dear friend, my shooting star." That was what he reminded me of, this incandescent trail of light that illuminated my life and touched my soul.

C H A P T E R
XXII

A week later, I was released from the hospital. Still fatigued and grumpy, Fred agreed to drive me home.

"Come on, Annie. Snap out of it. You're going home," Fred said, wheeling me to his car. I was still feeling sorry for myself and wasn't in the mood.

Sensing my lack of enthusiasm, we drove in silence. Peering out the window, I noticed he missed the turn and was heading in the opposite direction. "Fred, where are you taking me? I'm tired, and I want to go home."

"We have to pick Jack up at Mattie's," Fred interjected. "By the way, speaking of Jack, he's a great little guy, Annie. I hope you don't mind. I've been teaching him a little Nerf basketball. I think you'll be surprised. He's sure to beat you. That monster can wear a man out -- and stubborn. I don't know where he gets it, do you?"

I shrugged my shoulders, ignoring his attempts at humor.

"He's such a happy guy. He doesn't know a stranger when he sees one."

"He doesn't know a stranger because the whole world takes care of him," I said sarcastically. "His mother is always too busy forgetting her responsibilities. Like thanking you. I'm sorry I'm taking this out on you. You don't deserve it."

"All my women say that. As far as the lousy mother comment, I'll ignore it. Jack is a very lucky boy."

Fred turned the corner onto Holloway Street. "Don't be so hard on yourself. For Jack's sake, try to cheer up."

The street was lined with people. There was a banner that read, "Welcome back, Annie." Several of the children had balloons in their hands. My heart stopped beating. I took a deep breath as Fred pulled over to the curb.

"Surprise, Miss Grumpy," he said kissing me on the cheek. "I hope you're up to this. Try putting a smile on your sour puss face. Sweet Mattie has been planning this for days."

Fred got out, and, as gently as he could, pulled me out of the car. "Look at all the people who love you."

I couldn't move. Well-wishers enthusiastically surrounded the car. There were hundreds of people. I spotted Reverend Miles, Joseph Gibbons, Benjamin Goldstein, Paula Jennings, and even Ernest Moses. If I thought there weren't any tears left in my tear ducts, I was wrong. I cried like a baby. Unlike the rest of the ones I had shed, these were tears of joy.

As I approached the front sidewalk, Joseph Gibbons stood at the front gate.

"Thank you for saving my life," I said, shaking his hand. "Peter and Jason would never have found me if it were not for you."

Joseph nodded his head and smiled. His mouth moved, but because of the cheers I couldn't hear what he said. He noted my confusion and whispered in my ear. "You were worth saving, Miss Stevens."

Mattie stood on the front porch, counted to ten, and the balloons were released. Thousands of brightly colored balls flew into the air. The children, excited by the array of color, jumped as if they, too, could touch the sky.

I walked toward the steps and stopped in front of Mattie. I gave her a hug and whispered in her ear. "Have you lost your mind?"

"Hush up," she admonished. "Be a good girl. We need the publicity. People out there will see you on T.V. and send us money. Smile at the camera, my dear."

The Mayor, the same man Mattie had referred to as diabolical, came forward with a gold medal. Placing the medallion around my neck, he kissed me on both cheeks. Mattie wrinkled her nose.

Reverend Miles stepped up to the podium and gently took my hand. Approaching the microphone, the excited voices hushed as he spoke.

"My brothers and sisters, soon we'll be entering a new millennium. In the past, we have spoken a lot about black power. Black power is a good thing. We should always be proud of the color of our skin. But I want to speak to you today of a new power, a supreme power. One that is not isolated with the idealistic color of black, but filled with a multitude of colors, like a painter's palette.

"The proof of this power lies within each of us. The word for the power is tolerance. There have been many heroes who are long gone who have changed the course of history. Today, we honor a simple hero. She hasn't touched a nation like Abraham Lincoln or Martin Luther King. Instead, she has touched the lives of our own small community. The world may never know of her courageous spirit, but, nevertheless, unwittingly, she is the catalyst that brought us together."

Reverend Miles, still holding my hand, raised them carefully to the sky. "I believe it's the small heroes who will inevitably change this nation, one community at a time, one individual at a time. The wasteful blood of our brothers and sisters will no longer be shed upon these streets. We will help to rebuild our lives. More importantly, our families. There's a fresh hope for our future. The pestilence of hate and bigotry stops here."

Placing a kiss upon my cheek, the Reverend said three last words. "Thank you, Annie."

The church's choir began to sing. Mattie came forward and gently placed her arms around me. As I watched the brave men and women cheering, I felt proud. Not just a sense of pride in myself, but proud to have been born.

Under my breath, I thanked the two people who had helped me conquer my demons, Mattie and Peter. I thought about the promise I had made to Jack on the day he gave me my bluebird of happiness. I closed my eyes and felt his presence. I had fulfilled the promise I made to him and was worth saving after all. I finally understood. Guilt had only cheapened his sacrifice. I was setting myself free.

Standing at the podium, I had all these thoughts running through my head, but I was suddenly immobile. My mother was standing next to Jason. I was too overwhelmed to speak. They were standing apart from the crowd. She was holding my son. She flashed me a smile and suddenly the words were found.

"I don't deserve this medal. You do," I said, gesturing toward the crowd. "It was your courage that set Mattie's dream into action. I was the one who drove home at night to my safe bed on the other side of town. You were the ones who heard the sounds of gunfire and wondered when you would be next. You're the ones who watched your friends' blood as it filled the gutters of these streets."

I shaded my eyes to get a better look at them. "It wasn't until a week ago I saw what true poverty really meant. I didn't drive by in my car. I actually walked your sidewalks. Speaking of those sidewalks, a boy could never ride his bicycle, a mother could never use her stroller to take a child for a walk. They're in deplorable shape."

Knowing I was in front of the cameras, I turned toward Mayor Donovan. "Sir, is there anything the city can do about this problem? You should walk them yourself. They are like giant pieces of discarded concrete jutting out from the soil. They desperately need repaired."

Mayor Donovan cleared his throat. "I'll look into it, Miss Stevens," he said, uncomfortably pulling at his tie.

Taking off the medallion, I asked Reverend Miles to throw it at Jason. Its gold chain shimmered in the sun before he caught it in the air.

"This isn't about us. It's about them." I said, pointing to my son. "As a mother, I watch my son all the time. When I look into his innocent face, I see joy. His eyes light up with a special kind of magic. When I see discomfort, a tear rolls down his cheek. When I see love, I feel a priceless sense of overwhelming pride. When I see anger, a red glow burns brightly across his cheeks. But when I'm here and I see Mattie's kids, I'm deeply disturbed. They're beautiful, these kids. But in their eyes I see something unique, something children so young should never experience. That look is called fear. A child's eyes should be free from that face called fear."

An awkward silence fell across the yard. Not knowing what else to say, I put my head on Mattie's shoulder. She picked up the microphone and turned toward her people.

"We are a small town and, as such, we should feel a real sense of family. For many years now, we've lost our community. Hopefully, we'll get it back. This country spends millions of dollars warehousing our families. Your mothers and fathers are stealing and killing to get drugs, to get crack. It's a drug that keeps them away from the knowledge of who they are and prevents them from accepting what they've become."

Mattie pointed her finger at Goldstein who was standing a couple feet away. Most of you say, 'lock them up and throw away the key.' Thousands and thousands of dollars to throw away the key, never thinking to unlock their minds before they get to that cold, metal cell. Look around you! What do you see? Down the street there's a liquor store. Around the corner, a tavern, a place to take us out of our misery and have some fun. Where are the libraries? Where are the preschools?

"Studies have shown a baby's brain develops personality, develops a sense of self the first couple of years of life. The space they need to grow into decent human beings is empty, empty of love, empty of guidance, empty of parents. Empty!

"A couple of nights ago, we made this plaque to put on the wall at my front door. It'll be the first thing you see when you enter. It's the names of the children who are no longer here. Names that few of you remember, names of lost souls who were born in the wrong place, on the wrong street. Their lives were shortened through no fault of their own. Their crime was being born in an empty space."

She handed the plaque back to Reverend Miles, turning once again to her people. "What I'm asking for today will not take a miracle. This country spends a lot of money institutionalizing my family. I want it put toward schools, not just here, but throughout America. I'm not talking about public schools. I'm talking about schools like mine. I want volunteers like you making a difference. You're all beautiful. Every last one of you."

The band took Mattie's lead and sang the song I heard from my heart, "Everything is Beautiful."

Mattie walked me away from the podium where Reverend Miles gingerly took my hand. "You're learning, child," Mattie whispered. "You're learning. Next time ask for a park or a gymnasium."

* * *

For the next couple of weeks, Fred and my mother nursed me back to health. It was a strange feeling to finally be fussed over by her. One night, completely alone, we sat down and talked.

What I didn't know was on the night Jack was killed my mother was in a women's shelter. She'd been taken there by Jack himself that morning. She was leaving my father for good.

We had both spent many years blaming ourselves for Jack's death. Her, in particular. She'd spent the first couple of years confined in a mental institution. I had no idea the extent to which an ordinary functional person on the outside becomes what is conventionally described as insane. Perhaps we were both insane. What's true is my mental anguish had been spent in the outside world while hers had been spent behind more than the walls of concrete in an institution, she had built the walls around herself.

After being released, she made the adjustments in this outside world alone. Like me, she was merely dealing with it. When I called and told her I was pregnant, she knew it was time to face me. I wanted the baby to bring her back to me, to fill that empty spot left from Jack's death. Instead it brought out the jealousy I always felt when she loved Jack more. It was happening again. Maybe there is no excuse for a mother's lack of love. Perhaps we both loved Jack so much there wasn't room for a mother/daughter relationship. After all, we were competing for the same man. There was too much hostility and we weren't ready to bridge the gap when Jack was born.

Later Fred would pay many visits to my mother. He got to know her in ways I probably never will. He convinced her it was time to confront me, the damage she had done needed repairing.

It wasn't easy. We had to learn to accept what we couldn't change and go on living. I had more than the sores on the outside of my body to heal. The inside was finally healing as well. Now was the time to reactivate within ourselves the need for each other's love. The limitless burden of guilt, if not vanished, had been transformed into a new awareness of myself. I had learned to love me.

Fred and my mother put up with my complaints and my lack of patience. Unhappily, I watched them go back to Chicago and their work. He promised to return every weekend. She promised to appear on holidays and birthdays.

Soon the struggles with my own incapacitation lessened allowing me to become a fully employed productive member of society once again.

Mattie, Jason, and Paula Jennings continued to effectuate a miraculous change in people's attitudes inside the house and on the streets.

Crack was still a pervasive evil. Nothing would change that fact. However, there were fewer people partaking of its debilitating effects on their life. This was largely due to something that happened a few weeks after the broadcast. A large sum of money mysteriously appeared in Mattie's bank account from an anonymous donor.

The first thing done with this generous donation was to establish scholarships for some of the kids and a treatment center with actual in-house psychiatrists on staff for those addicted.

Thanks to the mayor's support, the city agreed to help clean up the neighborhood, starting with the sidewalks. The children and many adults picked up the trash and debris. The buildings and churches were free of graffiti. It had a new whitewashed look, and the people who walked the streets revealed a new attitude and a new found sense of pride.

On a daily basis, I received E-mail from Buddy. I offered him my home, but, unfortunately, he was not interested in coming back. He was another one of those special people I only saw on holidays and birthdays. There were too many painful memories, and, besides, he loved his new family, not to mention his new girlfriend. He was making good grades and seemed quite happy.

Of the three men who killed Michelle, two of them plead guilty and were awaiting sentence. They were cooperating with the state and hoped for a reduction in sentence. With their testimony, it was my fondest hope that Buddy's statement alone would be sufficient evidence to convict the third man.

As for Fred, his promise to be home every weekend came true. Slowly I began to see him in a different light. The connection between us had a special bond all its own. We took long walks, even went on a couple of weekend vacations. I found I wanted to be closer to him. The space between the seat next to mine lessened. The desire for flight turned gradually to a desire to stay.

The love I felt for Peter was becoming part of a lost dream, forever remembered, and where it should remain, forever a part of my past.

The turning point began the night Fred asked me to come up to Chicago for the weekend. His law firm had sent me a gold-embossed invitation. Fred's own handwriting had been inserted on a separate piece of paper. Inside it read: "Dance with me. Become aware of my body, the way I am aware of yours. I'll ignite your flesh, send you soaring to places in the world you've never been."

A couple of days later a box arrived at my office. Inside was a shimmering emerald A-line dress with a low-cut velvet bodice. Lying next to it was a matching velvet jacket to cover the scars on my arms, and a barrette with pearls and brilliant green crystals for my hair.

It was the first time I had been invited to stay in Fred's apartment. On the afternoon before the dance, my mother drove down, volunteering to babysit Jack. Before I left, she handed me a wrapped present, a rare occasion indeed. As I opened it, tears filled my eyes. It was an emerald green evening bag to match my dress.

"Don't forget to put a credit card and a couple of dollars for a taxi. Just in case. There's also a light brown lipstick I thought would go with the dress."

It was the first time this daughter had received a mother's advice. It felt oddly comforting. She waved good-bye with Jack in her arms.

Was I ready to make the commitment? I knew what would happen. A part of me wanted it, too. I drove up convinced I was making the right decision. We were such good friends. Could we be good lovers as well?

I was late when I finally reached Fred's apartment. He lived in a high rise on the Gold Coast overlooking Lake Michigan. I parked the car in the underground garage and entered the first floor. I gave the doorman my name.

"Oh, yes, Miss Stevens, Mr. Levine is expecting you." He buzzed me into a marble foyer to wait for the elevator. Riding up to the 33rd floor, I took a deep breath. What was wrong with me? I was a wreck. Calm down. It was only Fred.

When he opened the door, he was buttoning his shirt and tucking it into a pair of black tuxedo pants. His hair was still damp from the shower. As he grabbed my suitcase, he seemed to hesitate for a moment. "Hi," he said smiling.

He came forward giving me a hug. His sweeping eyelashes and clean shaven chin brushed against my cheek. After a couple of seconds, he gave me a peck on the cheek.

"I don't know about you, but I'm a little nervous," he said taking me by the hand. "Come. What do you think of my bachelor pad? I even cleaned it up."

It seemed strangely removed from the skyscrapers and concrete of Chicago. Fred had his own personal blend of interests displayed around the room. There was a lack of formal arrangement; pretty much what I expected. Strong sturdy pieces of oak furniture had been softened by dark green pillows. There were sports magazines, books and athletic equipment shoved to the side but neatly stacked next to the closet.

On the other side of the room, tall glass windows overlooked the lake. A large collection of antique scientific measuring instruments were displayed on a brass and glass etagere in the other corner of the room.

"It suits you. Expensive, yet cluttered," I said taking a seat in one of the matching winged-back chairs. It was surprisingly comfortable.

"Oh, Annie, I'm so glad you're here. We don't have much time, you know. Oh, no, lazy bones, you can't sit down. Go get beautiful. Look, I'm almost dressed."

I looked all right. He was damn handsome. It was I who got up, moving towards him and offering him my mouth. I kissed him long and hard on the lips wanting only to be held.

"Are you sure you want to do this?" he moaned, kissing me once again on the lips.

I took a deep breath and lied. "Of course I'm sure." I wasn't sure at all. Lately, the external feelings of our bodies had been getting in the way of our friendship. I didn't know what I wanted.

As he held me in his arms, I closed my eyes and felt his hands touching my breasts on the outside of my shirt. I moved my lips to where the crisp white collar of his shirt exposed his neck. Kissing his flesh, I moved further down his chest, unbuttoning his shirt as I went.

"I don't think I can wait any longer," he said, whispering in my ear. "I know I can't. Oh, what the hell!" He picked me up, carrying me to his bedroom.

An immense heavily carved mahogany bed stood alone in the middle of the room. The thick burgundy comforter he gently placed me on felt like I was floating on a cloud. I was uneasy and part of me still wanted to leave.

He sat down on the bed next to me, taking my hand to his lips. His eyes remained on my face all the time he talked. "Would you rather we waited until after dinner?"

"You mean keep the suspense of the final act until later?" I said, smiling. He nodded his head and smiled back.

I had reached the full pinnacle of emotions with this man. It was time to end it. I took off my shirt and laid my head back on his soft down pillows. I had no other garment on except my jeans.

"Oh, God, you're so beautiful. The only thing I want to eat is you!" He playfully moved forward taking a bite of my hand.

"Then come here," I said, extending my arms. He stood near the bed unbuttoning the rest of his shirt, exposing his muscular arms and flat stomach. I had seen his body many times before, but tonight it was different. It was meant for me.

He kissed me on the eyes, on the lips, moving down my neck. He kissed the scars on my arms, the wounds he had helped to heal. His hands were all over my body caressing me with a ferociousness born from too many nights laying awake dreaming of this moment.

I turned him over pressing my lips to his stomach, unzipping his pants. I half sat up and took my jeans off. He did the same. At last we were naked. Our mouths never stopped kissing every part of our bodies.

After what seemed like hours, I said, "I can't bear it any longer. Please, if you touch me anymore I'm going to explode." He moaned, his body trembling along with my own.

"I'm about to have everything I've ever wanted in my life. Oh, sweet heaven," he said, taking me in his arms. He covered me with his body and finally began to move inside of me. I felt the orgasm coming. I tried to hold back, wanting it to last forever. Fred heard my moans. The sensations were so acute I couldn't stand it.

I grasped his back, holding tightly. Explosions of pleasure burst from our bodies.

Several minutes passed. We laid there without saying anything. Still out of breath, he rolled me over and pressed many tiny kisses on my lips.

"That was unbelievable."

He was right. It was unbelievable. With my body entwined in his, I was magnetically drawn to his flesh. I wanted him again. In a weird way, I felt more alive than at any other time in my life. It's hard to explain really. When two people come together and are one in spirit, it goes far beyond having sex. This was entirely true.

"Thank you, Annie," he said burying his face in my hair.

"Oh, God, I love you!"

His words did not frighten me. I could now love myself so I was free to love him back.

"I love you, too," I sighed, squeezing him hard against my naked flesh.

He was someone I knew more than anyone else, someone I trusted, someone with no secrets. It felt like coming home and at last finding you're truly loved.

CHAPTER
XXIII

It was a crisp, refreshing Saturday afternoon, one of those days I'd call a ten. The sun was shining, and there was nothing to see but clear blue sky. A year had passed since that cold October evening, a year filled with a knowledgeable awareness of who I was and what I wanted. I could now stand as tall as the trees. Jack and I were in the backyard raking. It was my yard of multi-colored treasures and my life of blessed miracles.

Jack was a toddler now, a terrible two. Personally, I marveled at his keen intelligence and his wonderful sense of fun. He was a couple of feet away from me busily examining the bark on the tree trunk. It had been years since I'd studied tree bark myself. He was right. It was totally fascinating.

While we were standing next to this manifestation of nature, Mattie walked into the yard. She still carried a cane. This time some kid accidentally tripped her, sending her butt one direction and her leg the other.

Jack screamed out her name delighted to see her. Unfortunately, he ran so fast he smacked into her sore leg. She moaned and gave him a pat on the head. I slowly grimaced, getting off the ground. "Hey, Mattie, you should check out this bark," I yelled.

Jack took her hand and pointed to the tree, "Tree, Mattie. See pretty tree bark."

"Oh, Jack honey, Mattie's known the secret of tree barks for a long time now. All trees are beautiful. Not one of them is totally like another. Just look at how they almost reach the sky."

Mattie bent down and grabbed Jack's hand and turned it over. "Trees have fingerprints just like you do. In fact, if you count their ridges, you can tell how old they are. If I were a tree and you could count my ridges, they'd say this old lady's gonna kick the bucket."

Jack ignored Mattie's light-hearted banter and happily fell into a pile. I hadn't seen her for a while. I was glad she had dropped by.

"What brings you here?" I asked as if I didn't know.

Studying Mattie's face, I noticed she hadn't aged all that much, even though she seemed to think so. She looked tired, but working seven days a week would do that to anybody.

"I think I could use a stiff drink, Annie," she said pushing me in the direction of the house. "Reverend Miles and several members of his congregation have decided I need to expand. You won't believe this. They bought the lot next door. Guess what they want to do with it? They're going to build a new wing onto the house. They even showed me the floor plans. It has a gymnasium and a workout room where we could take dancing lessons. You'll be the first I put on the list. Teach you what a beat is.

"I don't know. I'm too busy. We white folks have trouble with that beat thing, remember."

"Oh, I told you that to get the kids laughing. You can learn. Look at what you've learned already hanging around me."

"Some of those lessons I could do without."

Mattie waved her arm, ignoring my retort. "Jason thinks we

need to start an animal shelter. I had to get out of there. Their philanthropic enthusiasms are making me feel old. To tell you the truth, they are driving me crazy!"

Jack followed close behind. Lucky for him, he didn't have a long trip. Hannah came up with another rake and asked to earn a few extra bucks. Obligingly, I pointed to the direction of the backyard and agreed to let them play.

Once inside, I made a pot of tea. Mattie sat down at the dining room table. I looked out the window as Hannah was burying Jack in a pile of leaves. I set the table and added a couple of homemade cookies. She looked suspiciously at me.

"Oh, don't look so skeptical," I muttered. "Don't worry. I didn't bake them. Fred didn't either. He bought them at a fine bakery in Chicago. So go ahead, you pig, eat Jack's cookies." Grabbing one myself, I sat down to join her.

As I poured the tea, Mattie was the first to break the silence.

"I stopped by today because I haven't been entirely honest," she said, with a wicked smirk on her face.

Placing my hand on my heart, I pretended surprise. "Oh, no. Really? Not my sweet friend, Mattie. Why if she were writing the 'True Confessions' magazine the pages would be blank or full of lies."

Mattie chuckled and in good humor continued. "Where do you think I get my material? Okay, okay. I deserve that. Don't give me any more of your lip. It's been almost a year now and with all these changes going on I haven't had the time to fill in the blanks. So shut up and listen to this feeble old woman before I suffer from Alzheimer's or something."

"Forget it. If I'm going to get mad at you again, why don't you keep it to yourself. Frankly, I have a few things to tell you. Let's pretend I'm Columbo and you tell me when I'm wrong. In fact, I've been waiting for an opportunity like this for a long time."

Mattie smiled. Contented, she sat back in her chair and folded her arms. "All right, Miss Smarty Pants, oh, I mean, Miss Columbo, out with it."

Taking one last bite, I swallowed hard. "Let's see now. We have to go back a fair bit to tell your preposterous story. All right. I've got it. First of all, you never really had agoraphobia. Oh, I will admit you had a few rough days after the rape, but you let everyone believe you had this psychological condition because it suited your plans. You and Peter were the masterminds, starting out slowly by setting up an office in your den. You filled your house with all the latest computer equipment. You and several other friends around the country hooked up your modems and fax machines."

I could tell I was not impressing her. "Don't interrupt. I'll get to the good part in due time. The concept of Mattie's House had been in your head for years. You even created a legitimate organization for adoption called The Children's Crisis Center. Today, it has become a multi-faceted network consisting of hundreds of people, hundreds of volunteers. That's where Peter came into the picture. He provided you with the sources. He moved from city to city, while you helped find homes for unwanted children."

Mattie interrupted my smug postulations. "May I point out, Miss Columbo, you already knew most of that."

Tapping her on the shoulder, I gave her a zip-your-lip look. "Don't be so sure of yourself. I had to start somewhere."

Pulling up my sleeves and rubbing my hands together, I started pacing. "Now, don't interrupt when Miss Columbo's on a roll here. What did you say revenge was? Orgasmic?"

"I never said revenge was orgasmic," she said, denying my accusation. "Food, maybe. This cookie isn't bad either."

"Shut up and let me talk," I demanded. "Not only did you find homes for these children, you also gave them new identities. Not too surprisingly Peter is not Peter Harrison, nor is he Reggie Parks. His real name is Brian Edwards. Brian sounds corny. It doesn't fit the man."

Mattie started to speak. I shook my head. "Shh, I'll get to it. You and Peter were in L.A. during the 1992 uprisings. While attending the grand gathering in the park, you watched the blending of the gangs in the inner city. That is where you got your ideas and began your campaign."

Judging by the look on Mattie's face, I was finally impressing her. "Who told you this? That louse of a grandson, I bet."

Nodding my head in acknowledgment, I smiled. "Don't you think I'm bright enough to figure this out for myself, my dear?"

"Never in a million years," Mattie responded.

I took another sip of my tea. "Of course, it was Peter. About six months ago, he wrote to me. It was a letter more along the lines of wanting to set the record straight. He figured his closed-mouth and sneaky grandmama would never tell me the truth. Unlike her, he felt he owed me an explanation for his misbegotten behavior."

Mattie stuck her tongue out. "He obviously didn't tell you about my financial condition. It was Peter's drug money that restored my house back to its original beauty. If it wasn't for him, I would have lost everything. For years, I only had money to pay the taxes. I couldn't afford the upkeep; so I allowed the house to fall into decay. What little I have comes from my teacher's pension. That's it."

Satisfied, the mystery was finally out, she wiped her brow. "Now you know absolutely everything there is to know about Mattie Turner and her perilous exploits. You're still talking to me, aren't you? No lectures."

I shook my head. "No lectures."

"Good. I'm in the mood for a celebration. Are you sure you don't have anything stronger than tea?"

I went to the kitchen to open the cabinet and do some rummaging. "Actually, I do have a bottle of wine around here somewhere. I've been saving it for a special occasion. Do you suppose Jason will pick you up if you get too drunk to drive home?"

"Of course he will," Mattie said, reassuringly. "He likes it when I'm a spectacle. Pour away, my dear. Speaking of Jason, I forgot one other thing. I guess I'm not through spilling my guts."

Reaching into the cabinet for the glasses, I found the corkscrew and opened the bottle. I poured the wine and handed a glass to her. "All right, Madam, tell me what you think."

As if Mattie knew the difference between a cheap bottle of wine or a *grand cru classe,* she twirled the wine in her glass, sniffed it like a true connoisseur, and rolled the juices in her mouth. She showed her approval by placing her right thumb in the air. I poured some more into her glass.

"This is not a very pleasant story. I probably shouldn't tell you," she mumbled taking another drink.

"While you were convalescing in the hospital, Jason wanted to speak to me in private. Our opportunity came the night you were hurt. He and his father were the two men who had broken into my house all those years ago. He raped me while his father watched. The one who'd left his mark forever on my flesh was his father, Rodney Thomas."

I choked down my wine. Mattie sadly continued to talk.

"Jason was fourteen years old at the time. The stories Jason told me of his father's cruelty would make your skin crawl. He learned long ago the consequences of disobedience."

Mattie shivered. "That was the other reason he cut Rodney Thomas's throat. Jason has a younger brother, Maurice. I know you've seen him around my house. Anyway, Jason's father decided it was time for Maurice to derive the same pleasure he himself felt when inflicting pain on others." Mattie grimaced as she spoke "Maurice was forced to rape--"

We said in unison, "--Paula Jennings."

Mattie nodded. "Right. Paula Jennings. That's why the MO's

matched. We bear the same grotesque marks upon our backs. The afternoon I went to see her should have put me in a mental institution. That's what snapped her out of her coma. Of course, my back would snap me out of a coma." Mattie took another drink. I was still too overwhelmed to speak.

"The father's manipulation of Maurice infuriated Jason. So much so it gave him the courage to kill the bastard. Jason wanted my forgiveness and was willing to accept his punishment. Of course, living with a father like that was punishment enough. Believe me. Jason's hell lasted longer than the night I suffered my own humiliation. Now, the rest you know."

There was a long silence. The full impact of her words hadn't hit me yet. I remembered that night quite well, the night Mitchell and Jeremy were killed. I remembered Jason's tears, his lack of self-control.

"Jason and Paula make a great couple. Has he told Paula the truth?" I asked.

Mattie shook her head. "Of course not. There are some things in life better left buried, and that story is one of them. Besides, Maurice will become Paula's brother-in-law. They've both been going to counseling sessions at the mental health clinic. It's helped tremendously."

I changed the subject to a happier note. "So, when's the wedding?"

Mattie picked up her glass and tapped it with mine. "Soon, I hope. They both deserve some happiness."

On the same vein, it was Mattie's turn to question me. "Oh, yes, and speaking of lovely couples, when is your wedding, my dear? You can bust your gut and tell ol' Mattie that one. Has Fred popped the question?" I rolled my eyes, trying not to choke.

"Don't you stare at me like that. I'm not stupid. I've seen the way the two of you look at each other. You belong together. You always have. It makes these old bones of mine very happy to see you smiling again."

"Mattie, don't push," I said, scolding her. "I don't need one of your lectures."

Mattie feigned hurt. "What, me push you into something you don't want to do? You're talking to grandmama here. Nothing moves Annie, the rock." She took a sip of her wine and waved her hand. "No, really, I'm proud of you. Not once in all these months have I seen you wallow in self-pity. A lot of people would have gotten agoraphobia."

Together we burst into a fit of laughter. Mattie decided to get bolder with her inquiries. "Annie, now tell me the truth. Are you finally over that rotten Peter? It truly saddened me to see you so hurt. I still feel responsible. I practically forced the two of you together. It's all my fault. I should've known you couldn't change him. It was only wishful thinking on my part. It's funny how we both ended up with men like Peter and my Daniel in our lives."

Mattie raised her glass. "I've just thought of another toast. Here's to us, to all women in the world who've fallen in love with a man whose cause was more important than our love. Fuck men with destiny."

Understanding her implication, I, too, raised my glass. "What about old women with causes?" I asked.

Mattie choked on her toast. "Fuck her, too."

"It's all right, Mattie," I said, handing her a napkin. "Take another drink and I'll tell you another secret. I came to terms with Peter the night he left the hospital. Peter was like one of those fireworks you see on the 4th of July. He came into my life like some huge incredible explosion. Disappointing, as it may seem, like all fireworks, the brightness dies in only a few short seconds. Believe me, if I'd have held onto Peter's flame, eventually it would have petered out."

Trying to get her to respond to my joke, I punched her on the arm. "Get it? Petered out. Okay, don't laugh. I thought it was pretty funny."

Mattie rolled her eyes and took another drink. I changed the subject to what she was most wanting to hear. "Fred, on the other hand, is like an eternal flame, burning forever brightly, creating a warm, perpetual glow. My support, not my rock. He shares his warmth because you're the most important person in his life. He shares his warmth because he understands what it means to love someone, to respect someone, and to be their best friend."

Changing my tone of voice, I whispered in her ear. "The flame is not extinguished because the feelings are real, Mattie. They're scary, but they're real."

I knew she would understand. She tipped her glass, emptied the last drops between her lips, and grabbed for the bottle to pour herself some more.

"Now you're learnin', girl," she said, proudly. "I'm not sure if I've ever told you this, another one of Mattie's magic philosophies. I look at life the way I look at art. You are the only one who has the power to turn it into a fine rich tapestry. Honey, you create the beauty within. The road you travel along yields the knowledge you need to continue on your journey. That's what you're doing. You're finding your path and sharing it with others."

Toasting me once again, tears filled our eyes. "You're a fine work of art, my dear friend."

"So are you. So are you," I said softly bending to whisper in her ear. "Are you ready for the real shocker? We're not drinking real wine. So much for your wine-tasting nose, Miss Mattie Turner. I'm pregnant."

She was too stunned to move. Giving me one of her surly looks, she picked up the glass to smell it. "Believe me, I've been around a long time, young lady, and I know wine when I taste it."

I pretended to go along with her. "Of course it's wine, silly. Alcohol free."

"Oh, my God," Mattie cried, as she examined the bottle. "You're telling the truth. I can't believe it. I didn't even know you were having sex. You know, you're turning into a real sneaky bitch. Why weren't you on the pill? Don't tell me you did it on purpose. You did, didn't you?" she asked, pointing her finger at me.

"When are you going to tell Fred? Are you two going to get married? Oh, what the hell, I don't care. Congratulations!" She stood up and gave me a hug around the neck. I wasn't sure if I could answer all the questions spewing out of her mouth.

"Miss Know-it-All, you're the one who hates the idea of marriage. And, no, I wasn't on the pill. I don't know why I did it. Yes, I do. I suppose deep down I did it because Jack needs a sibling."

"Does Fred know?"

"I haven't told him yet. I'm going to tell him this weekend. Fred's father has agreed to set up a satellite office here and he's moving in with me," I said unable to finish my sentence because the doorbell rang. It was Hannah and Jack.

"Is it all right if Jack comes to my house? I want to show him my new leaf collection from school." Jack looked anxiously at me in her arms.

"As long as you take his hand and walk on the sidewalk," I said. Before I shut the door, I glanced at the mailbox. A brown wrapped package was inserted in the slot.

Once again joining Mattie at the table, I noticed it was addressed to me in Fred's handwriting. Opening it with a small knife from the counter, I struggled with the lid. Inside was another blue crystal bird identical to the one my brother Jack had given me.

"Oh, what a lovely bird! What's it supposed to mean?" Mattie asked.

I started to place it back in the box when I noticed a smaller package laying in the corner. Taking it out, I unwrapped it and smiled. It was two crystal baby birds.

"I guess Fred already knows I'm pregnant," I said, handing her my present.

"Oh, how sweet!" Mattie exclaimed, taking them from my hand to study them. "Now you have a whole family. What a romantic thing to do."

Mattie was right. Fred understood me more than any man in my life, including my brother Jack. Once again, I remembered the promise I had made to him about finding love in *this* world. What I had come to realize was that was not my life's ambition. It was Jack's and Peter's.

When I was a little girl, I would sit for hours in my tall tree and daydream about this moment. All I ever wanted was what was in the palm of Mattie's hand, in every sense of the word, a family. They were my family, Fred, Jack, Mattie, Peter, my mother, Jason, Paula, Buddy, and all of Mattie's children. My family was huge, and I had found more than love in this world. I had found something more important, happiness. I had found a place to belong.

Placing the crystal birds back in the box, I remembered I hadn't answered one of Mattie's questions. I looked at her and gave her a sheepish grin.

"I still don't know if I'll marry him. I was foolish enough to do it once, perhaps I'll be foolish enough to do it again. Maybe I will maybe I won't. But I have it on good authority he'll make an excellent Lamaze partner," I smugly replied.

AUTHOR'S NOTE

You cannot love if your heart is made of stone. You cannot learn without accepting the challenging experiences in the journey through life. You cannot become who you are without opening and closing many doors.

There are many who will influence your life but none like the influence of a teacher.

IN MEMORY OF:
LaVada B. Thornton.
Born: June 19, 1915; Died: February 21, 1999.
She was a retired school teacher and continued to tutor at the Laura Lee Fellowship House up until the time of her death. She often asked me about this book. She was my Mattie Turner. She died before it was printed. It was a privilege to have known this outstanding woman.

A teacher affects eternity; you can never tell where the influence stops.